SOMEONE TO CATCH MY DRIFT

SOMEONE TO CATCH MY DRIFT

JACQUELINE POWELL

WARNER BOOKS

An AOL Time Warner Company

Copyright © 2002 by Jacqueline Powell
All rights reserved.

Warner Books, Inc., 1271 Avenue of the Americas, New York, NY 10020
Visit our Web site at www.twbookmark.com.

 An AOL Time Warner Company

Printed in the United States of America
First Printing: March 2002
10 9 8 7 6 5 4 3 2 1

Library of Congress Cataloging-in-Publication Data

Powell, Jacqueline.
    Someone to catch my drift / Jacqueline Powell.
        p. cm.
    ISBN 0-446-52748-3
        I. Title.

PS3566.O8318 S66 2001
813'.6—dc21   00-066264

TO EVERY MISUNDERSTOOD
SISTA
WHO HAS STROLLED OFF THE BEATEN PATH

Time to start blazing our own trails
The others can catch up later

Acknowledgments

Whew! I have truly healed during the process of writing this book and for that, I want to humbly thank the Creator for broadening my perspective and contributing to my growth. I can't wait to see what comes next.

I want to thank my mother, Williemenue "Penny" Powell, for your words of assurance and for being my constant cheerleader. My father, Larry Powell, for letting your little princess do her thing, her own way.

Thanks to all of my initial supporters including my sister LaNita Powell who read every last one of my rough drafts in the early years (she made me write that part). Debra Cottman, Valerie Noble, Daphne Rice, Nicole Rice, Robin Moore, Yasmin Thompson and Ray, too. John and Claudia Gatewood, Curtis Powell, Brenda Watson, Valerie Parks, Carla Williams, Charles and Ellen Cobbins, Curtis Young, Andrea Still, the Ward family, the Rice family, Velma Moore, Pearl and Luther Dave, Celeste Etherly, Judy and Gregory Gatewood, Kim Audrey, La-la and the entire Billups clan, Roslind Nelson, Reggie Ladd, Juan Hernandez, Xavier Hatcher, Dorothy Henderson, Tashara Jones, and all of my mother's co-workers who were there from the start. Evelyn "Sister" Williams, Gladys "Tookie" Allen, Regina, Pam, Tina Hicks and all of my Kansas City folks. Pam Grier and Valencia Seals.

Where would I be without Antoine and Theresa Coffer? Thanks to the entire Progressive Emporium family, and First World Bookstore. Thanks to Ramanu Ausar for the initial push,

Reginald Mitchell for critiquing my works like no one else could, and Brandeis Mitchell just for keeping Reggie together. Lisa Phillips, keep making it happen. Cheryl Anderson, here's the proof. Keep writing and I'll see you at the top. A special thanks to Ron Kirk for showing me as much of a firefighter's life as humanly possible.

Kenya M. Ford and Chrisman Harding. Where *are* y'all?

Thanks to the Remy family, and the entire Johnson family. I can't go without saying a special thanks to my heart, Robert Johnson. You were worth waiting for.

I have to mention Lolita Files and Eric Jerome Dickey for sharing all they knew about the business; my agent, Sara Camilli, for doing what you do so well; and my editor, Anita Diggs, for pushing the project the way that you did.

Last but not least, I want to thank my granny, Minerva Williams, for smiling down on me in a way that reminds me that God is steadfast in His love and mercy.

If I forgot to mention you it's only because you're so special that words can't express my gratitude. Much luv.

There was a time when I believed
that love meant the willingness
to sacrifice one's happiness for another's . . .
then I learned that was simply self-hatred.

—Jacqueline Powell

Part One

Out with the Old, In with the Untrue

Nikai

Silence is louder than noise.

It's funny what some women learn as little girls. I believe the things most remembered from a childhood can shape one as an individual. Makes you a kind, bitter, or misunderstood person. Me? I turned out to be a little of all three. Not because I lacked passion, but because my cries for attention were muffled. Silenced. The way that my mother put it was that people would take notice if they noticed me noticing them. And it was supposed to have been even better if I disappeared, because that would give them a chance to miss me—an opportunity to wonder where I was, to listen for the faint sound of my voice. Even in a world full of noise.

But for the three days that I tried this theory, it proved to be bullshit. I hadn't wandered outside the confinement of my half-empty apartment. I had stared at my black-and-white Wil Brent prints until they almost seemed to come to life. The tribal masks that decorated my walls were beginning to shift every hour, and I had lain in bed so long, I was sure there was an imprint in the mattress. After a while, I didn't so much as check the mail or pick up the phone, let alone go to work. And no one came by to see why Nikai had disappeared. Not my older sister, Taylor. Not my neighbor Sheila. Not even my mama, who has convinced me that she can't possibly be right about anything except my date of birth.

The hunter green-and-oatmeal curtains were drawn while my classic *Waiting to Exhale* CD was in place, working its healing magic. My phone was off of the hook because dumb Travis kept calling and asking me to bail his triflin' butt out of jail. First, he tried to sweet-talk me with the "Baby, I'm so sorry" line, but as soon as I told him that all of his stuff, which was small enough for me to carry, was out of the apartment and on his mother's porch, he started cussin' and yellin' like *I* was the one behind bars and in need of $4,500. Like *I* was the one with nerve enough to cheat on him with a *minor* and winded up getting arrested in front of *his* family. Like I even gave a *damn* if some six-foot-nine inmate named Bear turned him into his prison bitch. After what Travis had done to me, fate could have its way with him. And anyone he was locked up with could, too.

I had made it past the self-pity stage, waved good-bye to confusion, and abruptly arrived at revenge. I wanted someone to share in my pain. Particularly Travis. But anyone else who took a chance on coming around would be subjecting themselves to some serious anger displacement.

I reached over to turn the ringer back on and realized that I was still bleeding. Not heavily, but enough to soil the sheets if I rolled over the wrong way. As soon as I pulled my pink gown over my head, the phone rang and startled me. The sound of it had become unfamiliar after three days of that infamous silence. I checked the caller ID box and the prefix indicated St. Louis County. I guess there wasn't enough room for the word *jail* to pop up. But who needed to see that anyway? I knew who it was. I sighed, sat down on the edge of the bed, and answered it.

"Hello?"

A woman's recorded voice came over the line and announced that the call was coming from that loser behind bars.

"Nikai, can I please talk to you? I don't have long."

"You goin' somewhere?"

"All right, I'll let you crack your jokes if it'll make you feel better. Listen, my mama says she doesn't have room for my stuff, so can you *please* put it in the apartment until I can get this all straightened out?"

I sighed and massaged my left temple.

"Nikai, you there? Listen, I know I hurt you, and I'm sorry. . . ."

"You not only hurt me but you *embarrassed* me in front of my family!"

"I know, I know. . . ."

"No, you don't know how this has affected me! I haven't been to work or even to the mailbox in days!"

"Nikai?"

I fell silent as I felt my sanitary napkin becoming saturated.

"Nikai?"

"What, Travis?!"

"I want my family back."

"And I want peace of mind, but I don't see anybody dishin' none out!"

"Are you done yet?"

"I am now!"

I slammed the phone in its cradle and headed toward the bathroom. Maybe today will be better, I thought. Maybe I could watch something on TV without one of those judgmental Planned Parenthood commercials coming on and making me feel guilty for leaving that package in the clinic three days before. If I was lucky, I could miss the Pampers advertisements with the cute chocolate babies grinnin', with only two teeth at the bottom. Not to mention the precious newborns being cuddled in the Enfamil commercials. If I was lucky, just maybe today I could block the whole thing out.

I adjusted the water temperature right before the phone rang again. I couldn't understand the nerve he possessed even to *speak* to me, but Travis was a Sagittarius. And they're usually stronger than a cat's poop.

I picked it up on the third ring and waited for his plea.

He said, "Don't do that shit again."

I didn't respond.

"Nikai? Nikai?"

"*What?*"

"I can understand you being upset, but I need my stuff to be someplace safe."

"Is that all you can think about?"

"I told you that I wanted us to be together, but you're not

tryin' to hear that! You wanna slam the phone down and act all bad! Sometimes you act like you still need to grow up!"

"That must be what attracted your sick ass to me, you child molester!"

This time, I was the one getting my eardrum pierced. Travis slammed that phone down so hard, I was sure he had to have broken it in maybe three, four, or even five pieces. I could tell that he was getting frustrated because I still hadn't committed to holding his things until he got out or could afford storage. And the Lord knows that a statutory rape case will limit your financial flow.

The car rental company he managed called last week and wanted to know why they hadn't heard from him. I told them that I hadn't the faintest idea where he could have gone off to, empathized with them for a moment for leaving such an irresponsible employee in charge, only to screw up, and then promised that I would inform him that he was fired as soon as I had heard something. That was all before I decided that I didn't want to talk to anybody.

I took the cordless phone into the bathroom with me, stepped out of my panties, and discarded the messy pad, then slid into the steaming hot water and closed my eyes. Aretha was singin' about how the pain hurts like hell and making me more and more depressed. I lifted both of my hands, turned them over, and stared at my open palms. They were palms that could have been used to wipe away the tears of a newborn in seven months. Now the only rocking that I'd be doing would be rocking myself to sleep. I touched my vacant belly and felt water trickle down my face. That was the first time I had actually cried over what I had done. The first time that I'd physically acknowledged the death of my child.

The phone rang once more. Travis must have realized who had the upper hand and the *freedom* to go with it. I snatched the cordless off the white tile floor and pushed the talk button.

I screamed, "What do you want? You don't have any reason to call here anymore! Your job is gone, yo' baby is gone, and yo' stuff is, too!"

There was silence and then a female voice stretched across the line.

"Nikai, I'm on my way over."

It was Sheila from next door. I pushed the talk button and banged my forehead with the phone. *Damn. How could I be so stupid?* Throwing information around like that. And I had the nerve to call Travis dumb. Before I could even get out of the water, Sheila was banging on the door. I grabbed a hunter green bath towel off the rack and wrapped myself up in it, then headed toward the front door, leaving a puddle with every step.

Sheila rushed in and closed the door behind her. I turned and walked back into the bathroom.

"Nikai, don't just walk away from me. What is going on with you?"

"Everything I accidentally told you on the phone."

"Come out here and talk to me."

I yelled from the bathroom, "Hang on, I'm not done in here."

"Listen, I'll go home and put some tea on. Will you come over when you're done?"

"Yeah, just leave the door open."

The sound of Sheila exiting my apartment was interrupted by the phone ringing. It actually made me consider taking it off the hook again. That way, I didn't have to see anyone's number on my caller ID box. It was better to assume that no one cared. It was making me harder and more coldhearted by the day. If no one came by to see me, then that meant they didn't *care* what was going on.

"Hello?"

"Nikai, my stuff. Now are you gonna help me with it or not?"

"I'll tell you what I *will* do. I promise to ignore your calls if you promise not to call anymore. That way, if you slip up and dial this number by accident, I'll know that you can't possibly want anything. How does that sound?"

"Fuck it! If that's the way you want it, you don't have to worry about me calling there!"

"You promise?" I asked sarcastically.

"Not until my baby is born. So you've got seven months."

"Oh, I forget to mention that."

"Mention what?"

"I had an abortion the other day. And by the way, your job called and said you were fired."

I could hear him breathing heavily and switching the phone over to his other ear.

"This is all making you feel real good right about now, huh?"

"No, it isn't. I wanted you to be faithful. I wanted us to have the baby."

I needed to let him go, to get off of the phone. I could feel myself softening. Something I really didn't need to do, considering I had come that far and all alone.

Travis mumbled, "I gotta go. I'll call you tomorrow."

"For what? I thought you promised not to."

"All I can promise right now is that I'm not done with you. You'll be hearing from me."

I was dressed and knocking on Sheila's door within an hour. She greeted me with open arms and invited me into an incense-filled room with sounds of the ocean playing in the background. Two cups of oat-straw and squawroot herbal tea were resting on her wooden coffee table and she had changed into one of her colorful gowns.

Sheila was what some might consider eclectic, different, strange. I like to think of her as *special*. She wasn't the average, everyday person that you meet on the street. Sheila was one of those individuals that God puts in your life for a reason. But many people made the mistake of keeping their distance from her because she didn't fit the norm.

She was a rather tall, shapely woman and a few years older than I was. I once asked her how old she was and she only told me how old she *felt*, which was about twenty-three, but her face revealed her age, whether she knew it or not. I guessed about thirty-four, which made her nine years older than I was. Her skin was a dark, rich chocolate with a hint of red. She had rather large eyes and a broad nose. Full lips and cornrows going every which way on top of her head. When she let them fall, they hung down to her shoulders. And when Sheila got into one of her *moods*, she would put on these long gowns that gathered around her breasts and arms and flared out to about right above her ankles. Like something from the seventies. Except these gowns made noise. And if she got to doin' one of those dances, it was all over. My ears would be ringing for two weeks. She had little trinkets, seashells, cowrie shells, beads, and just about anything else she could find sewn onto those gowns. As if the blinding bright colors weren't enough.

Passing her threshold was like stepping into another dimension. Whereas my walls were all white, hers were lavender in the living room, green in the kitchen, and cranberry in the bathroom. She was the one who got me hooked on tribal masks, but hers were much larger. She had covered her walls with mud cloth and chimes. You know, the noisy kind that scream if you walk past them too fast. I can admit it took energy to hang out with Sheila. More energy than I actually had at that moment.

She said, "Sit down and tell me what's wrong with you."

"Well, I had an abortion three days ago, and Travis is in jail."

"*An abortion?* Why in the world would you do that?"

"What was I supposed to do? I just told you that Travis is in jail."

"And? What did he do?"

"I really don't feel like talking about it right now."

"So drink some tea until you do."

Sheila leaned back on her tan futon and began humming. I joined in because music usually makes me feel better. I'd like to sing professionally one day. I have a burning desire to deliver vocal inspiration to those who are down-and-out.

Sheila said, "I had an abortion once.

"And I regret it to this day," she continued. "The one thing that we can never run from is the unknown. It's like a prison, and knowledge is the key. You either step out of it or let it eat you up inside. I chose to let it eat me up for a while. I'll never know what that baby would have been like, and every day that I walked around that silent, empty apartment, I wondered."

"Thanks a lot, Sheila. That's just what I need right now, someone to make me feel even worse."

"That's not what I'm tryin' to do. You know what you need?"

"What?"

"You need to dance."

I doubled over with laughter and shook my head.

"I hope you don't think I'm gonna put on one of those dresses and let you sprinkle some dirt on the floor for me to kick around!"

"No, girl. I mean, you need to go out. Like to a club. I know the perfect spot."

"What kinda place, Sheila? I don't wanna be surrounded by a bunch of Rastas or weirdos or anything."

"I . . . don't . . . hang . . . out . . . with . . . *weirdos!*" She laughed. "And what is wrong with Rastas?"

"Nothing, they're just not my type."

"And what's your type, jailbirds?"

"Ha-ha. Real funny. I won't crack too hard while you're still wearing that getup. I wouldn't want you to put a hex on me or anything."

"Yeah, you betta play it safe," she said, jokingly waving her hands around and pretending to sprinkle invisible dust in my direction.

I reached over and gave her a hug, because at least she had managed to pull a laugh or two out of me.

"Sheila?"

"Yeah?"

"Statutory rape."

"*What?*"

"Travis got locked up for statutory rape."

"You're kidding me!"

"I wish I was."

"How long did he get?"

"Hasn't been sentenced yet."

"Well, I don't see him getting out anytime soon on something like that, so you know what this means."

"What?"

"You gotta put on yo' ho outfit. You know, there's a li'l hooker in all of us."

She was talking about my favorite size nine spaghetti-strapped black minidress that I had caught Travis's eye in. That was the last time I had gone out, too. Eleven months ago last week. I admit that that dress combined with my traffic-stoppin' booty and these perky size 36C's made me a lethal weapon. I had seen many men choke on a drink as I walked into the room swaying my hips to a silent beat. Nobody heard it, but they all felt it.

"All right, so what are *you* gonna put on?" I asked.

"Don't worry about all of that. You just be ready and over here by eight."

I laughed and left her apartment, but I couldn't do anything but worry about her. Sheila had been known to pick her braids out into a large Afro and take off out the door in a pair of bell-bottoms wide enough to sweep a small cat off the curb. But what could I say? My girlfriend was about to take me to therapy. And not the kind that required me to stretch out on a leather sofa. I was about to dance my problems away and grind on someone else's man until I had forgotten *all* about the one who used to be mine.

Around 6:30, I started curling my shoulder-length mane and pinned it up in a French roll with ringlets falling toward my face. Knocked the wrinkles out of my black weapon and loaded it up with ammunition. Adjusted the two cinnamon-toned cannonballs in the front so that they were centered, and then I jumped into a pair of black heels. I stood in front of the full-length mirror on the inside of my closet door and gave myself the once-over. Grabbed the brush off of the dresser and started singin' along with Gladys. I did a half spin to see how I looked at every angle and decided that a little makeup was in order. Just a dab of coffee bean lipstick and some black liner over the top eyelids would do. I puckered up and then practiced my seductive look by raising one brow and sucking in my cheeks. Who was I kidding? I hadn't gone out in damn near a year, and now I was supposed to strut in someplace that I knew nothing about and stop traffic? Yeah, right. Especially considering the fact that it was one of Sheila's favorite joints. I'd be lucky if the brothas in there even spoke English.

I grabbed my black handbag off the closet rack and walked over to Sheila's place. She opened the door. Her auburn hair was twisted up and she was wearin' a flamin' red strapless dress with a split so high that I could clearly see her tattoo. It was of a broken chain that started at the front of her thigh and ended in a beautiful string of cowrie shells around the other side. There was no linkage. She explained that it was a symbol of her freedom.

That she had liberated herself. Sometimes she ran off on tangents about freedom, but her attempts to take me there were futile. There are just some things I don't wanna get. But lookin' at Sheila in that dress, liberation would be the last thing on a brotha's mind. She was right. There *is* a li'l hooker in all of us. And she had more than I ever imagined.

"You slut! Look at you!" I screamed.

"I'm ready to put it *on* somebody's son!"

"And his daddy, too!"

"How you feelin'? You ready to do this? You ah'ight?" she asked.

"Yeah, I'm fine."

I felt like I was in a locker room getting a pep talk from a football coach. She even had the nerve to high-five me on the way out of the door. I knew that Sheila frequented the clubs, but she appeared to be a lot more excited than I'd imagined she would be. It almost seemed like she had something up her sleeve. Nothing like drugs or anything, but I wouldn't have doubted that she danced around some herbs, asking her friendly spirits to help me have a good time. Whatever it was, I could tell that I was in for something. Something big.

"All right, are you ladies ready for Chocolate Thunder?"

There was screaming and yelling all around my head. This was partly because I was sitting down and 120 women were standing. Over half of them had ten-dollar bills hanging out of their teeth. The music was bumpin', I was drunk, and Sheila had disappeared. She ordered another round of rum and Cokes and took off, saying that she would be right back. I was beginning to get a little worried, but Chocolate Thunder was slowly easing my concern. For a while, I had become bored, but it was still early. The club wouldn't be letting guys in until after the show, which would be around 12:30. I enjoyed it, but I just wasn't into jumping around with a bunch of other women over *one* fine man. I'd much rather hem some sexy stallion up in a corner to have for myself.

Chocolate Thunder left and was replaced with a light-skinned brotha in a blue-collar getup talkin' about layin' pipe. I finished my drink and started working on Sheila's. I wasn't too particular about redbones, but there was somethin' about this brotha. Maybe it was because he was giving me eye contact or maybe I was just flat-out drunk, but he was beginning to turn me on. He slowly removed his shirt to one of those late eighties "Freak me" tunes and tossed it to the left of the stage. Next went the pants, and just when I thought I had seen it all, everybody in the room looked down and realized that one of his red balls was hangin' out the side of his briefs. Most of the ladies fell out laughing as he indiscreetly tucked it back in without ever taking his eyes off of me. I raised my left brow just like I had practiced and shook my head. He didn't really need to tuck *anything, anywhere.*

At that moment, he stepped down off the stage and was heading toward me. Me, the only female still seated. The only silent mouth in the midst of all of this noise. And he was choosing me. My silence, or my drunken silence, had gotten his attention. I watched him push past women of all ages and approach the round table at which I was seated. Redbone extended his hand and waited for my drunk ass to stumble to my feet. He didn't utter a single word. Just grabbed me by the hips and rubbed that pouch all over my butt. And I let him. As a matter of fact, I *helped* him. I threw my hands in the air and let him run his hands up and down my sides. He stepped closer and I could feel his breath in my ear as he caressed the front of my thighs. Right there in front of all of those women, I let that fine stallion freak me like it was New Year's Eve 1999. I closed my eyes to the thought of Travis runnin' around a jail cell tryin' to get away from Bear, and laughed. By then, I had forgotten where I was. I could feel Redbone gettin' hard behind me and it was making *me* want to get carried away. He must've gotten embarrassed, so he backed up off of me for a minute. I turned around and gave him a wink. I wanted to ensure him that it was *all good.* He winked, too, and went back to staring at my butt in that dress. I laughed and shook it even harder. I was tryin' to hypnotize him right there in the club. That's when I heard those jealous heifers laughin'. Mad 'cause the brotha got good taste. I turned back around to get a little closer, and Redbone was gone. Had disappeared and darted back up on the stage. Left me standin' there lookin' like a damn fool, shakin' my ass like *I* was being paid to.

"You havin' fun?" Sheila asked out of nowhere.

"Where've you been?"

I was starting with my anger displacement again. I was pissed at every broad in there, but it just seemed easier to take it out on Sheila.

"I was in the back, making sure you got your full ten minutes."

"What *full ten minutes?*"

"You forgot about all of that stuff he was rubbin' against you that fast?"

"What are you talkin' about? You paid for that? He didn't come over here because . . ."

I fell back in my seat and took another swallow of Sheila's drink.

"You aren't mad, are you?"

"Of course I am!"

"Why? It's not like you want to marry him! It was just a dance. I didn't say I paid him to take Travis's place."

"Shut up, Sheila! If you wanna spend your money, buy me another drink. Got that fine mofo gettin' me all hot and bothered."

"The doors will be opening in fifteen minutes and you'll be able to pick and choose from a bunch of brothas who *ain't* showin' their *balls* for a livin'," Sheila assured me.

I sat at the round table, sippin' her drink, and envisioned Bear actually catchin' Travis by the back of the pants. The rest, I'm sure you don't wanna hear about. But by the time he was done havin' his way with him, a host of brothas in all sizes, shapes, and shades were steppin' up in the place. I stood up, stumbled over to the bar, and positioned myself to walk across the room when they all settled.

"You gonna be all right there, young lady?"

The bartender had sneaked up behind me and made me forget my seductive look. I couldn't remember if it was the right brow up or the left. And which way had I leaned my head?

"Yeah, I should be fine."

"Looks like you might need to slow down a bit."

"Maybe you're right. Let me get some water."

He slid me a glass of water down the bar like we were in a

western saloon. I caught it like a fool and then watched the water spill all over my hand in slow motion. Maybe I had had too much to drink. I started to pick up one of those small square napkins to wipe up the mess, when someone beat me to it.

"Let me help you with that."

A tall, dark, muscular brotha who looked like he could have jumped off the pages of the *Men of Color* calendar lifted my wrist from the small puddle. He gave a broad smile when he noticed me checking him out from head to toe. He was filling a pair of black linen pants and a black linen shirt quite nicely. His bald head had the lights above the bar bouncing off of it. For a minute, it looked like the light was coming down from heaven to feature this godsend. But like I said, I had had *tooooo* much to drink.

He asked, "You here alone?"

"No. You?"

"Me and my man just stopped through for a while. You here with somebody special?"

"No, he's probably cuddled up with Bear."

"Excuse me?"

I started laughing to myself until I looked across the room and spotted Redbone in plain clothes, talkin' to some tramp. Just like that, he had gone from some poor girl's fantasy to a regular guy. It made me question Mr. Wonderful standing here looking like a million bucks. He had probably shaken his butt for the crowd before Sheila and I arrived. Now he thinks he can play it off like he just got here with his *man*. Come to think of it, Sheila probably sent him over with a twenty tucked in his pocket. Like I couldn't pull one of these fine brothas on my own.

"How much did she pay *you?*"

"How much did *who* pay me?"

"Oh, that's real clever. She told you to play it off if I asked, too, huh?"

"Look, sweetheart, I think you need to have a seat. Those drinks are goin' to your head."

"I'm not drunk and I don't need *you, Sheila,* or *nobody else* to pay for me no time and attention!"

He leaned into me and whispered, "Unless you want to be

standing here by yourself, I suggest you calm down, sweetheart. Now, my name is Robert. What's yours?"

I looked up into his warm face and realized that he had no knowledge of who Sheila was or why I was yelling.

"I'm sorry. It's Nikai."

He extended his hand and shook mine.

"I knew a beautiful woman like yourself wouldn't normally act like that. You need to keep sipping that water."

He beckoned for the bartender to bring him a drink as I searched the room for Sheila. She was at the far end of the club, dancing with a tall caramel brown brotha donning dreadlocks and a dashiki. That's my girl. Always takin' it back to the motherland.

"So, Nikai, tell me a little bit about yourself."

"Well, I'm twenty-five, single, and drunk. How 'bout you?"

"Twenty-seven, single, and tryin' to get there."

"Then you need to have a seat," I said, patting the chair next to me.

He hopped up in the chair, grabbed his drink off of the bar, and lifted his glass to me in a toast.

"To Nikai."

I lifted my water and slurred.

"To Nikai."

He grinned and placed the drink back down.

"So where's your woman?" I asked.

"Don't have one."

"Oh really. You come here in hopes of finding one?"

"No. Moms told me never to get serious with women I meet in a club."

What does yo' mama know?

"That's interesting."

"But sometimes I make an exception to the rule."

You are just too kind.

"Yeah, I know what you mean. My mama never told me that about men, but I just consider it common knowledge. I'm sure just about every brotha in here has *someone, somewhere,* waitin' for them."

He took a sip and said, "Not true."

"And why do you say that?"

"I can't speak for every brotha in here, but I don't have anyone waiting on me. Actually, I kinda wish I did."

"So what part intrigues you, the idea of someone *waiting* for you or the thought of someone *being* there for you?"

"Both. We all get lonely, don't we?"

I started thinking about the three days that I spent in my apartment staring at the walls and waiting for something to happen. I don't exactly know what, but *something* was supposed to happen if I made myself miserable enough. Maybe I thought I would literally die from boredom. Or maybe I thought my disappearance would spark an interest in others. Cause them to posse up and rush over to my place, kick the door in, pull me from the bed, and try to figure out what was so wrong with me. I thought just maybe my silence would be heard.

"You all right? You look like you've got some things on your mind."

"I do."

"Wanna talk about it?"

"No, not really, but I *would* like to dance."

"Well, why didn't you say so?"

This Robert character took me by the hand and helped me down from the stool. Let me lead the way to the dance floor and started croonin' in my ear, right along with Luther.

"If this world were mine . . ."

I whispered, "You sound nice."

He held me closer and placed his hands on my hips. Patted them with every beat of the music and swayed from side to side like my body were his instrument.

"You *feel* even better," he said.

When he said that, I turned around and placed my butt right up against that bulge I felt in the front of his pants.

The DJ threw on Earth, Wind and Fire's "After the Love is Gone" and the crowd went wild. I could hear sistas hollerin', "Aahhh shit, that's my jam" all over the club. There was dippin' and grindin' from one corner of the dance floor to the other.

"I could hold you like this all night," he whispered.

I wound my hips like an old man's clock and wrapped my hand around the back of his neck. Pulled his head down to me and shoved my tongue in his mouth. Brothaman was shocked. He put a death grip on my waist and glued an even bigger bulge to my butt. Any closer and I would've been inside those linen pants with him.

"Damn, sweetheart. What are you tryin' to do, become Mrs. Hayes?"

I turned around and asked, "Oh, is that your last name?"

"You keep movin' like that and it'll become yours."

I rolled my eyes and turned back around. He didn't deserve my face after a comment like that. He was beginning to remind me of the prison bitch with his sorry pickup lines.

Once our slow jam ended, the DJ hyped things up with Jay-Z's "Can I Get a . . ." I took off toward the bathroom like my butt had been pressed up against a pillar and not some fine chocolate specimen. I could feel him reluctantly letting go, but nature was calling. On the way, I passed Sheila, who was lifting her *already* mini dress a little higher. Couldn't figure out if she was showin' Rastaman her tattoo or her pubic hair. I mouthed the word *slut* behind his back and caused her to lose the beat. Sheila fell out laughin', flipped me the bird, and moved in closer on her prey.

By the time I had eased my way across the dance floor and to the bathroom, it was like a henhouse in there. A lot of cackling and hardly enough room to squeeze through. Sistas were in there pinnin' up locks and combin' through perms. Linin' eyes and paintin' lips. Stuffin' bras and checkin' breath. I'm talkin' wall-to-wall competition.

I managed to grab a stall to relieve myself and involuntarily became about the twelfth party of a private conversation.

"Girl, don't even trip off of him. He ain't worth it."

Another sista said, "You know you can't trust a *fireman* anyway. Almost every man in a uniform is a dog. Think about it, all of that unaccounted-for time on their hands. Don't think he's out chasin' no cats out of trees all day *and* night."

"Yeah, he's chasin' *cat* all right!"

Someone else suggested, "Just go on home, girl. Sleep on it."

"Hell nah, she ain't lettin' no man run her up outta here! If anybody's leavin', it's *him! C'mon girl!*"

And just like that, they were gone. Left me standin' in the stall with my ear suctioned to the door and waitin' for them to drop a name or somethin'. I don't consider myself caught up in drama but I lived for stuff like this. I mean, how often do you get to see a sista pull out her clown suit in the middle of the club and act a damn fool on a promiscuous dog? Well, I don't know about you, but I'd waited eleven months and I wanted front-row seats.

I washed my hands and took off toward the dance floor to find Sheila, when some commotion to the left caught my attention. As it turned out, I walked right into the line of fire. The mad sista's ex-man was to my right and she was wieldin' a bottle of Dom, in an upright position, to my left. I felt the crowd getting thick around me and then I found myself being quickly pushed against a wall near the rest rooms. There was screamin' and then the distinct sound of an expensive bottle breakin'. More pushin', more shovin'. More touchin', more feelin'. A hand on my shoulder, a muscular chest in my face, and then a familiar voice.

"You all right? Did any of the glass hit you?" Robert asked.

He was moving my face from side to side and lifting my arms to check for cuts, bruises, and whatever else.

"I'm fine, really."

I felt him reach down and grab my hand. Then he used that massive body to part that crowd like the Red Sea.

I screamed, "Where are we going?"

"We're getting outta here!"

"I can't leave my girlfriend!" I yelled, trying to pull back.

"If your girlfriend's smart, she's already gone. Now, c'mon!"

I snatched my heels off and silently let that black stallion whisk me away in the midst of it all.

"So where do you want me to drop you off?"

"I don't know if I want you to know where I live," I said.

"Well, we can always go to *my* place."

Robert had a sly grin on his face as he slid a Dru Hill CD into his CD player.

"I like Dru Hill."

"Me, too. You know what else I like?"

"What?" I asked.

"Moments like this."

"Moments like what?"

"When both parties can make themselves sound bigger than life. Seem as interesting as we like."

"So in other words, you're excited about the lying process."

"No, Nikai. I just get to see how big your imagination is . . . and your apartment, too."

"I never said you could see my apartment or that I even lived in one."

"Well, I'm tellin' you that I live in one and would be more than happy to show it to you."

"At two-thirty in the morning, I guess you would be. Look, you've obviously gotten me mixed up with one of those sistas back in the club. I don't *fuck* everybody who wants to *fuck* me."

"You just *kiss* everybody you want to kiss. Am I right?"

I looked at Robert watching the road and grinning like a Cheshire cat.

"Take me to the Central West End. Euclid, specifically."

"That where you live?"

"No, that's where I get ice cream. At the Coffee Cartel, if that's okay with you."

"Whatever you want. But you have to let me check you and make sure you didn't get cut before I take you home."

"Yeah, right," I said, laughing. "I don't think it would take someone else to let me know if there's glass in my flesh. I had a few drinks, but I'm not numb anymore."

"Hey, I'm just doin' my civic duty," he said, holding his hands up in a surrendering position.

"Let me think about it."

"Take as long as you like."

Robert pulled his black four-door Maxima into a spot across the street from the ice-cream shop. Hopped out and ran around to my side. He waited for me to slip my shoes back on and then helped me out of the seat.

"Thank you."

"No need to thank me. That's part of the civic duty, too."

I laughed in his face, just to throw him off.

"You try, don't you?"

"That's all I can do," he said, making sure that I was on the inside of the sidewalk. "So tell me something else about you."

"What exactly do you wanna know?"

"Ever been married? Have any kids? Do you do drugs? Any jealous ex-boyfriends in jail?"

I tripped on the curb and almost twisted my ankle after that last question.

"You sure you're all right? I can drop you off at home if you need me to."

"I'm fine. It's just the heels. Why don't you tell me some more things about *you?*"

"All right. I'm a firefighter, so I live in the city—"

"Whoa, wait a minute. Did you know anything about the guy gettin' jumped back there in the club?"

"Yeah, we work at the same engine house."

"Was that your *man* you came with?"

"Yeah."

"So why did you leave him like that?"

"Well, for one, I just met him yesterday. I was actually sub-bing at *his* engine house. I didn't know what the situation was. That could've been his lady or anything. What was I supposed to do, pull her off and have him gettin' pissed at me for puttin' my hands on his woman? Or should I have helped a six-foot-four, two-hundred-and-thirty-pound *man* fight a five-foot-three, one-hundred-and-thirty-five pound *woman?*"

"Yeah, I guess you're right. So how long have you been chasing cats?"

He held the door open and asked, "Excuse me?"

"Just kidding. That was a joke I heard while those sistas were plottin' on jumpin' ya man."

"Oh, is that what they said we do?" he asked, laughing. "That's cruel."

"Well, if the truth hurts, you shall be in pain."

"No. I don't chase cats, but I give 'em plenty of reasons to purr."

I looked at Robert and couldn't help but blush. He was pullin' all kinds of tricks out of his bag.

A tall, thin white guy wearin' a white T-shirt and overalls approached us and asked for our order.

I said, "I'll take a scoop of black walnut in a cup."

"And I'll have two scoops of blueberry cheesecake on a cone."

"So do you have any kids? Jealous girlfriends? Drug addictions?"

"I don't have any kids, but I do have friends."

I should've known, with a chest like that.

"And drug addictions?"

"I *just say no*."

The guy gave us our ice cream and we took a seat by the large glass window, with an excellent view of the West End. All of the tables and chairs that lined the sidewalks outside of restaurants were filled with a rainbow of people walking, talking, and hanging out like us. Even at two o'clock in the morning.

"Nikai, tell me what your passion is."

"What do you mean?"

"There's got to be something you live for. Something that you would do even if you never got paid for it."

"That would have to be singing."

"You sing?" he asked with raised brows.

"Yeah. Would you like for me to sing for you one day?"

"I don't know," he joked. "Let me see how you sound first. I wouldn't want you doing any damage to my ears."

I leaned across the round table and sang Patti LaBelle's "If Only You Knew."

"I must have rehearsed my lines . . . a thousand times . . . until I had them memorized."

"Damn, I never imagined that a beautiful voice would be coupled with such a beautiful woman. You know any more *recent* songs?"

"Yeah, but there's nothin' like the old ones. There was more romance involved. It took Donnie to break it down in 'I Love You More Than You'll Ever Know.' "

"Donnie?"

"Yeah, Donnie Hathaway!"

"Oh, yeah. Forgot all about him. You know, it *has* been a while."

"Too long. I have some of his albums. Would you like to hear them?"

"Sure. When?"

"Now."

"I thought you didn't want me to take you home. A minute ago, I wasn't even allowed on your street, and now you want me to chill while you blow dust off some oldies."

I stood and put my hand on my hip.

"Is that a yes or a no? It's just an attempt to civilize you, not *sleep* with you."

Robert blushed and responded, "Well, since you asked so nicely."

I asked from the bedroom, "Would you like something to drink?"

I left him sitting on the couch so that I could cut through to the bathroom and handle my business. I washed up and grabbed some cutoff blue-jean shorts with beads dangling from them that Sheila had made for me and a white T-shirt that read WHEN GOD MADE THE BLACK WOMAN, HE WAS JUST SHOWING OFF.

"Yeah, what do you have?"

"Water, orange juice, Kool-Aid, and beer."

"Mind if I have a beer?"

"No, go right ahead."

I got dressed, pulled my hair back in a ponytail, splashed on some peach body spray, and slipped into my big bunny slippers. When I walked into the living room, Robert was sitting in Travis's favorite black leather recliner, sipping on a bottle of brew. Even had the nerve to be reclined.

I stopped in the threshold and asked, "You comfortable?"

"I am now. Thanks for asking."

I shook my head and dragged my bunnies over to my record player.

"I haven't seen one of those in years!" he said, sitting up.

"A lot of people don't care to."

"This is different. Or should I say unique?"

"What is?" I asked.

"The whole vibe in here."

Robert looked around the living room and made me question what exactly he meant by "unique." Unique in a good way or unique in a bad way? Was it creative or borderline strange?

I can admit, it wasn't the average setting. Travis and I had saved up for a black leather couch and love seat. The walls were white and all of the pictures that hung from them were black-and-white ones. Including the framed one of Bob Marley chillin' among his brethren that Sheila gave me as a gift for braiding her hair one day. The curtains were three shades of a linenlike material. Black, white, and tan—in order to pick up the hardwood floors. My halogen lamps were, of course, black, and so were the coffee and end tables. Even the large iron candleholders in the shape of village women holding a stick, which Taylor had brought me back from Singapore were black and tan. I guess I did see his point.

"So who are some of your favorite singers?" he asked.

"Patti, of course. I also like Chaka Khan, Stevie, Phyllis Hyman. The list goes on and on."

"What about more recent people?" he asked.

"You act like they're all *dead!*"

"I don't mean it like that. What about Toni Braxton? Now that sista can sing. And Faith Evans. Don't forget Mary J."

"Yeah, especially that Erykah Badu, and Lisa Larelle and Shanice Wilson."

"Lisa Larelle? Never heard of her."

"Keep ya ear to the streets, you will."

"I'm up on music a lot more than you think I am. I heard that L Boogie from the Fugees is comin' out with an album this year."

"Really? Now that sista can sing. I'll definitely be looking out for that one."

I put one of Donnie's albums on and sat down on the couch as his soulful voice spilled from the speakers.

"Love, Love, Love . . . Why'd you take so long to come to me . . ."

Robert asked, "Is there room for me over there?"

"Plenty," I answered, patting a spot on the couch next to me.

Robert joined me and took a long swig of his beer.

"So, are you gonna finish tellin' me who you are?"

"Well, I'm an administrative assistant at Livingston Brock. I have one sister, no kids, and plenty of dreams."

"Any drug addictions?" he asked, laughing.

"Crack, but only on weekends."

"You forgot to add your sense of humor."

"Yeah, well, I'm what most people consider cynical."

"People say the same thing about me."

I smiled and looked away from him as Donnie went on making the mood right.

"Your dreams. Tell me about 'em."

"Well, for one, I want what just about every woman wants—a healthy relationship."

"Is the situation out here with brothas that bad that you can only *dream* about a good one?"

"What do you think?"

"I think a lot of women have unrealistic expectations. They've got television mixed up with real life. I mean, there can only be so many handsome young millionaires with good table manners. I also think a lot of the time you all set yourselves up for disappointment."

I turned to face him and bent one knee up on the couch. He stared down at my toned thighs and then back up to my face.

"So you're sayin' the reason why we can't find a good man is because we don't know one when we see one?"

"No. I'm sayin' your shorts are loud."

I burst out laughing and slapped him on the arm. Didn't realize until then how tight it was, how firm *he* was.

"I'm just kiddin'. What I'm sayin' is that women need to understand that men think differently. The task of finding Ms. Right is like a field day for us. We get to try on new personalities and new faces. . . ."

"And new booty, too, huh?"

He nodded in agreement and shrugged his shoulders.

"And new booty, too."

I shook my head in disgust and said, "Go on."

"But for women, it's one big disappointment after another.

Eventually, they get tired and settle for someone who treats them halfway decent. Then when things sour, they stand around asking themselves what went wrong."

"So we set ourselves up?"

"Yep," he answered, finishing off his beer.

"And the dog who scarred us gets off that easily?"

"Nikai, love doesn't have a court of law. Women know when they get involved that if they get hurt, they can only do one of two things, get mad or get over it. I mean, it may sound cold, but I call it responsibility for your own decisions."

Robert did sound cold, but he was also making sense. I had a choice at that point. I could either continue to let Travis make my days longer and more miserable or I could just *get over it*. And with Robert sitting on my couch looking the way he was, it wasn't hard to choose the latter.

"So what other dreams do you have?" he asked.

"I want to sing professionally."

"Is that a professional *lounge* singer, or are we talkin' record-deal status?"

I laughed and said, "Record-deal status."

"I think I may be able to help you. A partner of mine has a cousin who produces music."

"I don't know about your friends. I'm not interested in ref-ereeing during studio time."

"I like that. Timing and delivery were on point, but don't quit your day job."

We both laughed, talked some more, and sorta dozed off at separate ends of the couch. Both waiting for the green light to get close, the way we had in the club. Both waiting to see if the other was in fact Mr. or Ms. Right. We both waited until the sweet sound of Donnie's voice had disappeared. And the energy to talk or even stay awake had gone with it.

Nikai

I was jolted from my sleep by the painful ringing of the phone. I sat up on the third ring, which was coupled with the annoying sound of beads dangling from my shorts. I searched all around me in an attempt to locate the faint tone of my cordless. My head was pounding, and my back was hurting from sleeping in a fetal position all night. I got to my feet and found a beer bottle on the floor by the couch. The record player was still on and there was a beautiful man sleeping at the other end of the couch—in that apartment—which was still in *Travis's* name.

The constant ringing of the phone had become a distant, irrelevant call from the bedroom. I was tryin' to remember how Sheila got home and, more importantly, what this brotha's name was.

He woke, stretched, and said, "Good morning, beautiful."

Since he wasn't calling me by my name, there was no sense in me trying to call him by his. Whatever it was.

"Good morning."

"How'd you sleep?"

How does it look like I slept? Cramped up on the couch with you!

"My back is hurting."

"Need a massage?" he asked, as though he had maybe brushed and gargled.

"No, I really don't have time. I've got a busy day today, but I appreciate you giving me a ride home last night."

He sat there on the edge of the couch, hanging from my

every word. I couldn't tell what the hell he was waiting on, but I needed privacy *immediately.*

"Did you happen to write your number down?" I asked.

"Are you saying you wanna hear from me again?"

"I do, but I'm in a hurry, so I'd appreciate it if you would write it down before you *go.*"

"Oh, I get it," he replied, jotting his number down on the front of an *Essence* magazine subscription card. "That's my cue to leave. Well, here you go. You have time to walk me to the door?"

I could detect a bit of sarcasm in his voice.

"Depends on if you plan to move as slowly as you are now."

"Ah, I see you keep that sense of humor twenty-four hours a day."

I shrugged my shoulders and said, "That's just me, I guess."

I walked behind him to the front door and unlocked it. Stood with one hand gripping the edge of it and the other on my hip.

"I hope I'll be hearing from you soon."

"You will."

"Here," he said, snatching a sheet of paper down from the outside of the door. "I believe this belongs to you."

I took the piece of paper from him, read it, and felt my heart sink. It was an eviction notice. I had a week to get out and turn in Travis's key. That old gray-headed man at the front desk mentioned on that dreadful day the police came and got Travis that he didn't think people like us deserved to live in such a nice area. Like there was any comparison between Travis and me. Travis was simply good-lookin', and if it weren't for my crush on Malcolm from *The Young and the Restless* and the resemblance between the two, I never would have given him the time of day. But none of that mattered at that point. I had to get Mr. Wonderful out of the door and Sheila face-to-face as soon as possible. I needed her reasoning, I needed her rationing, and, more than anything, I needed her reassurance that I would make it through another round of bullshit.

Sheila asked, "What do you mean, what are you gonna do?"

I was over at her place, sitting in the living room at a round table that she used for organizing her thoughts. I had the eviction notice in one hand and a bunch of Kleenex in the other. Sheila was on the floor doing some stretches. For what? I don't know. Maybe Rastaman told her it would be a good idea if she were limber. Whatever the reason, she was gettin' on my nerves. I'm big on undivided attention, and I didn't feel like I was getting that at all.

"Are . . . you . . . done . . . yet?" I asked, whimpering.

Sheila stopped pulling her chest down to her knees and looked over at me.

"Uh-uh. You are gonna have to stop all of that cryin', girl. Now, I told you that everything is gonna be okay. This is all in the plan."

"Whose plan? 'Cause I ain't planned on none of this happenin'!"

"The Creator's plan, silly."

She opened her legs and leaned into the right one, trying her best to get her knee to meet her forehead.

"Stop, Sheila! This is serious. I won't have a place to *live*."

"You can stay here until you find a place," she answered calmly.

"And what about all of the furniture?"

"Whose is it?"

"We both went in on the living room, but the rest of the big stuff is his."

She switched knees and suggested, "So sell the living room stuff."

"Why would I do that?"

"Do you wanna pay for storage *after* you buy the other half from Travis? You don't know how long it will take to get on your feet."

"But does it make sense to start from scratch?"

"Did it make sense for you to gap your legs open and let some strange man take your baby last week?"

"Well, it didn't make sense the way that you were out on that dance floor liftin' yo' dress high enough for Rastaman to see where yo' hipbone starts, but ain't nobody pointin' fingers at you!"

"His name is Byron and I was showing him a dance that I learned over in the islands."

"You ain't never been to no *islands!*"

"Yeah, but he doesn't know that." She laughed.

"You sound like you're planning to see him again."

"I am. Tonight."

Sheila had a smile on her face that was unmistakable. She was falling for Rastaman, or Byron. And I mean hard. She kept doing her stretches and started hummin' reggae tunes. Sheila had an extra pick-me-up attitude, and I don't mean the kind that comes in the form of herbs or tea. She glanced up at me, lookin' like the cat that swallowed the canary, and confirmed my suspicions.

I screamed, "You screwed Rastaman last night!"

Sheila stopped stretching and got up from the floor.

"No. I did not."

"Yes you did!"

"Nikai, have I ever lied to you? I'm tellin' you I did not screw Byron last night."

I closed one eye and turned my mouth up with skepticism. Sheila was usually a very health-conscious person, but I'll be damned if stretching ever brought a smile to her face. She stood with her feet wide apart and pushed one arm back with the other like she was trying to put herself in a headlock. The smile never left, and neither did the twinkle in her eye. But she'd never, ever lied to me. If Sheila said she didn't screw Rastaman last night, she didn't screw 'im.

"So you know what this means. The next time Travis calls, you have to answer the phone."

"Yeah, I know. I was thinking earlier if maybe getting out of that apartment is what I need. You know, just to get over it."

"I definitely think you do. A change of scenery will symbolize a step forward in your life. Out with the old and in with the new. You've just gotta get that property situation settled."

"I'm leavin' that up to Travis. He can have his *mama* come and get the furniture. I don't care."

Sheila sat down at the table with me and said, "There's no need to lie. You still care; you're just moving on. I'm assuming the brotha at the bar last night had something to do with you turning over a new leaf."

"Oh, yeah, he's okay."

"Okay, huh? You just gag everybody with your tongue who you consider to be *okay?*"

I fanned my hand as if to totally disregard what she said.

"I was drunk and he felt good. That . . . is . . . all."

"Yeah, right. He felt so good that you wanted that feelin' all night, huh?"

I didn't say anything. Although I wanted to know how long she had been watching my front door. But I just started staring at the eviction notice in my hand again.

Then Sheila shouted out of nowhere, "Nikai, you need to kill that stuff!"

"What stuff?"

"Actin' unmoved. Hell, black folks are an emotional people! We dance when we hear music, laugh out loud and stomp our feet when we're humored or filled with joy. Don't think you appear to be more *civilized* because you stay in your seat and mumble 'Oh, yeah, he's okay.' You wouldn't be afraid to diss the brotha if you really didn't like him, so if he's decent, smile and let the world know that you're pleased or that he's pleased you."

"All right, so I dig him a little. And as soon as I get myself situated, I *may* just call him. Now how's that?"

Sheila grabbed my hands across the table and said, "Now, that's what I like to hear. If you can't be truthful with yourself, you can't possibly be truthful with me. And vice versa."

I nodded and started toward the door so that I could wait for Travis's call to make arrangements, when Sheila stopped me.

"Nikai, call me later," she said, with that annoying smile back on her face. "And I meant what I said. I didn't screw Byron last night. I screwed 'im this morning!"

I was back at home under the hair dryer, giving myself a deep conditioning and reading an article in a local magazine. The title was "If You Can't Tell Who the Sucker Is, It's Probably You" and it was about being played without knowing it. I began to wonder if maybe the signs were there all along and I just didn't want to see them. There was a list of *red flags* in the article. And the more I read, the more I realized that about half of them should've gone up while I was dealing with Travis.

1. If your man deviates from a normal pattern: A sudden decrease in ability to get to the phone when you've paged him suggests that something is different in his life. He's unable to make promises anymore out of fear he might break them. Everything appears to be a toss-up, and there's a sudden uncomfortable level of spontaneity introduced to the relationship. If he can't justify this unusual behavior, he's probably hiding something.

2. If your man appears to have set new patterns where you are not concerned: Dogs don't leave the trail or they might lose the scent. He knows that in order to get what he wants from the other woman, he will have to be consistent. Therefore setting a pattern of being with her on time and, in turn, leaving home every evening with a new task and possibly a new glow. Watch 'im, girl . . .

6. If your man appears to substitute time with gifts: Guilt gifts are the oldest trick in the book. If you are busy unwrapping and marveling at what he's bought you, you don't have time to wonder why he's singing in the mirror before he leaves home *without* you . . .

8. If your man suddenly starts emphasizing the importance of privacy: Men don't usually keep little boxes filled with mementos. Request to have an Honesty Hour and both of you reveal your dear and nears. Make him feel like everything that matters to him matters to you, as well. If he appears reluctant, there's another red flag.

I lifted the hood of the dryer and walked over to the closet. Travis was always so organized that it was sickening. There was always a place for this and that. Although now that I thought of it, I'd never known where those places were. I got down on my hands and started pulling things out of the closet like a dog digging itself a hole. All I found were shoes, his dumb basketball, an unused briefcase, and a medium-size heavy metal box. I shook it and could hear not only that the contents were solid but also that there were other smaller things inside of it. More importantly, the damn thing was locked.

I sighed and sat back on my feet. I stared at that box so long that I could almost smell secrets brewing inside of it. There had to be a key. I got up and looked in the nightstand on his side of the bed but found nothing. Just as I was going for a fingernail file, the phone rang. I stopped in my tracks, jumped, and grabbed my chest. My heart was beating a mile a minute. But isn't that the way it usually goes when you're snoopin' around in somebody else's stuff?

I walked over to the caller ID box and saw that it was Travis making a three-way call via his grandmother. Made me wonder if maybe he had gotten some cameras installed in there. His timing was impeccable.

"Hello?"

"Who's been over there?" he asked, cutting to the point.

"What?"

"I said, who's been over there?"

"Travis, I don't have time to play games with you."

"Why not? You've got time to keep company in *my* apartment!"

I collapsed onto the bed. Didn't know what to say next. Couldn't tell if he was trying to get me to tell him something or if he really knew about Mr. Wonderful from the night before.

"I'm the only person who's been in this apartment, okay?"

"You think I don't have eyes out there? I won't be disrespected, Nikai!"

"Later for all that, Travis, 'cause I told you nobody's been in here. Now we have something more important to discuss, like what you're gonna do about gettin' your furniture outta here."

"For what? That apartment is in *my* name!"

"I know, that's why we have to go! Remember your little fetish for children under the legal age?" I asked sarcastically.

"You know what? I'm gettin' tired of your smart-ass mouth! I'm sittin' here locked up and all you can think to do is crack jokes!"

"I'm not crackin' jokes, because none of this is funny. You think I laughed when I pulled that eviction notice off the door?"

"No. But that's only because *you* weren't the one who pulled it off."

Travis got quiet, like he was giving me just enough rope to hang myself. He obviously had somebody watching me, so moving over to Sheila's wasn't gonna help one bit.

"Listen, I'm not gonna sit here and be accused of *anything*."

"Yeah, well keep your eyes open, because mine are."

He hung the phone up without saying good-bye, *or* how long I had before his friend came back to watch me. Suddenly, I felt a chill. I'd never noticed how alone I was in that apartment until then. Until I knew someone else was aware of it.

The sun was setting and I was sure that Sheila was getting ready for her date with Rastaman. The last thing she needed to hear was that I was scared to sleep alone. Normally, I would've beaten her door off the hinges before Travis had time to finish his last sentence, but I know what it's like when you haven't kept good company in a while, and she deserved that night. Without my untimely interruptions.

I got up, walked back over to the closet, and grabbed that metal box with the intention of pryin' that baby wide open. If Travis was gonna play private detective, then so was I. I stuck the file inside the keyhole and twisted it. Nothing happened. Next up was one of my bobby pins. Nada. Then came the hairpins, paper clips, steak knives, and finally the metal end of my rat-tail comb. Bingo! That sucka popped up like a timer in a turkey.

I lifted the lid and tried my best to pick my jaw up from my lap. There were nude photos of some young girl. She was everything that I wasn't. Dark-skinned, extremely thin, with long wavy hair. She didn't look African-American, but I couldn't really tell for noticing that she was wrapped up in the same damn set of sheets that were on our bed at that very moment. *Eewww!* I jumped up, grabbed the box, and sat on the floor with my legs crossed.

I went through just about every photo, until I simply couldn't take any more. I set them up on the bed and continued looking through the box of surprises. I found a little black book filled with numbers, an old worn picture of his mother and father when they were together, and a gun. It was a small unloaded silver .22. He had the bullets wrapped up in a cotton tube sock with a blue-and-red ring. I leaned my back against the bed and wondered what he had planned to do with such a small gun. It was the kind you expected a no-nonsense woman to keep tucked away in her handbag. Not some grown-ass man with an ego the size of Texas.

For the next four hours, I lay there on the floor among all of his mementos and silently waited. For what? I don't know, but I figured if I kept quiet long enough, I was bound to hear something or somebody. I glanced up at the clock and it read 11:23. *Damn, Sheila.* Rastaman hadn't brought her back yet.

I got up and tucked the .22 in the front waistband of my purple leggings. Tied my long red T-shirt up in a knot on the side, adjusted the plastic cap on my head like a beret, and pulled my crew socks up as high as they would go. Then I walked over to the long mirror and stood with my legs apart. Snatched the empty .22 out and aimed it at my reflection.

"Whassup now, Travis? Oh, you're at a sudden loss for words. Well, try explainin' these!"

I backed over to the bed and picked up the photos without taking my eyes off of the mirror.

"Oh, don't cry now, 'cause you're *busted!*"

There was a noise outside my bedroom window. I put the gun back in my leggings and hit the light switch. Got down on the floor and crawled on my elbows like I was under attack by an unknown enemy. One with no face or name. One who was sent to take me out, no matter what. The scary part was those were basically the circumstances.

I stood up alongside the window and peeped out of the hunter green blinds. It was Mr. Johnson from downstairs, emptying his trash in the Dumpster. I exhaled and felt my shoulders go limp. I was in that apartment, losin' my mind. Lettin' this fool scare me from behind bars. I had way more mind control than that. This was gettin' ridiculous. I grabbed a Will Downing tape, threw it in the stereo, and pushed the play button. It didn't matter which one of his songs came out. Just his voice alone was enough to take things down a notch. I looked over at the clock again and only six funky minutes had passed. Will was still doin' his best to keep me sane, while all I could think about was doofus down at the county jail.

Will sang ". . . guess you'll be glad to know that I've learned how to laugh and smile."

That's probably what Travis was doing, laughing at my nervous butt. Maybe this was supposed to be payback for having the abortion. Or maybe he was just taking a lucky guess about who took the notice off of the door. Maybe, maybe, maybe. Nothing appeared to be for certain anymore.

I walked over to the mirror again and raised my right hand.

"Do you, Nikai Parker, solemnly swear to keep your sanity, never take mess from another man, and bust a cap in *anybody's* ass who Travis tries to send up in here after you? I do."

I checked the time again and realized that the only way I was gonna make it through the night would be to try and get some sleep. I put my gun—that's right, I said *my* gun—on the nightstand and made a pallet on the floor. I lay there on my back, completely still, and tried doing that meditation thing that Sheila always did when she wanted to relax and become one with herself or something like that. I closed my eyes and began to feel light. Almost as if my spirit were floating. My breathing slowed and I could hear everything around me. *Including the footsteps outside my door.*

I jumped up and grabbed ole trusty off of the nightstand and headed toward the living room. The closer I got, I realized that there was more than one person. Guess Travis had planned on letting them ambush me. They were whispering and then laughing, like the possibility of my damn death was funny. There was a banging on the iron balcony, keys rattling, and then the sound of Sheila's "Come do me" giggle. I snatched that door open and watched their faces freeze in disbelief. I had forgotten about the gun in my hand, the plastic cap on my head, and the socks up to my shins.

"Nikai, *what* are you doing?" Sheila asked.

I put my index finger up to my lips and shushed her. Took a look around the complex and ducked into her apartment with them. Rastaman was looking good in his Fubu jeans and T-shirt. He wasn't very muscular, but his keen features gave him sex appeal. Sheila was in a long green summer dress, with her hair in cornrows going to the back.

"Travis has somebody watchin' the apartment," I whispered.

"What?"

"He saw my friend leaving this morning."

"You mean the guy you met at the club?" she asked.

"Yeah."

"How do you know this?"

Sheila was questioning me like she didn't believe me. And what made it worse was that Rastaman kept eyeing the gun like *I* was trying to hold *them* hostage.

"He called me today and told me that he knew I wasn't the one who took the eviction notice off of the door."

Rastaman asked, "Baby, you sure you don't need me to stick around here for the night? I'll stay up while you two get some sleep."

"No, no, baby. That's okay. We should be fine."

They were *baby*ing all over the place, when I could possibly have a bullet, rope, or butcher knife with my name on it.

"Um, excuse me, but I'd like a little attention here. This is my *life* we're talking about."

Sheila turned to her knight in shining armor and kissed him good night. Walked him to the door and then watched him until he pulled off in his white Suburban. She doubled back into the apartment and stood looking down her nose at me like a disappointed mother.

I defensively asked, "What?"

"You know what. Look at you. Do you know how crazy you look? You're not even wearing shoes."

I looked down at myself. I must've looked pretty stupid standing there in a plastic cap and that outfit.

"So are you sayin' you don't believe me?"

Sheila shook her head and stepped out of her black flat sandals.

"Go lock your door and c'mon back."

"Now, what exactly did he say?"

"Well, the time before when I talked to him, I told him

about the abortion and he said that he wasn't done with me. Now, I don't know what that sounds like to you, but it screams a threat to me."

"He might just be bluffing, you know. What you need to do is calm down and stop jumpin' around like you're Starsky without Hutch."

"Shut up, Sheila. I tried meditation."

"Did it make you feel any better?"

"A little, but when I heard some noise, I was back up again."

"I don't know, Nikai. Travis doesn't come across as the kinda guy who would have somebody watchin' you. He's so formal, ya know?"

"No . . . I . . . don't . . . know! That's all an illusion. Trust me, I've slept with the man for ten months. He couldn't bring *himself* to do it, but go to one of his family reunions and you can sell a proposal like this for as little as a rib sandwich and a Vess soda."

She laughed as though it hurt. Almost as though she was pretending for me.

"Sheila, you okay?"

She sighed and answered, "Yeah, I'm fine, considering."

"Considering what?"

"Considering the fact that Byron told me tonight that he's only here for another week and then he goes back home."

"Where's home?"

"He wouldn't tell me. He says the distance might make me want to forget about him."

I shook my head and rested my chin in the palm of my hand.

"Isn't that the way love goes? Just when you've found that person who is so unlike everybody else, circumstances pull him away."

"And that's not the bad part."

"What is?"

"The sex was better than any I've ever had *in my life*."

"Oohh. I'm sorry. I know how that can be. Travis's lousy ass used to put it on me like that."

"Well, I hope you weren't wearing that plastic cap at the time," she joked.

"You know I was."

Sheila issued an exhausted laugh, got up from the round table, and pulled the futon out for me.

"Here, you can sleep on this."

"Thanks, Sheila."

She turned to go to her bedroom and said, "Nikai, one more thing."

"What's that?"

"Put that gun away. Don't you know that guns are magnets for other guns? They automatically draw trouble to you."

"Okay, get some rest."

Sheila closed her bedroom door as I lay down and wrapped myself in a lavender comforter she gave me. I looked over at the blinds to make sure they were turned down and that the door was locked. Then I put the gun away—right under my pillow. Travis was obviously having fun playing his little mind games, but I was determined to keep my vow. I was gon' bust a cap in *anybody's* ass. Even if they were bad enough to show up in my dreams.

I had tossed, turned, and ended up on my back. All of the lights were out in the apartment. A sista couldn't even see her way to the toilet if she wanted to. I could hear the birds chirping on the balcony outside, and the living room floor settling. The sound was coming from over by the window. I opened my eyes and could barely see a tall silhouette of someone whose back was to me. I slowly reached under the pillow and grabbed that gun to shoot and then pistol-whip the snot out of whoever it was.

The floor creaked again and then I sat up. The figure quickly turned to me and started moving in closer.

"Back up off of me!" I yelled, aiming at the person's chest.

Sheila whispered. "Are you out of your mind?"

"Oooppps."

"*Oops* is all you can say? Gimme that!" she said, snatching it from me. "You need to get your butt up here to this window with me and try to figure out who this is standing at your door."

My heart stopped and then started at an extremely rapid pace. I threw the comforter back, tiptoed up to the window, and lifted one of the blinds. Sheila was right: There *was* someone outside my apartment.

"What am I gonna do?" I whispered, damn near in tears.

"If that's who's been watchin' you, then he already knows what you look like. It's time you find out what he looks like. It'll be harder for him to keep an eye on you if he knows you can recognize his face."

Sheila lifted the gun and asked, "Is this thing loaded?"

"Yeah."

"Well, here, you take it. I'll get my mama's cast-iron skillet. Be right back."

The person knocked on my door again. This time, it was a sort of impatient knock. Sheila came back with a black skillet that was bigger than life.

"Damn, he may survive a bullet wound, but that thing'll kill 'im for sure."

"Shut up, Nikai, and get ready to open this door. Now, on the count of three, we're gonna jump out on him, okay?"

"Okay."

Sheila started counting.

"One . . . two . . . two—"

"Quit playin', Sheila!"

"Hell, I ain't laughin'! Okay, one . . . two . . . three!"

I yanked the door open and we jumped out, lookin' like a broke-ass Cagney and Lacey. A tall, sexy man in a blue St. Louis firefighter's uniform, who was holding a box of Krispy Kreme doughnuts and two cups of coffee, fell out laughing at me and Sheila.

"What is this?" he asked.

"What are *you* doin' over here?"

"I thought I would bring you some doughnuts and coffee before I went to work. I figured you needed it after getting that notice yesterday morning."

Sheila said, "Oh, now isn't that sweet. I'll take this."

She took my weapon, placed it in the skillet, and walked back into her apartment.

I asked, "Listen, um, what was your name again?"

"Robert."

"Yeah, Robert. You can't just stop by here like this. I told you I would call you."

"I know you did, but you didn't."

"I didn't think I had limited time."

"Well, we all learn something new every day," he said, grinning. "So you're gonna make me stand here at six in the morning with unwanted coffee and doughnuts?"

I looked out across the parking lot and over the balcony. Everything appeared to be quiet, but there was really no telling. I walked back into Sheila's apartment and grabbed my key off her coffee table, then closed the door behind me and threw Robert a dirty look.

"You're very persistent, aren't you?" I asked.

"I try to be."

"Well, next time, don't try so hard."

I unlocked the door to my apartment and we went inside. The stereo was still on, but Will had long since stopped singing.

"Just let me get cleaned up. I'll be right back. Have a seat."

"Thanks, you were singeing my nostril hairs with that dragon breath."

I stopped on my way to the bathroom and couldn't help but laugh.

"And just think, you were having the same effect on me, and you already brushed."

Robert chuckled and said, "Timing was good, but delivery was off."

After I had gotten washed up, we sat and ate the breakfast that he was kind enough to bring by. His conversation was good, too. We talked about his job, my job, movies, our favorite restaurants, and what our childhoods were like.

An hour or so had passed and he left for work. I followed him out, the same way Sheila had done with Rastaman. I don't know what it was about Robert, but I *was* actually pleased.

Nikai

Growing up, I always knew that I was different, and not in a bad way. While my older sister, Taylor, played outside with the other girls on the block, I was at the mirror, mimicking Diana Ross or writing a song of my own. I was never the fun-loving extrovert that my sister, who entertained my parent's guests with the latest dance move she'd learned in ballet or tap class, was. My creative voice was muffled because I was measured on a scale of Taylor's accomplishments, and the math never added up.

Taylor always got the best grades, best boyfriends, and best reactions from my mother, who was big on appearances. She felt our success and failures were a direct reflection on her, and more times than not, I let her down. I struggled through high school, barely making C's, was cut from the high school volleyball team for fighting the visitors at a homecoming game, called home from college *every* weekend for money, but the statutory rape incident was the straw that broke the camel's back. Everyone we knew always appeared interested in Taylor's latest accomplishment. Winning the Talented Teen pageant, being awarded scholarships to colleges on the East Coast, and her stunning beauty made life with my mother a lot easier for Taylor.

As we got older, I broke free from the burden of Mama's expectations and started doing what I knew would make me happy. Or should I say doing what made the most sense to me at that time? Taylor did the same, but by then she was programmed to please my mama. She always showed out and generally showed up in the conversations about the few talented people we had in our family. Everyone else was either not mentioned or wondered about, and the latter consisted of Uncle Lucky and me.

Lung cancer snatched my father away during my senior year in college. All of my life, he'd been the only one on my team, until he died. It was really hard for me, and after a year, God brought Sheila into my life to help fill that void.

Uncle Lucky got his name from a habit he had. He used to gamble every day. Once, I overheard my great-aunt telling a story of how he'd been arrested for shooting dice and later had to be put in his own private holding cell for placing bets on who would post bail sooner.

My mother and her uncle Lucky live in a three-bedroom town house off of Highway 367 in North County. And Taylor spends most of her time flying in and out of the United States, detached from reality and her family as much as possible. I keep my distance also, but for different reasons.

Nevertheless, Uncle Lucky and Daddy were my favorites. Now at the age of seventy-two, Lucky has the daunting task of living with my mother—a stunt that even I found nearly impossible to pull off for another year. He usually lounges around in the family room, with his recliner stationed farthest from the window, claiming that the loan sharks are still after him. My mother stopped trying to get him to go out about a year ago. "Let him rot, if that's what he wants to do," she would say. Her words even penetrated my outer shell, because he would just look away, as if eye contact were the only way to the soul. But I know in my heart that he wanted more. He wanted to leave. Almost as badly as I did.

"Lucky, you gonna eat today?" my mother asked.

"Depends on what you got."

"You don't sound like a hungry man to me." She laughed.

I had come by to talk to Mama for the first time in almost two weeks. I was no happier to see her than she was to see me. When I rang the doorbell, she unlocked the door and turned the knob just enough for me to see that she was willing to tolerate my presence. I took a deep breath, jumped into character, and walked inside.

She had returned to her favorite spot in the house, the kitchen table. I followed, being careful to give her at least ten feet. She was chopping up onions, green peppers, and celery for a pot of chili that she had started. Gave me no eye contact at all but more attitude than I was prepared for. I took a seat, adjusted the collar of my short one-piece denim dress, and folded my hands in front of me on the round wooden table.

"Hey, what's goin' on?"

"Nothing, just making Lucky something to eat."

She got up and took the cutting board loaded with chopped goods over to the stove.

"Anything here to drink?"

"The refrigerator ain't moved since the last time you were over here."

She stood with her back to me, wearing a pair of black polyester pants, a blue short-sleeved blouse with a floral print, and a pair of black house slippers that snugly covered each of her feet entirely. She had pinned the sides of her dark brown hair back, so I could clearly see her biting the inside of her mahogany-toned cheeks. I had watched this habit form over the years. It had started back when I ruined my sixth-grade Christmas play by falling asleep while waiting to say my line, and the time when Daddy thought it was cool that I dug up the front yard while trying to run away to China. He applauded my efforts to be an individualist.

"Taylor in town?" I asked, grabbing a pitcher of water.

"Nope. Fiji Islands."

Taylor is a garment inspector for some big department store chain downtown. She flies into places like China, Singapore, and the Dominican Republic to make sure that the clothing is approved before it enters the United States. She gets paid pretty well, travels the world, and meets plenty of eligible bachelors.

"How long she been gone?" I asked.

"She left the day after Travis was incarcerated."

Oh shit! I knew where this was going. The heat was slowly rising like the fire under that pot. At that point, she was simmering, but, knowing Mama, she couldn't wait to bring things to a boil.

"Sheila told me to tell you hello."

"Oh really? How is she? She's not still practicing that voodoo, is she?"

"She never was, and she's doing okay."

"Mmmhmm. I'm just glad she didn't have to witness that mess with Travis being arrested. At least *everybody* you know didn't have to be embarrassed."

"Well, Sheila's one of those people who understands that people aren't necessarily guilty by association."

She gave a dry "Yeah, right."

"But speaking of Travis, I'm not with him anymore."

Without turning around, she said, "Well, according to the police, he was with somebody else anyway."

Now do you see where I get my sarcasm from? It was inherited.

"Okay, Mama. But I don't even plan to live in that apartment anymore."

"Oh, really? And why is that?"

I didn't want to say that I had been *put out,* because that would just be another notch in my belt of fuckups, as far as she was concerned. But at the same time, I had to make it seem desperate enough for her to take me in *and* try to prevent her from suggesting that I stay with Sheila.

"I just decided that it was time for me to move on with my life."

"Sounds like a wise choice. Where are you planning to stay?"

"Don't know yet. Maybe when Taylor comes into town, I can ask her to let me stay at her place."

She returned to the table to grab a can of beans and asked, "Ever think about getting a place of your own?"

"Of course I have. I just can't afford it right now. I'm only an administrative assistant."

"You don't have to spice the title up on my account. Secretaries live alone, too!"

"I know this, Mama. But right now, I could really use a roommate. I'm paying off credit cards *and* financial aid."

"Well, it just doesn't make sense to try to throw things off track with Taylor. You know, she's got a serious, steady relationship, and you being there might interfere. Why don't you ask Sheila? She doesn't look like too many guys are coming through to see her."

I had to take a deep breath and remind myself that I was on the asking end of this conversation. She was allowed to say whatever she wanted until I had established living quarters. After that, it was open game.

"Sheila only has a one-bedroom."

"Well, isn't she your friend?"

"You're my *mother and you have a guest room,* but you haven't offered to let me stay!"

She shook her head and turned back to the pot, which was boiling now.

"If you think I'm gonna have drama like that shit you and Travis pulled goin' on in my house, you are sadly mistaken."

"Why do you keep puttin' *me* in that? *I* didn't sleep with a *minor; Travis* did! And what ever happened to loving your children no matter what? What's goin' on inside your head that would make you believe that I can continue to survive without you showin' me some kind of love or concern? Take your pick! I'm up for either one!"

She turned around, her hands on her hips. Even had the nerve to have a tear in her eye.

"You think you're that grown that you can just tell your own mother off?"

That one softened me. My intentions weren't to hurt her, but to back her up off of me for a change. She was fully aware of the fact that I still needed a place to stay, but as long as I danced around it, she was gonna shuffle her feet until those house slippers no longer had soles.

"Listen, I'm sorry. I need a place to stay until I can get on my feet. Do you mind if I stay here?"

She was silent for a moment. I got up and stood beside her at the stove.

She looked at me and asked, "Nikai, when are you going to

get your life together? Nicholas isn't here anymore, and there's no telling how long I will be."

"I'm trying to, Mama. Just bear with me and stop talking like that. You're not going anywhere for a long, long time."

I gave her a hug.

"Have you gone in and spoken to Lucky? You know how he is about you. He's been asking where you've been."

I kissed Mama on her lightly perspiring forehead and joined Uncle Lucky in the living room.

"*Heeeyyyyy, Slim!* Where you been? I had a three-pound bag of pecans for you to help me crack, but you never came by."

"Oh, I'm sorry. I didn't know. But I'll tell you what I will do. The next time I come over, I'll have a *seven*-pound bag for you. And we'll crack 'em and watch the game together."

"Sounds like a plan, unless you pullin' my leg. You wouldn't do that, would ya, Slim? I get enough of that from ya mama. Always talkin' 'bout how she gonna bring me a treat home. Ben-Gay and ginkgo biloba ain't no treat!"

I giggled and rubbed his nearly bald head.

"Nah, that doesn't sound like a treat to me, either. You got something you'd like for me to pick up?"

It was understood that he was *not* leaving the house, so after a while, even I stopped asking.

"Yeah, you can bring me that voodoo friend of yours. Now, that's what I call a treat."

I lightly tapped him on the shoulder and whispered, "I think maybe she's a little too old for you."

"Yeah, come to think of it, maybe she is. But tell her she can come throw a hex on me *anyday*."

"Sheila doesn't practice voodoo, Uncle Lucky. She's what you call 'spiritually grounded.'"

"Spiritually grounded, summoning spirits—it's all the same."

"No, it's not. Hey, I've got a surprise for you."

"What's that?"

"I'm gonna be living here with you and Mama for a while."

"That's great, Slim. Now maybe you can take some of the pressure off of me."

"Nah, maybe we can share it."

Uncle Lucky got back into watching the television. I guess he had done his share of talking for the day. It wasn't that he didn't like to, but this was all that he was used to—a word here, a sentence there. And then it was back to his world of isolation. Mama never had much to say unless she was complaining, and Lucky usually followed her lead. The most disturbing part was that I was about to jump back into this emotionless system of living. This was a challenge unwelcomed. To see if love and concern for one another could become the norm, to see why for so many years we had shielded our fears and insecurities, and, finally, to see just what really was goin' on with my people.

By the time I made it home, Sheila was praying and burning sage. This was a ritual that she looked forward to in order to purify her apartment, but I dreaded it. Every time she lighted that stuff in a large silver tray, I had to wait three hours before the smoke cleared out. I wanted to give her the good news before I started packing up what was supposed to go with me. When she answered the door in one of those gowns, the smoke just about knocked me over. I turned around and leaned over the balcony to catch my breath. Thought about Travis's people watching me and flipped the bird to whatever eye was observing my every move.

"Girl, get in here. It's not that bad."

I put my hand over my nose and mouth and asked, "How long have you been doing that?"

"Oh, I went a little longer today. I wanted the house purified because I was praying for guidance."

"Guidance for what?"

Sheila fanned the extra smoke above the ashes, gathered up the front of her gown, and sat her bare behind right up close to me on the futon.

"Got somethin' to tell you."

"What?" I asked, leaning away from her. "You ain't about to have a little Rastaman, are you?"

"Girl, nah. I haven't known him that long."

"What, then?"

"Remember I told you that Byron's moving back home? Well, he asked me to move with him."

Sheila's mouth was smiling, but the rest of her face looked uncertain of my response.

"And where is home?"

"Oh, it's not that far."

"I thought you just said you haven't known him that long. How are you gonna move in with him? It's only been a week."

"I know this. That's why I prayed and asked the Creator to let me see what I needed to see and hear what I needed to hear. Trust me, I wouldn't do this if I didn't feel safe about it."

"And how do you know that he doesn't have a wife and kids tucked away somewhere? He could be *sacrificing sheep* every morning or even lying about his job! Do . . . you . . . even . . . *know* if he has one?"

"Yes, Nikai. He does construction work. I know what you're thinking, because at first I thought the same thing. I prayed on it and now I'm gonna leave it in the Creator's hands."

"So where is home? Kansas City? Chicago?"

"Nope."

Her smile grew more and more every time I guessed.

"Guess again."

"Indianapolis? Uh, Detroit?"

"Close. It sorta rhymes with Detroit."

By now, she was bouncing up and down and the beads on her dress were yellin' for me to keep going. I have to admit that I got a little excited. I really wanted to know, but I also wanted to be right.

"Illinois?"

"Nope. You already said Chicago. Guess again."

"Hell no! Tell me or *forget* it!"

She started guiding me along, *"De . . . tr . . . oi . . . t."*

Her hands were moving in a winding motion. Almost as if she were wrapping them both in tape.

"What? I don't get it!"

"Saint Croix, girl! *Damn!*"

"*Saint Croix!* What ever happened to 'not far'? That's the Virgin Islands. You're leavin' the *country!*"

"Oh, it's okay." She tried reassuring me by fanning at my concern. "It's owned by the United States."

"*Owned, my ass!* They still drive on the left side of the street! You don't know nothin' about livin' in the *islands!* See, that's what you get for lyin' and tellin' that man you've been somewhere you haven't! What do you think you're gonna do? Jump off the plane and go climbin' up coconut trees and shit? Are you *crazy?*"

Sheila's face turned cold and stiff as she stood and walked over to her "table of thought." I didn't say anything, because I really needed to hear what was going on in her head. She was planning to leave the country over a big dick and some dreadlocks. I can admit that I didn't necessarily have it all together, but even from where I was standing, this stunt she was pullin' looked like insanity.

"Nikai, leave my apartment," she insisted.

"But Sheila—"

"Now!"

"Sheila, just listen to me."

"*Now!*"

I got up, walked to the door, and tried one last time to get my point across. Sheila put her hand up in order to cease all comments and then joined me on the threshold.

"May the Creator and the spirits of our ancestors bless you with the wisdom and faith that you need to make it in this world. No wonder you have such a hard time trusting in people, Nikai. Sometimes you act as though you don't even trust in God."

At that moment, I got about ten feet of wood slammed shut in my face.

I never saw the inside of that apartment again, but what she said stuck with me. I fought faith. And lost the battle every time. Right along with the best friend I've had since my daddy.

I knocked on Sheila's door every day for the rest of that week, but she never answered. Eventually, I left a note informing her that I would be staying with my mother and included the address. On my last day of packing, I came home from work, to find that she had placed all of my things that either she had borrowed or I had left over at her place in a small cardboard box in front of my door. An old hot curler, a '98 issue of *Sister 2 Sister* magazine, a pair of gold hoop earrings, and, yes, even my gun. But she cared enough to keep the bullets. I cried until I couldn't any longer. I was starting over fresh and new. New people, new living arrangements, and a new frame of mind.

But that's the funny thing about life—sometimes you have to take a couple of steps backward in order to go forward. Which is definitely what God had in store for me. I didn't know if that was gonna happen with Sheila's new relationship, but there's one thing I did find out. It was that if I was going to make it in this world, I needed to start praying. And I didn't need sage, incense, or a dead sheep to do it, either. I needed that faith that Sheila spoke about. Faith to keep pushing, to make wise decisions, and, most of all, to believe that I wasn't ever alone. I think the most frightening part that I remember is that I needed it a lot sooner than I ever imagined.

Robert

Why is it I always have to meet the honey with problems?

I can take a kid here and there, even a little financial difficulty, but eviction notices spell one thing: Homegirl is eventually gonna need a place to stay. That, I couldn't provide. And the messed-up part about it is that this woman was *baaaddddd*. I'd say she looks like a high-powered Toni Braxton with lips like Sheryl Lee Ralph. You don't find women like her every day, I don't care where you look. Except maybe in one of those galleries featuring Egyptian divas from the early dynasties.

I know about that kinda stuff 'cause I'm always watching the Discovery Channel. Got *Wild Kingdom* tapes stacked up the wall right next to my pile of pharaoh footage and volumes of *Hieroglyphics Unfolded*. It's just something about the past *and* nature that intrigues me. If I had to pick between the two, it would probably be nature. Four years of watching a single lion take down a large buffalo in the humid savanna helped shape my "survival of the fittest" mentality. Some may call it selfish, but I call it *self*-preservation.

I got into these tapes during my senior year in college at SEMO, which was five years ago. No, I wasn't on the seven-year plan, I just didn't go right after high school. I was doing what I called finding myself and almost found myself at the courthouse marrying the wrong woman. That's when I decided to be a lot more careful with my pickings. A big ass and large breasts were no longer prerequisites. I've been there and done that. I decided a long time ago that the next woman I chose would have to have a good head on her shoulders *and* the personality to go with it.

I think that's why I couldn't shake this woman Nikai from my mind. She's the one who was on her way to homelessness. I didn't ask what the reason was for her getting put out, because I didn't think I had to. People will only tell you what they want you to know, anyway. I kept that in mind, even when we were discussing our lives one afternoon when I dropped by. I could tell she really needed someone to confide in, because she was doin' that woman thing. You know, talkin' about the last dog who stole her heart and ripped it to shreds. A brotha ain't tryin' to hear about somebody else's mistakes. That's like me explaining why I stuck it out with my ex-fiancée, Lana, even after I caught her servin' up my best man in our bathroom. To me, it's considered water under the bridge.

I hadn't heard from Nikai since that morning I took coffee and doughnuts by her place. I didn't want to come across as too pushy, but she had been on my mind all that day. I think the part that got me about her was that she could hang. She's a smart-ass, just like me. But she's sexy with hers. Most women write me off as a jerk, but that's only because, with me, they're forced to use their brains *or* get their egos crushed. But Nikai, I could tell that she could take me down if she really wanted to. And that was a serious turn-on.

On top of all that, she sings. And I don't mean no Broadway vocals. Nikai can sing a brotha up off his money clip. I told her that I would talk to my buddy Don about hookin' somethin' up. His cousin, Kalif, was supposed to be in producing. He'd been working with a group and trying to get a demo tape together. I personally saw it as an avenue back to Nikai. You know, like making myself the middleman.

That's how desperate I was to keep in contact with this woman. With just one kiss, she had put it on me like *that*. My piece was throbbin' so hard, you could've checked my pulse on it. And it wasn't just about layin' with her, because I could've tried something the night we met at Club De Ja Vu. She let me fall asleep at her place, listenin' to some old jams that I really didn't care to hear. Music is just one part of the past that I don't need. I mean, with all of the R. Kelly and Kenny Lattimore cuts, who needs to resurrect Donnie Hathaway's old jams?

But I let her have her moment, because that's just the kinda guy I am. Always trying to balance tasks and keep everyone happy. That is, if I can. And once it becomes too much to handle, my self-preservation instincts kick in. Then I quickly shift into "save my ass" mode. Unfortunately, often leaving the ones who are closest to me hurt. Like my younger sister, Kim, and my moms, who are really all I have. My pops, I couldn't pick out of a lineup. Never knew him. Moms had to be both parents and felt quite guilty for not picking a better man to procreate with. So ironically, I got spoiled, and Kim, since she knew her father, got whatever emotions were left, which helped turn her into Ms. Badass. She's got a mouth that won't quit and no body to back it up. Standing five foot three and weighing 120 pounds, she talks like a giant, even to me.

Kim can be humorous from time to time, but often she's a pain in the butt. Like I don't have enough stress from putting in extra hours at the engine house. Not to mention juggling all of these silly women who are eager to give it up all because of my size. But that's just some psychological shit. With all of this feminist talk goin' around, they still wanna be handled and controlled, if only for one night. And just about every brotha knows that you can't take every wrapped gift. Three or four of those babies are bound to explode, leaving you fucked up for life. That, I'm not tryin' to mess with. I take enough chances with my life just going to work. If I'm gonna get burned, it won't be the kind that'll affect me while I'm tryin' to take a piss. That's why I use a system that's called the process of elimination. It goes according to age, goals, wit, personality, and then body.

Prior to Nikai, the only woman I'd been seriously seeing was this beautician, Karen. Now, she's high-powered, too. Spontaneous, sexy, full of life, and owns her own shop. She filled every area except for wit. That's where Nikai was puttin' her to shame. But I just couldn't seem to get close enough to Nikai. She hadn't called, the way that she said she would, and according to the notice that was on her door, she was supposed to have moved ASAP.

One afternoon, about two weeks after we met, I was over to Moms's house, talking to Kim about why the guy she'd been dealing with was dating someone else. We were in the living room, waiting for the next commercial to come on the Animal Planet before I started lecturing again. She was in a plaid short-sleeved one-piece pajama set, sitting next to me on the couch, with folded arms, looking like a lumberjack with an attitude. I was in jean shorts and a white T-shirt, holding the remote in one hand and a beer in the other.

She complained, "Rob, you've seen this episode before!"

"I know, but it's always better the second time around."

I never took my eyes off the television as I awaited the cannibalistic act of one Komodo dragon in the Indonesian islands eating a smaller one. I could feel my pager go off, but I didn't move.

"Ah! He got him!"

"All right, a commercial's on now."

"Hold on a second."

I checked my pager, and it was Karen. I grabbed the phone off of the arm of the plastic-covered couch and dialed her number back.

"Hey."

"Hey, sweetheart. I miss you."

"Miss you, too."

"What are you doin'?" she asked.

"Sittin' here with my little sister watchin' TV."

"Well, we are still gonna catch that movie tonight, aren't we?"

I checked the time on my pager as it began to vibrate in my hand. I didn't recognize the number, but I knew the prefix wasn't from the city area.

"Hey, let me hit you back," I told Karen.

"Robert, I need to know *something*. Are we or aren't we going tonight?"

"I'll be there."

"What time?"

"Eight-thirty."

"Don't disappoint me," she warned.

"Do I ever?"

She let out a soft giggle and said, "Let's wait until the night is over and then ask me."

"Will do."

I pushed the flash button and dialed the number back. A woman answered the phone, sounding rather monotone. I wasn't used to that. Most of the ladies I'd dealt with anticipated my calls.

"I'm returning a page."

"Is this Robert?" she asked.

"Yeah, who is this?"

"Nikai."

"Hey, hey. How you doin'?" I asked, sitting up straight on the couch and adjusting my clothes, as though she could see me.

"Pretty good. I just got all of my things moved out of my old apartment and into my mother's. I wasn't really that tired, so I decided to call you and see if you wanted to hang out today."

"Uh-huh."

I was thinking about the promise that I'd just made to Karen, but this was *Nikai* finally pulling through. I could make that up to Karen. A wild Komodo on crack couldn't drag her away. She wasn't going anywhere.

"We don't have to, if you can't make it."

"No, no. I can make it. I was just trying to think of someplace nice to take you."

"Have you eaten lunch already? I know of a Vietnamese restaurant called De Nang over on the South side. The food is really good."

"I've seen that place before. Sounds good to me. What time do you need me to pick you up?"

The pissed-off lumberjack nudged me with her elbow before I could finish my sentence. Made me sound even more nervous than I already was.

"Coming to get me would be going out of your way. I'll meet you over there at around two. That okay?"

"Perfect."

"See you then."

I hung up the phone and must have looked real silly to Kim, because she broke into laughter.

"Well, well, well. Finally about to get a taste of your own medicine, huh?"

I straightened my face and asked, "What are you talkin' about?"

"Somebody's got you all giddy, and from the way you were tryin' to be all polite, it sounds like she's new."

"What it sounds like is you're crossin' your fingers and hopin' some man, somewhere, actually pays for what Kevin did to you."

"No, I don't, because he will suffer. *One way or another.*"

She leaned back on the plastic, folded her arms, and got a crazy look in her eye. You know that "woman scorned" look that always kept me on my toes. I never wanted some woman to sit back and stare at an empty wall while plottin' on takin' me down. That's why I was so careful. Never took chances with psychos like the one who was sitting next to me and never broke hearts unless it was *absolutely* necessary. And even then, I had a backup plan to *save my ass.*

Nikai had said she would meet me at De Nang at two, but I had been parked out front for almost an hour. I saw a green Camry pull up behind me after about ten more minutes had passed, and the beautiful driver innocently wiggled her fingers at me. I sucked my teeth, brushed the lint from my black jeans and T-shirt, and got out to open her door. I was a little irritated by her tardiness, but more happy to see her again.

Before I could close her door, she started with the apologies.

"I'm so sorry. My brother is in jail right now and he's been bugging me about helping him tie up some loose ends."

I found it rather strange for her not to have mentioned having a brother before, considering she had shared so much with me concerning her paranoid uncle, snobbish sister, and insensitive mother. But hey, she was there with me, and that was all that mattered.

"That's okay. You look wonderful."

She sashayed around to the sidewalk, making that black V-

necked T-shirt dress speak in a language that all men understood.

"Thanks. You look good yourself."

We walked inside and took a seat near the back. This was her
idea, but I wasn't complaining. That meant less witnesses. The
inside was rather small, but it was easy to tell that the decorator
was rich in culture. Even the music was Vietnamese.

I picked up a menu from among the salt, pepper, red pepper
sauce, and soy sauce.

"So what do you recommend?"

Her eyes peered above her menu and narrowed.

I asked, "What?"

"Nothing. Let's just say I like what I see."

"Oh really? Well, let me ask you this. Why'd it take you so
long to call me?"

"I was busy trying to move. You know that. Plus, my
brother's in jail, and that was taking a lot out of me."

There she went with that brother again. I wasn't gonna ask,
but she'd brought it up.

"What happened with your brother?"

"Um," Nikai started, sweating on her upper lip and stuttering.

"If you don't wanna talk about it, that's okay."

"I'd really rather not," she answered quickly.

There was silence between us. I wanted to give her a chance
to steer the conversation. That way, I wouldn't touch on any
personal subjects.

She said, "The chicken clay pot is really good. It's filled with
plenty of vegetables, baked rice, and chicken."

"Then I'll trust you and have that."

I closed the menu and folded my hands in front of me.

"So how's your partner in crime?"

She snatched the menu down with a confused look on her
face and asked, *"Who?"*

"You know, your girl who was ready to put my lights out
with that cast-iron skillet." I laughed.

"Oh, oh, Sheila. She's moved, too."

"Really? That must be a bad area, huh?"

"No. Actually, it was nice. She fell in love and moved to the Virgin Islands with some guy she met on the same night I met you."

"So that means if I ask you to relocate to Australia, you'd be game?"

"Of course not. I'm not Sheila. It would take a lot more than good sex and an accent to move me."

"So what *would* move you?"

"I don't know."

Nikai began to look around the restaurant, hoping that I would let her off the hook, but I wanted badly to know the route to her heart.

"What do you mean, you don't know? You should know what gets you going and what doesn't."

She looked at me and said, "I do. I'm just not telling you."

"As of right now, you mean?"

"For as long as I'm feeling this way."

A young Vietnamese girl came and took our order for two chicken clay pots and left us alone in our corner.

"What way are you feeling?"

She fumbled with the silver rings on her index and ring fingers.

"Right now, like I'm under investigation. You mind not asking so *many* questions?"

"That's cool. My fault. You got some you wanna ask me?"

"Yeah. Does that offer to see your apartment still stand?"

"*Hell yeah!* I mean, of course it does."

I was losing my cool too soon. She was trying to get close to me, and I don't necessarily mean sexually. She wanted to know me, or at least a little more than she already did.

"Good, now maybe I can see if *your* taste is unique."

"I don't know about my taste in furniture, but my taste in women is definitely on point."

"You'll have to excuse the place," I said, picking up beer bottles, empty plates, and clothing.

I walked into the bathroom and grabbed the can of neutralizing air freshener. Sprayed every room in the apartment except for the one she was sitting in and hoped like hell the odor of my sweat socks didn't linger too long.

"You don't have to do all that, Robert. If this is you, this is you."

I stopped and checked her expression in order to determine whether or not I was being insulted in my own place.

"What are you tryin' to say?"

"That I don't believe in perfection. I didn't expect to walk in here and be able to see my reflection in your coffee table, so sit down. Relax and entertain. Isn't that what I'm here for?"

Damn, Nikai was cool. Straightforward without being a bitch and open to my insecurities. I closed the door to my bedroom and joined her on the navy blue sofa.

"You know what, Nikai?" I said, resting my arm behind her.

"What?"

"You ah'ight with me."

"You cool people, too. Now show me some of those movies you've got piled up over there."

She was pointing toward my wall of videos. It was across the room from the one sofa I had and adjacent to the twenty-seven-inch set that I got from my man on discount. The rest of the room was practically empty, unless you counted some old-ass end tables and the beanbags that I still had from college, which were cleverly hiding a nasty spill on the worn brown-and-tan carpet.

"I don't know if you'd be interested in these. They're mostly wildlife footage and blaxploitation films."

"Which ones do you have? I bet you don't have my favorite with 'Too Sweet' and 'Half Dead' tryin' to kill each other for an hour and a half straight."

"What is a blaxploitation collection without *Penitentiary Two*? Of course I have it!"

"I see we have a lot more in common than I thought," she said, smiling.

"And what did you think, that we were from two different worlds?"

"You know, it's possible. Especially considering the fact that I would've offered you something to drink by now."

I jumped up, rubbed my palms together, and asked, "Would you like something to drink?"

"What do you have?"

"Grape Kool-Aid, beer, and water."

"I'll have a beer."

I headed toward the kitchen, when the damn phone started ringing. My instincts told me that it was Karen trying to confirm our date, but I didn't know how long I was gonna be with Nikai. I took my time pouring the beer into a tall glass as each ring became louder and more annoying. Finally, when it stopped, I bit my bottom lip and walked back into the living room.

I handed Nikai the glass and said, "Here you go."

"Thank you, Robert."

She grinned and batted her eyelashes. I wondered if she'd even heard the phone.

"That's another difference between you and me."

"What's that?" I asked, going back into the kitchen for another beer.

"*I* would've answered the phone."

I laughed nervously and shook my head. She had actually left me stumped, without a comeback. I grabbed myself a bottle of beer and sat down next to her in the living room.

Nikai looked at me and asked, "You smoke?"

I immediately grabbed the ashtray filled with butts that was on the coffee table and took it into the kitchen.

She laughed and called, "Robert!"

I leaned against the island in front of the fridge and banged the side of my head with the heel of my hand. Paced back and forth. Wished I could undo what she'd seen and just be "cool people" again.

"Robert!"

Nikai's voice was getting louder, until finally she was standing in the kitchen with me.

"What are you doing?" she asked.

"Nothin'. What's up?"

"C'mere."

She held out her hand for me to take. I felt like a six-foot-four, 235-pound punk. No woman had ever made me feel this way. Want to hide certain parts of me that may not be considered acceptable. I was never the one with sweaty palms and a case of the jitters. It was always the other way around. And the most baffling part was that none of this was intentional. Nikai *wanted* me to relax and enjoy myself. But I couldn't. I wouldn't until I was sure she really dug me and wasn't just killing time until the next guy with more shit and a bigger chest than mine came along.

Okay, so I'll be honest. It did have a little to do with the fact that she had so much class. I actually wished for a moment that I'd had something to impress her with, but I didn't. I had nothing but a classic film that I couldn't even show her because my damn VCR was broken. But I couldn't tell her to ignore the smell coming from my closet, never mind the constant ringing of the phone and taking a rain check for the film feature. She would have laughed me right back out to my car. Which was the only nice thing that I did have. And I must admit, it fooled a lot of women. But that wasn't what I was tryin' to do with Nikai. And the desire to do whatever it was I was trying to do was killing me.

She took my hand and said, "I don't care that you smoke. I just found it kinda strange for a fireman to involuntarily *and* voluntarily draw smoke into his lungs. Now, what did I tell you about perfection?"

"I don't remember. What?"

"That as far as I'm concerned, it does not exist."

She winked, pulled me back into the living room, and asked the question I was hoping she wouldn't.

"So are you gonna let me see one of those movies or am I gonna have to put one on myself?"

"Good luck. The VCR is broken right now."

"All right, how about some music?"

"How about you providing the music?" I proposed.

Nikai started out with a low humming and then began to serenade me with one of Minnie Riperton's oldies.

"Loving you is easy 'cause you're beautiful . . ."

I was on the couch, watching her slowly walk over to me and

then finally sit on my lap. Her hips spread like butter over morning toast and she smelled of sweet, ripened fruit. Nikai put her arm around my neck and began whispering the words to the song in my ear until they had faded somewhere between a mumble and a lick. I shivered and put my lips to hers. They were soft, much softer than I'd imagined, and tasted like sweet butterscotch candy. Took me back to my childhood. To a time when a feminine stroke on the back would make it all better.

She pulled away and surprisingly went back to singing, as though she had never stopped.

"Hold up!" I interjected.

"What's wrong?"

"Look at what you did!"

I pointed to my crotch and she fell over laughing.

"Self-control, Robert. You need to learn some."

"C'mere, I've got some self-control for you."

I stood up and held her around her narrow waist. That T-shirt dress was allowing me to feel just about everything I needed to store in my memory. She placed her hand in the middle of my chest and gave a little push.

"Let's leave something to be desired."

I lifted my hands and said, "Whatever you say."

Just as we sat down, the phone rang again. Nikai looked at me and smiled.

"I'll be right back."

I walked into the bedroom, snatched the phone from its cradle, and yelled, "Who is this?"

My buddy Don answered, "You must be in the middle of somethin'."

"Somethin' like that. Whassup?"

"Yo, bruh, I talked to Kalif and he said it may be a couple of months before he can start working with your friend, but he definitely sounded interested."

I sat down on the edge of the bed and asked, "Nothin' he can do now though, huh?"

"Nope. You still tryin' to link up later?"

"Nah, got company now."

"That's a first for you. Thought you said your home number and address were off-limits. Who is it? The songbird?"

"You know it. But look, I'll hit you back tomorrow, ah'ight?"

"Peace."

I fell back on the bed for a second and tried to figure out how I was gonna break this news to Nikai. This was what I got for trying to make myself look bigger than life. I decided to wait until she mentioned it. Then maybe I'd explain that Kalif was layin' so many tracks in preparation for her that he needed more time.

"Robert!"

"On my way."

I walked back into the living room and found her standing in front of the television with her handbag on her shoulder.

"You have something else to do today?"

"Nah. What about you?"

"I was thinking that we could get out for a while. I wanna take you to my favorite spot. That is, if you don't mind."

"That's cool. Let me get my keys."

"You okay? You look like you've got something on your mind."

"I do. I'm just not tellin' you," I joked.

"Ah, cute," she said, smiling. "Timing was good, but originality needs a little work."

When I say this woman was driving me crazy, I mean just that. Crazy enough to give her the keys to my '98 Maxima. Which was another thing I had never done. Not even to get a piece, which wasn't my primary objective this time around.

I asked, "Where are we goin'?"

"I don't like backseat drivers."

"Well, it's a good thing I'm riding shotgun."

"You know what I mean. Relax and enjoy the scenery."

I reclined in the peanut butter–colored leather seat and let her take control. She turned the radio on and changed the station to one that specifically played old songs. I smiled to myself at her persistence. She was determined to be different from any woman I had ever met.

We rode another five miles or so and ended up at Forest Park, next to several hills.

"C'mon."

Nikai got out and sat on the front of the car. I heard the hood fall in and thought about another place she could set those hips.

"My father used to bring me here when I was little. We'd run up and down this hill right here. Go back into the woods over there and chase snakes all afternoon. I think it's because he always wanted boys."

I asked, "When was the last time you were here?"

"Oh, about three months ago. Back when it first started warming up. My ex and I would come out here to sit and talk."

"So does this make me a prospect?"

"No. It just makes you a man in the park with me."

"You are so tough," I said, pulling her by her waist. "C'mere."

"Chill, black man. I can hear you from here."

"So what happened to that man who was once so lucky?"

"He just sorta left one day."

Nikai looked off toward the hills and appeared to be upset by the thought of this guy. I didn't want to delve into her past, because that way, I didn't have to feel bad about not allowing her to do the same to mine. Besides, recalling exactly where things went wrong might make her want him back.

"Now this song, I can get with!" I yelled, running back to turn the radio up.

Her attention still hadn't drifted back to me, us, or the moment.

"Do . . . what you want to do . . ."

"C'mon, Nikai. This was when Mike was black!"

I sang and danced around in front of her, tryin' to pull a smile from her beautiful face. Broke out doin' every move from the cabbage patch to the robot.

"Robert, people are beginning to stare at you."

Popped and locked like I was auditioning for a break-dancing documentary.

"I know. So how long are you gonna make me do this before you smile for me?"

Wopped and smurfed my way back to the eighties.

"All right, all right!" she screamed, laughing. "You . . . are . . . crazy!"

"Nope, just fallin' for you."

I stopped making a fool out of myself long enough to kiss her full brown lips and felt a serious case of blue balls comin' on.

She pulled back and said, "Robert, I don't do public displays of affection."

"How about private displays?"

She was silent until I leaned my piece into that warm haven between her legs.

"Maybe, maybe private."

I can't quite remember who was all over whom, but in the next fifteen minutes, we were back in my bedroom, making something that came strangely close to love. Well, at least that's the way it was for me.

Once she fell asleep, I rolled over, turned the ringer off, and held that beautiful work of art in my arms until the sun had fallen on both of us. Until I could no longer visually admire her mahogany profile. And until I had thought of a damn good lie to tell Karen.

Robert

I was drifting in and out of sleep until I heard the irksome sound of a siren going off. *Damn.* I had missed another run. I knew then that when the captain got back, he was gonna have my butt in a sling.

I sat up and looked around the sleeping quarters. I was the only one left in the engine house. As I got to my feet, I heard the beeping of my pager. Karen had been all over me since that morning, and I had slept through that, too.

After serving each other up again, Nikai had silently ducked out of my apartment in the middle of the night. And she hadn't called to say *anything* about what we had done. I got nothin' except a note informing me that she would call. Didn't say when. Today, tomorrow, when she needed some more. Nothing. I actually entertained the thought of calling *her,* but pussy-whipped was not the look I was goin' for.

After about thirty minutes or so, I heard the pumper pulling back into the engine house, the sound of firefighters making small talk, and then the captain yelling my name.

"Hayes! Upstairs! My quarters! Ten minutes!"

I could smell a write-up in the air. This was the second time in two months that I had stayed up all night sexing and missed a run. The first time, Karen had worked me over at her place. Made one of those baked Italian dishes because she knows that's my favorite food. Gave me a hot-oil massage and served dessert while I lay in bed. Now that time, it was worth it to hear Keates's bitchin'. By the time she turned me loose, I was limber, my stomach was full, and my crotch felt light. What more could a man ask for?

I started up the staircase to the captain's quarters. He had shut his door, indicating that he intended for it to be a private yet lengthy discussion. I knocked and waited for permission to enter.

"Come on in."

I walked in and greeted him with "What's up, Captain?"

Keates, an older white guy with thinning gray hair, was sitting in a chair behind a short wooden table, clipping his nails. He nodded his head for me to close the door behind me. I did so and stood beside his perfectly made iron-post bed. The white bedspread had a cigarette burn in it near the foot. He noticed me noticing it and got right down to the point.

"Hayes, this is the second time in two months that you've missed a run because you were snoozin'. Now, we'd all love to get a little extra rest, but lives are on the line. People depend on us."

I shoved my hands into the pockets of my blue uniform pants and responded, "I know this."

"I'm beginning to think you don't."

"Keates, I understand what you're sayin', but my aunt was in a fatal car accident last night and I was up with my mother at the hospital."

He sighed heavily and looked up at me with doubtful eyes.

"You sure about that? The last time, your father died from a heart attack. Things keep goin' this way and there won't be anyone left for a family reunion."

Keates sorta laughed, because he knew I was lying. I had stood before him and practically killed off about half of my family in an attempt to *save my ass*. But something told me that he understood that life was full of surprises.

"Look," he said, leaning forward on his elbows and pointing his finger, "I'm gonna let you off this time without a write-up, but I *swear to God*, Hayes, you pull this shit again and it'll be your ass. Got that?"

"Yeah, my ass. Right."

I smiled, turned, and walked out of his quarters. I could hear him still speaking to me as I left. But he knew as much as I did that the rest of that stuff was goin' in one ear and out the other. I was still a grown man. A fact that he better not ever forget. Even if I fell asleep *makin' a run.*

I walked down the stairs and could hear that the kitchen was busy with men flocking over food. The smell of baked lasagna hung in the air. I turned the corner, to find Karen in a pink ankle-length summer dress, instructing everyone to have a seat so she could prepare a plate for them. That woman knew how to work magic on a man. When the other firefighters noticed me, a roar filled the engine house. Thank-yous coming from every direction. As though it'd been my idea to have her come up there and look me in the eye as I concocted another bold-faced lie.

"Hey, baby." She greeted me with open arms.

Hodges yelled, "Enough with that! We've got starving men over here."

I told them, "Help yourself, fellas."

The sound of chairs scooting across the floor and spatulas hitting the Corning Ware dish rang through the kitchen.

"I brought something special for you, baby."

"What?" I asked, feeling like a spoiled kid again.

"Peach cobbler."

"That's my favorite. Is it cold, the way I like it?"

"If I can't serve it to you right, then I might as well not serve it at all."

She tossed her long dark brown hair over her shoulder and revealed the set of twins that I had fallen in love with. They were full, round, and perky, like an eighteen-year-old's. Even though it had been almost ten years since either of us had seen that age.

The fellas' attention was beginning to drift in the direction of the twins and not the lasagna, so I put my arm around Karen and walked her out to her car.

"I have to leave so soon?" she asked.

"I'm sorta in the hot seat with the captain right now."

"What'd you do, *miss another run?*"

"Yeah, only about an hour ago."

"Robert, you seein' somebody else? You know the last time you missed a run, we stayed up all night."

I shifted my weight a couple of times and glanced back into the engine house. Karen stared at me.

"We both know you're fine and all, but I can only tolerate a dog for so long. Then you'll be set out to fend for yourself."

"Karen, baby, please don't start that again. If I were ready for a relationship, you would be the *first* person to know it."

Never said you'd be the *first* pick.

"I believe you, but only because of your backstroke," she assured me while grabbin' my butt in front of everybody.

I could hear the laughter all the way out on the street. I opened the door to her white Jeep Laredo and signaled for her to climb inside. She stood her ground and stayed there, still grippin' my butt and laughing.

"You think that's funny?" I asked.

"What I *think* doesn't matter. What I *know* is that you're due for another hot-oil massage."

"If you let my butt cheek go, I'll be there the first thing in the morning."

"Deal. Bye, fellas!" she yelled, waving at everyone inside the engine house.

I watched Karen pull off and then walked back inside. Prepared myself for whatever jokes were coming my way.

Hodges suggested with a mouthful of food, "Now you should make *her* your wife. Have you tasted this food? It's *unreal*. And her timing was perfect. By the way, I wanna speak to you about that bowl of peach cobbler."

"Hands off. You can have the lasagna, but the cobbler's mine."

Surprisingly enough, nobody had anything to say about Karen's showing out. They were too busy watching the dish to make sure it wasn't getting low. I grabbed a plate from the cabinet and felt my pager vibrating on my waist. Someone had left a verbal message. I walked into the TV room to replay it in there.

"Hi, I just wanted to say that last night was really nice. So nice that I was late to work this morning. Well, I'm gonna go to lunch now, but I hope to talk with you soon. Bye."

Soon? When exactly was soon? I wanted so badly to hang that phone up and dial Nikai back, but I didn't have her work number. Just her home number. But it would be worth it to try to contact her. After all, she was no Karen. I pressed the flash button and dialed her mother's house. An elderly man answered the phone, sounding bitter.

"Yeah!"

Yeah?

"Hello, is Nikai there?"

"Nah, she at wurk! Who this?"

"Uh, this is Rob. Do you have her work number?"

"Hol' on," he said as he called to someone else. "Esther, what's Nikai's numba at wurk?"

The woman answered, "Who is that? Don't be in there givin' information out! It could be Travis or anybody! Lucky, what did I tell you about answering the phone, anyway?"

Travis? The woman, who I assumed was Nikai's mother, picked up the phone and sounded about as bitter as the old man.

"Who is this?"

"How are you doing, ma'am? This is her friend Robert."

"Hhmm. Never heard her mention *you*."

Made me wonder exactly who she *was* mentioning. Could it have been Travis?

"She just paged me, and I wanted to call her back."

"She didn't leave a number?" she asked.

"No, ma'am."

"Then she obviously didn't want you to have it."

And that was that. She disconnected us before I could inhale enough air to respond. I pulled out a pack of Newports and stepped outside to the iron bench. Keates was out there with his sleeves rolled up, taking long drags off a cigarette, too. I guess he knew he had to be careful, since I had seen that burn mark in his bedspread. Him fuckin' up made it a lot more difficult to get on my head about simple things like oversleeping. At least I was just *missing* fires. He was up in his quarters damn near *starting* them.

I asked, "You get something to eat?"

"Nah, this is food enough for me," he said, lifting the half-smoked cigarette in the air.

"You ah 'ight? You look like you're thinking too hard."

"That's got to be impossible. Especially when you're making up for lost time. Time when you *should've* been thinking."

"Your woman?" I asked, detecting a broken heart.

"What used to be my woman."

He took another long drag off of his cigarette and continued.

"She used to do the same stuff that yours is doing for you. Brought me cakes, snacks and shit. Never enough for the rest of them, though. But she made me feel damn special."

The entire time he talked, Keates never looked me in the eye. Just stared at a tree in full bloom across the street, where Karen had parked her Jeep.

"What happened to her?"

"Came up here one day and said she found somebody else. Somebody who could give her the time and attention she needed. Somebody who would be there to hold her at night. She took all of my purpose away. Left me with a lot of undedicated free time. Shit like that will make a man lie in bed and smoke at night, Hayes."

I sat there next to Keates, focused in on that same tree, and wondered about the possibility of that happening to me. If maybe one day the peach cobbler would stop coming. The late-night lovin'. And the phone calls, too. If just maybe one day I'd have holes in my sheets from smoking a woman's memory away.

Keates was starting to depress me, so I left him to be alone. To wallow in self-pity over his memories. When I strolled back inside, Don, a six-foot-four but thinner Gerald Levert look-alike, was wiping Parmesan cheese from around his mouth and stretching out on the couch in the TV room.

"Your girl hooked it *up!*" he said, rubbing his stomach. "The songbird cook like that?"

"Don't know yet."

"That's somethin' I think you need to find out. You know,

the other night I was returning some movies and met this honey named Theresa. Pretty as the sunshine. If she can cook like this, I won't *ever* let her go."

I sat there and envisioned Nikai's face as I kissed her in the park. She was much prettier than sunshine even after a midday rain. She kept me on my toes mentally and she made them curl physically. That was the person I never wanted to let go, but there was only one problem. Who was Travis?

"You still here?" Don asked, rolling over on his side to catch some z's.

"Yeah, but one day you'll learn that your mama lied. The quickest way to a man's heart ain't necessarily through his stomach."

"Karen, I'm *not* into that shit! What do you women talk about all day in that beauty shop?"

"Men like you. Now c'mon, Rob, just try the handcuffs on and see if they fit. That's a shame. All that I do for you and you can't do this one little favor for me."

"Fine. Put them on and take them *right off!*"

I'd promised that I would drop by Karen's place that next morning, and now I found myself regretting that I had. She was gettin' kinky on me again. Pullin' out motion lotion, pornos, and handcuffs. Whatever happened to normal sex? I was just looking forward to the hot-oil massage, but she had planned a three-ring circus act, with me as the main attraction.

I stayed up the entire night waiting to hear from Nikai but didn't get one page. Except from the Barnun and Bailey protégée. When Karen said she'd call, she did just that. Over and over again.

The only problem I had with her was the fact that she hung every little thing she did for me over my head. I felt like I owed certain things to her. And as sick as it sounds, sex was one of them. She was hornier than any *man* I had ever met. If she wasn't bleeding, she was begging. For a piece of me. I didn't mind at first, but with Nikai holding my attention, it seemed a bit difficult to give all that I had. Women can tell when a man has been saving up and when he hasn't. That was one of the few pieces of knowledge that Kim had shared with me.

Karen and I went through about an hour and a half of rubbing and kissing and massaging before she realized that my thoughts were no longer in her pastel and floral print-filled bedroom anymore.

She fell back on the bed with a dispirited look on her face and asked, "Who is she?"

"Who is *who?*"

"The woman on your mind."

"I don't know what you're talking about. I'm here with you, aren't I?"

"That doesn't mean anything. I've never seen that look on your face before. Something's goin' on and I wanna know what it is before we go any further."

I sat up and tried to hold her, then remembered that my hands were tied. She looked down at them and then back up to my face. Karen had no intentions of making this easy for me. She had gotten to know me almost as well as I knew myself. Once those handcuffs were removed, I was gonna be out the door.

"Baby, do you know how hard it would be to find someone else like you? Like searching for a needle in a haystack."

Her expression softened.

"Can you take these off? I hate the idea of not being able to touch you the way that I want to."

"That's the purpose. To increase the desire."

"What if I told you I couldn't possibly desire you any more than I do right at this moment?"

"I'd think you were tryin' to talk your way out of those handcuffs. You want something to drink? I've got some zinfandel."

She switched subjects like we were discussing the weather. Karen got up to go to the kitchen and then doubled back.

"You want yours in a glass or on me?"

"A glass will be fine."

I sighed and leaned my back against the headboard. After just two hours over there, I was ready to go. I heard my pager vibrating against my pants and wondered if maybe that was the call I had been waiting for. Karen came back in the bedroom with two wineglasses and a bunch of black grapes.

"Looks like somebody's callin' us," she sang, picking my pants up from the floor.

"Stop it, Karen."

"Let's see. Five five five-one seven four three," she said as she grabbed the pager and checked the number. "Now, who might that be? You gonna call it back, or would you like for me to?"

"I'd like you to take these handcuffs off of me."

I was trying my best to remain calm. Anger would have only given her incentive to act a damn fool.

"I'll tell you what I'll do. I'll set this down and go bake you that apple pie that you've been bugging me about. How's that sound?"

"Like a really bad idea, Karen. Hand me my pager, please."

"Tsk, tsk, tsk. Aren't we feeling rather feisty today?" she asked while holding the pager over her head. "Now, I promise I'll be right back. I've just got to peel these apples, make the crust, and pop it in the oven. Don't you go anywhere."

She exited the room laughing as I used my feet to scoot to the edge of the bed. Karen left the pager on the dresser, knowing that I could get to it. At the time, I didn't realize that that was part of the fun for her. I would know who it was calling and just not be able to call them back. And as fate would have it, I was right. It was Nikai.

I called into the kitchen, "Karen!"

She appeared in the doorway naked, with an apron on that read KISS THE COOK. As far as I was concerned, the cook could *kiss my ass.* I wanted to talk to Nikai. Karen walked into the room without uttering a single word. Seductively stared at me for a minute and then dropped to her knees. Threw my piece in her mouth and gave it a one-on-one with her tonsils. I bucked and bolted for a minute and finally fell back on the bed to surrender to the feelings. I ran my fingers through her hair with my cuffed hands and tried desperately to think of a reason for taking so long to explode in her mouth. A purpose for leaving that apartment immediately afterward. And, unfortunately, an excuse for burning a bridge with Nikai that I was sure I still needed to cross.

Nikai

Three more weeks had gone by and I still hadn't heard from Sheila. No letter stating that she was happy she'd moved or even a postcard to say that they hadn't crashed and burned on the way down there. I had begun to worry. Not so much about her well-being as about the state of our friendship. Whether or not she had decided to be done with me or if there was still hope.

As it turned out, Travis was bluffing. It was either that or he had finally fallen in love with Bear. I didn't hear anything else from him after the day I met with Robert for lunch. He did the usual "It's not over; I'll be back for the woman I love" speech. But if he wanted to keep in heavy contact with me, it would've been easy. The closest I came to talking to him after that was his mother calling and cursing me out for leaving his furniture in the apartment. Like I actually valued the opinion of the mother of a pedophile.

Surprisingly enough, the relationship between my mother and me was going pretty good, at first. That was mostly because Taylor hadn't returned from the Fiji Islands, coupled with the fact that Mama was helping me dodge Robert's phone calls.

The morning after we had sex, I called and told him how good it was, and I guess it went straight to his head. The bastard didn't even have the decency to call me back. I figured it was mostly my fault. He had basically warned me about the process of finding Ms. Right. How much fun it was to go through new faces, new personalities, and *new booty*. Which, I might add, he did an excellent job of on mine.

My mother did more hanging up in those three weeks than I had ever seen, and believe me, she can be a rude woman. It sorta gave her a high, I think. But none of that mattered. I was only interested in knowing that Robert had gotten my point. I was *not* to be used. No matter how good a man looked. I could hold out longer than Mother Teresa and not even flinch. Which is what I did until the day things started to change.

One evening, I came home from work and discovered that my mother had company. One of those women from her coupon-clipping group. They were sitting in the living room and ignoring Uncle Lucky, as usual. I walked in, gave him a kiss on the cheek, and turned to greet the two of them.

"Hello. How's everybody doing today?"

"Fine. And you?"

"Pretty good."

I asked my mother, "Did I get any calls today?"

She turned her mouth up in disapproval and said, "No one but that Robert. He left a number for you to reach him. I put it on the fridge. He mentioned something about a guy named Kalif having room for you now. What's that all about?"

"Oh, he's a producer I was going to try to work with."

The woman dressed in khaki pants and a white button-down blouse nudged my mother. Uncle Lucky looked over at me with a glare of warning. They had probably been sitting there the whole time discussing whatever it was in front of him as though he were deaf.

My mother jumped into an almost-extreme level of excitement and said, "Lula Mae's son does music, too!"

I looked back at her friend and responded, "Oh really? In what capacity?"

"Well, he has his own studio, and he's been looking for a beautiful young lady to sing on some of the music he's recorded."

"He's really attractive, too, Nikai. He makes good money and he even has his master's degree."

"No disrespect, Ms. Lula Mae, but, Mama, producing music isn't really that lucrative unless you're on Babyface status."

They both looked at each other and asked, "Who's Baby-face?"

Then Mama said, "No, what I mean is that he's a stockbro-ker. Wears a tie to work every day. Now, that's what I call a good catch."

"Does the tie help him to produce music any better?" I asked sarcastically.

Lula Mae's upper lip stiffened as she silently suggested that my mother check me for the disrespect. But I could see through all of that. Mama was tryin' to set me up again. She wanted me to be with someone in corporate America more than she wanted me to breathe. I guess she felt a grounded man would help me to do what she considered *getting myself together.*

"It was nice seeing you again, Ms. Mae."

"Mmmhmm."

I laughed to myself, grabbed the message from Robert off of the refrigerator, and headed upstairs to the guest room, which had turned into my own personal cluttered hole. I had so much stuff that was still in boxes and more outfits than the closet could hold. I had laid some of my work clothes across the arm of the light blue recliner and my knickknacks were strewn all over the place. The day before, I had begun taking a lot of my books, pictures, and stuff like that down to the basement. It was becoming a challenge for me to live in such disorganization.

I sat down at the head of my bed and stared at the scribbled message. I guess Robert thought he could just ease his way back into my panties as if his name were written on them. Like I was one of those cheap chicks he was obviously used to dealing with. Just screwin' for sport. Well, I didn't get down like that. I gave him a little trim, but I still had some sense of self-respect. And I kept all that in mind as I dialed the number of the paper.

On the third ring, I heard him answer, "Whassup?"

"Is that how you answer the phone?"

"Oh shit! Nikai, baby, where've you been?"

He was really pressing it with the dramatics.

"Working and handling my business. And you?"

"Thinking about you. Wondering why you wouldn't take my calls. I didn't know what happened."

"So you can imagine how I felt the day I paged you and you didn't call me back."

"Sweetheart, I was at another engine house subbing. I'm sorry. I promise it won't ever happen again."

"Oh, I'm sure of that, 'cause I don't have any plans of paging you again."

"I know, baby. That's why I left my home number with your mother. Something tells me she doesn't like me very much."

I cut him off by saying, "That's neither here nor there. The message read that Kalif was ready to work with me."

"Um, well, uh . . ."

"What, Robert?"

"To be honest, that was just to get you to call me back, but he *is* looking forward to hearing you sing."

"So call me when he's ready."

"Wait! I wanna see you."

"For what? I'm *not* going to sleep with you."

"Woman, I don't care about that. I wanna see *you*. Now how about it? Can I come and pick you up now?"

I sighed heavily and said, "I don't know, Robert."

"Would it help if I begged? Plleeaassse, baby, please, baby . . ."

"I don't—"

"I've got something for you," he sang.

"Really? What is it?"

"You'll have to let me come and get you."

"And take me where?"

"That's a surprise, too."

"Okay, but I've got to work in the morning, so it can't take long."

"I promise it'll be worth every minute."

I gave him the address and directions to my mother's town house before hanging up. He told me he'd be there in forty-five minutes, which meant I had ten to jump in the shower, ten to bump the ends of my hair, fifteen to decide what to wear, five to do my makeup, and another five to relax and act like I could take him or leave him.

As I pulled out a short khaki skirt, a sleeveless denim top, brown sandals, and a matching purse, I remembered what Sheila once told me about expressing the way I felt. Maybe there was nothing wrong with letting him know that I had missed him that entire three weeks. That I had entertained the thought of giving him a little bit more of me. That I remembered the way that he held me until the sun set on us after we had sexed all over his bedroom.

Once I was done getting dressed, I walked downstairs, where my mother and Lucky were sitting. I guess Ms. Mae had left after her son's talent had been questioned in front of others. Mama looked at me and shook her head in disgust.

"And just *where* are you going?" she asked, stretching out on the couch.

"A friend of mine is coming to get me. You want anything while I'm out?"

"Yeah, if you could pick up a little common sense while you're out there, I'd really appreciate it."

"Where did that come from?" I asked, my feelings a little hurt.

There I was, a grown woman, and my mother was debating whether I had common sense. And by the way she was staring at me, I could tell she'd use a comment like that to support her argument on why I was still living with her.

"You act like you don't know a good thing when you see it. *I'm* trying to help *you*! Not the other way around. Don't you ever wish you had all of the nice things Taylor has?"

"Like what?"

"Stability, for one!"

Okay, so she had me there, but Taylor wasn't the kind of person I envied. She was usually uptight and stressed about thoughts that never passed her lips. If that was stability, then maybe I didn't want it.

"I'll be back later," I responded as I turned to answer the doorbell.

Mama jumped up from the couch like the Road Runner. I guess to see what kind of pathetic company I planned to keep for the evening. When she saw Robert standing on the step in a pair of cargo shorts and a blue Old Navy T-shirt, she sighed loudly enough for Lucky to feel the wind in the living room.

"And you are?" she asked.

"Robert. How are you doing?"

"Up until now, I was fine."

"Okay, Mama. See ya later."

I looked back at Robert and rolled my eyes to the ceiling in an effort to excuse my mother's behavior. When they landed, they were on her as she stood holding the edge of the door in one hand and a sheet of paper in the other. She glanced at Robert long and hard, then at me.

"Nikai, you make sure you call *this* young man. Lula Mae left the number and said she'd *make sure* he expects your call. I can imagine that he'd be worth your time and effort. Good day, *Robert.*"

I asked, "Okay, so where are we going?"

He stared at the road and grinned.

"I don't like backseat drivers."

"Well, nobody's back there, so tell me where you're planning to take me."

Robert didn't answer. Just pushed an Earth, Wind and Fire CD in and pressed the review button to number three.

"Remember this?"

It was "After the Love Is Gone" flowing from his back speakers.

"No."

"This song was playing the first time I held you."

"Wrong! It was Luther's 'If This World Were Mine.'"

"I thought you didn't remember."

I laughed and said, "Selective amnesia. I thought you were into more *recent* songs."

"I am, but it's not about me right now."

I blushed and asked, "So this is what you had for me?"

"Nope, got the CD for me," he answered, reaching into the backseat. "I ran all over St. Louis searching for the *album* because I know you're into the vinyl sound."

"That was sweet, Robert."

I leaned over, grabbed his chin, and kissed him on the lips. I had *him* blushing then, but I'd wanted to do that more than he knew. I'd missed the taste of his lips and the gentle way that he held me.

"Have you eaten?"

"It's after seven. It's too late to eat."

"Says who?"

"Says me!"

"Look at my baby. Stuck in a time warp, and a health-conscious freak, too. That's cute."

I dulled his sarcasm by saying, "You said we were going *where?*"

"I didn't, but since you're so persistent, I'm taking you to my favorite spot."

We headed downtown and got out on the arch grounds. Walked up the grassy hills and over to the long drop of steps that were situated out front and in between the legs of the monument. Robert stood behind me and warmed me with his muscular arms. Rocked from side to side as we watched the barges go up and down the Mississippi. We could see the lights from the casino shining brightly alongside the dim McDonald's boat, which was closed for the evening, and others that were used for throwing parties and functions.

He said, "This is where *I* used to come. Actually, I still do. I park up on Thirteenth Street and walk all the way down here. Get lost in thought and hours go by."

"So if you ever disappear, this is where I can find you?"

"I'm not sayin' that." He laughed. "Nikai, you feelin' lucky tonight?"

"What?"

"You feelin' lucky?"

"Why? You thinkin' about going on the casino boat?"

"Yeah. I figure if I'm lucky enough to get you here, then I may just be on a roll."

"Robert, I'll go with you, but I can't afford to blow any money right now. I'm trying to save up to do the impossible."

"What's that?"

"Get my own apartment."

"Okay. I'll make a deal with you. I've got one hundred dollars in my wallet. We'll split it fifty-fifty. Whoever walks away with the least amount cooks dinner tomorrow night."

"Deal."

We shook on it and started off down the long descent of steps. Hand in hand, as if there were something more than three weeks of no communication between us.

As we boarded, I noticed women of every nationality all over the boat, staring at Robert like they dared me to leave him alone, even to go pee. They were whispering and making comments about his chest, all of which went totally unnoticed from his end. Robert seemed more preoccupied with getting to the crap tables than with all of the *new booty* scopin' him out in the room.

He eased his way up to the table and found himself a spot to start either winning or losing. I could hear brothas yelling and talking shit over the sound of coins hitting the bottom of slot machines. Bells were going off and a pregnant waitress in one of those booty-high red-and-black dresses with swollen cleavage spilling onto the tray of drinks she carried was scooting past me and practically begging gamblers to order cocktails.

Robert turned to me and said, "I'm feelin' lucky, baby. You gonna go get busy?"

"Yeah, I'll be over on the slots."

He opened his wallet, pulled out fifty dollars, folded it on the down-low, and handed it to me. I reached out to take it as Robert pulled me close and planted a wet one on me. Took me by total surprise that he was kissing me good-bye when I was only gonna be across the room. Now that I look back, it was the little things he did that made him so special to me.

Still smiling, I strolled over to the cashier's gate and changed that fifty for five rolls of quarters. Pivoted toward the slot machines and took a seat in front of three empty ones. When I first sat down, I was hittin' pretty good. Playing three coins at a time seemed to pay off. And that's when the two hundred popped up. I jumped off of that stool and screamed like somebody was about to wheel a brand-new car out for me. I looked around, but nobody seemed to notice. I was alone in my aisle except for an elderly woman who had already filled four buckets and was on her way to five. She didn't bother to bat an eye at my mediocre winnings.

I danced and scooted around on that stool until I had finished scooping my coins into the buckets. That was when my baby showed up. Placed his arm on my shoulder and gave it a light massage with his massive hand.

Then he said, "T gon' be happy to hear about this."

I turned around to the unrecognizable voice and realized that it wasn't Robert at all, but one of Travis's ghetto-ass cousins. He was standing behind me, grinnin' and suckin' on the diamond in his front gold tooth. He had a drink in one hand, while the other was checking to make sure not one strand of his process was out of place. His heavy, slanted eyes were bloodshot, which probably explained how he ended up walking out of the house in that tacky-ass royal blue silk pants outfit.

"What do you want, Tyrone?"

"Ah, Shawtie, don't be like that. I just wanted to come over and congratulate you on yo' winnings. See if yo' singin' career is takin' off like my rhymin' is."

Tyrone was one of those aspiring rappers with no skills but a pocketful of dirty money to pay his way into the business. So you can imagine why I was insulted by him comparing our talents. I stayed true to my art. The fame and fortune would only be a perk.

"So what was the comment about Travis for?" I asked, peeking around the corner to see if I saw Robert coming.

"You lookin' fu somebody?"

"Who in the hell are you tryin' to get loud with?"

"Oh, now you tryin' to disrespect my boy? Out here shakin' yo' ass when you supposed to be somewhere gettin' ready to drop his load!"

"Drop his load?" What the hell was he talking about?

"You wait 'till I tell my boy his baby's mama was on the boat wit' somebody else. And don't let *me* catch you wit' his ass!"

"I ain't nobody's *baby's mama,* Tyrone! And until I start fuckin' around with children under the legal age like Travis's triflin' butt, don't say shit to me! I'm grown and I ain't fuckin' *you*! So if you see me with somebody, *anybody,* you betta act like you don't!"

He sipped his drink, sucked his gold tooth, and walked away toward the exit, nodding his head. I peeked back around the slot machine to make sure Robert was still playing. He spotted me and raised his hands while smiling. I took a seat back on my stool and slumped over. Couldn't believe the nerve Tyrone had to step to me like that. It didn't take a lot of deductive reasoning to figure out that he wasn't that set of eyes Travis said he had out on the street. The sole desire to open his mouth would've blown Tyrone's cover a loonnnnggggg time ago.

After that, I didn't feel much like playing anymore. I gathered up my winnings and took them to the cashier's gate. I walked away with eighty dollars and a headache. Rejoined Robert at the crap tables and wrapped my arms around him. He didn't move a muscle. Just concentrated more on his money and the pair of dice being tossed across the table.

"Ah, damn!"

"What happened? You lose?"

"Everything but the drawers on my butt. How about you?"

"I walked away with eighty."

"Well, I hope you like Top Ramen noodles 'cause that's the only thing I know how to make." He laughed, holding the exit door open for me.

"I think I'll cook for us this time and just give you a few lessons."

"'Preciate it, baby."

Robert kissed me on the forehead as we walked along the ramp to the cobblestone parking lot near the boats. Upon approaching the sidewalk, I felt a serious pain in my temple and began to massage it. Robert was busy watching for traffic and waiting for an opportunity to cross. When I looked up, a white Acura was pulling in front of us, with a woman driving and ignorant-ass Tyrone hangin' out the window.

He yelled, "Nikai, I ain't playin'! Travis is gon' find out about this shit!"

Then the car sped off, leaving us standing in a dusty cloud of misunderstanding. Robert didn't comment, and neither did I.

Just took off toward the arch and pulled those steps like I was Jackie Joyner-Kersee.

"Nikai, Nikai, wait a minute!"

I could hear him behind me, calling my name beyond the roar of thunder and lightning in the sky. Heavy, plentiful raindrops saturated my hair and clothes as I tried to find my way back through the darkness and trees.

"You're going the wrong way! The car is over here!" Robert yelled.

I shifted my direction, still walking quickly and folding my arms close to my abdomen. I met up with him, as he insistently remained by my side with every step.

Then he asked, "Don't you think we need to talk?"

I didn't say anything. I wanted badly to get out of the rain. My sandals had small puddles in them, I was getting cold, and my headache still had not gone away.

"Who was that?"

"Take me home."

"Tell me who that was," he insisted.

"Take . . . me . . . home!"

Robert stopped walking and grabbed me by the shoulders. The rain seemed to come down even harder now that we were standing still. My hair was stuck to the sides of my face and my fingers were beginning to prune.

"I think you owe it to me to let me know who that was!"

"And I think the least you could do is open the *goddamn door* so I can get in the car!"

"Fine, you wanna get in? Get in!"

He slammed the door so hard that the CD cases rattled under the armrest. I considered reaching over and unlocking his but decided that would've been a sign of weakness. He hopped in, started up the engine, and took off into the night. Didn't call my name, didn't ask any more questions, and didn't even play our song.

I pushed the button on the side of my seat and leaned back. He had the heat on full blast as the windshield wipers drummed a beat that soon put me to sleep. I quickly woke when I felt the car stop. Robert was sitting there staring at me, with the side of his forehead resting in the palm of his hand.

"Good night, Robert," I said, turning to open the door.

I looked out and realized that we were not in front of my house, but his. I swiftly turned to him with a look of annoyance.

"Why are you playing with me?" I asked.

"It seems like you're the one full of games."

"Didn't I ask you to take me home?"

"Well, it appears that neither of us is getting what we want, because I asked you to tell me who that was yelling out of that Acura."

I looked down at my wet purse in my lap and said, "That was nobody."

"It's funny how *nobody* could know the same Travis your mother knows."

It was right about then that my heart stopped beating. My jaws tightened and my muscles felt like they were spasming. All at once, I was falling apart in front of the man who was beginning to mean so much to me.

"It's time we start coming clean and being honest about everything."

"What makes you think I haven't been honest?"

"Because I can tell you're upset. Now, who is Travis?"

I took a deep breath and popped my neck from side to side. "He's my ex-boyfriend."

"And who was that in the Acura?"

"His cousin, Tyrone."

"Is there anything else I should know about this situation?"

"Travis is in jail for statutory rape."

"Anything else?"

"I think he may still want me."

"Anything else?"

"He's upset because I aborted his child two months ago."

"Anything else?"

"I don't have any intentions of ever speaking to him again. I hate him, and so does my mother."

"Well, at least I know I'm not alone in that area."

Robert gave a slight chuckle and looked out across the street for a while. I assumed that he was taking in everything I had just told him and deciding whether it would be a good idea to remain involved with me. He did that laughing thing again, shook his head, and looked at me.

"Nikai, I want to be with you."

"I guessed that was the point of bringing me here," I said.

"No, no, no! Don't you understand? I can get *that* anywhere! You're more than that to me. The sex was good, too, but I want *you,* exclusively. Just me and you," he explained, pointing back and forth at the two of us.

I laughed at his urgency to get his point across.

Then I asked, "Just me and you?"

"Just me and you. How about it?"

I leaned across the armrest and answered with the same kind of kiss I'd planted on him the night we met on the dance floor. I wanted him to feel what I was saying. Especially since everything else I had said or not said, up until that point, had been misleading.

By the time we got out of the car and went into the house, it was about 10:30. Our clothes were soaked, I had the sniffles, and Robert, well, he had an erection that would darken the brightest room. I fell asleep there at his place after a long evening of horizontal poker, if you know what I mean.

In the middle of the night, while we were lying buck naked under the sheets, I woke from my sleep and replayed the entire evening. Tyrone steppin' to me and all. I felt relieved as I thought about the fact that Robert knew everything—everything from the jail sentence to the abortion—and it was all okay with him. I looked down and rubbed his bald head, which was resting gently on my breast. That's when the one lie that was left occurred to me. I shook his back and called his name to waken him.

"Robert, Robert, wake up. I have something else to tell you."

"Whassup?" he asked without opening his eyes.

"I don't really have a brother."

"I already knew that, baby. Now go back to sleep."

*   *   *

The next morning when I arrived at home, I went up to my bedroom and found a note on my pillow from my mother that read:

Last night I stayed up for hours trying to think of one man who would buy the cow when he was already getting the milk for free, but I couldn't think of anyone. Can you?

I balled it up and tossed it in the wastebasket by the door. I was used to that kind of cynical behavior. This was just another attempt to plant seeds in my head. My mother never actually *told* me what to do. She just set up situations and circumstances and let me draw my own conclusions. But no harvest ever flourishes under harsh and ill-nurtured conditions.

I jumped in the shower, then threw on a pair of black slacks with a chartreuse button-down short-sleeved shirt for work. Brushed all of my hair back into a neat little bun and prepared a cinnamon raisin bagel with strawberry cream cheese before walking out the door. I picked up my black handbag off of the stand by the front door and noticed that an envelope had fallen from the side pocket. I figured my mama was so disgusted with me that she stuck it there, where she knew I'd see it. The return address was from the U.S. Virgin Islands. I sat down in the kitchen and ripped it down the side. There was no paper, no letter, not even a Post-it note. Just a picture of Sheila hanging from a coconut tree and smilin' like a fool. I turned the picture over, to find that she had written a few words on the back.

*I didn't get up this baby as soon as
I jumped off the plane, but I made it.
I miss you and I still love you.
          Sheila*

I arrived at work a little later than usual that morning. I had a bit of emotional regrouping to do from crying and thinking of a future without that friendship. I didn't have a girlfriend to talk to anymore. Things were beginning to happen in my life and I had no one to share them with.

Robert and I had officially become a couple, Travis had decided to do a disappearing act, and I was eagerly awaiting an opportunity to work with a producer.

I got up from my desk and went to the bathroom to check my makeup and see how I looked in the full-length, never-lying mirror on the wall. I had smeared my eyeliner when the mascara started making my eyes itch on the freeway. *Damn.* I was looking bad and feeling worse.

Linda, one of the secretaries, met me at the coffee machine and asked if I was okay. I put on my "Couldn't be better" face and did a half skip back to my office.

I made a practice not to air my dirty laundry at work. But to be honest, there was one exception to the rule—Dorothy. She was an older sista, about fifty-five or sixty. I found it impolite to ask her age because, after all, she was my elder. She'd been looking out for me from the moment I arrived, but in an eerie kind of way. Apparently, I looked just like her daughter, who had died two years prior in a car accident, and that was as close as she could get to being with her baby. At least that's the way that she put it.

That particular morning, I had my door open. Dorothy stopped right outside my door and waved. I straightened my back, cleared my throat, and belted a "Good morning. How are you feeling today?"

"I'm too blessed to be stressed," she said. "But what's going on with you, chile?"

I ran my hand over my hair and asked, "What do you mean?"

I knew exactly what she was talking about. I couldn't manage to get rid of the bags under my eyes. Not to mention the fact that Dorothy could tell if I was lying, regardless of how hard I tried to hide it.

"Don't tell me nothing's wrong. You look like yo' best friend died next to ya in the middle of da night."

I laughed at her blunt response. It was funny how tall and plump Dorothy could switch up from being so professional one minute to acting like she had just fallen off a turnip truck from Paducah, Kentucky, the next. She would step into my office, close the door, and get "good and southern" with me. Read me up one side and down the other if I wasn't working up to my potential. In some ways, she was like family.

"I didn't get a lot of sleep last night," I said, kicking my black pumps off under my desk, since my door was now closed.

"And why not, Miss Thang? You lettin' a man keep you up at night?"

She placed one hand on her hip and leaned heavily on my desk with the other. Stared me down like I was on trial and would get life, with no chance for parole.

"No, ma'am." I laughed.

"What did I tell you about that 'ma'am' stuff? I'm not *that* old."

"I know. Actually, my best friend moved away. Just packed up one day and flew away with a guy she loved."

"She happy?"

"Here's a picture of her," I said, handing the photo across my desk.

"She looks pretty damn close to happy from where I'm standin'. Did she marry him?"

"Nope, not that I know of, anyway. She didn't send a letter. Just the picture."

"Well, Nikai, you're a pretty girl, too," she said, glancing back at the photo of Sheila. "And yo' eyes ain't half as big as this chile's here. You'll find somebody to love someday, too. And the best part is that he'll truly love you back."

"Yeah, I know."

I was thinking of Robert as she talked about this Mr. Right stepping into my life and being good *for* me as well as *to* me.

"Well, cheer up, Tracey. Tomorrow's a new day."

"Sure. Will do."

I didn't mention that she had accidentally called me by her daughter's name again.

As Dorothy left, Linda came hopping by, smiling and tossing her hands about like she had knocked off a pot of coffee by herself.

"Good morning, Nikai. How ya feelin'?" Linda asked.

"I'm doing okay. How about yourself?"

"What is it Dorothy says, 'I'm too blessed to be depressed'?"

I leaned forward and laughed at the fact that Linda not only paid attention to what countrified Dorothy was saying but was actually trying to recall it, word for word.

"No, it's 'too blessed to be stressed,'" I said, correcting her.

"Oh well, same thing."

She shrugged her shoulders a couple of times and bounced over to my desk. Linda was one of those rebellious girls in her early twenties who still lived at home and usually did things to tick her parents off. She would come in from time to time and tell me how they waved money under her nose and hung the Mercedes car over her head to keep her in check. Something that I could never relate to.

She was more into the alternative crowd, but she could win an Oscar for the performance that she put on at work. So professional from nine to five and then that bobbed blond hair turned blue after hours. Out with the business attire and in with the cargo pants and tie-dyed shirts. I guess, in a way, that was one of the reasons why I didn't mind her stopping in so often. It's as though I wanted to draw some of her energy. It's strange how two people from two different worlds can want the same thing so badly and the only thing separating them is the fact that only one has the courage to make herself happy.

She slumped down in the chair in front of my desk and grabbed a pen and pad, as if she were taking notes.

"Ming is ignoring me again," she said, sighing aloud.

Ming was her Vietnamese boyfriend—a senior in college and apparently a bookworm.

"Well, did you talk to him about it, like I told you to?"

"Yeah, and he says that I should understand how busy he is. That he's only trying to make things better for us in the future."

"Well, you know, you've got to honor that. If this guy is really trying to include you and you are *certain* that he is studying, then you should sit back and count your blessings."

"I know. It's just that I would like for us to be a lot closer."

"You mean physically?" I asked.

She got up to close my door and then resumed her frustrated position.

"I mean that I'm ready to have sex or at least go down on him."

I covered my mouth and cleared my throat to hide the grin on my face. It seemed kinda backward to want to have sex that badly and then take going down on *someone else* as a consolation.

"I'm assuming you've talked to him about this."

"Nope," she said, smiling and sitting up straight. "I thought maybe I'd show him."

"And how exactly do you plan to do that?"

"Well, that's where you come in."

"Me?"

I leaned back in my chair and gave her that Gary Coleman look, like when someone ran an idea by him that he didn't agree with.

"What are you talking about?" I asked.

"Not like that," she assured me. "I want you to help me pick out some lingerie and maybe some body gel. And I thought that maybe you could share some of your tips with me."

Linda was a sweet girl, but it was becoming apparent that she was taking these chat sessions a bit too seriously.

"Well, I can't imagine my advice being of much use," I said.

"C'mon." She stood there, jumping in front of my desk. "I know you've got somethin' up your sleeve to keep your guy comin' back every night."

I faked a smile for a moment.

"C'mon, Nikai. Just this once. Pleeeaaassssse."

"All right."

Linda bounced out of my office like she had found the answer to all of her woes. I just hoped that I could be of help. I mean, I imagined that there had to be some kind of differences in our cultural ideas of sexuality. A line so thick that it almost seemed dangerous to cross. Especially since we were talking about someone who wasn't of either of our races.

I reached behind my chair and turned the radio on 100.9 FM. The morning talk show was on and the topic was "black-on-black crime." A young woman called in, complaining, "I just wanted to comment on an experience I had the other day when I went downtown to an office building. There was a guard at the front desk who happened to be a brotha and he was talking to a woman when I walked in. I pushed the button for the elevator, and by the time it came, three young brothas and a white guy joined me. Well, the three brothas were telling me to smile on such a beautiful day and making small talk with me. We all got on and rode up together. Well, on my way down, I was joined by two white guys dressed in business suits. When I got off the elevator, the guard immediately stopped me and apologized. For a minute, I wondered why this total stranger was so sorry. Then he asked, 'Did they scare you?' And I realized that he was talking about the three brothas I rode up the elevator with. What I want to say is that it's a shame that this black man felt that he had to protect me from my own people, based solely on the fact that they were young black men who weren't afraid to say what they felt at the time."

The host asked, "Well, what did you say when he asked you that?"

"I told him that I didn't have a reason to be afraid. I also asked him why he didn't apologize for me having to ride down the elevator *alone* with two white men. In my eyes, a man is a man."

The host turned the comment over to the guest, who was a professor of African-American studies. She went on to thank the woman for not perpetuating the myth that only white men can be trusted in an elevator or that a brotha will put his foot on your throat and take your purse before you can push the floor you want.

The host added, "You know you were right, but there is sometimes an ugly truth to that myth. You can take a lot of these brothas out here who commit crimes, put them in a white neighborhood, and tell them to run wild and rob whomever, and they won't touch a thing. But take those same brothas to a black neighborhood and tell them the same thing and they'll take their time going from house to house, whether they know the occupant or not."

I bit down on the tip of my pen and gave an amen to that. I turned around to surf the stations for some jazz, when I heard

Dorothy coming down the hall. She stepped into my office and glanced behind her to make sure no one else was around.

"Guess what I just heard Marion saying?" she asked, tapping the corner of a stack of manila folders on my desk.

"What?"

"They're looking for leasing consultants, and she mentioned you as a good candidate."

"Are you serious, Dorothy?"

"Yeah, chile. And you know what that means. More money, a bigger office, and time away from this place."

Leasing consultants were the employees who went out into the field and showed property to prospective residents. It was a chance to be free from the daily routine. I could meet new people, use my own discretion when it came to getting back to the office, and I would be compensated for gas.

"You know I'm gonna keep my fingers crossed for you, Nikai."

"I know you will, and I appreciate it, too."

"You feel like going to the St. Louis Centre for lunch? I can tell you about all of the little extras I did to land my position. Don't believe it's all about the quality of work you do."

"All right. I'll meet you down the hall at one."

"Don't keep me waiting."

"I won't," I told her, glancing back down at the photo of Sheila.

Although waiting was all I seemed to do—for an opportunity to move out of my mother's house, for certainty that Robert was the real deal, for a reunion with my best friend, for that mystery producer to find time for me, and, as of that moment, for the decision about whether I was a positive candidate for a position that I could fill with my eyes closed.

Once that day had ended and I was back at home in my room, I closed my eyes and wished for all of this waiting to be over. That became the first of a long string of prayers that didn't necessarily come in that form. I had ventured from the traditional folding of the hands and scarring of the knees. I was trying the candlelit room and peaceful chant route. My mama swore that I had begun to hang out with cult members in my free time. Warned me not to let Sheila's silly voodoo make me wind up homeless again. I think that was the comment that hurt the most.

After a couple of weeks, she began to suggest that drugs were bad and then checked for my reaction. As though I was gonna jump up on the kitchen table, pull a bong from my handbag, and start singin' "No Woman No Cry." Drugs had nothing to do with my sudden desire to have peace of mind. Sheila's consistent letters did.

After that picture came letter after letter after letter. Then more pictures of her and Rastaman kickin' it like lovers from way back when. To be honest, I began to envy their relationship, because mine and Robert's had sort of become stagnant. He thought what I was doing was mimicking Sheila, trying to become someone that I wasn't. Told me that I couldn't live in her world, that I had my own to flourish in. And finally, he told me to get all of those *goddamn* candles and chimes out of his apartment.

We'd argue and then make up between the sheets. My long-distance friendship with Sheila became a subject of daily debate. He'd argue his point and then I'd make him see things my way when the sun fell. Rob didn't mind the candles so much then. That is, until I'd gone over to his place after talking to Sheila on the phone and used the candles to cry over memories that seemed a lifetime away.

One night, while we were lying in bed, he suggested that we take a trip to Saint Croix to visit Sheila and Rastaman. I was so ecstatic, I lighted some candles, worked him over, and had him climbin' the walls and callin' for his mama. Afterward, we lay there on fresh sheets, cuddled up and thinking. He, probably about how much the trip would cost. Me, about how much fun it would be to get up that coconut tree with Sheila.

"If that's the way you feel, we can go to Jamaica, too!" he said, propping himself up against the wooden headboard.

"For now, I think one trip will be enough. Besides, once I get this promotion, we'll be doing a lot of things right here in St. Louis."

"Promotion? You're getting a promotion?"

"Yes, baby. Remember my friend Dorothy, the one I told you about? Well, she overheard Marion saying that I would make a good candidate for a leasing consultant."

He mumbled a dry "Ah, for real?"

Robert grabbed the remote control for the nineteen-inch TV off of the nightstand and began channel surfing. After finding nothing that interested him, he turned the TV off, tossed the remote across the room, and rolled onto his side. He lay there like that with his naked, dark back to me. Silent. Except for the loud sound of wind darting in and out of his flared nostrils.

I asked, "Is there a problem?"

He didn't respond.

"Robert!"

"Whassup?"

"I asked you a question."

"I heard you."

"Then act like you did and entertain it with an answer."

"What do you want me to say? That's great that you're climbin' the ladder of success. I'm happy for you."

"You done patronizing me?"

"Then don't ask me anything, Nikai! Whatever I say won't be good enough, anyway!"

"I don't get you. One minute, you want me bad enough to sprint after me in the middle of a thunderstorm, and now that you see I'm ecstatic about something other than this relationship, I get attitude. If I didn't know any better, I'd think this wasn't about my happiness."

Still no comment.

"Robert, you know what I've been going through. I don't really have any friends anymore, my money has been short, and the whole Travis situation. I just wanna be at peace with—"

"You don't wanna be at peace; you wanna be *Sheila,* and you can't!"

I had formed my lips to mount a rebuttal but found myself speechless. And as strange as it may seem, his brusque response reminded me of how naked I was next to him as I drew an invisible line with the side of my hand down the sheet between us.

I backed away from him and turned over to face the armoire.

There was nothing left to be said on that subject. And there was no need to defend myself. I could put on one of those loud-ass gowns, dance around in circles, build an indoor bonfire with *his* coffee table, beat the walls with bamboo sticks, sacrifice a wild yak, and kick dirt up to the beat of a drum in the middle of his damn living room if I wanted to, but I still wouldn't have to answer to him.

The remainder of that night was a quiet one: no talking, no sexing, and no morning apologies. Which was basically because I sneaked out around five and locked the bottom lock on the knob.

When I made it home, I found my mother in the kitchen, still wearing her lavender gown, sitting in the dark.

"Mama, you okay?"

She lifted her head from her hands and answered, "Yeah, I'm fine. Where you been?"

"Over to Robert's. Why are you sitting here like this?"

"Just thinking about your father, Nikai."

I joined her at the table and asked, "You miss him, too, huh?"

Tears streamed down her face as she lifted her head to the ceiling. This was the first time I had actually seen her look weak in a long time. She always appeared to be in control, always emotionless.

"Yeah, he's been on my mind a lot lately."

She wiped her cheeks dry and cleared her throat.

"So, have you talked to Jason?"

"Who?" I asked.

"Jason. Lulu Mae's boy!"

"No, I haven't. Haven't really had time to get back to him."

Mama looked at me as though she would have preferred that I'd lied. As if I was insulting her by not squirming in my seat and fabricating a story, like I'd dialed the wrong number or that *he* wasn't getting back to *me*.

"If you spent a little less time playin' house and more time concentrating on what you're gonna do with your life, I'm sure you'd have a minute or two to pick up the phone!" she replied while getting up from the table. "I don't know how long you expect to lay up on me like you're fifteen, but you got anotha thing comin'!"

I slid down in my chair and rested my forehead on the corner of my hand as she took off toward the stairs, leaving me in what she considered to be more than the mere darkness of the kitchen—the darkness of ignorance. I closed my tired and tearful eyes and listened as her voice slowly drifted away to an angry mumble of unclear words.

". . . runnin' around here tryin' to *play* grown . . . using my house as a dressin' room . . . can get yo' shit and go!"

"Are you serious? Thank you, Marion! You won't be sorry."

I was leaving Marion's office, feeling better than I had felt that entire day. She had given me news of my promotion and the first reason in a long time to put a smile on my mama's face. I was suddenly beginning to feel like I *was* fifteen again. Searching for something to make her proud of me. A reason for the spotlight to shift from Taylor over to me. Even if it was for one day.

I pulled up into a parking space directly in front of the town house, took a deep breath, and grabbed my purse off the passenger seat. As I got closer to the door, I could hear my mother laughing. And I don't mean a little dainty laugh. I'm talkin' the kind you do when you want to convince the person talking that he's interesting when he really isn't.

When I stepped inside, I found my mother standing across the room from Uncle Lucky, talking to a light-skinned man who was wearing a dark blue suit, and carrying a briefcase. He was dressed to kill. To kill what? I don't know. Probably nothing over three feet. He was so short that my mama could eat off the top of his head, which was half-bald, and not by choice. His hairline was literally adjacent to his ears. Neither of them noticed me right away, as they went on discussing characteristics that closely resembled mine.

"She's about my complexion with long, pretty hair. She keeps in shape and she has her own car. I'm sure your mother told you all about her. I mean, I don't wanna brag about my own daughter, but she is definitely a sight for sore eyes."

"And she can really sing, too?" he asked.

"Like Whitney Houston!" my mother bragged.

"I've never dated anyone who—"

Their eyes quickly shifted in my direction as I eased over to Lucky's chair.

My mother jumped into character and said, "Here's the little songstress now. I was just telling Jason here how well you sing. He's been so eager to work with you that he rushed right over."

"On his own?" I asked, with absolutely no expression on my face.

"Well, after your mother called and told me about you being a little nervous, I . . ."

Her eyes fell to the floor.

"A little nervous? About what?"

"The dinner."

"What dinner?"

He looked at my mother as though the fact that we were all on different pages had just occurred to him.

"My mother's church is having a dinner this Sunday to celebrate raising enough money to pay for a parking lot that includes a two-car garage for the pastor's Mercedes and Jaguar. Your mother was kind enough to inform me that you were willing to sing at the service and be my date for the dinner."

If it had not been for Lucky nudging me in my side with his elbow, I might not have realized that my mouth was hanging open. This miniature man had run down a full plan for my Sunday, short of what I would be wearing.

"I just thought I'd inform you that the pastor would like for everyone to dress in white to symbolize how giving this money helped to cleanse our souls. And by the way, your donation will be due on Thursday."

"*Donation?*"

"Yeah, it's the only way that you'll be allowed to perform at the service."

"Well, just count me—"

"*In!*" my mother interjected.

"I think I can finish my own sentences," I told her.

"Obviously not the way that they should be finished, or I wouldn't have to stop you from making a fool of yourself."

"Oh, is that what I'm doing? I thought *you* had that part covered."

In my peripheral vision, I could see Jason nervously shifting his weight from one foot to the other, but I refused to back down. Not when I knew that I was in the right.

"Well, maybe you should stop making it so easy for people to do. If that dumb Travis could do it, *anyone* can."

I looked over at Jason, smiled, and asked, "Now you wouldn't want the daughter of a woman who talks like that to accompany you to such a God-fearing function, would you? I'm sorry about the misunderstanding, but I won't be going anywhere with you on Sunday."

I turned to my mother and continued, "I'll be *moving* that day."

She rotated her neck from one side to the other while Jason was beginning to sweat a puddle in the middle of the living room floor. Lucky turned the volume up on the television and started his agitated habit of rocking back and forth. I placed my hand on his shoulder before he reached up, took it, and rested the side of his warm, wrinkled face on it.

Mama told Jason, "You know, you don't have to mention this to your mother. I'm truly sorry about my daughter's behavior. It is simply ridiculous, but it definitely shouldn't be looked at as a reflection on me."

"No, no. I can tell she really has a *mind of her own.*"

I looked at both of them standing there performing for each other. My mother tryin' to play civilized and Jason makin' a desperate attempt to pretend like this wasn't the first time he had seen some crazy shit like that. Mama walked him to the front door, still showering him with apologies, as I let Lucky go and took off upstairs to my cluttered room. When I heard her walk back into the house, reality set in. I had let my mouth write a check that my butt couldn't cash. There was no way I could find a place to stay in four days.

Things were beginning to move backward, and I mean at a scary pace. I stretched out on my bed and stared at the ceiling for what seemed like twenty minutes, and then the phone rang. I looked over at it, not knowing whether I should answer or assume that it was more bad news. After three rings, my mama called for me to pick up the line in my room.

"Hello?"

"Hey, sweetie. What's goin' on?" Sheila asked, sounding cheerful.

"Nothin' much. I just got promoted to a leasing consultant today."

"That's wonderful! Why aren't you out celebrating?"

"Because I have more news."

"Well, out with it!"

"Robert is planning a trip for us to go down and see you guys, he's not too happy about me getting a promotion, and I have to move out of *here* by Sunday."

"Whoa, wait a minute. Now, back this up. When are y'all comin' down here?"

"He didn't say exactly when, but he surprised me with the news last night. Right before I gave him mine."

"So which one of y'all will be pullin' in more money?"

"It'll be about the same, but I don't see what the big deal is."

"Nikai, the big deal is that some men want to feel needed. Like the breadwinner. Robert might feel as though you're taking his manhood from him. Some brothas need that damsel in distress to stroke their egos from time to time."

"So what does he think I'm gonna do, pass on the promotion?"

"No, silly. All you have to do is remind him of how much you still need him. You know, ask him to open a jar that's too tight for you, or ask him something about the car. Pretend like you still don't get it and tell him you don't know what you'd do without him around. They love that. But whatever you do, don't start throwing your weight around. No matter how mad at him you get. Watch your mouth. Don't go into that 'I don't need no man' mode, 'cause that's bull anyway."

"But it's true. I *don't* need a man."

"Shut up, Nikai. It's not true! You know what it is? It's cliché. And I'm tired of hearing sistas sayin' it. The Creator put man here for woman and woman here for man. We *do* need one another. Look around you. Notice it's mostly lonely *sistas* singing that song. The same sistas who make *bad choices* with men and then raise their sons on the philosophy that all men are dogs. If they start them with low expectations, they can't expect much more than a dog to come of them. It's nothing short of a conspiracy to keep the black family apart."

"There *you* go again."

"That's right; it's the truth. Until we demand that slackin' brothas stand up and be men, they won't. If you keep telling a child he's bad, Nikai, he will eventually believe it and live his life accordingly. You have set the pace and inadvertently helped him to define who he is as a person."

"Is it time to pass the collection plate yet?" I asked sarcastically.

"All right, peanuthead. You'll be hopping on a plane to visit me by yourself. So what happened that you decided to move?"

"My mama started actin' crazy again. Told some man that I would be his date for a church dinner and had him waiting to meet me when I got in from work today. We had some words and I told her that I was leaving."

"With no idea where you were gonna stay?"

"Not a clue."

"Well, you know what you gotta do."

"No, I don't. What?"

"Either apologize to your mother or get over to Robert's and hope like hell he's in a good mood. Help him to understand how much both of you will benefit from your success. I mean, it is that serious, isn't it?"

"I'm sleeping with him, and in my book, it don't get any more serious than that!"

"Then show that brotha where you're comin' from! What's goin' on with the Travis situation?"

"Girl, don't you know his country-ass cousin, Tyrone, tried to blow up the spot one night when Robert and I were at the casino! I only talked to Travis once, though. Way back when I first moved."

"How was he talking?"

"Like somebody praying for freedom."

"Ain't we all," she said. "Ain't we all."

That was one of those comments that meant something more than the obvious. Something I didn't necessarily feel like getting into, because Sheila was bound to get emotional, start rambling on about ancestors, and forget how long we had been on that long-distance call. Somehow, the conversation shifted back to me needing a place to stay and I allowed her to go through the pep-talk motions. The seemingly endless litany of "Keep yo' head up," "It's always darkest before dawn," and "Be good to a good man."

After praying for me, she let me go so that I could prepare myself for an evening of convincing Robert that I would be a lovely addition to his apartment and that I needed him. Not just for the roof over my head but for the feelings in my heart. And what I needed more was to know that he still felt the same.

Robert

I caught a page from Nikai about five minutes after we had come back from a run, but Don was on the phone making love noises and puckering up to his new woman, Theresa—this mystery chick that had stepped into his life and changed his whole way of thinking. He no longer hung out with me four days out of the week. It had decreased to one afternoon or maybe a whole day, depending on what *she* had planned. And the sick part was that he didn't appear to have a problem with it. Even seemed like he was adapting to this new way of life.

I couldn't understand it. Don had been like a brother since graduation from the fire academy and the two of us getting hired at the same engine house. We were the same height, with the same build, except he had about fifteen pounds on me. With that pretty-boy light brown skin, he liked to consider himself a ladies' man.

He was an attractive guy. And I don't mean that in any other way. I ain't into that other stuff. But it wasn't like ladies never approached him when we were out. Yet lately, I had seen him turn down some *baaadddddd* women. Ones who live in *Hooter*-ville, with bangin' backyards. Small waists, the kind of thick thighs that a man dreams about being wrapped up in, and pretty faces to match. Not to discredit Theresa, but all I had seen of her was the photo he had begun carrying around in his wallet. Protecting it like it were a piece of gold, like maybe she were even a piece of gold.

I really had no room to diss him, 'cause by then Nikai had

me breaking bachelor rules left and right. Before, I might've said that it was the sex, but I know it was more. It was the way she rubbed my back when we were in public, the way she would look up at me when we were alone. It was as if she was proud to have me around, even when I had done nothing at all. Yeah, we would have our little tiffs about her runnin' around actin' like she was a fifty-year-old Haitian voodoo priestess, but we found ways to compromise.

Well, to be honest, that shit was starting to take a serious toll on me. The incense, I could deal with. I could maybe even see past the roomful of candles, but those wild-woman gowns, indoor wind chimes, and funky-ass sage had to go. She was makin' a brotha nervous about company dropping by. There was no telling what they would think about the noises and smell seeping through the front door.

I admit that one night I threw it up in her face because I was feeling stupid about a promotion she said she was up for. That news made my already-unfit apartment look like a shack. Nikai was *moving up* and I was *fucking up* at the engine house, fallin' asleep and missin' runs, comin' close to losing my job, while her employers felt her qualifications were too high for the one she was presently holding. To be frank, I was jealous. *I* wanted to be the provider. Wanted to have a nice place to take her to. Not just sex her up and down on a raggedy mattress and box spring. I had decided at that point that I wanted to be her *man*.

I walked up behind Don in the kitchen and asked, "Hey, lover boy, you think I can use that device you've glued to the side of your face?"

He raised his index finger, signaling for me to give him a second. I guess maybe to go through one last round of "I miss you more." After two minutes of schoolboy whispering, he hung up, leaned back in the black swivel chair, locked his fingers behind his head, and sighed.

I asked, "It's like that?"

"Like that, man," he responded, nodding his head and smiling.

"So when do I get to meet the mystery woman?"

"Why don't we get together for dinner tomorrow night? And you can bring the songbird."

"I'll see what she says," I said, dialing Nikai's number.

I could tell by the way Nikai answered that something was different, something was wrong. There was a long drawn-out sigh before she even brought herself to mumble a pitiful greeting.

"Nikai, you all right?"

"Thanks for calling back, Rob. Yeah, I should be fine."

"What do you mean 'should be'? What's wrong?"

"Besides the fact that I'm homeless, nothing."

Damn! I knew it! Didn't I say that she would eventually be needing a place to stay and that somehow the ball would find its way over to me? Now it was my choice either to keep it or to knock that baby clear to Kansas City.

I fell silent and tried to come up with a plan to buy myself a little time to think. She was asking me to go against everything that I knew to be normal. Women never got my home phone number, but Nikai was the exception. Visiting my place was not even *open for discussion,* but I had let her do everything in there short of kicking up her leg and pissing alongside my couch. I was beginning to feel trapped. Like my every move would be caught on film and played for me when I got in at night. I was going for being her *man* and suddenly I felt as though I was getting *married*.

"Robert . . . Robert! If it takes that long to think about it, then for—"

"When do you want to move in?"

She instantly humbled herself and answered, "Whenever's good for you."

How's July of 2009?

"First of all, tell me what happened."

"It was my mother."

"Enough said. Get your things together and you can come by the engine house to pick up the key."

"You sure?" she asked.

"Of course I'm sure. You okay?"

"I am now."

"All right, see you shortly."

I hung up the phone and rubbed both eyes with the palms of my hands.

Don lowered the top corner of the newspaper he was reading and asked, " 'Come by the engine house to pick up the key'? 'When do you want to move in'? Is that what I heard you say?"

"Never thought you'd see the day, huh?"

"Not while I was still able to move around on my own." He laughed. "So I'm assuming that you'll be busy tomorrow night."

"Try for the next three months. I've got to get used to this. I never wanted to bring a woman into my apartment with the way that it is."

"Man, there's nothin' wrong with the apartment. Hell, I'd move in there any day. It's your furniture, bruh! It looks like somebody paid *you* to take it off of *their* hands."

"Fuck you, Don."

"No thanks. But seriously, maybe a woman's touch is what you need in your life."

"Maybe. And then again, maybe I just need *that* woman."

Whatever it was, I could feel it in the air that things were definitely about to change.

Part Two

Everything Must Change

Nikai

I can remember moving into Rob's apartment that next day. The following six months seemed to fly by at the speed of light. We spent Thanksgiving at his mother's and Christmas at mine, after endless attempts at reconciliation. What really softened Mama's heart was the obvious changes that were beginning to occur in my life. It even got to the point where we could hold a pleasant conversation as long as I wasn't talking about moving back home. To my mother, it appeared as though I was actually getting myself together for once.

Robert got a part-time job cleaning offices so that we could buy new furniture and fix his place up. Although I had received a promotion, I hardly even felt the raise in my pocket. It was as though I was working harder for fewer peanuts. Most of my extra change went into buying knickknacks like better curtains, throw pillows, figurines, and decent-looking ashtrays, since Robert insisted on smoking more frequently. I got the VCR fixed, the carpet cleaned, and made the bathroom look like a female had actually taken up residence there. It required a lot of work, but before long, we had a home.

That part of our lives seemed to come together like the pieces of a puzzle, while our relationship was slowly doing the opposite. Robert stopped giving me the majority of his checks to pay the bills and buy what we needed for the apartment. He began making promises that he'd get around to it. That is, until we were sitting in the dark. He complained about me trying to take too much control of his life. Reminded me numerous times that he was a grown man and should be keeping his own checks. It was beginning to sound as if someone else were speaking *through* him.

Then one night, he came home from the office cleaning gig smelling brand spankin' new, when normally he would've reeked like a vacuum cleaner had exploded in his face. There was wine on his breath instead of cigarette smoke. And he didn't appear to be as tired as he usually was. I found it to be a little strange, but when one goes looking for trouble, one will surely find it. I didn't want to believe that Robert could possibly be another Travis. So I lay in bed and convinced myself that he and Don had had another guys' night out. But the truth of the matter is, I was content.

I would walk around the apartment and marvel at the empire that he and I had built together. I had even invited my mother and Taylor over to view my accomplishments. This was my sophomore attempt at living with a man, but I promised myself that this time things would be different. I was gonna *make* this one work. I would be willing to go to any extreme to keep another woman away, even if it meant taking Sheila's advice on how to keep Robert satisfied. And it was apparent that that girl-friend knew just what to do in that area.

Eventually, communication failed between Sheila and me. Not because we had fallen out again, but because her *wifely* duties called for her to look after her mother-in-law. She wrote one day, informing me that she had had a small wedding, and enclosed photos of the two of them. She looked beautiful with her minibraids pinned up and her kente cloth draped over her shoulder. Rastaman's even longer locks failed to hide the noble smile that was sprawled across his face as he held my best buddy from behind, with his bare chest and a kente cloth wrapped from the waist down. They stood in the sands of the Virgin Islands, underneath a large shady palm tree, looking like royalty.

Apparently, his mother, who lived on the opposite side of the island, had fallen ill. She was unable to leave her home and had practically no lines of communication. Her neighbors would visit and they were the only ones she expected to hear from. Sheila didn't seem to have a big problem with the relocation, but I did. I wanted to talk to my friend every weekend. If it were possible, I would've called every day. But she had an undying love for Byron and an even larger amount of respect for his mother. Family was sacred to her and not to be trifled with.

When Robert learned of Sheila's absence from my life, he tried to fill that void with his younger sister, Kim. But she was far from being Sheila. Kim was what one might consider animated and high-spirited. She definitely brought a lot of energy with her presence.

Robert began arranging things so that we would be able to get to know each other. For example, he said he didn't have time to find his mother a birthday gift, so he asked me to go with Kim to help her look, since I had no idea what his mother would like. I didn't see how it would be difficult to find something for a condescending, insensitive old hag. A burnt-orange shawl or a set of lima bean green doilies would do just fine, if you asked me.

Aside from the time we had her wait at the apartment for the cable man and she took the liberty of opening my mail and reviewing the results of my pelvic exam in hopes of becoming a grandmother, this evil woman personally saw to it that I was uncomfortable at Thanksgiving dinner by relentlessly asking off-the-wall questions. She wanted to know why I had pushed myself on her son without getting married first. What plans I had for bearing children and which one of us was footing most of the bills at our place. She went on drilling me like that for hours. Yet she acted totally oblivious of her daughter, who was arguing and mushing her man, Kevin, in the side of the head at the dinner table. It was like a circus in there, and I was the only spectator.

After a while, Kim began to grow on me, although her antics never did. We started hanging out on a regular basis, but Sheila stayed in my heart. I never intended to substitute one for the other, but it sorta happened that way. I didn't pray as much anymore, and all of my beaded gowns were put up in a cedar chest that I bought for our bedroom. The only part of our friendship that I didn't let go of was the fascination with astrology that Sheila started writing to me about. And that was partly because it could be perceived as normal, since the horoscopes were in the daily paper. There was no room for the rest of our rituals in the new world that I was building around myself.

Deep down, I became ashamed of what I enjoyed, ashamed of that peace of mind I had. And Robert loved it. He no longer had to worry about sage burning or wind chimes making noise as he left the room. Didn't have to concern himself anymore with whether Don and Theresa thought I was a carnival freak. I was what he considered normal again. But looking back at it all, Robert never even knew what normal was. Neither did I, but instincts told me that I was closer than he was to finding it.

Our relationship began to closely resemble a roller-coaster ride. Up in the clouds one day, and before I knew it, it was shootin' to hell the next. A carefully prepared dinner would start out with romance and end with a petty argument over fictitious characters in a movie. We would crawl between the sheets pissed, but in minutes we would be drawn to each other like magnets. If I didn't scream loudly enough or it took him too long to ejaculate, there was another argument. And it went that way for months, until one night we sat down for a real heart-to-heart. Tried to come up with a strategy to make our bond stronger, something to build a greater appreciation for each other.

Before long, Rob and I decided to start a family. You heard me right, not a marriage and not a wedding, but a family. I admit that it was mostly my idea. I had received that promotion, I was sick of taking birth-control pills, and the truth of the matter is, I wanted a part of him inside me.

So we stopped using condoms and I got off the pill. Screwed like wild jackrabbits every chance we had, and the only damn thing he put inside me to grow was a chronic yeast infection. You know, the kind that's been passed on by more than one party?

One afternoon when I got home from the doctor's office, scratchin' like Cooties was my middle name, he was outside washing his Maxima. Had it shining like a brand-new penny when I pulled up and pinned him between my bumper and his trunk. I jumped out with a poker face and stood next to his car while he squirmed around trying to get free. After a minute, he stopped, realizing that I'd only been kind enough to leave room for blood to maneuver through his veins.

"Hey, Rob, got a trick question for you."

"What the fuck is wrong with you?" he yelled.

"No, me first, then you," I said calmly. "Can you tell me why it hurts me to wear drawers?"

He got quiet and sort of tilted his head to the right and stared at me like I had eight heads and they were all spinning.

"Answer me!" I yelled.

An older white lady sat outside on her balcony, watching the whole ordeal, and actually started snickering.

"Answer me, Rob!"

He stood there looking about as nervous as a hooker in church. Fumbled for his Newports. Weeble-wobbled back and forth trying to keep his balance and not fall into his open trunk. Basically unaware of everything around him, which gave me room to pick up on certain things—like the beautiful wicker picnic basket that I had never seen before. Wondering what the hell his nondomesticated ass was doing with a white miniature table-cloth in his trunk, I pointed at all of this stuff that should have been used to try to make me happy.

"What?" he asked, this time with a more gentle, defensive tone.

"Planning to take me on a picnic?"

"Huh?"

"If you can 'Huh?,' you can hear me!"

"Well, it's kinda hard to with all of the blood rushing to the upper half of my body!"

"Don't get cute or I'll have that sweet old lady call and ask for an EMS unit to be dispatched. Now, what are the odds of you knowing the driver? I'd say pretty good."

I gave him a sort of psychotic grin and grabbed the basket out of his trunk.

It was filled with dishes and silverware, which wasn't that un-usual, but they were dirty, and unless he was getting down with the man by day/woman by night scene, someone was definitely sharing my lovin'.

"Whose lipstick is this on this cup, Robert?"

"Huh?"

I looked down my nose at him like a grammar teacher reminding a student not to use the word *ain't*.

"I don't know whose lipstick it is because it's not even my basket!"

"Then whose is it?" I asked.

I knew there was nothing coming but a lie about the size of Texas, but I listened, just to see how far he would go to keep us together.

"*Don* put that in there the other day."

I folded my arms securely across my chest.

"And why in the hell would *Don* be putting a *picnic basket* in *your* trunk, Robert?"

"He needed the room in his trunk for a used tire he was picking up," he said, lifting each object up, including the ones that I hadn't noticed. "Where did you think this tablecloth and tote bag came from?"

So maybe I had jumped the gun on that one, but it still didn't ease the pain between my legs.

"Now what did the doctor tell you, baby?" he asked, faking genuine concern.

"Don't 'baby' me! I have a yeast infection that measured off the scale."

"Well, this isn't the first time you've had a yeast infection, is it? You know, I read that it's possible to get recurring infections from oral sex. That's probably what it is. We'll go to see your doctor together and ask her about it."

He was talking a mile a minute, and the scary part was that I found myself actually listening.

"I've got a better idea. Why don't we visit *your* doctor together and see what we find floating around your genital area."

"Don't play—you know I don't go to doctors or hospitals unless it's an emergency."

I looked down at his legs, which were trapped between his bumper and mine.

"I see I haven't gotten serious enough with you, huh?"

"Move your car so we can go in the house, Nik."

I shifted my weight a couple of times, looked up at the old lady on her balcony for the go-ahead, and finally decided to free him.

We did schedule an appointment to see my doctor together, but when the day came, Robert claimed that he couldn't make it. I was given a prescription for a one-dosage pill, and after a week or so we were trying for a baby again.

Months went by—I'd say about three, actually—and I still had not become pregnant. I prayed for a child, even went out and bought an ovulation kit, but my period always came like clockwork. Convinced that a precious baby girl would bring us closer, I stayed up at night and touched my womb in hopes that life was occurring inside of me, but nothing ever happened. Most of the time, I was in tears. Felt like I had been cursed for not appreciating the blessing that I had aborted before. Was less of a woman because of my unspeakable malfunction. Soon after, Robert confirmed that his beliefs coincided with mine.

We had just made love one morning before he was to go to the engine house. I was in the bathroom, drying off from a shower, when I heard him call my name. There was no specific tone in which he did it. It was almost as if he was searching for the right one, and before he knew it, I was standing there before him. He sat on the side of our bed with his elbows resting on his knees and stared at the floor.

"What?" I asked.

He didn't look up, just sort of let the question hang there for a second, and then he stared up at me, confused. As if out of all the inconceivable things he had seen in his life, I had presented him with the most baffling.

"What's wrong with you? Why can't you get pregnant?"

I stopped moving, can't really remember if I bothered to breathe. I got full; my eyes were heavy. *What's wrong with you? What's wrong with you? What's wrong with you?* I heard it over and over and over. It wouldn't go away. A tear fell, and he couldn't stand to look at me. My emotions were sentencing him to life with guilt. I lost control of my legs *and* my facial expressions. Couldn't pretend not to be moved. He had shaken me to my foundation. The only thing that I had left to hang on to was hope. And if it was apparent to him that there was none, then maybe I really *was* wasting my time—and his.

"I don't know what's wrong with me!" I cried.

I couldn't stand to see him or have him see me with my inadequate body. Women have been having babies since the beginning of time. Getting pregnant was something that could be done on one foot with both hands tied behind your back, and yet I couldn't manage it for the life of me. I hadn't been able to look at Robert the same since then. I guess because I knew how he truly saw me. Sex with him would only resurrect that question: "What's wrong with you?" One I didn't necessarily have an answer to and one that I was too afraid and embarrassed to ask.

And so I shut down, just like that. Without consideration of how he would feel, his sexual needs. And then, things got worse. Robert stopped coming in at the regular time, stopped trying to touch me, and if I'm not mistaken, he came close to not loving me. The pressure made me want to ball up and disappear. Remain silent and wait for him to come looking for the woman he'd fallen so hard for eleven months before. But it didn't happen, nobody came looking. I started considering a move. And I don't mean to another country. I was trying to leave the state of Missouri in hopes of leaving the state of misery that I was in.

I needed to talk to Sheila more than ever before. These were things that I wouldn't dare share with Kim. She wouldn't understand, and trying to explain would require me telling her about my abortion.

I found myself praying in private, asking the Creator to help me. To do what? I had no idea. I just wanted to be at peace. I didn't know if having a baby would bring it, if Robert's presence would or my absence. But as it turned out, a late-night phone call did.

"Hello?" I answered.

"Sweetie, are you okay?" Sheila asked.

My eyes welled up with tears as I whispered a quiet thank-you to the Creator for answering my prayers.

"Sheila, I'm a mess."

"What's wrong, baby?"

"My relationship is falling apart. I don't know if I'll ever be able to get pregnant again, either. And I miss you."

"Oh, Kai, I miss you, too. Why don't you think you'll get pregnant?" she asked.

"Robert and I have tried over and over again," I whined. "Now he won't even touch me."

"Sweetie, calm down first. Now tell me what happened."

I wiped the snot from my top lip and grabbed a Kleenex off of the wooden nightstand.

"We started having arguments almost daily—about money, about bills, my promotion, my praying, sex, the weather, a movie. It seemed that we were arguing over everything. He would say that he was going to work, but when he got home, something inside me told me that he hadn't been there at all. Then we would argue about that. The only thing that seemed to keep us together was the sex. But after failing to get pregnant, I didn't want to do that anymore. He says that something is wrong with me."

"Wrong with *you?*"

"Yeah. That's what he asked me, 'What's wrong with you?' Like I were a walking defect or something. Now he's developed a habit of drinking."

"Drinking what?"

"Wine is what his breath usually smells like when he comes in from work. But since we don't do very much talking anymore, it's hard to tell. I don't know." I sighed. "I think I want to go away for a while."

"Away *where,* Kai?"

"Out of town someplace. Away from all of this."

"Are you saying that you want to leave him? Because if you are, you need to slow down and do some serious evaluating. You can't just jump up like Betty Badass when you don't have anyplace to go. Look what happened the last time you needed a roof over your head. You couldn't afford to move alone and your mother made your life miserable."

"I know, I know."

"Kai, there's a time and purpose for everything, and I don't think that right now is a good time for you to leave that apartment. Note that I didn't say Robert. I can't tell you that you're wrong for feeling the way that you do, because you're there and I'm here, but don't cut off your nose to spite your face. You'll only end up hurting yourself. Have you done all you can to make your relationship work?"

"Like what?"

"Like sitting down and talking out your feelings. Sharing what's on your mind. He won't know how you feel unless you tell him. I can see you're going into your shell again. I told you that's a no-no. You need to stand up and be a strong woman."

"And you need to record yourself and sell some cassettes," I joked.

"All right, peanuthead, you better start taking me seriously."

"I do. How's Rastaman?"

"*Byron* is fine. He's out here visiting for the weekend, but he has to go back to work Monday."

"Well, tell him I said hi and give his mother my best wishes."

"Okay, baby. You gonna be okay?"

"I'm a big girl, Sheila. I ought to be able to deal with Rob until I'm able to take off."

"Don't say it like that! You make it sound like I won't be able to find you for a while."

"Well, you better keep in touch."

"Okay, good night, sweetie."

"Good night."

I placed the phone in its cradle and my problems in the Creator's hands. Said a prayer that night that Robert and I both would make a change for the better.

But as fate would have it, we didn't.

Later that month, things only got worse.

Robert

Before you take Nik's side, let me explain. First of all, I *paid* on the lights; the electric company's computer systems shut down that day and the order to disconnect had already been given. Second, I should be able to keep my own damn check. Nik wasn't there draggin' a hose with me when I made it. Third, a man being cut off from all sexual contact is incentive alone to drink, and considering I'm over the legal age, I didn't feel like I had to clear it with *anybody.*

She's right about things taking a ugly turn. We argued like strangers, until we began to look like strangers to each other. The sight of her body had become foreign. My touch always brought about a startled stare. I hated the way things had become between us, and me working my ass off didn't seem to make her love me any more. So I quit the night job I had but continued to take off out the door at the regular time every evening. She never even found out until much later, on the night I had the accident in her car, which I'm sure she's gonna tell you about.

Before all of that, I slowly began to regress. Started seeing Karen again. Good ole reliable Karen. Even after nine months, she was still willing to bake pies for me and treat me like a king. *That's* why I was coming home smelling like wine and peach massage oil. I was being loved. Or at least it felt like I was.

Nik started spending a lot of time with my sister, Kim, when the voodoo broad stopped calling. That meant that a lot would change, and it did, including the smell in the apartment. As long as she was in contact with Sheila, Nik wasn't concerned with how *"praying"* would affect my guests. She would tell me to bring my air mask from work if I had a problem with it.

The very same smart mouth that had intrigued me a year ago was starting to piss me off—to the point where I slapped her one night. I cried like a baby afterward because I was truly sorry. But even more sorry when she tossed that skillet of hot grease in my direction after one of those big-ass three-wick, seven-pound candles she used came flying at my head and *didn't* miss. I told you she was high-powered, but I had no idea she could throw like *that*.

I came in the next day with flowers and good news. Kalif was ready to work with her and wanted her to be a part of a group he had started. Without an ounce of enthusiasm, Nik cut her eyes at me and turned her face. My chest sunk when I could still vaguely see my handprint on her skin. I had hurt my baby, which was something I never really wanted to do.

It seemed as the weeks went by, she would go further and further into isolation. We went from being lovers to being roommates. I tried to talk things out, but Nik didn't seem to want to talk until *she* got ready. And by then, I was usually on my way out the door to Karen's place. Although as far as Nik knew, I was just running late for work.

Karen and I were spending almost as much time together as we had before Nik even entered the picture, except after the accident, we stopped leaving her apartment. I didn't want to take any more chances on being seen with her, because I was still in love with my baby at home. It didn't take long for Karen to pick up on that, either. She didn't like the idea of me being in a relationship, but not much had changed, because it wasn't like she'd ever had my home number or knew where I lived.

Karen's place had become like a spa for me. I could relax and get pampered without the nagging or uncomfortable silence that Nik dished out. My only beef with Karen became her thing about condoms. She never wanted me to wear one. Even after I got on her head about the yeast infection that I'd passed on to Nik. Then I began to trust her enough to let her put them on me, until I realized that it was all a game. So one day, I scheduled another appointment to see the doctor. I had every test they could possibly perform run on me. I realized then that I had to gain control of the situation or Karen just might destroy my relationship.

The only thing that bothered me after that was not being able to talk to Nik—not only about the doctor's appointments but about everything that I wanted from her, everything I needed from her. She was changing, and so was I. So quickly that we didn't know how to catch up with each other. We didn't know how to say "I'm sorry." And as the quiet, empty, listless weeks went by, we had almost forgotten how to say "I love you."

Nikai

Midnight Madness is probably what I would call that moment. Whatever it was, it was definitely far from Standing on Sanity. Robert left about three hours earlier for another guys' night out with Don, and as soon as I heard him turn the burglar alarm on, I made a beeline for the hall closet for the rest of my luggage. That three-digit code seemed to take forever, but when you've got one foot on the floor and the other ready to push off of the bed, everything starts to move at the speed of tooth decay.

I had been rehearsing for weeks how I would bow out of the relationship gracefully. Keep some sense of dignity and my two front teeth, if possible. Robert had been known to have a bad attitude, quick temper, and unpredictable spasms in his right arm. In all honestly, I wasn't what one would consider a victim. I had been known to cause him to clock in with a few bruises myself. Like the time he allowed his mother to open a letter from my OB-GYN. And I mustn't forget when he borrowed my Camry because his car was in the shop and I got a late-night phone call informing me that it had been run into a tree, "And by the way, Ms. Parker, the young lady driving didn't have a license." "The *young lady* driving?" I screamed.

By the time I *left* the hospital, they had moved Robert from the emergency room, having first listed him in stable condition, to the intensive care unit. They said he had suffered a slight heart attack. I guess the sight of a pissed-off sista stompin' through the silent halls of a hospital wearing curling rods and mix-matched pieces of a warm-up suit at two o'clock in the morning will cause any patient's EKG to dance a jig. But before his slow-dragging nurse could respond to his call, I gave him a quick right and wished him a speedy recovery. He just sort of tilted his head to the side, grabbed his cheek, and bucked his eyes the way he always did when he wanted to warn me that revenge was his.

The insurance company had my car fixed in a week. As for Robert's jaw, six to eight is what they told us.

I didn't know if he had been smart enough to notice, but, contrary to what Sheila had suggested, I had been packing for about four days. Removing a few shirts from the closet here and a couple of pantsuits there. No sudden moves like marked boxes or masking tape lying around, but I was almost sure that the map of Georgia he found the other day would raise a few eyebrows.

Maybe the reason it didn't was because before the serious decline in emotions, I started talking about a trip to the South for us, since it seemed we would never be able to save enough for the islands. Robert agreed that we needed time away from our routine lives. A chance to get things back to the way they used to be when his happiness was my concern and vice versa. Back when Fridays meant unexpected gifts, emotions were nothing to be toyed with, and sex was the norm. Back when it wasn't necessarily a bad thing for the two of us to be cramped up in that apartment at the same time, in the same room, breathing the same air.

Most of the furniture was his: The couch, bedroom, and dining room things all belonged to Robert. Now, all of the black-and-white Wil Brent prints, Afrocentric art, curtains, throw rugs, knickknacks, plant life, and cooking utensils belonged to me. Which, I might add, helped bring that place to life. I mean, yeah, it was a two-bedroom apartment with a sunroom and walk-in closets, but until I arrived, it was not yet a home. And with my departure being so abrupt, I had hoped that he and that place would both return to a lifeless state.

I had my sights for a permanent move on Miami, Houston, Los Angeles, or Atlanta. And I knew absolutely no one in any of those cities. But compared to the company that I'd been keeping, loneliness looked pretty promising. I guess I should rephrase that, because there's a distinct difference between being lonely and being alone. Okay, well, maybe I would've been a little of both, but at least I would've had my sanity.

I guess you're wondering why I choose sanity or the lack thereof to describe the void in my life. Why an attractive twenty-six-year-old UMSL alumna who has advanced from administrative assistant to leasing consultant in just six months would've arrived so quickly at a breaking point and packed her clothes at midnight like a fugitive on the run. Just be patient and stick with me.

I stood in the middle of our bedroom and gave it a final once-over to make sure that all of my things either had been loaded in my trunk the day before or were stacked up by the front door. I had even stripped the bed of my satin sheets and taken down the shower curtain that I'd bought the month before. I took a deep breath, hit the light switch, and closed the bedroom door behind me. My footsteps echoed on the hardwood floors while I paced myself as if an electric chair were all I had to look forward to. The kitchen was clean, but the smell of Newports still lingered in the air. I grabbed the Post-it pad off of the counter and scribbled, "You doubted I would leave; now watch *my* smoke!" I stuck it to an ashtray, where I knew he would find it.

The light on the answering machine was still blinking and brought the last message to mind: "Mr. Hayes, this is Carol at Dr. Sullen's office. Your test results are in. Please give me a call at five five five-zero zero two nine. Thanks."

I sprayed some smell-good air freshener to clear the stench he'd left behind and then glanced at my watch. I knew my time was up, so I pivoted toward the door and continued my leisurely stroll toward a new life. My heart beat quickly, but it was the kind of beating that came from anticipation, not agony. I dimmed the halogen lamp in the corner, put my purse on my shoulder, and bid that apartment an untimely farewell.

Robert's face crossed my mind, the dark, smooth skin and keen features. His clean-cut face and bald head were what had hooked me in the first place. Suddenly, my heart got heavy and I could smell him. No wait—the scent of those damn Newports is what hit me like a sucker punch in the dark. The dead bolt turned over and the bottom lock clicked. I didn't move, too afraid even to breathe. Didn't know whether to stare up or down, to watch for facial expression or hand movements. The knob turned, the door opened, and I sweated—the kind of sweat that would steam up the mirror of a medicine cabinet in ten seconds flat. The alarm beeped. Once, twice, thrice. He looked at me and then down at my bags, but he didn't miss a single drag off of his cigarette.

Robert asked, "You have somethin' that you wanna get off of your chest?"

I didn't respond. Just sort of stared at him like a scolded child waiting for the next belittling comment. I was willing to do whatever it took to make him believe that he was in control of the situation. Didn't want any casualties, on my part or his.

Robert threw the Newport that I had smelled on the ground and stepped on it. Sucked his teeth, then threw me a dirty look, along with the bouquet of flowers he had brought with him. The alarm blared like a cat dying a slow death, silencing him, silencing me, not that there was really anything left to say.

He walked in, disarmed the screaming gadget, and asked, "Why are your bags packed, Nik? Be a woman and speak your mind."

I was tired of "speaking my mind," and tired of hoping that things would get better. Tired of pretending that my feelings were numbed by the sole desire for male companionship. Men like Robert didn't seem to understand monogamy until their well had run dry. Until their women had one hand on the doorknob and the other on the garment bag.

"Your test results came back. There's a message from your doctor's office on the answering machine."

His eyes shifted a couple of times before he said a dry "Thank you."

"You didn't tell me that you were having any tests run."

"And *you* didn't tell me that you were leaving me, either!" he snapped.

He shook his head as though he pitied me and asked, "So were you gonna cancel the appointment at the studio Friday, or what? I put my name behind you and now you're ready to bounce. That shit costs money!"

I had forgotten about the studio time and the arrangement with the producer that Rob had made. He'd been backing me in my pursuit of fame and my burning desire to deliver vocal inspiration to the lost and less fortunate. He had promised months before that he would talk to Don, one of the firefighters he works with, about getting his cousin to commit. His name is Kalif. He produces tracks for a local group called N-Sight, and he had mentioned that he was looking for a sultry voice to complete the trio. That's when Jackass stepped in and seized the moment. It's not that I'm not grateful, but he reminded me of his overrated efforts every chance he got.

I dropped my purse by my side and closed the front door.

"I'm still going," I said, sitting down on the arm of the beige leather couch.

With my back to him, I could hear him laughing. Everything had become a joke to Rob—me, the relationship, and apparently his health, too.

"So, are you gonna tell me what kind of test you had run?" I asked.

"Blood tests."

"What kind of blood tests, Rob?"

"I got tested for HIV."

There was no emotion in his voice, but then, there hardly ever was. I paused and thought about the last time we'd had sex, which was several months ago, but there'd been no protection involved.

"Why were you getting tested for HIV?" I asked.

"Why not?"

"Let me rephrase that. Why didn't *we* talk about needing to get tested?"

"Okay, so we're even," he said, looking down at my luggage. "You kept your departure time from me and I kept this from you."

He was working toward his nomination for Asshole of the Year award again.

"Robert, is there something that I need to know?"

"You *know* all that you need to know. Did they leave the results on the answering machine?"

"No."

"Then I don't know any more than you do right now."

He was calm as a cucumber. Poured himself a glass of water

and leaned against the island in front of the refrigerator. He stared
at me until he was done. I cut my eyes away a couple of times and
then checked to see if he looked like he was losing any weight.
Robert was a sexy six-foot-four, 235-pound chocolate man with
eyes that would make you change your religion. But I didn't appreciate his nonchalant attitude about a life-or-death matter, so at
that moment, his looks were beside the point. I had a bigger
problem, and it was called going back to the drawing board.

I was stuck. Caught between what I wanted and what I
needed. And to spice things up, he was throwing in a side order
of worry.

He sat next to me on the couch, grabbed the VCR remote,
and pushed the play button.

"You can thank me for the flowers later," he said sarcastically.

"You mean the lovely ones on the floor by the ottoman?"

He looked at me and sucked his teeth again. This was his way
of minimizing my sarcasm. We were usually all over each other
with it. He'd snap and then I'd snap, occasionally leaving us
laughing. But things had gotten too far out of hand to grin or
do anything of that nature.

We had been depriving each other of the simple pleasures in
life. Holding out to see who would give in first, and I must admit
that I was impressed. I expected to see *his* bags at the door by the
fourth month of my abstinence spell. Nonetheless, I'm *more* than
certain that he was maintaining. But me, my needs were totally
different from Robert's. I wanted a man to walk up behind me
and remind me of how much he loved me. Surprise me with gifts
without a bottle of *motion lotion* being tossed into the package.
And not bullshit me about something as serious as HIV.

I had a career to consider, and Robert knew this. He also
knew how to hang his input over my head. "If I don't talk to
Kalif, how will you ever make it? Singing in the shower won't
get you a record deal. You *need* my connections, so don't get
tough," he'd say. That alone was enough to send me walking.

Don't get me wrong, there were times when I got that tin-
gle inside at the sound of his voice. At one point, the way that
he walked into a room, closely resembling a tribal warrior, had
me beaming with pride to be the chosen one. The one to stroke

his head at night as he nestled deep into my lap. Back then, I was the heart of this man, the one in his corner, cleaning his bruises and sending him back out into the cold, cruel world to fight another day.

Robert stepped into my life at a time when I needed reassurance that my entire existence was adequate, to say the least. He invited me to share his apartment when my own mother made me feel as though I was under surveillance in hers. When loneliness was beginning to take a toll on me, along with the pressures of a competitive, successful sibling. Not to mention the death of my father, the prison conviction of my ex, and a prior abortion. When tackling the cold, cruel world, which I later prepared him for, was becoming more and more of a daily task, Robert showed me how to laugh again, and love like I'd never been hurt. And there hardly ever came a time when he needed reciprocity. That was what made it so sweet—he really was a warrior. My warrior. Until the day that I sexually fell back into my slump and my wonderful, dependable, courageous man never showed up to make it all better.

I try not to think about the past anymore, though. It only makes me wonder if those things were still being done for him. And if I wasn't the one doing them, someone else probably was. I mean, how else would he be holding up? Where would he get the energy to be so harsh and insensitive? Wouldn't he have longed for my touch? Wouldn't seeing my face in the morning be of more importance to him? And what about all of the shocking evidence against him? There was no doubt that there had been someone else taking my place, being me, or coming frighteningly close to it.

"Wake me up before you go to work," he said, yawning. "I wanna call the doctor's office back."

I saw room for compassion and ran for it.

"What do you think they'll say?"

"The psychics are on Channel Five," he replied, stretching out and rolling onto his side. "Since I'm so unpredictable, see if you have any better luck with Ms. Warwick."

Robert often said things of that nature because he knew that I really believed in psychic abilities, horoscopes, astrology, the whole nine yards. He used to say it was ridiculous how I allowed a newspaper's prediction to dictate the way the rest of my day would go. I say it was taking necessary precautions.

My horoscope for that day stated that an immediate change would occur. Uncertainty would be in abundance and I might find myself backtracking in order to keep peace. Now, didn't that sound like my situation? His said something about a future battle between mind and body. Happiness would surely find him in the end because loss is sometimes greater. I didn't understand what that meant and didn't bother to share it with him, because I knew he'd give me one of those stares that would make me question whether or not the analytical side of my brain was even operating that day. Robert possessed that silent ability to convey messages that otherwise would have gone over my head. But at the same time, he was too blind and headstrong to realize that I was tired of living in uncertainty and that something had to happen, whether it be good or bad.

You guessed it right. He is a Libra. In search of constant balance, and he would have left me tipped over if I hadn't continuously competed with everything else that mattered to him. Me? I'm a Capricorn. The goat, alone on the top of the mountain, observing everything. That's why Robert usually got caught: I was always watching. But could I honestly be any other way, with him sneaking around and getting tested for HIV behind my back?

I can't say that I believe there is a need for balance. Things are either one way or the other. You are either in love or you're not. A door is either closed or it's not. A woman is either pregnant or she is not. There are rarely in-betweens, except in certain situations like my own. For example, "Distance makes the heart grow fonder" is to "Out of sight, out of mind" what Robert was to me. They can't both coexist at the same time and fill the same space. But both are true and exact, yet so imperfect, as were we. And I guess maybe deep down inside, this was part of the reason that I was still there—my infatuation with that perfect imperfection.

Robert

"Listen, we've gone through this before."

I was naked and on my back in a spread-eagle position across my lady friend's bed. Blindfolded, with my wrists and ankles tied to the bedposts. Karen's down with that kinky stuff. Borderline dominatrix. She's into role-playing, and that time we were supposed to be in a hostage situation, which I really didn't have time for, but she was pretending to be some freaky broad from another country who couldn't speak good English and communicated by touch. So I figured it was worth it to see how that shit played out.

I just learned that morning that I was HIV-negative, which called for a celebration, so I told the captain that I had an important run to make, because I thought that it would only take thirty minutes to get the foreplay over with, blaze it, and get cleaned up. But it was apparent that Karen had other things in mind.

"And I told you that I'm wearing a diaphragm, Rusty," she insisted.

"Rusty" was the stupid nickname that she came up with for me when we first started messing around again. I told her about Nik holding out on me. So she told me that she was gonna help me to get back into the groove of lovemaking. That I was *rusty*.

"Look, I have a woman at home and I can't take chances."

"Don't remind me of that!" she yelled, loudly enough to make me wanna open my eyes and maybe ball up to protect my jewels. I felt cool air on my chest and then a wet tongue on my side. I jerked and eased to the right, then felt fingertips on my left.

"Do you have the condom or not?" I asked.

There was silence and no movement. I worried for a minute. Envisioned somebody finding my decomposed body in that very position 'cause she had gone mad and killed me. At least I wouldn't have had to explain my death to Nik the way I would another yeast infection or something worse.

I felt her warm mouth enveloping my piece. It made me arch my back like someone had yelled, "Clear!" in an attempt to restart my heart. All of my energy went to the middle of my body. It formed in my stomach, causing me to pull at those satin ropes that she had my wrists and ankles tied with. I moaned and so did she, only louder. I couldn't see anything, which was probably good, because I was hittin' it from behind. I could have made her look like Vanessa Bell Calloway, if I'd wanted to. I mean, it was supposed to be partly *my* fantasy, too.

Karen climbed on top and took the best seat in the house. I felt her moisture only a bit too well.

"Karen, get up! I told you about the fuckin' condom!"

"And I told you that I was wearing a diaphragm."

She moved up and down, rocked back and forth. Wet pelvic thrusts clouded my reasoning. The words formed at my lips and then fell somewhere between a hiss and a moan. I pulled my wrists free and grabbed her under her armpits. Lifted her with all of the strength that I had left. She pounced back down and did circles until my toes curled. Then up and down. I could hear it and feel it but didn't want to see it. Or have it see me. Not Karen, but the guilt.

"Get up. I'm coming!" I yelled.

"So am I!"

"Then get up!"

She shoved me in my chest and held me down with her weight. Then I did it, let go of all my fluid. My piece throbbed inside of her while she kissed my chest and wiped the sweat from her forehead. Breathing heavily, she thanked me in what sounded like a different language.

"What?"

"I said, *Gracias.* That's 'thank you' in Spanish. Remember the hostage negotiation that you ruined with your paranoia?"

Karen owns and works as a beautician over at Hair by Mona, or so she said. I didn't really know that much about her private life except that she had my juices floating around in her. I had taken her to a couple of Cardinal games with Hodges from the engine house and his wife, but that was only because Nik was always too busy meditatin' or vibin' to some reggae. No doubt, this broad had nothing on my baby but personality. She was down for whatever. It was all good to her—*in* the bedroom and *out*.

I remember the night that I met her; she told me something that's stuck with me, even to this day. We had received a call over the audible about smoke in the kitchen of an Italian restaurant. When we arrived, the manager had everything under control, which was a relief because it gave me a few extra minutes to speak to the attractive woman seated alone in a far corner. She had been staring at me from the moment I stepped in the door, but I was sure the odds of her being alone weren't too good—that is, until she beckoned for me.

She said, "I was wondering how long it would take you to come over and speak to me."

"Do I know you?" I asked, shocked by how comfortable she was with herself.

"No. Do you have to?"

"I guess not. Are you dining alone tonight?"

"No. Should I be?"

"So where's your husband?" I asked.

"I don't have one, but my date is in the men's room."

"So why am I over here?"

"Because I didn't think that I could throw my phone number as far as you were standing."

I laughed and instinctively glanced toward the men's room.

"And how do you think your date will feel about that?"

"I can imagine he wouldn't like it," she said, handing me a business card decorated with a pair of scissors and a blow-dryer.

I wrote my pager number on the other side and handed it back to her.

"You know, you have a lot of nerve," I said.

Without even considering the crowd in the restaurant *or* her date approaching the table, she gave me a wink and said, "If you don't have nerve, you don't have any business in this world."

And she meant just that. Karen had more nerve than a lot of *men* I knew. Did whatever she felt, whenever she felt like it. We went on to become friends, if that's what you want to call it, and I actually enjoyed our time together. We did little things, like hung out in the park on Mondays, when she didn't have to work and everybody else in St. Louis with a job did. She would bake pies and cookies for me and bring them to the engine house. Sometimes she'd stay for a while, play a few games of spades with the other firefighters, and keep us all laughing until it was time for visitors to leave, which was usually nine o'clock. None of the guys could understand why I didn't trade the often-unseen Nik in for Karen. Except for Don. He usually stayed up-stairs lifting weights or watching television, saying that just because I was disrespecting my woman didn't mean that he had to. So I decided to stop Karen from coming to the engine house. And for a long time, she remained my little wild, high-spirited secret. But as time went on, I began to realize that she had no problem making her feelings for me very vocal. That was her sword, her big mouth. Along with that pocket between her legs.

Karen loosened my ankles, removed the blindfold, and stretched out across the bed.

"Rusty, you aren't mad at me, are you?" she asked, kicking her legs like a lovesick teenager.

"I don't wanna talk about that right now, because I told you what *not* to do."

I got up to go to the bathroom, when she sprang from the bed and stood in front of me.

"Listen, you knew what time it was when you walked through that front door, so don't come at me like I *took* some-thin' from you."

"You wanted this," she said, pointing to her crotch, "just like I wanted that."

"Yeah, all right," I said, reminding myself that this was my last trip over there.

"Robert, I'm not trying to break up that sorry-ass relationship that is apparently falling apart whether I come around or not!"

I sucked my teeth and retreated to the bathroom to wash away the feeling of her body and any other memories that I had of her. She stood on the other side of the door, yelling like I owed her money. I sat down on the edge of the tub to think about what I had just done, but all that came to mind was Nik. And what we had coming to an end. I turned the shower on to drown out Karen's yelling and to steam up the mirror on the back of the door. I didn't want to see myself in her bathroom, naked, limp, sticky, and on one knee, praying that I wouldn't start itching in a week or so.

I jumped in the shower, to find that there was no soap. I stepped out, leaving a trail of wetness almost as bad as the one she had left on me. I opened the linen closet and moved some sanitary napkins, toilet tissue, and an EPT test to the side. Found the soap and went back to the test. It hadn't been opened, but there was more than one. I thought about all of the buildup that I had just left inside of her and cringed. Closed the closet and cleaned myself as close as I could get to my soul, but just short of my conscience.

"Robert, come on outta there. I've got things to do!"

By the time I came out, she was in a T-shirt that I had left over there the time before. She looked good enough to eat, with her skin the color of lightly browned corn bread. She almost made me not mind the two prints that she was leaving in the shirt with those size D cups. I wiped the smile from my face when I saw the one on hers.

"This doesn't change anything between us, does it?" she asked, crossing her legs and revealing those calves, which she knew I was a sucker for.

"If there's nothin' there, then how can it change?"

"And what's that supposed to mean?"

She uncrossed her legs and rolled her neck like a cobra.

"It means that what we do can't leave this room."

"As long as you leave this room, so will your business."

She leaned backward and gave me a mischievous grin.

"If Nik finds out about this . . ."

"Fuck her!"

I grabbed my clothes and said, "I don't have time for this."

"Oh, you've got more time than you realize!"

Karen climbed up on the dresser and jumped out at me with claws extended. I stepped to the left and she fell short of the bed. Kicked, screamed, and grabbed at my ankle. I tried to shake her off and only managed to kick her in the shoulder, which made it even harder for me to understand why she grabbed her lip, which was already bleeding from her attempt to fly, and screamed, "Someone, anyone, call nine one one."

"Karen, get up and be quiet."

"Oh God! Somebody help me."

"Karen, this shit ain't funny. Get up!"

She rolled around on the floor for a second and said, "Stop yelling at me. My head hurts."

"Will you please get up and stop that yelling before somebody hears you."

"Well, it'll be nice to get through to *somebody,* 'cause you sure can't hear me."

She moved to get up, but she slipped back down.

I sucked my teeth again and asked, "What's wrong now?"

"I'm hurting, Rob. It won't kill you to be a little more compassionate. I mean, I *could* be carrying your baby."

I had her up by her arm and let her fake butt drop like a ton of bricks.

"What the fuck do you mean, carrying my baby?" I yelled.

"You know what just went down here. Don't play stupid with me!"

I stared at her as she laughed at me before getting up on her own and dusting herself off like the great Houdini after escaping from the inside of a chained box. It was at that moment that I saw Karen in a whole new light. She was a drama junkie looking for her next fix and she had found it—in me. The only thing left for me to do was see how much this stunt was gonna cost me and, more importantly, how far she would let this sick addiction carry her.

* * *

I was on my second mile when Don finally pulled up. We usually met at the community college track every Tuesday, Thursday, and Saturday, but I'd switched up on him. I needed to be alone to think some things out. Not that I didn't value his opinion, 'cause Don was truly my right-hand man even from the first day at the engine house.

Man, we watched brothas lose their lives trying to be tough before the fitness test. They dragged hoses and carried a ladder a little over thirty feet and collapsed on some fatal asthma shit. That's enough to make you find a sane individual on the squad and stick with 'im. Whether he's keepin' you in check or vice versa. And that was our duty to each other. I felt I had to be there for him because he led his life based on emotions. At one point, Theresa had him in therapy for some nightmares he was having. Flashbacks of individuals he just couldn't get to in time had him up at night. I was the one who taught him to distance himself. "Leave your work *at* work and save your emotions for your woman" is what I told him. I think he listened, but I often caught him falling off, and that's when I got on his head. Which made it even harder to admit to him that I wasn't in control myself.

"Hey, whassup?" Don asked.

I slowed down to a light jog for him and wiped my face with the gray T-shirt that I was wearing.

"You knew where to look, huh?"

"Yeah, what was up with that? You need time to get in touch with your feminine side?" he joked.

"Naw, just heard that this track is better."

"So whassup for the weekend? We still shootin' out to Chicago?"

Chicago is where Don was from, but I'd lived in St. Louis my entire life. Never even thought about living anywhere else. He was supposed to be partners with his old man in a family lounge, but they couldn't keep the money straight. He said his family drank so much that if he didn't go up there every weekend, the joint would get shut down. That time, he wanted me to go with him to check out the nightlife. So I had a choice, stay home with Nik, who probably wouldn't *sell* me a piece, or go to Chi-town and give my money to nameless, faceless women whom I couldn't *buy* a piece from. I was better off sticking with Nik. At least she might've looked out for me with *my* money. But blue balls are blue balls, no matter how far you drive to get 'em.

It kinda made me wish for the times when seeing Karen was a weekly event. And I do mean an *event*. She used to arrange what she would call "Evenings to Remember." And she knew just what to do in order to lodge things deep into my memory— way back there next to the first time I rode a bike, kissed a girl, or learned a dance move.

Karen loved to laugh, so we'd spend a great deal of time going to comedy clubs. Next came dinner and then dancing until just before the sun came up. We'd go back to her place, have a few drinks, and then connect. She never brought up my relationship, never asked why I found it absolutely necessary to leave the next morning. Her only concern was making sure my eggs were scrambled hard enough, my bread was toasted dark enough, and that I didn't have to want for anything as long as I was in her company.

It seemed as though the more Karen did, the less Nik did. And I found no need to demand from Nik what I was already getting somewhere else. I let her hold out with the sex and I did the same with affection. The difference between the two of them was that Nik needed me and Karen needed me to need her. Karen wasn't looking for validation. All she wanted was to give me a reason to keep coming back. She didn't drain me; she filled me up—almost to the point of overflowing. I was smart enough to beware of the bearer of gifts, but the truth of the matter is that it felt damn good to be *taken care of* in every sense of the phrase.

"Man, I gotta see what Nik is talking about doing first. We've got enough things going wrong. Spending the night away from home isn't what I need to do right now."

"Hey, you know I'm with that. Handle yours."

Don messed me up, 'cause sometimes he could be extremely sensitive. The type who surprises his woman so often that she's not even surprised when he does romantic stuff. Actually, he was the one who gave me the weak idea to give Nik those flowers.

And what did that get me? Walking papers and attitude. He told me that I needed to stimulate Nik's sexuality by taking her places that she didn't expect me to, like going ice-skating, fruit-picking, catching plays at the Fox, or even going on picnics. I did take his advice once and used the picnic theme, just not on Nik. That turned out to be more trouble than it was worth, especially when Nik found the evidence in my trunk. After that, I wasn't trying to hear anything Don had to say about women *or* sex. 'Cause with or without the gifts, I'd still get mine.

I gave him a pound and dusted him off on my fifth lap. If he had known what he was dapping me up in agreement with, he would've been pissed. He liked Nik a lot. Was always telling me about the "gem" I had. How someday I'd wish that I had taken better care of my woman. And to some degree, I knew he was right. I didn't wanna become old and gray and have no one to share my life with. I wanted that wife and kids that society says makes life worth living. But it was beginning to look like the man upstairs had another plan mapped out.

Things weren't the same between Nik and me. Hadn't been for a while. The midday lovemaking had ceased months before and late-night conversations were a thing of the past. I tried being spontaneous and offered to take her to the Ozarks on the weekends, but she only accused me of having bad timing.

We could have one small misunderstanding and it would be blown out of proportion before I could fully grasp what had just gone down. The mood swings were a bitch and the tears had been flowing so often that I didn't know whether to walk in the house or backstroke through the side door. If I tried to touch her, there was instantly ten feet between us. She'd sprint across the room as if I were wielding a machete. And *then* she started doing her PMS thing.

The biggest beef I had with Nik was that she saw things in black and white, with no room for gray. Now, I, on the other hand, saw in many shades. Rules were made to be broken. Somebody's dream has to be deferred. It's all about who's smart enough to play the game of life *and* win. Yet all Nik seemed to want to do was pack her bags and renege. Something Karen would never do. At the card table or not.

*   *   *

"So you mean to tell me that you knew she was gonna try to leave?"

I was in the kitchen at the engine house talking to my younger sister, Kim, on the phone. She and Nik had become close, a little too close, since we'd begun dating almost two years before.

"I didn't say I *knew;* I just said she mentioned a change of scenery."

"Whose sister are you? I swear that sometimes you look out for the wrong person."

"Listen, big bro, don't get mad at me 'cause you can't keep your butt off of the streets and your hands to yourself. I don't have anything to do with your affairs. Now, I tried to get as much information from her as I possibly could, but she sounded pretty pissed at you."

"Yeah, well thanks for nothing. Where's Moms?"

"She went to bingo with Mrs. Banks. Hey, are you still gonna let me get that loan?"

"I shouldn't give you anything."

I tried to sound as unmoved by her begging as possible, but Kim was my one and only baby sis. Besides, I was so used to her begging that it had become a regular part of every conversation. You wouldn't think that she'd graduated from MU and had a decent-paying job at Southwestern Bell. She usually begged so much that for a long time, I thought her hands were cups.

I *can* say that she came in handy when I just couldn't manage to get inside of Nik's head. A lot of times, women talk to one another about their men. So it was the perfect hookup. I basically knew what I'd done and what I needed to do to try to correct it in time for dinner. All it took was a simple phone call to Kim.

"What if I talk to Nik again for you?"

"Let's see what you can do first."

"Don't expect a miracle, especially if all you plan to take home are some tired flowers and a cloud of smoke around your head. When are you gonna stop smoking, anyway?"

"Who is four years older than who here? I don't need a lecture. Just get off of this phone and do your thing before she really *does* leave me."

"Consider the job done."

"Peace."

"Hey, Rob."

"What?"

"I'll take those in twenties, fives, and tens." She laughed.

"Yeah, the *only* way you'll get it is to *take* it."

I hung up, leaned back in the swivel chair, and stared at the ceiling. The engine house was noisy, with Hodges and Fuller playing cards and other small talk that filled the air, but to me, there was nothing going on. For a fireman, anything but a *run* is considered peaceful. I had big problems in my personal life, but everything had to take a mental backseat when it came to saving the lives of others. I relaxed while I was there so that when the time came to haul ass, I'd be focused.

I washed up the last of the dishes from dinner and read the paper until the news came on. Channel 5 was running a story about a little girl on the South Side who'd died from smoke inhalation that morning. I cringed and changed the channel to something more upbeat.

I dozed off for a minute and was awakened by my pager. It was Karen. She'd left a message, complaining about back pains, how I had caused them, and saying that she needed to see me again—ASAP. I checked the time, which was 10:23, and called her back at home.

"Whassup?"

"What did I tell you about greeting me like that?" she asked.

Karen sounded as though she had some heavy things on her mind and I played a big part in it all.

"Yeah, I'm returning a page," I said.

"Ha-ha. Real funny, Rusty. I need you to come over here."

"For what?"

"For free! Now are you coming or not?"

"I'm working right now."

She sighed, as though her patience was wearing thin, and said, "That never stopped you before."

"Let's just say that it's reason enough to stop me now."

"What did you do, go somewhere and fall in love?"

I didn't entertain that last comment. Silence stretched across the phone line, making her uncomfortable.

"Whassup? I need to get back to work."

"And I *need* to see you. I don't know why you keep playing with me, Robert, because you know that I'm no joke."

I switched the phone to the other ear and sat up straight in the swivel chair.

"You threatening me now?"

"I don't have to threaten you. Anything I say, I can back up. Now, like I said, I need to see you. We can schedule a time now or I'll try to reach you at *home* tomorrow."

At home? I could see that Karen was playing to win. But then again, she could be bluffing. Strangely enough, that was what had attracted me to her from the beginning. That woman had spirit. Even if it meant losing, it was worth it to her if she was simply allowed to play. But her award-winning performances were starting to piss me off. Partly because she was taking them out of the bedroom and into the streets. Using them to fight dirty and break up homes. I couldn't take a chance on her running into Nik, so I agreed. Gave in, as if I really were in a hostage situation.

"I'll be there on Friday. Whatever it is you want, you better rehearse that shit now so that you can say it fast! I don't have all day to play with you."

Being rude to her was my only way of staying sane, but it really didn't matter, because she wasn't even living in this world. My comments meant nothing to her. As long as Karen got what she wanted, she won. In her eyes, that is.

I heard a dim laugh and then the phone being dropped into the cradle. I could imagine her scoring another mark on the wall for herself. Probably high-fiving another one of her sick beauty shop girlfriends. And rambling on about my backstroke, which she'd never see again.

Nikai

I hadn't heard from Sheila in a month and a half. I couldn't tell who had done a better disappearing act, Sheila or Travis. Upset and frustrated, I began going to work and pouring my heart out to Dorothy. She listened like the concerned mother I never really had. Gave good advice, too. But I still insisted on using my own discretion. I was the only one feeling what I felt at night. I had let the idea of leaving rest, but it still lingered in the back of my mind.

When I arrived at work one morning, Dorothy and I started with our therapy sessions. And as usual, I was the patient.

"Remember when you told me always to do what I feel is right, even when everyone else is screaming against it?"

"Mmmhmm," Dorothy said, straightening up and folding her thick arms across her chest.

"Well, last night I packed my things up to leave Robert."

"And go where?"

"Atlanta." I busied myself with the pens on my desk and then began doodling.

"Did it occur to you that today is a workday?"

"I know, I know. I was just ready to make a move in my life. I was ready, and that's all that matters. I was willing to leave all of this behind—this job, Robert, the apartment, everything."

"Chile, when I told you to do what makes you happy, I didn't mean go with the first idea that comes to your head. You've got to use some common sense, think it out, weigh your options, not just take off like some immature teenager in the middle of the night, expecting home, stability, and everything to be there whenever you get ready to come back. Besides, *home* is where you are loved. Don't you ever forget that."

She finally took a breath and was back at it.

"And I don't care what you say—it's got something to do with that Robert fella you're seein'. Get yourself together. We're gonna run down to the St. Louis Centre for lunch."

"Can't. I've got showings at one o'clock and two-thirty."

She waved her index finger and squinted one eye before opening my door. "You betta start thinking."

"I do and I will," I said, half-smiling at the fact that she felt she had to remind me to do something as simple as thinking.

My phone rang as my door finally closed.

"Hello?"

"Whassup witcha?" Kim asked.

"Nothing. I'm just tired as hell."

"Why? What did you do to my brother now?" she joked.

"Girl, don't even—"

"You know you're the one always starting things." She laughed through just about every other word. "What about the time you went crazy and gave him a heart attack *while* he was in the hospital for something else? Punching on him like a madwoman."

"Yeah, and you also know what your *wonderful* brother did to land himself in the hospital in the first place."

"I'm just messin' with you, girl. What's goin' on with y'all now? Why are you tryin' to leave him?" she asked.

"I can't talk about this right now. Some of us do respect the workplace."

"Look, I'm just gonna be honest with you. He called me this morning because he didn't know what else to do."

"So why didn't he try calling me?"

"I don't know, but he wants to talk to you. Now, I've got this guy I met last week, and he's been wanting to take me out, so why don't we all go out together? That way, y'all can get your anger away from the household and have a good time tonight."

"Why don't you just come up with another idea?"

"Well, because I didn't want to be alone with this guy on our first date?"

"Guess what? That's a red flag. Fear should not be an initial emotion when dating someone."

"How about it?"

There was a knock at my door and I instinctively slipped my shoes back on.

"I gotta go."

"Well, how about it?" she insisted.

"Fine, fine. Let me talk to Robert."

I slammed the phone in its cradle. "Come in."

Linda walked in with a stack of folders and placed them on my desk. "Marion asked me to get these to you. They're residential complaints."

"Thank you," I said. "And please leave that door open for me."

I needed the air to circulate a little better. Open up those isolating four walls that stunted my perception. See more than what was just before my eyes and basically do what Dorothy suggested—*think*.

I got home around a quarter to five, thanking God and sweating bullets. After showing property to two inconsiderate newlywed couples who had no concept of time, I headed down Market Street and made a right onto Jefferson. The sun was leaning on me like a drunk at a two-drink-minimum bar, and Robert had never gotten around to putting that Freon in my car that I had asked him about a week and a half before.

But anyway, I was letting the wind blow through my shoulder-length mane and listening to Bob Marley and the Wailers telling me to "get up, stand up," when I saw blue lights flashing in my rearview mirror. The first thing that came to mind was my stack of parking tickets, which was thick enough to level a coffee table. He sped past me and continued on up Salisbury toward I-70 while I exhaled and thanked the Lord for not letting them decorate my wrists with steel bracelets in front of all of downtown. You ain't been caught up in prayer 'til you pull over, get out, and circle the car the way I did. Out on Jefferson, looking like I was about to perform a one-woman séance.

The thought of handcuffs escorted my memory back to the last time I had seen Travis. The way the police carelessly showed up at our apartment while I was entertaining my family and the horrible accusations of statutory rape that later proved to be true. The tone in which that old gray-headed landlord used to refer to *me* as a "disgrace . . . unfit to live around such nice people . . . promoter of molestation . . . and a threat to society." All in front of my mother. As though I would allow the man that I was sleeping with to date a seventeen-year-old, or even a twenty-one-year-old, for that matter. I'd stood on the front lawn, staring at those blue lights and waiting for an alarm clock to go off, because I knew it had to be nothing more than a nightmare. But as it turned out, it wasn't.

When I got back home, I walked through the front door, dropped my bags, washed my hands, put Bob on again, and started some red beans and rice with chicken for dinner. There'd been too much tension in the apartment the night before to try to put things back in their proper place.

Robert had sat in the living room the night before, smoked at least a pack of cigarettes, and watched a "survival of the fittest" *Wild Kingdom* tape that he knew from start to finish. Didn't mention the note I'd left, didn't speak any further about his health concerns, and didn't bother with the fact that there were no sheets on the bed. He intended to sleep right there on the couch, alone.

After fixing the chicken, I wrapped my hair up, drew some bathwater, dropped in stress-free crystals, and lighted four candles. Hit the light switch, disrobed, and slid in. I leaned my head back and closed my eyes. Steam caused beads of sweat to form on my skin. I began praying a different kind of prayer this time, not the "Save my butt" kind, but the kind that comes from the soul, the kind that makes you stop whatever it is you're doing. The kind of praying that I had been made to feel ashamed of. I was praying and meditating for peace. Happiness that didn't come in the form of a man.

Tap, tap, tap. "Nik, you there?" Robert asked, breaking my train of thought.

"Yeah."

"Did you know that this stuff is burning out here?"

"Would you turn it off, please?"

I sat up in the tub and began to lather up.

Tap, tap, tap. "Can I come in?"

"I'm already in the tub, Rob." I sighed aloud.

"*I'll* mop the floor, then. Just open the door. I wanna talk to you."

"Can't it wait 'til I'm done?"

"It's important, it's about us. I wanna apologize for the way I acted last night."

His attempt to smooth things over was practically futile, because it wasn't the first time he'd hidden information from me. Things had been rocky for a while and I just didn't know if I could take it much longer, if I even wanted to talk things out. *Tap, tap, tap.* I got up out of the tub, water dripping everywhere. Some even dropped on a candle, killing the flame, making it darker and harder for me to see, harder for me to *think*.

"Have you talked to Kim today?" I asked, slowly descending into what liquid was left.

He walked in quietly, paying attention to my dark nipples, which stood up like pencil erasers. It was as if I had said nothing at all. He rubbed my shoulder and kissed behind my right ear. I placed my hand on top of his and quickly moved it away.

He sighed, locked his fingers under his chin, and asked, "What were you saying?"

"I asked you if you had talked to Kim today. She mentioned us going out with a guy she met."

"I don't have money for that kinda thing right now."

He gave me a "You scratch my back and I'll scratch yours" sorta look. Like my coochie was negotiable—no dice, brotha.

"That's good, because I really wasn't lookin' forward to it anyway. Did you call the doctor back yet?"

He didn't say a word, just kinda gave me a blank stare before standing and stretching. "Were you gonna put some sheets on the bed?"

Just like that, with no emotion in his voice whatever.

"Did you say you were coming in here to give me an *apology* or something?"

He sucked his teeth, which was a habit of his that I hated. Then squinted his eyes as though he despised me and said, "I guess there's a whole lot we've *both* got to be sorry for."

Robert stood up, turned to close the door behind him, shook his head, and left it open instead. My candles blew out one by one, leaving me in the darkness, but not much more than I was already in.

The following Saturday, I stopped by my mother's house for a brief moment to sift through some boxes of old albums. I had to be the only person left in our family to have a record player, and for that reason, along with many others, I was considered a misfit. Even my father had done away with the old Patti LaBelle and Donnie Hathaway albums. But Daddy, may he rest in peace, wasn't into the latest technology, so he understood my appreciation for yesteryear.

"Nikki, you can have all of that mess if you want it. It's only taking up space in the basement, and nobody's gonna come by here to help me clean it out. So do what you can now."

I piled Gladys, the Temptations, Marvin, and a host of others into one slightly water-stained cardboard box. By the time I had made it to the middle of the stairs, Taylor was coming through the front door, wearing a white nylon jogging suit and high-stepping like she was leading a parade.

"Mama, sit down. I've got something to tell you."

"What is it?" Mama asked, dropping *everything* and taking a seat in the family room next to Uncle Lucky.

"James asked me to marry him this morning!"

They held hands and jumped around in a circle, like Taylor was single-handedly responsible for finding a cure for cancer, while Uncle Lucky turned up the volume on the television. He didn't care for this showing off any more than I did, but those two were demanding everyone's attention. This was Esther's baby, giving her something else to brag about. A reason to call

all of her friends and explain how naturally success and happiness came to her daughter.

And just as I turned to head back into the basement, Mama called my name.

"Nikai's here?" I heard Taylor ask. "Nikai, look. Isn't my engagement ring beautiful? It's three karats, girl."

I pulled the fakest smile that I could scrounge up and said, "Yeah, congratulations. I know you're so happy."

James, her fiancé, was a New York attorney. We'd seen him only three times in the year that they'd been dating. But from what I'd seen, he was definitely a good catch. Kind to my mother, a gentleman toward Taylor, and he even went as far as to stand before any woman at our table sat down. And the way he'd had those women swooning two Sunday services before, when Taylor brought him in to meet the pastor, was ridiculous. It's sad the way that sistas act when a Tyson Beckford look-alike comes to town. The reverend shouldn't have to remind grown women to "keep ya mind on Jesus."

"So when is the big day?" I asked.

"We haven't set it yet, but when we do, you will be one of the first people I'll call."

One of the first, huh? How sweet. All I'd wanted to do was go over there and get a few old jams to ease the pressure from the fucked-up relationship that I had. And suddenly, I'd been painfully reminded again of how abnormal my entire existence was. Other people were getting married in half the time it had taken Robert and me just to see eye-to-eye on certain things. Hell, we still argued over what cereal to buy, and Taylor's selfish butt had gotten somebody to plan the rest of his life around her.

I set my box of oldies but goodies down by the front door and said, "Hey, everybody. I'm about to get out of here. I'll see you guys later."

Nobody responded but Uncle Lucky.

"See ya, Slim."

"See ya, Uncle Lucky. I love you."

He didn't seem to hear that part. I understood that he had probably gone back to wherever it was he found serenity. The sad part was that I wanted to do the same but just couldn't think of anyplace to go.

That evening, Kim and I were riding downtown to a Dillard's clearance sale when I noticed some Scripture posted on the lawn outside of a church. It read, "Every plant which my heavenly Father hath not planted shall be rooted up. Matthew 15:13." The thought of just leaving St. Louis because it was what *I* wanted at the time crossed my mind. Not having any sense of direction, just floating out in the world to fall where I may, didn't seem like such a good idea anymore.

I stared out the window as Kim did sixty-seven in a fifty-five zone down I-70. My nerves were getting worse because nobody really knew why I needed to run, nobody but Robert and me. And sometimes I wondered if he was cognizant of it all. I cracked my neck from side to side, the way I always did when things built up.

"Can you do me a favor and just *try* to be a lady for the next couple of hours? You crackin' your neck like you're about to put a quarterback on his ass or something."

Kim was usually like that, loud and obnoxious. Even got kicked out of her mother's church bingo group for announcing her winnings in surround sound. And doing the tootsie roll in a miniskirt at the deacon's birthday party didn't gain her too many points with the Mother Board, either. There's one good thing that I can say about her: She was one of the most honest people I'd ever met. There had been a couple of times when she'd been forced to choose between Rob and me. She pulled us to the side for separate counseling and sent us back to each other. But it's hard to fix something that you don't even know is broken. I guess deep down that's why I couldn't tell her how serious things had become, because she'd do everything in her power to make him see the error of his ways. And that's not what I wanted. At that point, I think I might've been inadvertently searching for something new and improved.

I reached down and turned the radio on. Kim had it tuned into a hip-hop station *again*. I looked at her to get the go-ahead to change it and she put up her index finger, signaling for me to wait a minute. I took a deep breath and leaned back in my seat. Looked out the window as we sped past everyone else who had at least the slightest bit of respect for the speed limit. She started snapping her fingers at the intro beat of a rap. I looked over at her and shook my head.

She said, "Girl, please. This is my song!"

Kim started dancing around in her seat as though *I* was the one driving and *she* was the one riding. The DJ started talking about some local artists and introducing the song. Suddenly, Kim stopped moving.

"Ah, damn! That's a fuckin' sample! You can change that."

The DJ continued, "For all you hip-hop lovers out there, here's a group that just got signed from the STL. Many of their peeps might know 'em as Raquon Spencer, Leroy Davis, and Tyrone Givens. But the world is about to know 'em as—"

Tyrone Givens? That was Travis's cousin. The country tacky-ass fool who was hangin' out the Acura window like a brotha fresh off of house arrest. I couldn't believe that he had landed *any* kind of contract other than one on his life.

Kim said, "So what did you decide to do?"

"About what?" I said, trying to remember what we could possibly have been talking about before.

"Leaving everything that you're familiar with."

I glanced over at Kim and went back to staring out of the window. We had been through this a thousand and one times and I wasn't in the mood to back my decisions.

"What?" she asked.

"What?"

"What was that look for?"

"What look are you talking about?"

"The dirty one that looked like I was being damned to hell."

"I don't know what you're talking about."

"So answer the question."

"What difference does it make whether I leave or not? I'm not hurting anybody, am I?"

I was getting upset because she was pushing my buttons to see which one was programmed to get me to talk.

"And what about Robert? You planning on telling him first

or sneaking out 'Dear John' style again? He told me about the other night, and you know that wasn't right, Nikai."

"You don't really wanna talk about what's not right. *Not right* is your mama opening my mail."

Kim laughed and slightly swerved into the next lane.

"All right, you got me there, but I just don't see what's down there in Georgia calling your name so loudly that you can't concentrate on your life here."

"What *life* here?"

"You've got your job, your family, friends, a beautiful apartment, and—"

"And what, your brother?"

"All right, so he's not a knight in shining armor, but how often do you find those, anyway? Besides, I know you're not so weak that you would let a *man* run you out of town."

"Nice try, but the reverse psychology ain't working."

"Okay, well, maybe I *was* grasping for straws, but I just think you need some time to consider what it is you're doing."

"And how do you know that I haven't done that already?"

"Because if you had, you would either be in Atlanta now or on good terms with your man. You don't know what you wanna do, but staring out that window ain't gonna help you find it. The way that I see it is that there's a part of you that wants to stay here, just long enough to see what Rob is gonna do."

I searched outside the window for the right words to say. Ones that would convince her that I'd given it a substantial amount of thought. We rode another five miles, when she looked at me, put her hand on mine, and asked, "You ever thought about giving him a baby?"

I froze for a moment, blinked heavily, and tried to push that lump out of my throat. You know, the one that keeps you from speaking as well as breaking down when you're not quite ready to. Thought about all those times when I'd tried and failed at doing just that.

"I think a little baby would soften Rob up some and make things better for you," she added.

I narrowed my eyes and said, "I think that *love* should be enough to soften him up."

"C'mon, Nik, you know what I mean. He probably needs some incentive."

"Well, if it's such a good idea, why haven't you done it?"

"I don't get the kind of complaints that you do."

"What complaints?!" I asked.

"That's not the point. The point is that you have got to make your man happy or he will go elsewhere and won't *care* if you leave."

"So that's what this is about? You're on his team now?"

"I'm not on anybody's team, but I *do* know what a man needs."

"Well, I don't see you picking out china patterns and heading for the bridal registry."

"And you don't see any of my men beatin' on your door for advice, either."

"Then maybe it's your brother and not me!"

"Maybe, and then again, maybe not."

Kim got quiet and so did I. Mainly because I didn't know what else to say about Robert or anything else. But what I did know was that I had just experienced a huge epiphany. Kim's relationship with Robert was permanent, but my relationship with her was in and of the moment. She had a burden of responsibility to both of us, but something deep inside told me that when push came to shove, I would be left alone. Without that baby, without my friend, and, more importantly, without Robert.

Kim looked over at me with bugged eyes and asked, "Well, are you gonna change the station, or what? You know you don't like that kinda flava anyway."

My mind drifted back to the moment and I put the radio on a R&B station, one that I could relax and calm my nerves to. The idea of a no-talent, uncouth jackass like Tyrone making faster and more lucrative career moves was starting to piss me off. The soulful sounds of Sade put my blood pressure back to normal as I assured myself that everything was gonna be okay. After all, I was meeting with a producer soon.

Robert

The alarm clock blared in my ear Friday morning and woke me from a deep sleep. Thought that I was at the engine house until I heard the shower running and Nik's sweet singing. She had vocals like Billie Holiday. Could sing a brotha into a frenzy, the way she would hit those high notes and move her body slow and smooth. Like the music was carrying her to another place. When it stopped, she came back, usually as unresponsive as she'd been when she first drifted off.

I pulled the sheet back and walked into the bathroom. Stepped out of my boxers and opened the glass shower door. She kinda jumped and looked at me for a minute, like she was trying to remember where she knew my face from. I took the washcloth from her and placed the soap back in its dish. She stood, vulnerable and naked, with her back to me. I wrapped my arms around her and felt her nipples stiffen.

"Sing to me, baby."

She was quiet. No humming, swaying, or pelvic thrusts.

"I don't feel much like singing," she whispered.

I started to argue the fact that she'd just been singing a second ago, but I realized that would do me no good. "Well, would you wash my back?"

She turned halfway around to look at me and then changed her mind. "Gotta be at work in thirty minutes. I'm already late."

She turned and stepped out of the sprinkles that I'd hoped we could use to wash away some morning lovin'. I watched her long enough to see that she didn't bother to look back at me for a response. I guess I stared because there was something I wanted to know, like who she had turned into. But instead of inquiring, I just envisioned Karen going down on me. Making me weak the way that Nik used to do, all before we started talking about that baby shit.

It was all her idea to change the level of the relationship. She said it was either that or marriage, and we both knew that I wasn't ready for marriage, so I tried to give her what she wanted. But for some reason, she wasn't receiving. She did a lot of reading up on it, but she never went to the doctor like I told her to. She said some shit about the way she would look *trying* to get pregnant *without* a husband. I don't know if that was supposed to be my cue to get down on one knee and pop the question, but I ducked and dodged it like a brotha was being paid to.

It's not that I didn't love her, but my lady could put some serious pressure on me when she came up with a bright idea to improve *our* lives, like when she wanted to move to a bigger apartment so that her gambling uncle could move in and hide from God knows who. That incident had me making a pallet on the living room floor for about a week.

We'd been told by one of the psychics she dragged me to that our relationship wasn't exactly what would be classified as healthy. We were so much alike that sometimes it scared me. Stubbornness, leadership skills, and initiative are all qualities that we both possessed and, way too often, used on each other.

"You gonna be free for lunch?" I asked as she finished dressing and grabbed her pocketbook off of the closet door.

"Dorothy is taking me downtown today."

"Well, would you at least make time this weekend to talk to me?"

"We'll see, Robert."

"'We'll see'? 'We'll see'? See, this is the shit that I'm talking about! Are you fuckin' Dorothy now? 'Cause you sure ain't fuckin' me!"

She gave me a blank stare, almost as if she was looking at something else on my side of the room.

"We have to talk about what's goin' on between us. Sometimes you act like you hate me or somethin'! I already know from the shit you pulled earlier this week that you don't wanna be here, but stayin' just confused things even more. If you want the little bit of this relationship that's left, let me know. Page me before nine!"

By the time I had finished, Nik was at the front door. I had practically given her an ultimatum, but she didn't even break her stride. Strutted like the Queen Mother of the Universe or somethin'. Shit like that will make a brotha snap. Pack yo' shit up to leave, reject my sexual advances, tell me about what you *ain't* gon' do, and then act like I'm not even there. Women have been left lonely for *a lot* less.

I picked up the phone and dialed Karen's number, but there was no answer. She was probably out somewhere, thinking of new ways to piss me off. On the third ring, the answering machine picked up, so I left a brief but descriptive message: "Hey, uh, it's me. You said you wanted to see me, but you're not home, so I'm assuming you changed that sick-ass mind of yours. Listen . . . I don't even know how things got to this point . . . how we even ended up in this cat and mouse chase . . . but I'm tired of it. Page me when you get the chance."

I hung up the phone up and lay back on the bed. As soon as I closed my eyes, it rang. I reached over, picked it up, and put it to my ear.

"What's with the message, Rusty?" Karen asked.

I sat straight up, so quickly that the bath towel came undone.

"How did you get this number?"

"I used this sick-ass mind of mine." She laughed.

"Look, you know that you can't call here!"

"So which one am I, the cat or the mouse?"

Her voice was calm. It was as though she found peace knowing that she could stir my world up. I tried to regain my composure, because it was obvious that this was the only way I could deal with her.

"Karen, can you do me a favor and not call here anymore?"

"Why not? Nicole has been gone for, uh, let's see, about seven minutes now."

"Her name is Nikai, and how the hell do you know when she left?"

Karen was silent. I grabbed the caller ID box and saw that the call was from outside the area, which meant one of two things: She was either out of town or on her cellular, watching my fuckin' apartment. I jumped up and ran to the front window, but I didn't see her car anywhere.

"Karen?"

"Yes?"

"Where are you?"

"Rusty, you never answered my question."

"What question?"

I could feel sweat forming on my forehead and my armpits began to itch. I was walking toward the bathroom to put some deodorant on when I thought about the fact that Karen had kicked off this game again and hadn't warned me about her head start.

"I asked you if I was the cat or the mouse."

"Right now, you can be whoever the hell you wanna be."

"Don't say that. That's not true. I wanna be that special someone in your life again."

"I hear you, but don't you think you're going about this all wrong? Shouldn't *I* be seducing *you?*"

She fell silent again. I wondered for a second if she was going for that bull, and just as I was about to score a point for myself, she called my name in a seductive tone that made me remember that last hostage situation that we'd pretended to be in.

"Yeah, baby?"

"*Tell your bitch that those shoes don't go with that dress!*"

Just as she disconnected us, I could hear keys jingling in the front door, and then the sudden slamming that usually followed when Nik had forgotten something. She walked into the bedroom and began pushing hats and sweaters to each side in the top of the closet. Carelessly shoving things that did and didn't belong to her. I waited. She kept looking. Dropped her purse like the brick she was toting in it had finally gotten too heavy.

The digital clock on the nightstand read 8:30, the exact time that she was expected at work. I was tempted to ask if I could help her find whatever it was she was looking for, but when I stood up to adjust the navy blue towel that was wrapped around my waist, she stopped, as if she didn't even know I was there. Turned her head but not her body, arms still extended. Her eyes darted around the room, from the nightstand to the dresser and back over to the armoire. She gave me, the bed, and everything else an unfamiliar glance and then walked into the kitchen. Her green ankle-length dress was billowing as she turned the corner and tucked her hair behind her right ear. I guess maybe to see better. I followed, but not too closely.

"Have you seen that brown paper bag that was in the bedroom closet?" she asked.

"No. Uh, what was in it?"

She leaned over on the counter, showing the first signs of relaxation. I stepped closer and wrapped my arm around her. She shook for a moment, even though it was the middle of August. Leaned away, looked at me, and asked the same question again.

"I said no! Why don't you tell me what was in it; maybe I can help you find it."

"No thanks, I'll find it," she said, freeing herself and making her way to the bedroom.

Before I could mumble another word, she had slammed the door and picked up the phone. I grabbed the other line in time to catch her calling in sick. Made me wonder even more what was in that damn paper bag.

She pulled the door open and asked, "Around what time are you leaving?"

"Why?"

"Because I wanna know."

"When I'm done getting dressed," I said.

The bedroom door slammed again, only a little louder this time. I rushed into the front room and peeped out of the blinds to see if Karen was circling the building, but there was no sign of her.

"Looking for somebody?" Nik asked, standing in the threshold of the living room.

"What?"

"You heard me. Why the hell are you peepin' out the blinds like you owe somebody money?"

This was the most conversation I had gotten from her in weeks, and I cherished it, even though it was negative.

"So you're speaking to me now?"

She rolled her eyes and turned around to go back into the bedroom. I gave a sigh of relief and sat down on the sofa. I could feel the leather sticking to my bare back as Nik slammed the door again. I adjusted the towel around my waist and rested the side of my head in the palm of my right hand. I closed my eyes and a car horn blew. It sounded loud enough to wake the dead, probably because my instincts told me that it was Karen stepping up for another show.

Nik opened the bedroom door and asked, "Are you expecting somebody?"

"No, no. Why'd you ask that?" I said, trying to remind myself not to stutter.

"Because there's a blue Neon pulled right outside that window, blowing."

"I . . . I . . . I don't know who it is."

She gave me a look as though she was questioning my honesty and retreated back to her haven, this time leaving the door open. Someone finally came out of the neighbor's apartment and got into the noisy Neon. Cleared my suspicions. It was becoming apparent that riding around in an unmarked vehicle at 8:30 A.M. was not beneath Karen.

I walked into the bedroom and saw a brown paper bag lying on the bed just behind Nik. She was sitting with her back to me, facing the dresser.

I asked, "So you found what you were looking for?"

She didn't move. Concentrated on whatever it was resting in her lap.

"Nik."

"*What?*" she asked, turning halfway around and revealing what looked like medical gadgets.

"What are you doing?"

"Looking out for myself!"

I walked around the side of the bed and snatched from her lap a box that held a home HIV test. She looked up at me. Finally showing a sign that she cared what I thought. It was almost as if she was waiting for me to tell her that all of this wasn't necessary. That I wouldn't hurt her like that. That I wouldn't infect her if that had been the case.

"This is what you've been looking for?" I asked.

She lowered her head. I guess I didn't give her what she was hoping for. I failed to deliver assurance. I took the kit and laid it on the dresser. Sat down next to her and wrapped my arm around her. Waited for her to snatch away but got another reaction instead. I felt her break down in my arms. She leaned into me as I held her tighter. I searched for the right words to say. Something more powerful than "I'm sorry."

"I love you, baby."

She didn't respond. Broke down harder and finally looked me in the eye.

"I don't wanna keep hurting like this, Rob. I don't wanna keep hurting you like this."

"I'm sorry," I said.

"I'm tired of trying to show you that I don't need you. I guess that's because there's a part of me that really believes that I do."

"We need each other, baby. We're gonna make this work, but we've got to stop looking at each other as the enemy. Baby, I need you to make love to me sometimes. Rub my back when I come home from work. *Treat* me like you need me."

She wiped the tears from her cheek and asked, "Well, what about the things that I need?"

"Tell me what it is that you need."

"I need to know if you're HIV-positive or not. I need to know that you aren't seeing somebody else. I need to know that this relationship is going somewhere. I wanna get married someday, Robert."

I leaned out of our embrace and sighed. Not because we were getting somewhere, but because she was taking her requests too far. If she was willing to give me the affection that I needed, I could leave Karen alone. In fact, that was the plan. But marriage? I just wasn't ready.

"Well?" she asked.

"Well what?"

She pulled away and said, "Taylor is getting married. She's known James for one year and he's ready to make that final move. She doesn't have to worry about him sneaking behind her back to get blood tests and shit!"

Her voice got more intense. I started checking the room for heavy objects like three-wick candles or nearby lamps.

"She doesn't have to worry about him fuckin' around on her, talkin' shit, and lettin' his dick run the relationship!"

I got defensive and said, "Well, that has nothin' to do with me."

"Goddamn it, that *is* you!"

She sprang from the bed and stood over me. I then stood up and put a little distance between us.

"Here we go again."

"That's right, here we go—"

"Does it make you feel any better to know that the test results were negative?" I asked.

"No! What *would* make me feel better is you not taking so long to share something with me that could alter my life! What *would* make me feel better is you thinking about someone besides yourself all of the time!"

I grabbed that kit off of the dresser to throw it away, when the phone rang. I stopped dead in my tracks, waited to hear who had such bad timing. Nik was still yelling when she went to answer it. I loosened up a bit and took the kit into the kitchen. Stepped on the lever at the bottom of the garbage can and heard her say, "No, honey. No Rusty lives here."

Nik put the phone back in its cradle and continued to complain. I didn't hear her. Only pictured Karen laughing and scoring another point for herself. Pictured myself actually choking the shit out of her. And then for no apparent reason at all, I pictured her pregnant with my child. As much as I hated the thought of it, I had to see her again. Not just to settle the score but to settle my suspicions, as well.

Nikai

Robert told me that Kalif's studio was located downtown. Somewhere between Market Street and Olive. I was supposed to see a tall office building with large glass windows on a corner across from a Nationsbank and Calico's Restaurant. None of these directions was correct.

I had stopped at a pay phone and called Kalif, who had an unusually deep voice. I could hear a session going on in the background. Sounded as though the Supremes had gotten back together with a new flavor and were holding the reunion in his studio.

"You're gonna make a left off of Tucker and come down to Seventh. The building will be on your right. You have the address, don't you?"

"Yeah. It's eleven forty-two. Right?"

"That's right. I can stand outside and watch for you if you need me to."

"No. I should be fine."

An older man in soiled clothing walked up to me and leaned on the pay phone that I was using. I looked over, waiting to hear his reason for stepping into my comfort zone. He smiled and I saw pieces of lunches from three weeks ago still in his teeth.

Kalif said, "So you're on your way?"

"Yeah, I ought to be there in five minutes."

The space invader began tapping the side of the phone booth and humming an unfamiliar tune. I put my purse on the other shoulder and glanced back at my car to make sure my doors were locked.

"I'll be off in a minute," I told him.

"Take your time. That's all we've got, anyway."

"Some of us, that is," I added.

Kalif said, "I'll be waiting."

I'd hung up and started toward my car when the stranger yelled, "Excuse me, young lady. Do you have any change to spare?"

I could see that question coming from way back when he leaned on the phone booth, but something made me want to give to him. I felt around in my pocket, while he did the same. He was digging around as if he remembered that he had a one-hundred-dollar bill in there somewhere. My hand reappeared with a dollar, two quarters, a dime, and a nickel, while his came back with a torn piece of paper. I chuckled at the idea that maybe he was trying to slip me his digits.

"Here you go, young lady. I can't take your money without giving you something."

I looked down at the torn edges and what looked like dried catsup mixed with sticky candy and declined.

"No, sir, I can't take anything from you."

He looked me in the eye as though he could read my thoughts, maybe even see my soul. Right through to my unhappiness. He grabbed my left hand and made me grab my heart with the right.

"What are you doing?"

"Take it," he said. "I know it's dirty, but it's worth more than any money you can give me."

He placed the paper in my hand, took the change, and started off into the darkness, that too-familiar darkness. I looked down and cringed at the thought of where that paper had been. Folded the dollar bill around it and shoved it into the side of my purse.

Kalif was waiting on the corner in a pair of baggy jeans, large tan boots, and a black T-shirt. Dark brown dreads rested on his shoulders as he shoved his hands into his pockets and leaned against the brick building. A broad smile covered his face when I pulled up and cut my engine off. I pulled my visor down to get a final glance in the vanity mirror, wiped the oil from my nose and forehead, and then did a quick check of my breath. With dreads blowing in the wind, he rushed over to the driver's side and attempted to open my door, before realizing that it was locked.

I rolled my window down just enough to reach out and say, "You shouldn't walk up to an unfamiliar lady's door and pull on it."

"I apologize for that."

He smiled, extending his hand. "I'm Kalif."

His frame was that of a boxer, but his smile was that of a gentle being. He had a childlike gleam in his eye that made me not mind his rough hand and the tattoos up each arm.

He grabbed the handle a second time and said, "Let me get that for you."

"Thanks."

"You didn't have a hard time finding it, did you?"

"Yes, the directions I had were all wrong," I said, stepping out and adjusting my clothes.

I was wearing my favorite pair of snug blue jeans and a black fitted shirt that Robert had bought me last summer.

"The girls are upstairs and ready to meet you."

He was rubbing his hands together like his big plans were finally beginning to take shape. Truthfully, I was hoping for a good chemistry among us all, but it takes more, much more, than a vocal mix to keep things intact.

We hopped onto a dark elevator before pulling the wooden cage down and riding up a few floors. There was only enough light for me to see the whites of his eyes, and that was because he was staring at me. I cleared my throat and looked straight ahead.

Kalif said, "Sorry about the light. It blew out this morning and I haven't had a chance to replace it."

I gave him a brief "Mmmhmm" and began tapping my foot.

"Here we go, the fourth floor. Ladies first."

He pushed the cage up and I stepped out into a dimly lighted loft with large plants, three black futons, abstract wood carvings, African art, and pieces by Seitu and C'Babi decorating the walls. There was brown carpet in the living room area and a thirty-one-inch-screen television. Large colorful pillows were tossed about the floor, along with a host of CDs, tapes, and albums.

"I have to apologize about the mess, too," he said, noticing the unusual amount of attention that I was giving that area.

What he didn't realize was that I didn't mind it at all. There was something about the dark earthiness that drew me closer. Reminded me of Sheila and, ironically, it reminded me of a me. The one that I had begun to suppress. I wanted to relax on that thick carpet, stretch out and chill on those large pillows, and groove to the surround sound that the entire section held.

I smiled and asked, "You always keep it this dark in here during the day?"

"Oh, it gets darker. C'mon, so you can meet the girls."

Kalif led me to a set of closed double doors and then stopped.

"You can take your shoes off, if you want. Everybody else has."

I kicked my black sandals off and set them against the wall in the row of other shoes. Two pair that belonged to women and one pair of Lugz boots that belonged to a man.

Kalif did the same and asked, "You ready?"

It made me wonder exactly what it was that I was getting ready *for*.

"Yeah. I guess."

I watched him turn the knob and then saw three heads turn. Two were adorned with long braids and another with dreads. Those were shorter than Kalif's. I counted four large auburn three-wick candles, three keyboards, two guitars, and a small drum over in the corner.

"Everybody, this is Nikai. Nikai, this is Janae, Maurie, and Ahmad."

"Hey, Nikai. You got here just in time."

Maurie got down from her stool and asked, "You sing soprano?"

"Yeah. How'd you guess?" I asked.

"I've got an ear for it," she said, smiling.

"She really does," Janae added.

"How quickly do you think that you can learn this song?"

Maurie handed me a sheet of torn-out notebook paper while Ahmad stood up to give me his seat. I squinted in the candle-light and then Kalif flipped the light switch.

Janae hummed along as I read the words:

> *You watched me grow, now you seem so unsure*
> *And now I know that I need so much more*
> *Than what you try to give, the way you try to live*
> *Ain't for me, now I see*
> *That we both should be free.*
> *I shift my faith, just not in your direction*
> *And now you say that I need correction*
> *And you're the man for it, but now I can't forget*
> *What you did, you hurt me*
> *So now we both should be free.*

Maurie and Janae sang the song at least three times, and by the fourth, I had joined in and completed the trio.

Then Kalif said, "I think we've found our missing link. You ready to become part of the group?"

I blushed at the response that I was getting from everyone. They seemed as excited as I was to be there, making music and making friends. Our voices swayed with such harmony that Kalif and Ahmad were moved to give us a standing ovation.

I looked at the girls, Kalif, and Ahmad and finally around the candlelit room. Maurie was paper sack brown, had shoulder-length braids, and was in excellent shape—a perfect 36-24-36. Janae was dark brown, with thin braids down her back, a natural face with no makeup, and a skinny yet fit frame. Both were dressed in loose clothing and adorned with silver and copper jewelry.

I felt commercial and phony with my tight blue jeans, relaxed hair, and makeup—like the brothas you see in the club draped in gold jewelry, a diamond stud in each ear, processed hair, silk outfits, and alligator shoes. Maurie and Janae had a vibe going that I wasn't in tune with. As a sista, I was welcome to it but just not in tune with it. And in my world, I didn't know if that natural, earthy, dreadlocked look was appropriate. In fact, I knew it wasn't. I just wondered if I possessed the nerve to try to get away with it for the sake of my singing career and for the sake of becoming half as centered as they were.

I had wanted change for so long, but not what came with it—the responsibility, the scrutiny, the task of justifying my actions. For me, at that moment, freedom just didn't seem worth it. And out of nowhere, I found myself searching for differences between us. I mean, they weren't necessarily like Sheila and me. *We* were spiritual. *They* were Afrocentric. And whether I liked it or not, that drew a serious line between the two sides.

My proud smile changed to a look of concern, concern about our level of compatibility. Sure, we could make the music sound good, but did it mean relatively the same thing to all of us?

Janae asked, "What's wrong?"

I shook my head and said, "Nothing. Just thinking."

"About what?" Maurie asked.

"Nothing important."

They looked at each other. Made me wonder if they already knew what I felt. How badly I wanted to get back to my world of comfort and confusion.

How badly I just wanted to be me.

Whoever that was.

Robert

Our two-year anniversary had arrived. The only reason I remembered was because Don and his lady, Theresa, had celebrated their anniversary last week and he'd made such a big deal out of it. Dragged me from one florist to another, one jewelry store to another, got personalized cards made, and even ordered some of Chaka Khan's Chakalates just to show how *sweet* he could be. Or at least that's what the card read. So with the pressure that Don was putting on me and all of the trouble I had caused, it only made sense to grab some stuff for my baby while I was there.

Nik and I had made plans to spend the evening out, celebrating with Don and Theresa. Well, actually, I had. She wasn't even speaking to me after the last argument. I had to sneak up on her that morning when I came in from the engine house with flowers and a tennis bracelet. At first, she gave me one of those "I can't be bought" looks, but after opening the slender black velvet box, she wrapped those sexy brown arms around my neck the way that she used to. I planted a couple of soft, wet pecks on her neck just to see how much of an impact my gifts had made. But I soon learned that she had only forgiven, not forgotten.

We all decided on dinner and a movie. I would've loved to have gone dancing and then gotten served up afterward Karen-style, but I had to remember that I was dealing with two totally different characters. Nik wasn't big on clubs anymore and I hadn't felt her crotch since her crotch felt me.

I was on the couch, waiting in a pair of black jeans and a charcoal gray fleece button-down shirt. Rewinding my second-favorite *Wild Kingdom* tape and smoking on a square. I could hear Nik in the bedroom jingling necklaces and other trinkets in her jewelry box. The scent of her perfume was drifting out into the living room and instantly seized my attention. I got up and stood in the doorway of the bedroom, watching her put on finishing touches. Watching her presence fill a room for the first time in a while.

My woman was beautiful in her black midthigh skirt and a gray shirt that accented her perfect waistline and perky breasts. Nik looked sexy and high-powered, like one of the great queens of Africa. She made me want to walk up and hold her from behind, but I didn't want to disturb her. For the moment, it was enough to stand back, admire her beauty, and thank God that she was mine.

She noticed my reflection in the mirror, smiled, and asked, "What are you staring at?"

"You."

"And why would you be doing that, Mr. Hayes?"

"Because I love you."

She turned to me with a look of desperation, a look that clearly illustrated how much those words meant to her. The reflection was no longer enough. She had to look me in the eye to see if it was the truth, to see if the whole moment was true.

"I love you, too, Rob."

"Nik, you're still the one I'd stare at across a crowded room."

"Well, can we kill some of the distance between us right now?"

I walked over and held her in my arms for what seemed like forever. I couldn't get enough of what was already there for me. A woman with a good heart and strong mind. A woman who didn't embarrass the hell out of me when she didn't get her way or try to threaten me when I didn't jump for her. A woman who had tolerated my games much longer than she should have. A woman who was soulfully mine.

While still locked in an embrace, my pager went off and partially killed the moment.

Nik asked, "Are you gonna leave that thing on for the entire evening?"

"If you don't want me to, I won't. It's your call. Tonight is your night."

"And what about every other night? Who do those belong to?"

"If I belong to you, then who else *could* they belong to?"

"Sounds good." She playfully turned her mouth up with skepticism. "But do you mean it?"

I made a sign of the cross over the left side of my chest.

"Cross my heart and hope to die."

Nik gave a soft, gentle laugh, looked across the room, and then pulled away. I could tell that as normal as the moment was, it still felt awkward. It was times like those that had brought us so close in the beginning. Laughing, joking, and preparing to face the world as a couple. But we were so used to fighting that it seemed as if we didn't know how *not* to. It had become a foreign thing to be in the same room without tension bouncing off of the walls. Having a decent conversation at that point was not likely to happen. But something else was happening. Nik and I were falling in love again. And it felt good, maybe even better than the first time.

Don and Theresa met us at our favorite Italian spot in the central West End. It was one of those restaurants that's usually learned about through word of mouth. It was actually back off a side street, located in what used to be the basement of a building, but the setting made you glad to keep the word to yourself. Nik and I dug it because it was intimate, with limited space. You didn't have to worry about a football team going there after a big game. The ceiling was low and the lights are always dim. Candles decorated the tables, and several mirrors, along with pieces of history, decorated the walls. Documents from many years ago took you back to a time that you otherwise might not have known about.

Theresa said, "So he pulls out this little box. He wasn't on one knee, so I knew it wasn't a ring, but when I saw these diamond earrings, I didn't care. My baby is so good to me. Give me a kiss."

Theresa leaned over and locked lips with Don as Nik looked at me and smiled. Then Nik proceeded to tell the story of how I had given her the bracelet. Of course she didn't add the dirty look she'd given me that morning, but I was happy to hear her sharing our good times. Don nodded his head and then dapped me up as if to say I had done good. It made me realize how negative I must have seemed to everyone. Did I appear incapable of having a heart just because I occasionally slept with another woman? Was I such a bad guy just because there was a part of me that Nik wasn't nurturing? It didn't make me love her any less. In fact, it had built up my tolerance. Why hadn't anyone asked her what she had gotten me? Was she no longer responsible for making me feel good? The longer I sat in that restaurant, the more pissed I got. That shit was all backward, or should I say one-sided? The fact that our sheets hadn't been moistened in several months never occurred to anybody. Nobody wanted to know if she'd blessed me that morning after I wrapped those expensive-ass diamonds around her wrist, either. I wasn't proud anymore. Actually, I sat there in my own little world and realized that I had not been adequately thanked. Where was Nik's appreciation? I looked, but I didn't see it. Not even in that exaggerated-ass story she had concocted to try to make Theresa jealous.

I wanted gratitude.

And I planned to get it. *That night.*

Nikai

Robert had been a total gentleman for the entire evening—pulling out chairs, opening doors, holding my hand, and giving me an occasional kiss when I caught him staring at me. It reminded me of the old Robert: the provider, the nurturer, and the lover. Speaking of the lover, it was killing me not to be able to make love to him that night. But I was bleeding like a wounded field animal and that, coupled with some serious cramps, put me in no mood to be touched *anywhere* below the collarbone.

He'd awakened me that morning with a dozen roses and a beautiful diamond tennis bracelet. I could barely move then, but with all of the fuss that was being made over me, I hugged him as tightly as I could. And as soon as you give a man a rope, he's bound to try to become a cowboy. I felt Rob working his hands up under the blankets, and that's when I tried to take his arm off of me. Not because I didn't want to bless him, but I didn't *owe* him anything. And then the strangest thing happened later that afternoon. I caught him staring at me, and not with a lustful look in his eye. He didn't appear to be trying to remember what my body looked like without the clothes, and it made me feel special. It made me feel loved. And that's exactly what he told me, that he loved me.

After a long, tiring evening, I had taken my shower and dressed in a pajama shirt with some shorts in order to keep from soiling the sheets. I grabbed my pen and pad off of the nightstand and began working on a song to show the girls, when Rob stepped out of the bathroom in nothing but his birthday suit.

He casually walked around the bed as though he were fully dressed. Applied some deodorant, lotion, and then climbed between the burgundy-and-cream sheets like he didn't notice me staring at him.

I asked, "You comfortable?"

"Am I making you uncomfortable?"

"No. I want to thank you for everything today."

"Did you have a good time?" he asked, turning over and facing me.

I immediately looked down at the hair on his dark chest. His naked body lying so close was turning me on. I could feel my bleeding slowing up and being replaced with female lubrication. I wanted to reach out and touch him, but I knew what would follow. Me disappointing him by saying I could go no further for at least another six days. Robert didn't want to hear that any more than I wanted to say it, but the need to be close to him was strong. Much stronger than the will to stay away.

I dropped my pen and pad on the floor next to the bed and pulled Rob toward me by the back of his neck. I could hear him breathing heavily and felt him running his hands up and down my thighs. Getting closer to that bulky layer of cotton that stood in the way of our satisfaction. I stopped, pulled way, and looked him in the eye.

"What's wrong, baby? What's going on?" he asked with an almost-terrified look on his face.

Robert appeared to be that afraid of *not* having me.

I thought about all he had done to make me happy that night. All he had done just to see me smile and share with our friends the joy he had brought me. I had given him nothing all day, not even a card. And now, now all I was about to deliver was bad news, disappointment, and, if I wasn't careful, blue balls.

"Lie down," I told him. "Just lie down and relax."

I pushed Rob onto his back and disappeared under the covers. Kissed his chest and worked my way down to his jungle of love. I could feel the muscles in his tight dark thighs tensing up as his piece grew before my eyes. It advanced to a size that I hadn't remembered seeing but was quite pleased to claim as my own. As I parted lips not exactly made for enveloping genitalia, that damn pager went off again. And again, and again, and again.

I threw the covers back and silently retreated back to my spot on my side of the bed. I could hear Rob sighing as though he was half as upset as I was. And maybe he was.

"Who was that?" I asked.

"Huh?"

I turned over, looked at him, and again asked, *"Who was that?"*

"Oh, you mean paging me?"

"Yeah, paging you."

"Oh, that was, uh, Don. I hope he and Theresa aren't having another fight. I'll wait until tomorrow before I call him back."

I turned over, with the palm of my hand cushioning my face, and stared at the bathroom door. He was lying to me again. The call was probably from the same person whose lipstick had been all over those picnic cups. The same person he had been sipping wine with. And the very same person I feared would come into our lives and tear our love apart.

I was learning more and more with each anniversary, each new day, each new tear. The night didn't belong to me, and neither did Rob. As for the person calling his pager, well, she was obviously trying to locate the part of him that I did have, the twelve inches poking me in the back. But she already had the part I wanted, the part I needed most at that point—Rob's heart.

Robert

Crazy-ass Karen had been blowing my pager off of my waist since last Sunday. The latest page I received was at 2:30 in the morning. I guess by then she realized that I wasn't going to call her back.

I ran by the shop she owned, on my way to Don's place, to see what was so important. As usual, she fell into character the moment that I set foot in the door.

"Oh my goodness, I'm so glad you came by," she said dramatically, placing her hand over her mouth and walking toward the front entrance, where I stood.

"What the *fuck* do you want now?" I asked in a direct tone.

"That's awfully rude of you to greet me like that in my place of business. I don't go up to the engine house acting like that."

"You don't go to the engine house *at all*," I said, giving her a scornful look.

She leaned into me and whispered, "Now you don't really believe that, do you?"

I took a full step back so that I could check her facial expression, because I knew she couldn't be suggesting what it sounded like.

"Whassup? What were all of the pages for?"

"What, I can't miss you now?"

She grinned and batted her eyelashes like an innocent schoolgirl. Moved in closer and wrapped an arm around me. Made me remember where we were, in view and earshot of other people. I took another full step back and freed myself. Karen's facial expressions deepened. Tension spread throughout her body as one of her hands came up to her abdomen and the other covered her mouth. She gagged. Her eyes grew to the size of grapefruits; then she broke, her black smock swaying in the wind, and ran toward the bathroom.

One of the beauticians braiding a woman's hair looked at me with a twisted grin and said, "She's been doing that all day. She says she might be pregnant."

She waited for a reaction from me, assuming that I was the father, I guess, which pissed me off, because I couldn't honestly say that I wasn't.

I darted toward the back of the salon and found the door to the women's rest room closed. I knocked, paused, and then knocked again. The door opened slightly. Karen was sitting on the toilet, with her face cupped in her hands.

"You all right?" I asked.

There was silence. Her curved back rose and fell as she sighed aloud.

"Karen, what's going on with you? I know about the phone call you made to my apartment. You *knew* Nik was home."

She stood and turned to look in the mirror over the sink.

"Rather impressive, huh?" she asked, staring at me through my reflection. "You know, Rusty, I really want this to work between us. What we have is unique."

I leaned against the door, and for some strange, unknown reason, I wanted to listen. Wanted to know why she felt the need to act out so often. Wanted to know what had happened to the fun-loving, cookie-baking, card-playing, attentive woman I used to look forward to seeing.

"When we first met, we did picnics and plays. Now all we do is each other."

She ran her fingers through her hair, wiped away the excess mascara, and turned to me.

"I don't want our baby to be born out of wedlock."

"What?"

"I want a family, Rusty. It's not like you're happy where you are, anyway. She won't even make love to you."

I stood at attention and tried to back away, then realized that

I didn't have a damn place to go. I was trapped. In more ways than one. My problems at home didn't have anything to do with what went on between us, between Karen's sheets. Suddenly, I regretted confiding in someone so shaky and fickle. The moment I made her mad, she would load up with about a week's worth of emotional ammunition and blow Nik away.

"Listen," I said, grabbing her by the shoulders, "I told you when we first met that I wasn't in it for the long haul. I'm not ready for this. I've got my life to live."

She placed her hand on her stomach and asked, "Well, what about *this* life?"

"Look, you wanted that baby, not me!"

"Well, it will be here eventually, so it doesn't matter whose idea it was!"

"Not necessarily."

"Not necessarily what?"

"Karen, you don't *have* to have that baby. You can get an abortion."

She was quiet. Gave me that same deviant, psychotic look she'd given me when the little bastard was being conceived, leaned into me as if she didn't even want the walls to hear, and whispered, "Now, you don't really believe that, either, do you?"

"Don, what am I gonna do?"

We were already on our fourth mile at the track, and even with the strong breeze, I was wearing Don out. He'd been prepared to run only three miles, but Karen had my head so twisted with that baby shit that the first few had gone by unnoticed. We had lapped two brothas who were dressed like members of a track team in black tights and thin white T-shirts, twice. But I was zoned. Runnin' and thinkin' made me forget a couple of times that I wasn't even alone.

"I think . . . you need . . . to slow . . . down," he said, gasping for breath.

We came to a complete halt and then proceeded to do a final cooldown.

Don asked, "Did she look serious?"

"It's so hard to tell with Karen. She's always acting like Spike

Lee is in town scouting for new talent. Everything is overdramatized with her."

"Well, did you tell her that you weren't ready for any kids?"

"Hell yeah! It went in one ear and out the other. She thinks she's slick, tryin' to stick a brotha. Just as Nik and I were trying to talk things out, Karen called the house the other day."

"*What?* How'd she get the number? Because I know you weren't stupid enough to call her from home."

"That's not the point."

"No, Rob. I think that you are *missing* the point. *You* brought all of this about and now you're afraid that someone will actually point the finger at you. Yeah, you can be upset with her, but who is really to blame here?"

"Yeah, I know what you mean."

Don was making sense, the way he usually did, and inadvertently showing me how my life could be as worry-free as his.

"So what happened when she called?"

"Nik picked up."

"And?"

"She has this stupid name that she gave me back when we first started messin' around again. She used that name when she called. So Nik assumed that she had the wrong number. But the thing that pisses me off is that she knew Nik was home and did it to see how much she could make me sweat. It's like a fuckin' game to her or somethin'."

"Well, how did she guess that Nik was home?"

"She was somewhere outside, watching the apartment."

Don came to a screeching halt and asked, "*What?* How in the hell does she know where you live?"

"Man, I don't know."

"You should never let the other woman know where you rest your head."

"But that's the thing—she's not the other woman. She's an intriguing woman who let her emotions get involved. Now she thinks that I'm supposed to suffer because *she* fell in love."

"Well, you look like a man who's suffering to me."

"Not for long, though."

"So what do you plan to do?"

"I don't know."

"I warned you about this back when you had her hangin' around the engine house, long after you met the songbird." Don shook his head as if to say I deserved what I was getting. "You ever thought about telling her how much Nik means to you? That usually pisses the other woman off enough to make her go away."

"You just don't know Karen. I think that might be just the excitement she needs to take things up another notch. She's disturbed like that."

"You sure that isn't what attracted you to her?" Don laughed.

"I told you that her spirit did."

"Which one?"

Don went on cracking jokes as though someone, somewhere, had made the mistake of even chuckling at one of his pitiful punch lines. He had gone through a whole twenty seconds of careless comedy before he realized how serious I was.

"All right, all right. I've got an idea. She sounds like she's no dummy and she knows how you are. So why don't you switch up on her?"

"What?"

"You say you haven't been nice to her, so do that."

"It's that simple? Just be nice to her?"

"If she gets off on you being the way you are now, switching up ought to make her get out."

"And if it doesn't?"

"Then I'll be happy I'm not you."

Nikai

At Mama's house, the topics of the day were wedding colors and guest lists. Two things that didn't exist in my life and things that I didn't see coming up in any more recent conversations between my *in*significant other and me. Taylor was completely ecstatic, while Uncle Lucky was everything but. He sat back and watched an old cowboy flick and occasionally beckoned me to come over and talk to him.

"Hey, Slim, you know your sista's gon' be ugly in whatever she's wearin'," he said, tapping me on the shoulder with his wrinkled sandy brown index finger. "You the pretty one."

I laughed and took his hand in mine.

"You are still crazy, Uncle Lucky."

I caught myself and made a note of not saying that to him. He was reminded that people sincerely felt that way when my mother had company over and he'd remain in his chair. Never moving and never asking for anything. Not even a glass of water. If my mama wasn't halfway attentive, he'd probably sit right in that chair and die without even a whimper.

"I ain't too crazy to know ugly when I see it," he assured me with a straight face.

"What are you in here talking about, Lucky?" asked Taylor.

He didn't say anything. Just went back into his trance, as though the television were hypnotizing him. His eyes were narrowed, and if I watched long enough, I could count the times that he blinked. Without making a sound, he'd let those who weren't welcome in his world know it.

Taylor turned to me and said, "You know we decided on pink and silver."

"And you know that I don't do pastels, either," I answered.

"Well, it looks like you will on October fourteenth."

She smiled and bounced upstairs like she was marrying Michael Jordan instead of some lawyer. I walked into the kitchen, where my mother was resting her feet on one of the wooden kitchen chairs. She had the white pages, Yellow Pages, and even black pages open, circling numbers and addresses with red ink.

"You know, you could be a bit more excited about this. I mean, this is your sister who's getting married."

"And how happy, for me, do you think she would be?"

"You all need to be closer. I would hate to think that if I left this earth tomorrow, you and Taylor wouldn't know how to get along."

She shook her head and pushed her reading glasses back up on her nose.

"It's very important to her that you be there and be happy. This isn't easy at all. Having to rush this thing so she won't be showing when she walks down the aisle."

"*Won't be showing?*" I asked. "She didn't tell me that she was pregnant."

"Well, that's probably because you all aren't as close as you need to be!" she scolded.

I looked up the stairs, where Taylor had gone, and thought about her standing before me with a life inside her. I wanted that feeling so badly that I wished it were pinkeye she had. Something contagious. It seemed as though Taylor always got what she wanted. Even when she didn't want what she got, it was considered a prize possession by others.

I wanted to run upstairs, rub her stomach, and ask her what it felt like. Whether or not she was ready. What James thought and how far along she was. She had something in her life that she probably considered minute, when it wouldn't take much more than one to make my life complete.

I could hear her flush the toilet upstairs and then come out singing out of tune. *Damn her.* I was the singer *and* the one who wanted a baby, and if the Lord was kind enough to throw a wedding in there, that would be cool, too. Taylor strolled down the steps, rubbing her stomach under her shirt until she saw me.

"Oh, girl, you scared me." She laughed.

"Sorry, didn't mean to. You okay?" I asked.

"Yeah, fine. Why do you ask that?"

She gave a sort of nervous smile and trotted down the rest of the steps and into the kitchen. I followed close behind in hopes that one of them would slip up in my presence. Taylor went into the pantry and got the saltines out. She sat down and put her feet up on another chair. Now, let me remind you that there were only four kitchen chairs and my mother's feet were already airborne.

"I guess I'll get a seat out of the dining room," I mumbled.

"Here, you can have this one," my mother insisted.

I pretended as if I couldn't hear her, simply because I didn't want to, either of them. I just wanted to hear Taylor say that she was expecting, look into her face, and wonder what she felt. Then I could leave. Then maybe I could go on, once I knew that it was real. Had heard it from the horse's mouth. But conversation was nonexistent while I was in the room. Nobody but me could think of anything to say.

"So, when is James coming back in town?"

"I don't know." She sounded irritated. "I'm supposed to be going there next month."

"That's wonderful," my mother said. "I can't wait to meet his parents."

"And what does he think about the pastels?" I asked.

"He *thinks* whatever *I* think is fine."

Taylor looked at me in a matter-of-fact fashion, while my mother shook her head like I'd asked if James were gay. Uncle Lucky called me from the family room in time to save me from the gruesome twosome.

"Yeah, Uncle Lucky?"

"Watch this horse come in first," he said, pointing to the races on television.

He was into it. Moving around in that recliner as if he had saddled up a horse and was ready to take off.

"When was the last time you went to a racetrack?"

He got quiet on me all of a sudden and stared down at the remote.

"It's been a while, Slim."

"You wanna go one day? I'll take you, if you like."

"Nah, nah. I don't do that no more, can't do that no more!"

He sighed heavily and poked his chest out, like the brave man he really *wanted* to be. His face held so much tension that it looked like his eyebrows were about to go to battle.

"You can do anything you wanna do, Uncle Lucky."

"Nah, Slim, not that. Now, I don't wanna talk about it anymore!"

"Go on in there with ya mama," he said, fanning me away and changing the channel.

I looked in the direction in which he wished I would go and realized that I wasn't welcome in that room, either. So I made my exit. As I unlocked the door to my hunter green Camry, I remembered that Dorothy had told me that home is where you are loved. I pulled away from the haven in which my entire family dwelled and couldn't come up with a name to call it. But there was definitely no love in there for me.

Dorothy tapped on the door to my office and let herself in before I could answer. She wore a tan pantsuit and her long hair was curled and pinned up in the back. She wasn't smiling or frowning. Just nonchalantly strolled in and closed my door behind her.

"Good morning," she said as she stood in front of my desk.

"Hi, Dorothy."

"You know, Marion has been complaining about Linda hanging out in your office so much."

"No, I didn't know that. She didn't mention it to me, and neither did Linda."

"Well, you might need to watch her, because she's got a net to catch her when she falls, but how about you?" she asked, doing her customary lean on the corner of my desk.

I thought about the fact that Marion was the one who had hired Linda. She was supposed to be dating Marion's nephew or something like that, but apparently Linda had broken up with him, for Ming. This was information that Linda had dished out on one of the many days that she had shared her life story. She usually told everything, whether I wanted to hear it or not— from her parent's sex life to the frequency of her bowel movements.

"I'll ask Linda about it when she comes back from lunch."

"I hope so. And you look so much better today. I see your hair is done up so pretty, chile. Going somewhere special after work?"

"Nope. I wish. Just home and to bed."

"Why don't you have that fella of yours take you out to a nice restaurant tonight?"

"We're having a few problems right now."

"I knew it, I knew it. Let me sit down so you can tell Mama Dorothy all about it."

She dropped the pile of folders that she was carrying on my desk and pulled up a seat.

"Now, what's the problem? You still trying to leave him to go to Atlanta? I told you that home is where you are loved. Now, all of your family is here in St. Louis. You won't have anybody to look out for you when you're hundreds of miles away. Don't make that mistake and have to come back here trying to save face."

I got defensive and asked, "Save face with who?"

"Everybody. Everybody who knows that it would be a waste of time."

"How can everybody know what I consider wasted time? And why should I really care what *everybody else* thinks. *Everybody else* doesn't consult with me before they make a change."

Dorothy stood up straight and grabbed the folders off of my desk, cut her eyes away, and opened my door.

"You remind me of stubborn-ass Tracy. Thinking you know everything. Just remember what I told you."

I sighed with relief when my door finally closed. Slumped down in my chair just before the phone disturbed the quiet atmosphere.

"Nikai Parker speaking."

"Well, well, well. It's nice to know that we're movin' on up like the Jeffersons."

I massaged my left temple and asked, "What is it, Travis?"

"Is that any way to speak to the man whose child you once carried?"

"Does the word *harassment* mean anything to you?" I asked.

"Do the words *I don't love you any more than you love me* mean anything to you?"

"Well, I'm glad as hell to know that we're on the same page. Now, why are you calling me? Shouldn't you be somewhere jackin' off to junior high school yearbooks?"

"Don't make me break out of here solely for the purpose of kickin' yo' ass, Nikai."

"Hol' on. You hear that?"

"What?" he asked.

"My hands shaking. I'm so scared, Travis. Like yo' punk ass would even make it past the front desk anyway."

"All right, we'll see how you're talkin' when I get outta here."

"By that time, you'll be tryin' to remember where you know me from."

"Are you done?" he yelled, sounding frustrated.

"If my memory serves me correctly, *you* called *my* office!"

"Listen, right before I got locked up, I took out a loan and put your name down as a contact reference."

"And?"

"And they've been calling my mom's house on a regular basis."

"And you're tellin' me this because of what?"

"Because I need a favor. I need you to call the woman for me and tell her that you have not seen me in two years. Then back up my mother by saying that she hasn't, either."

"Is that all?"

"Not exactly. I need you to get some money from my mom and put it on my books."

"Why me?"

"Because I can't depend on anyone else."

"And what makes you think that you can depend on me?"

Travis got quiet. I could hear other inmates on phones, probably making the same pleas to their ex-girlfriends, whom they hadn't seen in years. Instantly, I felt powerful. Like I had the chance to show him something after all of that time. I leaned back in my chair, the tip of my pen in the corner of my mouth, pondering the thought for a second, and then Travis broke his silence.

"If you do this for me, I'll leave you alone for good. You and the fireman will never hear from me again. It's not personal; it's business."

I damn near fell backward and hit my head on the windowsill. How did he know about Rob after all of this time? And how did he know about his occupation, too?

"What've you been doing? Hiring somebody to watch me again?"

"Again?" he asked.

Travis was ignorant like that. He'd leave a question open so that I could drive myself crazy trying to figure out exactly what he meant. I tapped my heel on the floor as I thought of a lie to put a little heat under his butt and back him up off of me.

"Fine. I'll put something on your books, 'cause I'd hate to have to bust a cap in the ass of one of yo' peeps with this twenty-two I found a while back. And by the way, your parents were such a cute couple when they were together. And very photogenic, too."

"Nikai . . . I'm gonna kick yo'—"

"It wasn't business, Travis. It was personal."

Robert

I arrived at the engine house about 8:00 or 8:15, depending on whose clock you were looking at. Keates was in the downstairs TV room watching ESPN. That was his usual spot, other than his quarters upstairs. Keates was as cool as could be expected when he wasn't reminiscing over the woman who'd left him. He often made fighting fires his entire purpose in life. Nothing else seemed to matter when we had a run. Possibly because he knew that there would be no one waiting for him whether he made it home or not.

He wasn't the type to throw his weight around and wouldn't think twice about getting in his gear and beatin' a blaze with us. If we were in it, he was, too. And for that, I could respect the man, but for many other reasons, I couldn't. He seemed to get off on rescues, but in my eyes, no one had to die or be injured for there to be a tragedy. If you ask me, it's tragic when someone has lost property. He didn't seem to see it that way, though. I just tried to make every fire a damn good one, and that meant that if four of us went in, four of us would come out.

I had just taken my turnout gear out of my locker and put it down on the floor next to the pumper when a call came over the audible. "Pumper twenty, pumper twenty. Fire in house, two-story brick, heavy smoke showing." I hadn't had time to check the schedule, but I did know enough to realize that I was the leadoff on that shift. Which meant that I'd be the first to tackle those hot-ass flames. I got situated behind Keates, who was riding shotgun, and fastened the tank on my back. The dispatcher rattled off the address a couple more times before Hodges pulled out of the engine house.

Keates went on and on and sounded pretty upset about there not being any people trapped inside. I just looked out the corner of my eye in hopes that he would kill that shit before we got to the scene. I felt like I shouldn't have to remind the captain that sick small talk like that should remain in his quarters.

Hodges pulled up in front of a four-family flat over on the South Side of town. Two elderly women stood on the front lawn, screaming about how their neighbor's granddaughter was stuck inside, couldn't make it to the door, the smoke was so thick, and other calls for help. I looked back in time to catch Keates getting excited.

When I reached the porch, I could see that the door was slightly cracked. I figured maybe one of those old ladies must've tried to do my job and hadn't succeeded. I pushed it and it didn't budge. Kinda stuck like a rug was caught between the floor and the bottom of the door. I put a little more pressure behind it and shoved whatever it was out of the way, kicked part of it when I walked by, and proceeded to the back of the apartment.

The ladies were right: The smoke was thick, black, and blinding. I moved toward the kitchen, feeling my way through and hoping I would bump into the girl on her way out. I could hear Keates yelling behind me, asking if anyone could hear him, if anyone was inside. There was no sound except for the fire tearing someone's life apart, all that they had worked for.

"C'mon, Hayes," Keates said to me. "We've got to find her."

He was charged up, like someone had plugged him into a battery on the way over there.

"Are they sure she's still in here?" I asked.

"They said she was. And that means that we're not leaving until we come out of here with someone!"

He was starting to piss me off with his Hercules mentality. I didn't have anything to prove to anybody outside. So coming out empty-handed didn't make either one of us less of a firefighter, in my eyes.

As I walked across the threshold leading to the living room, flames rose to about six feet behind me. I could hear the fire burning through wood, causing the dining room chairs to collapse and a wooden beam in the ceiling to fall across a queen-size bed. The flames burned closer and closer to the living room. I got hotter, more mad, more impatient.

"Keates, if she's in here, she's gone by now!" Don yelled.

I couldn't see Keates's eyes, but I heard him taking a deep breath. The kind that let you know you were disappointing him.

He yelled, "I'm gonna run through here one more time!"

"Let's split up and go through again," Hodges suggested.

I felt bad for the victim, but I would have felt worse if one of us had died unnecessarily. I turned toward the main entrance and walked through the living room. Kicked that familiar object by the front door for the second time and tried to clear out enough smoke for me to see. I pulled the front door open for light and saw a hand, then a leg with a ruffled sock burned into the flesh. The skin didn't look real. Almost like a life-size rag doll that had been tossed into the flames. I shook my head and made a sign of the cross over my chest. A feeling of guilt rushed over me. I had been kicking and pushing that young girl the entire time.

"Let's get out of here!" Keates yelled. "She must have made it out. The fire's getting too bad."

"No!" I said, pointing to the corpse behind the door. "I found her."

They all sighed, paused for a minute, and then rushed outside to put the flames out.

Don asked, "You all right, man?"

"Yeah, I'm fine."

I was bent over, with my head hung low. Tired, sad, and frustrated all at once.

When we made it back to the engine house, I got washed up and dialed my mother's house. Kim answered, sounding as though I had awakened her.

I asked jokingly, "When are you gonna move out and get your own place?"

"When you learn how to please a woman!" she snapped.

"Where's Moms at?"

"Definitely not looking for you."

"You must have gotten paid this weekend, because you forget how to act when you get a little change in your pocket."

"Oohhh. Save that one for Russell Simmons. Hol' on—I think I've got his number right here."

"Put Moms on the phone, Kim."

"First tell me where Nik is."

"I don't know. I'm at the engine house. Why don't you try calling her at home?"

"I already did that. She didn't answer."

"Well, I don't know what to tell you."

"She *should* be somewhere gettin' some real lovin'."

She laughed so hard that I was sure she would burst a blood vessel. I was silent until she was done and had come to the conclusion that I wasn't in the mood for any more of her jokes.

"Hol' on—here she is."

"Hello?"

"Hey, whassup? What are you doin'?"

"Nothin', sitting here watching a little television. What are you doin'?"

"Thinkin' about you. Did you ever get those batteries for those smoke detectors in the hallway?"

"Yeah. Kim said last week she would call you to put them up."

I ran my hand over my sweaty bald head and shook it in frustration.

"That girl didn't call me at all," I said.

"Well, it's okay. Just get over here when you can."

"No, that's important. I'll be over there in the morning. What are you doing for the rest of the day?"

"I was thinking of going to bingo and then maybe shopping for a soon-to-be grandchild," she said, laughing.

I sat up straight, felt tension in my back, and thought about Karen.

"Ma, I told you that Nik and I aren't ready for kids yet."

"Well, I don't see what y'all are waiting for."

I cleared my throat and said, "Well, I think she might be

waiting for you to start respecting her and not opening up her mail."

She got quiet and then whispered something to Kim. I could hear her loudmouthed laughing in the background.

"Well, I was only checking to see if she was going for a pregnancy test or not."

"Did you find out what you needed to know?" I asked.

"Yeah, and I hope she got that taken care of. You know, that kind of infection can cause problems when you're tryin' to have kids."

"Listen, Ma. I'm at the engine house, so I've gotta go. Why don't you start running that baby idea by Kim for a change?"

"Not living up in here on me!" she yelled.

I laughed and let go. Too bad the rest of my life couldn't be that simple.

Nikai

Maurie, Janae, and I had been going over songs one Wednesday evening. Reviewing tracks, learning tunes, and lighting incense was the agenda for the day.

I left work early, ran by Travis's mom's house, picked up five hundred dollars, stashed it in an empty purse at home, called back to the office to remind Linda that I would get back with her about Ming and told her to pile the paperwork for the following day on my desk. What the girls and I had planned was more important. There was gonna be an open mike session down at a club in the Delmar Loop area that next week. A part of town that looked like it had been built solely for youthful expression, with its vintage shops and free-for-all atmosphere.

Kalif told us that this spot packed a mixed crowd, which generally led to acceptance, because they could appreciate diversity. In a place like that, you could embrace your own culture and not be viewed as a separatist.

Maurie was stretched out on one of the large pillows in the living room, while Janae switched the CDs according to her mood. Both were in black ankle-length dresses, with their braids tied up in a colorful head wrap. I had stopped home in time to change into some shorts and a T-shirt and ran into Rob, who was giving the apartment a full fire inspection.

Janae sat down next to me on the couch, propped her feet up on the coffee table, and asked, "So, what are you gonna do about your hair?"

I looked at Janae, and then Maurie looked at me as though

the topic of my hair had come up in a previous discussion, only I hadn't been around.

Knowing what she meant, I touched my head and asked, "What's wrong with my hair?"

"It's not you!" Maurie barked.

"Well, I think that it *is* me."

Maurie tilted her head, raised her right brow, and stuck her mouth out in a "Don't even go there" fashion.

"Let me rephrase that. It's not *us!*" she added.

Janae said, "We don't mean it like that. What Maurie is trying to say is that it symbolizes your lack of self-awareness."

It was apparent that Janae was trying to soften the blow, but at the same time, I felt like I was being ganged up on. Maurie sat up on her pillow and turned the volume down on the CD player.

"How can you say that you love God and who he has made you when you undo what he has blessed you with? Do you feel like he made a mistake? Or are you letting society convince you that in order for you to be beautiful, you have to mimic someone else?"

"Maurie, stop treating that girl like she committed a crime!"

"I'm serious!" Maurie yelled in obvious frustration. "Because sistas like her are the main ones complainin' about our men runnin' to white women, but they never realize that imitation is the highest form of flattery. Nobody has to convince our men of anything. We do by fryin' our hair!"

Janae turned to me and saw the look on my face—one that said her homie had three seconds to check herself.

Janae asked, "How do you feel about your hair?"

"I haven't actually felt the need to sit down and analyze it."

"So you're saying that you don't analyze things that are important to you?"

"No. I'm saying that I don't analyze my hair."

"So in other words, your hair isn't important to you?"

"Yes. But . . ."

"But what?" Janae asked.

"But the key word is *my*. It's my hair, so I do what I like with it."

They both looked at each other and then back at me. Whispered something about ignorance being bliss and turned the music back up. Tuned me out as if I weren't there. Like my general miseducation made any further comments that I may have cared to share irrelevant. Like maybe I wasn't even a sista.

"Do you believe in multiple orgasms?"

Linda and I were sitting outside a deli in University City for lunch. I was having a bagel. She was having coffee, a cigarette, and daydreams about a porno she and Ming had watched the night before.

"You're too pretty to be smoking, Linda," I said, fanning the smoke in the other direction.

"Is there anything else you wanna complain about before we finish this conversation?"

I crossed my legs, rested my arm on the back of the iron chair, and apologized.

Linda asked, "What's been going on with you lately?"

"A lot of stress," I answered, massaging my temples. "Has anyone spoken to you about the way that you frequent my office?"

"No. Why?"

"I didn't think so."

"Why?" she insisted.

"Let's just change the subject."

I wanted to ask her what she thought about me growing my hair out naturally, but something told me that she wouldn't understand. I had been raised to believe that the closer I got my hair to hers, the more beautiful I would be. The complexity was too extreme for her to grasp.

"I've never personally had any."

"Had any what?" she asked.

I leaned across the table and whispered, "Multiple orgasms."

"Oh, later for that. Let's talk about what's been bothering you."

I took a sip of my bottled water and leaned forward, resting my elbows on the glass table. Sighed and looked Linda in the eye.

"Remember when I told you about that singing group that I made it into?"

She put her cigarette out and said, "Yeah."

"Well, in the music industry, there's this thing called 'artist development.' Your appearance, the way that you carry yourself, and the way that you speak are all taken into consideration. You know, to determine whether you're marketable."

"You speak fine to me."

"Thanks," I said, touching her hand. "But my appearance isn't quite what it needs to be."

"Nikai, you are a beautiful woman. There's nothing wrong with you, and anyone that says differently is obviously blind or jealous."

I was flattered by her opinion of me, but she just wasn't getting what I was trying to tap into.

I sat up straight and asked, "What do you think about my hair?"

"Your hair looks great. Honestly, Nikai, I don't see what the problem is."

I decided to take another approach.

"Do you believe in God?"

"Yeah."

"Do you believe that He made everyone the way that He intended for us to look?"

"I guess you could say that," she answered, shrugging her shoulders.

"Then why do you dye your hair blue sometimes?"

"Because I like to wear it that way. The same reason I wear red lipstick on Monday and brown on Tuesday—for variety."

I thought about the answer that she gave and realized that the difference in the way we altered ourselves was that Linda always came back to her natural state, while I continuously ran from mine every time there was the slightest indication that I wasn't the person I *thought* the relaxer made me appear to be.

I had spent a lot of time trying to create differences between myself and Maurie and Janae so that I could justify living in a fantasy. Going as far as to say that spirituality and Afrocentricity were like apples and oranges. I mean, when I really sat down and thought about it, it made no difference whether or not they thought pigs could fly. We all possessed a distinct, undeniable identity. Our skin and hair would follow us all the days of our lives. And so would the long-term effects of it being tainted. At one point, the thought of looking the way that I was meant to frightened the hell out of me, but suddenly, for some unknown reason, it brought about a childlike excitement. Now there was only one question left: For whom was I doing it? Maurie and Janae? Myself? Or to prove to society that I *did* know who I was? When actually, I still didn't have a clue.

That following Saturday morning, I got up and out of the apartment in time to avoid Robert, so quickly that I accidentally forgot to take Travis's money to get a money order. Lately, Rob had been going over fire-evacuation plans, like we lived in a five-bedroom, two-bath house. I stopped at the grocery store, did a little shopping, and picked up two glazed doughnuts, a bottle of orange juice, and a bouquet of flowers, the nicest ones they had.

It had rained during the night and most of that morning. The sun appeared to be playing a game of hide-and-seek with me. But on that particular day, I wasn't in the mood to play, kid, or joke around. I needed a friend.

I pulled up to plot 46B in the Calvary Cemetery and got out of my car. The ground was wet and soggy. Destroying my Nikes and the lower portion of my denim pant legs. Paying respect to everyone I passed, I stepped in between every plot until I found the one I had been searching for. I stooped down and placed the flowers in the pot in front of a tombstone that read HERE LIES A WONDERFUL FATHER AND LOYAL HUSBAND—NICHOLAS JAMES PARKER.

"Hi, Daddy. It's me, Nikki. What do you think of the weather? Horrible, huh?"

I looked across the cemetery at the rows and rows of plots and then back down to my father's and laughed.

"I guess you know that's not why I'm here, huh? Yeah, you always did know, didn't you? Taylor's getting married in a couple of months. Yeah, to some nice lawyer she met. He's from New York. Don't worry, he's a good guy. You know her type. She's got a little one on the way, too. Me? No, I'm just trying to get my singing off the ground. I've got to worry about the important things first. Isn't that what you always told me? Uncle

Lucky? Oh, he's fine. Still in the house, afraid to go out. Yep, he's still afraid."

I stuck my hands in my pockets and rocked back and forth a couple of times. Looked around the cemetery again. No one was out there. Just me, alone. I began to think about my uncertainties and my eyes got heavy. They overflowed at the thought of my never getting married or having children. Possibly not ever having a singing career or peace of mind. I turned back to my father.

"Daddy, I'm scared."

I waited. Waited to hear him answer out loud. Waited to feel an arm wrap around me and tell me that this life is only temporary. I waited to hear that maybe I wasn't alone.

"I wish you were here, Daddy. Nobody really understands me. Mama and Taylor have got each other and I've got no one. Her baby and wedding are all that seem to matter to Mama now. Sometimes, I don't feel like I'm really living. It's like my life is just passing away so fast and I have no control of anything."

I wiped the tears from my face and raised my head to the sky.

"God, does my daddy hear me?"

I sighed and pulled my hands from the pockets of my navy blue raincoat. Brushed the leaves from around his tombstone and adjusted the flowers that I had just brought.

"Well, I guess I better go now. I'm sure you're up there looking out for a lot of people. How come they don't visit you? Daddy, I really don't know. Mama always says that it hurts too badly to come. Taylor's always out of town, you know. I guess it's possible for you to get lonely, too, huh? I love you, too, Daddy."

I stepped away and smiled. Basically because he was there for me when no one else was. He showed up when I needed him, and that was more than I could say for the living.

I got into my car and wiped my face with a Kleenex from the box on the dashboard. Just as I prepared to pull off, I felt compelled to step outside of the car. The clouds had parted and the sun had given up the game. Finally, I had won at something.

I leaned my head back to the heavens and whispered, "Thanks, Daddy, for keeping your promise."

Robert

"When you hear these smoke detectors beeping, that means that it's time for the battery to be changed."

Kim was sitting on the couch, painting her crusty toenails and tuning me out as much as possible. I had come over to help fireproof my mother's house and was getting no cooperation whatsoever.

"I'll try to remember that. Oh, and I meant to thank you for inventing electricity and the wheel, too. I don't know what kinda flames you've been running into, but you need to chill out with all of the drills."

I sucked my teeth, shook my head, and went into the kitchen, where my mother was. At least in there, I knew that my warnings would be heard.

"Ma, do you remember how to use this fire extinguisher?"

"Yes, Rob," she said, lightly tapping me on the cheek.

"Ma, I just wanna know that y'all are safe. I don't want a call to come over the audible with your address in it."

"You won't, you won't. Now, stop nagging. I think you've been working too hard."

"No, I haven't been working enough. I was thinking about taking Nik on a trip in December. That way, we can escape the cold weather for a few days."

"Yeah, take her somewhere and see if you can talk her into giving me some grandbabies," she suggested, pulling a brown paper bag full of greens out of the refrigerator.

"Ma, I thought we already had this talk before."

"We did, but you didn't tell me what I wanted to hear."

I reached across the table, kissed her cheek, and retreated to the living room, where smart-ass was on the phone, talking loudly.

I asked Kim, "Can you keep it down some?"

"Can you go home?"

She shifted back into her conversation as I began to channel surf.

"Yeah, girl. Yo' man is over here actin' like he's lost his mind."

I extended my hand and said, "Let me speak to Nik."

She looked me up and down like I'd asked for her left kidney.

"Give me the phone!"

"Gimme got shot."

"Would you tell her to page me?"

"Smokey the Bear wants to know if you would page him, and do your share to help stop fires, as well," she told Nik.

I felt my pager vibrating on my hip and pulled it off of my belt to check the number. It was Karen. I hadn't heard from her in four days. It's funny how a crazy person's absence can make you just as nervous as her presence.

"Let me use the phone."

"Nik wants to know when you will be coming home."

"Tell her that I will be leaving here as soon as you let me use the phone."

"She wants to know who it is you have to call so urgently."

My jaws tightened and I squinted my eyes to let Kim know that I wasn't joking anymore.

"All right, Nik. I gotta go. I'll call you back when I'm done helping my mama pick these greens."

"Thank you," I said, snatching the cordless phone from her hand. "Now, get out!"

"Why? I still wanna know who it is you have to call."

"You said you won't be needing any more loans from me?" I asked sarcastically.

"You aren't funny, Rob."

I dialed Karen's number as Kim headed toward the kitchen.

Karen answered. "Hello?"

"Hey."

"Hey, where are you?"

"Mom's house. Whassup?"

"I just wanted to tell you that I went to the doctor today."

"And?"

"And I'm pregnant, for sure."

I sighed and leaned back on the couch.

"So, what do you want to do?"

"What did I tell you I wanted to do?" she asked.

She was calm. Almost sounded sane. I guess reality had taken a good swing at her and didn't miss. Whatever it was, I liked it. She seemed rational, approachable.

"Karen, you know that this won't change anything between us, don't you?"

She was quiet for a second and then whispered, "Yeah."

"So, you still wanna do this?"

"You sound as though you don't. I mean, this *is* your child inside of me, Rob."

"You think I don't know this? Listen, take some time out and think about what you wanna do. Call me tomorrow. Maybe I can come through there for a minute or so."

"Yeah, all right."

I hung up with Karen, but she stayed heavy on my mind, even after I had arrived back home with Nik. It scared me to be concerned about someone I despised, but I figured the game was over. Karen was no longer the opponent, but a team member. She was helping me to live forever, through her womb. Little would change, but little would stay the same. I didn't want to lose my lady at home, but Karen had a part of me, my child, inside of her, and that was more, way more, than I could say for Nik.

Nikai

Hello?"

"Hey, Nik. Is Rob home?"

"How are you doin', Don? No, he's not in right now. You wanna leave him a message?"

"No, actually I was calling for you."

"Me? Whassup?"

I stopped putting canned goods in the pantry and sat down at the kitchen table. It was 10:00 A.M. and too early for anything to be wrong. Especially anything that I could help with.

"Kalif wanted to speak to you, but I didn't want to give him your home number without your permission."

I thought about the time when I was verbally pushed around down at his loft, and I felt a bit uneasy, yet curious.

"That's fine. You can go ahead and give it to him."

"You sure?" Don asked.

"Yeah, it's okay. And thanks for calling and asking first."

"No problem. I'll let him know. Hey, when Rob gets in, tell him to call me."

"All right."

I hung up and finished piling my groceries into the pantry and refrigerator. Glanced over at the cordless. Wondered what Kalif had on his mind that early in the morning. And why was I specifically a part of it.

I began steaming a pot of broccoli and cauliflower, when a call came through. I put the bag of frozen vegetables down on

the island and walked over to the phone. It rang again. I picked
it up, stared at it. On the third ring, I pushed the talk button.

"Hello?"

"Good morning. May I speak with Nikai?"

"This is she."

"This is Kalif. How are you feelin' today?"

"Pretty good. And you?"

I was getting sick of the preliminaries. Tired of the polite talk.

"Good. Yeah, I got your number from Don this morning. I
wanted to make sure that it was cleared with your husband first."

I blushed and said, "I'm not married."

I never thought I would see the day that it didn't hurt to say
that phrase.

"Oh, okay. Well, listen, I was going over some tracks and I
just thought since you were so new to the group, it would help
for you to get a feel for the music."

"That sounds like a good idea."

"So, do you think you could come down to the studio
around noon? It shouldn't take too long."

The other phone line rang.

"Can you hold on a second?"

I pushed the flash button and said, "Hello."

"Are you gonna get fitted for your dress, or should I just
have the seamstress guess at your size?" Taylor asked.

"Depends on if you can ask me with a smile."

"I'm pressed for time, Nikai," she sang.

"Well, you never even officially asked me to be in your wedding."

"Well, I thought you would assume it. I mean, you *are* the
only sister I have."

I could tell she meant what she was saying, and as sweet as
the compliment was, Taylor still managed to make it sound belittling.

"Listen, I'm on the other line. Can I call you right back?"

"Nikai, this is important!"

"To whom?" I asked.

"To me!"

"So I'm assuming you can understand how I feel about my call on the other line, huh?"

Taylor slammed the phone down hard. Then probably went to tell my mother that I was single-handedly trying to destroy her wedding.

I pushed the flash button again, but Kalif was gone. I grabbed the caller ID box to get his number, but as I began to look, Rob walked through the front door. I pressed the review button a couple of times but went back a few calls too far. Noticed that there had been a lot of anonymous calls being made there. About ten in just that last week. *Anonymous, Blocked,* and *Unknown* is what just about every call read. I put the phone down in its cradle and went to greet the man who wasn't quite ready to become my husband.

Rob was sitting down in the living room, facing the front window. He had tilted the blinds enough so that he could see out but no one could see in.

"Hey, you all right?" I asked.

He jumped, as though his mind was in another place. Turned, looked at me, and then relaxed.

"C'mere," he said, his arm extended.

I walked over and sat down on the couch next to him. He held me close, which was something that I didn't expect. Rob was silent. Yet at the same time, he was telling me that something was wrong.

I looked up at him and asked, "You sure you're all right?"

He didn't answer. Kept looking out the window. His facial expression was one of sadness. He looked as though he saw something further than the parking lot. Further than my eyes could see.

Robert kissed me on the forehead and said, "I love you."

"I love you, too."

We sat there for an hour or so, worrying. Only I didn't know exactly what it was we were supposed to be so worried about. But Rob, he saw something coming.

Something big.

Big enough to make him stop and contemplate his next move. Whatever that was to be.

*   *   *

"Is anybody else coming?" I asked Kalif.

"Maurie didn't have a baby-sitter, Janae was meeting with somebody for lunch, and Ahmad works on the weekends."

Kalif turned toward the double doors and strolled like the man of all men. He had his dreads tied up in a ponytail, with one strand dangling on the side. He wore a Wu Wear T-shirt, a pair of baggy black jeans, and those same untied boots. Looked like he had just fallen out of a Wu Tang Clan video. Which I didn't particularly find attractive. I preferred the clean-cut type with close shaves and clothes that fit.

"You mind if I light a few candles and cut out the lights?" he asked.

"No, it's okay."

"That's usually the setting we have in here," he added, laughing. "I'm not trying to romance you or anything."

He lighted the candles as I sat up on one of the stools, crossed my ankles, and straightened the leg of my khakis.

"So, how long have you been producing?" I asked.

"Uh, about nine years."

"How long have you been singing?"

"Well, I started taking it seriously about three years ago."

He came over and pulled the stool that was next to me across the room, then sat down on it and leaned his back against the wall.

I smiled and asked, "You like to lean a lot, huh?"

"Why do you ask that?"

"Because when I first met you, you were leaning against the building outside."

"I guess I just like to be comfortable."

Maybe that explained his clothes being large enough for two more people to fit into.

"I see you're very observant."

I blushed and said, "I try to be."

"That's good. You need to be."

As he got down from his stool to play a couple of tracks, I noticed a cigar tucked firmly behind his right ear. I thought about mentioning it but then remembered that it was *his* loft we were in.

The first track was a ballad, soft yet abrupt. He danced across the room, over to his stool. He was in another world. I guess the same way I was when I was singing. His head was bobbing slowly. That loose dread was swaying to the beat. Then he stopped, turned to me, and smiled.

"You like jewelry, Nikai?"

"Doesn't every woman?" I asked.

"You feel like making some?"

"*Making* some?"

"Yeah, making some." He laughed.

"I'm not sure I know how to *make* jewelry."

"Well, I'll show you a few pieces that I've made. Then you tell me if you're interested."

He walked into the other room and shut the door behind him. I looked around at all of the darkness, smelled the African Wind incense burning, and listened to the music. It all brought back the memory of the girls questioning my knowledge of self. I wasn't quite sure that it wouldn't turn into four against one this time around. So I had pulled my hair back into a bun that particular day. Possibly to minimize the attention that the relaxer was bound to draw.

Kalif walked back into the room holding a bag and said, "Hey, I forgot to ask you if you wanted to take your shoes off."

"Is that some sort of ritual?" I asked.

"We just like to be comfortable when we create. But you don't have to, if you don't want to."

I looked at him standing in his socks and decided not to rock the boat. I stepped out of my brown loafers and set them against the wall next to his boots. He smiled, which made his five o'clock shadow even more uninviting.

"C'mere and stand by the candlelight for a second so you can see," he said, beckoning for me to join him on the other side of the room.

I stepped well into his comfort zone. My arm brushed against his. I looked down at his tattoos instead of at the jewelry that he was showing me. There was a large ankh on his right arm and a verse from Scripture on his left. I stared, used the candlelight to see what it was that meant so much to him that he felt he had to mark his body with it.

"Something wrong?" he asked.

"No," I said, collecting myself. "I was just checking out your tattoos. That's all."

"Why were you frowning like that?"

"Um, they just look painful. Did they hurt?"

"Nah, not really," he answered, pulling his T-shirt over his head. "This first one did, though."

His chest looked like it had been carved from chocolate, just not as dark. It was as though he'd been molded and shaped by a skilled hand. The flames that danced off of the walls gave him an appeal that I wasn't quite ready for. Had to remind myself that he wasn't my type. That he was rough, rugged, and raw.

"This one is of my son," he said, pointing to a picture of an infant on his chest, right above his heart.

"How old is he?" I asked.

"He died when he was one week old. Respiratory problem."

I looked him in the eye to acknowledge his emotions but also to get my mind off of his body.

"I'm sorry to hear that. How long has it been?"

"Two years. You have any seeds?"

"Seeds?" I asked.

He laughed and said, "Yeah, seeds. Children. Kids."

"Oh, no. None for me. Not yet anyway."

"So, you say you're not married, huh?"

"No, haven't done that yet, either." I laughed nervously. "How about you?"

"No. I have people I see occasionally, but nobody special."

I looked away. Wondered how long it was gonna take him to put that damn shirt back on. When he would finally get down to showing me the jewelry in his hand. When he would get off the subject of our personal lives.

"So, what do you think of the girls?" he asked.

"They're nice. I was here with them a few nights ago."

"Oh. I hate that I missed you."

"Why is that?"

"There's something about you. It's your spirit. Maybe the innocence of it. Whatever it is, I like it. It's what makes you you, for now."

"What do you mean, 'for now'?"

"There's a lot of you that's undone. It's like a queen living her life and not knowing that she's royalty. Your humbling innocence is what makes you you."

I was confused but too afraid to show it. He seemed to be good at pointing out things. I didn't want my lack of self-awareness to be one of them.

"So when did you become so good at figuring people out?" I asked.

"Figuring people out is not what I do. I try to *understand* people. For every effect, there is a cause. A reason for people to react the way that they do."

"So, what have you been able to tell about me so far?" I asked.

Kalif laughed and walked back over to his stool. Sat down and leaned against the wall again. He pulled that cigar from behind his right ear and asked if I minded him lighting up.

"It's your place," I said, shrugging my shoulders.

"I don't think you're really sure what you want."

"What do you mean?" I asked.

"I think you've got the drive to get what you want; you just have to figure it out first," he said, taking a drag off of the cigar.

"So, doesn't everybody?"

"Yeah, but you seem to let your environment and circumstances determine where you go, instead of using wisdom."

I got defensive and asked, "What's that supposed to mean?"

"Calm down. I didn't mean it in a negative way. For example, you probably had something else to do today. But instead of doing that, you came here. Now I've been talking to you about everything *but* these tracks. And not once have you stopped me and demanded that we get down to business so you can carry on with your day."

"So what would you suggest I do, cut you off?"

"No, but I *do* suggest you get what you came for and *not* what you're given. That should be applied every day."

I thought about the fact that the last time I was in that place, I'd felt the very same way.

Stupid.

It seemed as though this group sought out victims to tear

limb from limb and then sent them back out into the world even more unsure and insecure than they'd been when they arrived.

"If you're done analyzing, I'd appreciate it if you would put that cigar out. Something tells me that's not tobacco inside of it."

Kalif coughed like a lung was on its way up and said, "That something must be right, 'cause it's not."

Just as he was putting the cigar out, a car horn blew three times. He got up, walked to the window, and gave a call that sounded like something dying in the jungle.

"I can leave if you have company," I told him.

He smiled, winked at me, and said, "Something tells me that you don't really wanna do that."

He rode the elevator down to open the door for his visitor. I was relaxed. It could have been because I wasn't wearing shoes or maybe because I had caught a whiff of secondhand smoke. When Kalif came back up, he was being followed by Don. He stepped into the smoked-filled room. Half weed, half incense. Saw the four scented candles burning and looked as though he was wondering why we were sitting in the dark at one o'clock in the afternoon. Don looked me up and down with curiosity, then at Kalif, who still hadn't put his damn shirt back on.

"Hey, Nik. How's the music coming?" Don asked.

"Fine."

"Uh, Kalif. Let me holla at you in the other room for a minute."

They both left the room and I tried to imagine the conversation. What warnings Don was giving Kalif about moving in on his best friend's woman. What reassurances Kalif was giving Don, like the fact that I wasn't his type, that I didn't even know that I was royalty, that I still had a perm.

When they came back, Don had an uneasy look on his face, but Kalif wasn't letting either of us kill his high.

"Um, I got in touch with Rob," Don told me. "He seemed a little upset. You know what's bothering him?"

"Nope. I've just decided to give him some room to breathe. When he's ready to talk, he will."

Kalif gave a short chuckle and then asked Don if he was done playing private investigator. Don looked at us both, one by one.

Me, sitting on a stool in a candlelit, smoke-filled room, with no shoes on. And Kalif, bare-chested, blasted out of his mind, and holding on to the corner of the open door, waiting for Don to leave.

"If I see Rob, what do you want me to tell him?" he asked.

Kalif answered, "Tell him she's down at the loft working on some tracks."

I glanced at Kalif for a minute, as though I wasn't quite sure if that was the truth.

"Okay," Don said, looking at me. "Is that all?"

Still holding on to the door, Kalif laughed and began rubbing his chest with his free hand. It made me want to see what he felt like.

I told Don, "If there's anything else, I'll page him."

"You done now?" Kalif asked Don.

As he escorted Don to the elevator, I turned around on my stool and picked up the bag of jewelry that Kalif had laid down. When he got back upstairs, I heard him come into the room and close the door behind him. I didn't turn around, though. Didn't want to see if he had actually put his shirt back on.

"Something told me that you didn't really want to leave," he said.

"Maybe it was the fact that you didn't *want* me to leave."

He smiled, stepped up next to me, and said, "I see you catch on fast."

His eyes were low, red, and glossy. His cheekbones rose higher with every grin.

He slowly walked back over to his stool, allowing me to see the muscles rippling in his brown paper sack–colored back with each stride. He sat down and slumped over even more than usual. Grabbed a crocheted yellow-green-red-and-black hat off of a nearby nail in the wall and placed it on his head. Rocked back and forth to the beat of the music.

Then he looked up at me and asked, "Did you see anything you liked?"

"Um, uh, yeah. This bracelet."

It was a string of black leather with red, black, and white wooden beads on it. The center bead was decorated with an ankh.

"This is actually an anklet. But you can have it. You know once you tie it on, you shouldn't take it off. Some things are forever."

He walked across the room to me and took it from my hands. Lifted my right leg and removed my sock. Braced my foot against his bare stomach. I could feel his treasure trail of hair, below his navel, between my toes. He tied the anklet around my ankle but held on to my foot.

"This is a gift. From me to you."

I looked him in his eyes, those blazing, glossy eyes, and pulled my leg away.

"Thank you. You mind if we talk about the tracks now?" I asked.

He laughed hard. Hard enough to make me wonder whether he was intrigued or intimidated by my statement.

"I like that," he said, shaking his index finger at me. "But it doesn't count if that's not what you really want."

"What are you trying to say?"

"I'm *sayin'* that you haven't been watchin' my every move because you *didn't* want me to touch you. Nikai, I'm not gonna do anything to you that you don't want me to."

Suddenly, I saw the blame shifting. He was touching me because he could sense that I wanted him to.

I jumped down off of my stool and grabbed my shoes.

"This is all making me a bit uncomfortable."

"Nikai, I told you that I liked you. I don't wanna make you uncomfortable."

He shoved his hands into his pockets.

I turned to him and asked, "Is that supposed to be a sign of surrender?"

"What?"

"Putting your hands in your pockets like that?"

"No. Just a force of habit. Is that what you want me to do, surrender?"

I didn't say anything.

"I can't do that, either. You have to be at war to surrender. And I don't hurt my own. Besides, I've got something better planned for you."

Robert

Ｈow are you feeling?" I asked Karen.

I was at her place, preparing myself for whatever decision she had made about having that baby.

"I've been throwing up all morning, but I think I'll be okay."

She gave me a pitiful look and leaned away from me on the sofa. Picked the remote up off of the glass coffee table and flipped the channels as if her thumb was having uncontrollable spasms.

"You want anything to drink? There's some white zinfandel and soda in the fridge."

"You haven't been drinking, have you?" I asked.

She didn't respond. Just leaned more heavily into the arm of the couch.

"If you're gonna have that baby, you can't drink, Karen."

"*That* baby?" she yelled.

I sighed and rested my elbows on my knees.

"You know what I mean."

"No, I don't. I *do* know what you said, though."

"I'm not here to argue. I'm here to talk about what you're gonna do."

Suddenly, she came to life. Sat up like she had been struck by lightning.

"Have you told Nicole?"

"Her name is *Nikai*. And no, I haven't told her. What does that have to do with your decision?"

"Have you told anyone?" she asked.

"No. Why should I?"

"Well, my mother isn't alive and yours is."

"So?"

"So, the baby will need to know his or her grandmother! What were you planning to do, keep it a secret?"

I was fed up with her running the show, and just when I thought I saw some sense of decency, the actress in her popped up again. It was becoming obvious that being nice wasn't going to work.

"Listen, Karen, you betta calm your ass down! I'm under enough stress as it is, okay?"

She settled like a storm had passed.

"Am I ever gonna meet your mother, Robert?"

I cupped my face in my hands and, without looking up, asked, "For what, Karen?"

"Because I think that it's important for us to have a relationship. Whether you like it or not, I'll always be a part of your family."

"Don't you mean that that *baby* will be a part of my family?"

She fell silent. Got that crazy look in her eye that she always did when she had silly shit on her mind. Then she gave a wicked grin.

"I saw Nikai in the grocery store this morning. I started to speak, but I was running late. Maybe next time I'll stop and have a chat."

I lifted my head and looked at Karen. By this time, she had gone back to flipping the channels. Like she had said nothing.

"Don't play with me, Karen."

"Do you see a smile painted on my face? I told you a long time ago not to play with me. But I can tell that you still think I'm joking with you, Robert."

We stared at each other. Daring the other to look away.

"So, I'm assuming you've decided to keep this baby."

She adjusted the pillow behind her back and said, "Let's just say that I'm praying for a boy. Robert junior has a certain ring to it, don't you think?"

She made me wanna *ring* her neck. Karen rubbed her stomach and began making little baby noises. Told me that those were the sounds that I needed to get used to. Then she informed me that her out-of-state hair shows would allow a lot of bonding time between me and my firstborn. Stressed the importance of us having a close, healthy relationship. Then said that I needed to familiarize myself with her body because, after all, that's where the baby would be coming from.

Karen also mentioned that she was gonna eventually need to meet Nik. That since I wouldn't break up with her, she had to give her the once-over. Claimed that she couldn't trust just *anybody* around her child, especially some jealous girlfriend. Said Nik might try to harm the baby in retaliation.

It all came across as insanity to me, because I had no intentions of those two being in the same room together. There was no way that Karen would take the lead again. Not in my life.

"Have you thought about how us not being together will affect the baby?" I asked.

She looked at me as though she wanted to turn the question around and shoot it back in my direction.

"Why are you asking me? You *should* be asking yourself that question. You are the one who has decided not to bring him or her up in a family environment."

As she was playing mind games, her pager vibrated across the coffee table and onto the floor. She picked it up, looked at the number, and sighed. Put it down and it went off again. The second time she checked the number, she called whoever it was back.

"What is it?"

She sounded irritated. Like the individual on the other end of the line never failed to deliver bad news.

"So what are you calling me for? I don't have it."

I listened closely. Couldn't make out any words that were being said, but I could tell that it was a male she was speaking to. I admit that a taste of jealousy rushed over me for a second. I mean, this woman had a part of me inside of her and another man was upsetting her. And possibly upsetting my child.

"Listen, it's your turn to do that. Remember, you decided what you wanted, not me. Okay, okay. But I've got company now."

The guy's voice got louder. He was yelling at Karen. Possibly about whatever it was she'd refused to do, or possibly about me.

"Didn't I just tell yo' silly ass that I have company?" she yelled.

Karen fell silent, pulled the phone away from her ear, and stared at it for a minute. Like there were no good-byes, like she had just been hung up on. She sighed again and put the phone down. Went back to channel surfing as if nothing had happened.

"Well, I'm about to get out of here," I said.

She turned to me like she had just snapped out of a hypnotic state and said, "Don't go yet, Rob. My back is hurting. Can you rub it for a little while?" she asked.

She licked her lips as if her tongue were searching for something to do, and then she grabbed my piece. She massaged it until it stood at attention. I thought about Nik being down at the studio, mixed with the fact that all I would be doing at home would be watching a couple of wildebeest mating in the wild on the Discovery Channel and reminding myself of what Karen was practically begging me to do. So I didn't stop her when she began unzipping my pants with her teeth.

She stood up from the couch, took me by the hand, and led me to her bedroom. Karen disrobed me and then herself. Stood close enough for me to feel the heat from her body and then placed my hand on her stomach. I rubbed the small pouch that hadn't been there the last time she had invited me to dance around inside her.

She looked at me and whispered, "That's you. That's us."

I did circular motions with my hand and then brought it up to her face. Kissed her honey brown forehead lightly, because for that moment, she was precious, delicate. Everything about her well-being suddenly seemed to matter to me.

She wrapped her arms around my back and held me close, as though my existence meant hers and possibly our child's. She released the grasp as I pushed her down and took her nipple in my mouth just as her head hit the pillow. She melted onto the bed and parted the doors that held my immortality. With my tongue, I drew a line, from her breast to her navel. Down to her moist, sweet opening. Sucked her pearl tongue and wrote my

name in her heavenly hole. She bucked and bolted. Grabbed the
sheets. Swayed from east to west. Called my name and then
God's. His again, and then mine. She raised up off of the bed
and my mouth followed. I wouldn't let her go, wouldn't let her
lose the feeling. I held her by her sweaty hips and licked from
corner to corner. One opening to the other. And then she
stopped in midair. The calf muscles that turned me on so much
got tense as she froze and let her liquid love flow. Onto the
sheets, and onto me.

I crawled on top of her and massaged her body. Kissed her
neck and then slid inside of her. Made my place between her
thighs and took my time feeling her.

Karen whispered, "I love you, Robert."

She wrapped her thighs around me tighter and moved her
hips like she was trying to take me somewhere. Somewhere deep
between her legs, a place that no man had ever known about.
Someplace I wasn't sure I wanted to go. She moaned and
screamed as though trying to convey a message to someone in
Uganda, when there was a knock at the door. I stopped
midthrust. Remembered the brotha who was so pissed at her
that he'd hung up in her ear. I looked down at Karen. Her eyes
were still closed, as though she had not come back from that
deep, dark place yet.

"You expecting somebody?" I asked.

"No. Don't stop," she whispered.

The knocks got louder. Turned into a beating and then kicking. I got up and put my boxers back on while she grabbed a
pink satin robe and headed toward the front door. I could hear
a man's voice, Karen's, and then the voice of a child about four
years old.

"I told you about coming over here without calling first!"
Karen warned.

"Look, I don't give a shit about you fuckin' some sucka!
Who in St. Louis ain't ran up in yo' ass?"

"Do you honestly think that I'm gonna stand here and listen
to this *shit?*"

"Until you give me what I came for, you will."

By then, the child had started crying and mumbling words

that I couldn't quite make out, but it was obvious that he or she knew Karen very well.

I heard footsteps getting closer as the guy yelled, "Ay, brotha, whoever you are. Save yourself some time and trips to the clinic! Unless you have plans of taking—"

Karen cut him off and blocked his way, somewhere between the living room and the hallway. I jumped up and grabbed my pants, because he didn't sound like he had plans of going anywhere anytime soon. I pulled my shirt over my head and slipped into my Nikes. By the time I was done lacing up and dressing, Karen was walking back into the bedroom. She closed the door behind her and then began looking around the room. Spotted her purse, snatched up her wallet, and then ran back out of the room without uttering a single word.

The brotha had obviously gotten what he wanted, because he left without a fuss and took his whining child with him. I opened the bedroom door and found Karen lying on the couch in the fetal position. Tears were rolling down her face and she rocked like she was two screams short of a nervous breakdown. I walked over to her and knelt down beside her. Ran my hand across her ruffled hair and rubbed her shaking back.

"Karen."

She looked up at me with eyes that begged for understanding.

"Who was that at the door?" I asked.

She looked back down and continued to rock.

"Karen, why did you give him money?"

She stopped rocking and her mouth fell open. Words looked as though they were a half a breath away when she looked at me again.

"They're turnin' my baby against me," she whispered.

"What? What baby?"

"That was my baby who was just here, and Derek's family is turning him against me. Did you hear the way that he cried when Derek threatened to leave him with me?"

"I didn't hear that much of the conversation. When were you gonna tell me that you had kids already?" I asked.

"I don't know. Probably when it was too late for you to try to convince me to abort ours."

She looked away and continued. "Derek thinks that it doesn't hurt me not to see Alex, but it does. I miss him. Every time I go over to Derek's mother's house to see him, he's bigger and bigger. And less interested in me. I wanna be an important part of his life, too. I want him to look at me the way that he looks at Derek."

As she continued to pour her heart out, I sat down on the floor in front of the couch and tried to soak all of this in. The idea of her having a child already and her failure to take on her present responsibility. The fact that my involvement with such a fickle person could seriously jeopardize my relationship with Nik, despite my efforts to keep it all under wraps. The thought of me being that brotha knocking at her door, two or three years from now, asking for some help in raising our baby. The idea that maybe I *was* being the sucka that he'd said I was.

Her love was beginning to dry on the side of my mouth. It brought back the reality that I was in a place where I had no business. Karen had talked herself into a light sleep. Dozed off while still lying in the fetal position.

I got up and walked to the bathroom to clean myself up before returning home. I grabbed a washcloth out of the linen closet and saw those same two EPT tests that had been in there the day of conception. Then it occurred to me that if a woman suspected pregnancy, she would immediately go to the one of the *two unused* pregnancy tests in her linen closet and not seek an outside opinion first. Unless, of course, the day of conception hadn't actually been the day of conception.

I could see then that Karen was trying to cook with too many pots on the stove. And it was becoming more apparent that mine wasn't the only stick stirring up the goods. What I needed to do was find that brotha who'd been there earlier. And then find out all that he knew. Get a few warnings and possibly decrease the chances of ending up the sucka that Karen had planned for me to be.

Nikai

Kim and I were supposed to be meeting Taylor over at Mama's house so that she could take me to get fitted for my bridesmaid's dress. It was noon and I was pressed for time because the girls and I had a show that night down at a club in the Delmar Loop. That's why I'd brought Kim along, to help me find something appropriate to wear while we were out.

I'd called Don that morning and asked him to take Rob to the club that night. I wanted to surprise him and also show him what had kept me so preoccupied. Don told me that he would try, but I could sense a bit of reluctancy in his voice. As though he couldn't get that day Kalif and I were at the loft together out of his mind. In a way, I understood, because, as hard as I tried, I still couldn't get it out of mine.

"Hey, pretty lady," Uncle Lucky called to Kim.

She sashayed over to him, anchoring his recliner. He was still wearing his pajamas.

"You shoot dice?" he asked.

"No, Uncle Lucky, Kim doesn't shoot dice, and you don't, either," I interjected.

"That's a shame. You wanna learn?" he asked.

Kim laughed like he was doing a thirty-minute stand-up routine, but what she didn't realize was that he was serious as cancer. Lucky seemed to love it when pretty young women came around. He suddenly came to life. He, for once, wanted to be funny and interesting. It was as though the young reminded him to do the one thing that kept slipping his mind—to live.

"Girl, you look so good, I don't know whether to poop or go blind. I think I might just fart and close one eye."

"Lucky, leave that girl alone," my mother scolded. "She didn't come over here to be harassed by an old man!"

At that moment, Lucky shut down. Maybe it was from embarrassment or maybe it was because Mama had reminded him of what he was, an old man. Whatever it was, he slumped down in his recliner, stared at the television, not paying any particular attention to what was on, and went back to his place. The place that sheltered him from her comments, the place that made other people look distant and far away. The place where he could pretend to be a stubborn, brave, and strong old man. Even though an old man was never actually what he really wanted to be.

"Nikki, Taylor's on the phone," Mama called. "She wants to speak to you."

I stood up from the couch, kissed Lucky on the cheek, and walked into the kitchen.

"Hello?"

"Hey, I need you to meet me at the seamstress's," Taylor said, sounding out of breath and irritated, as usual.

"What happened to you coming over here?"

"*Who's the fuckin' bride here, me or you?*" she screamed.

I pulled the phone from my ear and looked at it for a second. I couldn't believe what she had just said and whom she'd said it to.

"Assuming you live that long," I answered.

She sighed as though *I* was getting on *her* nerves and asked, "Do you know where it is, Nikai?"

"Yeah, but what's *your* problem?"

"*You* not knowing how to follow directions. Now, I need you over there in thirty minutes or less. James is leaving town today and I want to see him off at the airport."

"All right, we'll be there."

"We? Who is we?"

"Oh. My friend Kim. We're going shopping after I'm done with the seamstress."

"You know I don't want anybody else seeing my dresses *or*

material before the wedding! I had this stuff shipped in from Italy, and *nobody* is gonna steal my ideas! Put Mama on the phone!" she cried.

I called Mama back into the kitchen and whispered to her that Kim and I were about to go and meet Taylor at the seamstress's. She nodded and took the receiver from me. I walked into the family room, where Lucky had Kim watching an old black-and-white flick.

"You ready?" I asked her.

"Yeah."

"Well, we're about to go," I told Lucky as I grabbed my purse off of the couch.

He didn't turn around, didn't speak, and didn't even nod his head. Just raised his hand and wiggled his fingers. Kim and I got the message, though.

"Let's stop and get a drink," Kim suggested as we got into my car.

"A drink? I have to meet my sister in less than thirty minutes."

"I didn't say get *drunk*. I said get a drink. How far do we have to go to meet her?"

"Chambers and West Florissant."

"Oh, girl," she said, going for her wallet. "You know we can be over there in fifteen minutes. Pull into that liquor store. I'm buying. What do you want?"

I pulled up in the store's parking lot and cut my engine.

"I'll take whatever you're getting," I said. "And hurry up."

Kim danced into the liquor store like she was cashing in the winning lotto ticket. She drank, but not very often. Her personality was so strong that she didn't have to be under the influence of anything to leave a lasting impression on people. Whether she was inebriated or not, those she encountered never forgot the first time they laid eyes on Kimberly Hayes.

I remember the first time I met her. Robert had taken me home to meet his family. It was the summer of '98. It was extremely hot that summer and Robert had gotten three shades darker than pitch-black. He warned me that his father was deceased, his mother was ready for grandchildren, and his younger sister, who happened to be the spitting image of him, only in a petite and feminine sense, was rather impulsive. And also that if I pretended to be shy, the evening would fly by smoothly.

When Robert pulled up in front of his mother's house, Kim was standing outside, next to a car with a man and a woman seated inside. She dangled keys in front of the window and then stood there with her hands on her hips, as though she was waiting for something to happen.

"Do you have all of my money, Kevin?" she asked, tossing her long jet black hair over her shoulder.

The guy inside the car was leaning forward on the steering wheel and his friend had her eyes on Kim. Stared as though you couldn't have *paid* her to look elsewhere. Kim walked around to the passenger side of the car, bent over, and tapped on the window.

"Girlfriend, did he tell you that we were together last Friday?"

The sista in the car looked at the driver, then back at Kim. Cracked the window enough so that only words could get through.

"That's okay, we just met on Saturday," she answered in a timid tone.

Kim's eyes began to twitch the way they always did when she got mad.

"Honey, could you roll your window down just a little bit more, please?" she asked in a June Cleaver voice.

The skinny, light-skinned sista glanced apprehensively at the driver, who was still resting his forehead on the steering wheel, and then slowly rolled the window halfway down. The next thing I knew, Kim was airborne and that terrified brotha looked up as though death were on its way.

"Kevin, you don't even know this bitch and you're bringin' her to my house?"

Kim had half of her body inside of the car and across that poor girl's lap when Robert ran over and pulled her by the feet. Gave the brotha his car keys back in exchange for his word that he would deliver whatever money he owed Kim by the following day. She kicked and screamed as if she were possessed by the devil. I stood on the porch, feeling nothing short of amused. I thought it was all sort of funny. It was like one of those stories that you always hear about but are never lucky enough to witness. I could tell from that incident that she had spunk. She had the kinda drive that you don't find in very many people. Not many who aren't under the influence of a controlled or uncontrolled substance.

Kim came out of the liquor store carrying a large brown paper bag and sporting a smile as wide as the bumper. Jumped in the car and then waved a bottle of brandy in my face.

"I didn't take too long, did I?" she asked.

"Would it make a difference if you had?" I answered sarcastically.

"Shut up and drive. You're startin' to sound like Rob. Always got jokes."

On the way to the seamstress's, Kim made herself a drink and gave me a couple of sips of her brandy and Coke. Heavy on the brandy. She pushed my *One Day It'll All Make Sense* tape in and rolled the window down. Danced around in the seat like it was her last chance to qualify for Soul Train.

I pulled up in front of the little dress shop and spotted Taylor's champagne Q45 Infiniti parked nearest to the front door.

I turned to Kim and asked, "Hey, you wanna calm down before we get in there?"

She stopped dancing and looked at me like I had broken up a one-woman party.

"*I'm* waiting on *you*," she said, and opened her door to get out.

Taylor met us at the glass front door in a mauve short-sleeved business suit, her curled hair falling heavily over her right shoulder. She looked at me and then cut her eyes at Kim. Turned away from us and began talking to the seamstress, a quiet elderly woman who looked like she was in her mid-seventies.

"Emma, could you size her up quickly?" she said, pointing to me. "They're in a hurry."

I walked over to the woman, who didn't appear to have any intentions of getting up, and lifted my arms. As she wrapped a tape measure around my breasts, I glanced over in time to catch Kim introducing herself to Taylor.

"Hello, I'm Nikai's friend Kim," she said, extending her hand.

Taylor pulled a smile from deep down inside and responded, "Hi, I'm her sister, Taylor. Are you Robert's sister?"

"Yeah. That's how we met. What colors are your wedding gonna be?"

Taylor looked at me, rolled her eyes, and mumbled, "Pink and silver."

"Sounds pretty. You have a lot of bridesmaids?"

"Eight. But I guess that could be considered a lot."

"Well, it's *your* day. You should make it unforgettable. What do the dresses look like?"

"Um, they're still being made," I interjected.

Emma finally opened her big mouth and blabbed that she had a copy of one in the back of the store. Taylor's eyes got bloodshot as she folded her arms across her chest and damn near cussed Emma out.

"I said they don't have time for that! Now get finished, Emma, or I'll find someone else to do the job!"

The room got so quiet, you could've heard a rat pissin' on cotton. Kim looked at me and I looked at my big sister. Didn't need to look at Emma to know that her feelings were hurt, because her hands began to tremble as she continued to size my butt up.

"Taylor, I think you owe Emma an apology," I suggested.

"And I think you owe *me* an apology for bringing your *drunk* friend in here, thinking I wouldn't smell the alcohol on her breath! This is my *wedding* we're preparing for, not some *backyard barbecue!* What did you do, stop at the liquor store for a forty?"

At that moment, things began to move in slow motion. Or maybe it was because it didn't seem like I could move fast enough.

Kim yelled, "Bitch, it wasn't a forty! Try a fifth of brandy, and I ain't Emma. I'll—"

My older sister backed up against a wall of dresses and screamed like she didn't quite know what Kim would do. Probably because she didn't. And the scary part was that I didn't, either.

"Kim, leave her alone," I said.

"Did you hear what she just said to me?"

"Yeah, but leave her alone. She's pregnant!" I warned.

Taylor looked at me and immediately brought to mind the fact that I wasn't supposed to know that information.

"Who told you that?" she screamed.

"What difference does it make? *You* should have told me; you're my sister."

"But that has nothing to do with you! It has nothing to do with any of you!" she said, pointing at us all.

Then Kim said, "Well, personally, I don't give a shit."

I nudged Kim and moved closer to Taylor.

"Mama told me, Taylor."

Her eyes narrowed and her nostrils flared. She exhaled so heavily that I could clearly see her chest rising and falling. Taylor clinched her fist and then pounded it on the wooden measurement table.

"So you think you're special, huh? You think you know something now, huh? Well, if you're so close to Mama, why didn't she tell you about the lump in her breast? Where was *sorry-ass Nikki* when she needed somebody to go to the doctor with her? Where were you then, since you're so *fuckin' special?*" Taylor asked.

She had moved within inches of me. Made me wanna knock the wind out of my own sister. Not because of what she'd said, but because of the way she had said it. My mama was sick, hurting, and never told me.

"I've spent more damn time with Mama than you ever will!"

"Well, I guess you would, messin' with the kind of men you choose! You don't have much choice but to move back home every weekend!"

The only thing that prevented me from completing what

looked to be Kim's contemplation of a violent swan dive across that sewing room at Taylor were the forty common pins that Emma had lined up and down my back. That was bound to be a painful experience, even if Taylor never laid hands on me. As for Kim, her only prevention was a little thing called *probation*.

"Don't even waste your time with that dress Emma, because she's *out* of my wedding!"

After hearing that I was no longer a member of the wedding party, shock was what caused me to freeze in place. I couldn't believe how irrational Taylor had become over a wedding, or a man, or a pregnancy, or whatever it was that was causing her to turn into a woman I didn't even know.

I guess I realized then how betrayed Taylor must have felt. She had confided in Mama and Mama had broken that vow of silence. But Mama's situation was different, life-threatening. Taylor's would eventually bring joy. Something she apparently hadn't had much of lately, yet feared that those around her would obtain before her. And in a sick, twisted way, it occurred to me that sharing Mama's illness was not an action of concern, but one of revenge. Revenge for telling *me* something so near and dear to her. Taylor's facial expression clearly illustrated that she despised Mama for that. That there was more to this pregnancy and possibly this wedding that no one but Taylor knew about. And now she was out to hurt Mama, be it in sickness or in health.

Robert

Don and I were on our way back from the Anheuser-Busch tour. We usually went twice a month. I would meet him over at his place and we'd ride together. Reminiscing about a hard week's work, venting any frustrations, and confiding in each other the private thoughts we had about the engine house, our significant others, and our future endeavors. And we both agreed that a brewery was the perfect place to start the day. We made friends in the factory, learned a little bit more about how things worked, and, more importantly, got free beer at the end of each tour.

"Do you believe how Keates was actin' on that last run?" Don asked.

"It's one thing to put *your* life on the line unnecessarily, but to do it to other people is totally different."

"He thinks every run will make the front page if he's pictured carrying somebody out of a burning building. That shit is sick."

"I know. But I'm willin' to take a chance on gettin' suspended rather than fuck around with him."

"Man, I don't know if I could afford that, what with all of the problems that we've been having at the lounge in Chicago. Every day, there's something new. I've been thinking about pulling out of it. Just doesn't seem lucrative anymore. Plus, I'm thinking about popping the question to Theresa."

I looked at him in total disbelief. Waited for him to turn around and tell me that he was only joking, but he didn't. Just stared straight ahead and then mumbled some shit about shopping for a ring.

"What the hell is this, the year of the bride and groom?" I asked.

He shook his head at me as if to disregard my comment totally.

"If anybody needs to follow my lead, it's you."

"Oh, I've got mine together," I said defensively.

I gripped the top of the steering wheel and stared at the highway. Didn't want Don to think that he could convince me that I was doing otherwise.

He laughed, saying, "You've got yours together, huh? You're starting a family and *forgot* to tell your *woman,* who happens to be living with you. Oh yeah, as a matter of fact, maybe I *should* follow your lead. You seem to have it all figured out. You've got the excitement of a maniac on one hand, and a woman seeking love somewhere—"

"What?" I yelled.

Don's smile immediately turned upside down as I pulled the car over to the shoulder of the road. I shifted into park and turned to my best buddy, who was nervously grinding his fist into the palm of his hand.

"What did you just say?" I asked again.

Don was quiet and then began the fakest laugh I had ever heard coming from his mouth.

"Don, don't bullshit me about something like this! What did you say about Nik?"

He batted his eyes and rubbed his forehead, like eczema ran in his family.

"I was just sayin' that I had a talk with Nik and she's hurtin'. She says that's why she's been buryin' herself in her music. She loves it, but it bothers her that she has to seek love in music instead of with her man. That's all."

I lost the tension in my shoulders and faced forward again. Thought about what Don had said and the sadness of the fact that he had to tell me.

"Man, sometimes it's hard to face her," I said, gripping the steering wheel with both hands again and yanking at it. "I know what I've done to her isn't right. And it's like I don't even have a chance to correct the shit before she finds out. Don, I truly love Nik with all of my heart."

"When are you gonna tell her?"

"When I *absolutely have to.*"

"She wants to see you tonight. She's performin' with that group she's in. She asked me to make sure you're there."

"I don't even know that I have any business representing her," I said.

"But you're not makin' her look bad, if she doesn't know yet."

"Yeah, but *I* know. And *Karen* knows."

"How do you know that Karen's really gonna have it?"

"I don't. I mean, she said she wanted it, but now I'm not quite sure it's mine."

"What?"

"Yeah. The other day, I was over there—"

"Big mistake," Don said, interrupting me.

"I know, I know. But I needed to see where her head was."

"Yeah, and see where you could put yours!" Don scolded.

"That wasn't the plan. It just worked out that way. She's real aggressive. I just wish you knew."

I leaned back against the headrest and thought about the times when she was outside watching my apartment or calling when she knew Nik was home. Demanding to see me and even acting a goddamn fool at her own place of business. And then the fact that she apparently had the same irritating effect on other men, too.

"This brotha came over with a kid, asking for money. And it just so happens that the kid was hers."

"What?"

"Yeah. She has a kid already, but not custody of him."

"And what do you expect of her for this one?"

"But see, that's the point. The time before that, when I hit it, I noticed some shit in her bathroom."

"What?"

"She had pregnancy tests before she even had reason to believe that she was pregnant."

Don got quiet again and started rubbing his chin.

"And that's not the most confusing part. The tests were still there after she confirmed the very suspicions that should have caused her to get the tests in the first place."

Don looked at me and asked, "What the hell did you just say?"

"Man, I think that broad was pregnant long before I came along and hit it."

Don laughed and banged on the dashboard with his fist.

"And what makes you think somebody sees you as a model parent? I mean, why *you* and nobody else?"

I checked my rearview mirror and pulled off into traffic.

"I don't know. But what I do know is that Karen's still playing games. And with all of the time and effort she's putting into this, she obviously sees something to gain. I've just gotta find out what it is."

Nikai

"Hey, Mama, it's me. I was calling because I needed to talk to you about something. I just left Taylor at the dress shop and I dropped Kim off. And uh . . . You know I've got a show tonight, so I'm over at the loft with the girls. Mama . . . I need to, uh, talk to you as soon as possible. Love you with all of my heart. Bye."

It was 6:45 P.M. I'd tried calling my mother's house but only got the answering machine, so I left a message and then finished getting dressed. Well, to be more specific, I allowed Maurie and Janae to dress me. I was so upset after hearing about my mama having a lump in her breast that I couldn't shop. So I called the girls and attempted to bow out of the performance that night, but they insisted that I come over immediately. Said they would pull something together and that I would look fine, and that after performing, I'd probably feel better. I didn't really see the possibility of that happening, but I dropped Kim off and rushed right over.

Janae pulled my permed hair up into a ponytail on top of my head. Pinned down what was mine and gelled it so good that it didn't look as relaxed. She took half of a bag of Afro Curl weave and wrapped it around the knot in the top. Teased the weave good, until it napped up and laid heavily to each side. Then she sprayed some luminating shine to make it look natural, and I was ready to go from the neck up.

Maurie gave me one of her brown baby doll–style dresses and copper jewelry to match. She even handed me brown high-heeled sandals that laced up around the ankle to complete the outfit.

I stood in the bathroom, yelling from the other side of the door.

"Y'all ready?"

"Yeah, girl," Maurie and Janae said in unison. "C'mon out."

But when I stepped out of the bathroom, all I could focus on was Kalif. And it appeared that I had the same effect on him. He was standing next to the girls in absolute awe. Looked me over from the coily weave on my head to the shiny brown nail polish on my toes.

"You wanna close your mouth and stop slobbering on my shoulder?" Maurie asked him.

He laughed at her suggestion and then, without speaking a word, walked over to me. Smiled broadly when he noticed his anklet still decorating my leg.

"Sista, *you are beautiful!*" he said, emphasizing each word.

I blushed and responded, "Thank you, brotha."

"Well, I hate to be the one to stop you two from running toward each other in slow motion, but we've got a performance to give. Can we leave now?" Maurie asked.

She and Janae were both in black baby doll–style dresses, with their braids tied up in a black wrap. They accented it all with cowrie shells in their hair and as accessories. For a moment, they reminded me of Sheila. They were free to make their own choices, and in that sense, we were different.

We had agreed to sing a song we'd written two weeks before that allowed me to do the lead vocals, since my look called for me to remain in between them at all times. Everybody piled into Ahmad's Explorer and headed to the University City area. Kalif made sure that he rode next to me. It all made me feel as though he was trying to put claims on a woman who was already spoken for, a woman who was preparing to make things right with her man.

A loudmouthed DJ had the crowd amped and ready for a live performance, one that I wasn't so sure I could give. The girls and I prayed before going on, but I couldn't remove my problems from my mind, not even for the fifteen minutes that it would take to bring down the house.

"And finally what you've all been waiting for, N-Sight."

We held hands and approached the stage. Took our separate mikes and dropped our heads as the drummer counted us in with three rim shots. I stood slightly ahead of them and gave a private prayer of my own for Mama *and* our relationship, as well as for the one with Robert and Taylor.

Maurie and Janae started with their background vocals as I grabbed the mike and gave the audience everything that I had. I closed my eyes in hopes that I would travel someplace else—a place where babies are born to people who deserve them, a place where Uncle Lucky would be strong enough to leave the house, where fathers never died, mothers were invincible, and sisters showed one another love.

I opened my eyes to a smoke-filled room and thought about Robert. Searched throughout the audience to see if he'd made it. I wanted to make up for not singing to him in the shower the way that I used to. I had stopped rubbing his head at night and singing him to sleep, too. But that night, he could hear how I felt, because the song I was singing was for him. For all of the times that I walked out when I should have stayed and talked it out. For all the times that I gave up on us.

I belted out notes that earned applause even before I was done. And I made the girls proud; I made myself proud. But not Robert, because I still hadn't spotted him out there yet. The audience gave us a standing ovation, which made it difficult to see any farther than the first three rows, but my heart felt something that I didn't actually need to see. It felt emptiness, like the seat Robert should have occupied.

I put on a face for the crowd as we exited at the left side of the stage, but I didn't absorb much. No one was saying what I wanted to hear—that Rob was waiting for me at the entrance of the club or that he had tried his best but was caught up with a four-alarm blaze. Anything would have been better than the obvious, because the truth is always painful. I guess that's why most of us lie to ourselves so often. Take our daily dosage of fan-

tasy and act oblivious until the sun goes down, only to have to
face it all again the next day.

My father used to tell me, "When you're in a bad situation,
you'll do whatever it takes to get out of it. And if you don't, it's
simply because you haven't had enough." Maybe I hadn't had
enough of Robert; maybe I thought that if I pretended things
were good between us, they eventually would be. And maybe,
just maybe, I was OD'ing on fantasy.

Maurie, Janae, and Ahmad surrounded me as Kalif stood
back calmly.

"Girl, we did it! They loved us! Can you believe this?" they
screamed.

I remained silent during the group hug. Stood emotionless
as the girls went on crying like *Cooley High* was on. I looked
across the club one last time and sighed with disappointment.

"You lookin' for somebody?" Kalif asked.

"No, not anymore."

"Is something bothering you?"

Kalif and I were back at the loft, alone. I grabbed one of the
large pillows on the floor and stretched out on it.

"Don't ask questions that you already know the answer to!"
I snapped.

Kalif raised his hands and sort of laughed.

"You want anything to drink?" he asked, kicking his boots off
and heading toward the kitchen.

"You have anything strong?"

"Like what?"

"I don't know. Something to take the pain away."

"I've got just the thing for that."

He smiled and grabbed a cigar off a nearby counter. Dragged
his feet as he strolled across the room, picking up lint and whatever else with his lengthy pant legs. Kalif sat down on the couch
in front of the wooden coffee table, scooted his butt toward the
edge, and set a place for himself.

"So he didn't show up tonight, huh?"

I rolled onto my stomach and answered, "No."

"How do you feel about that?"

"What are you, a doctor now?"

He shrugged his shoulders and picked up a razor blade. Sliced the cigar in half and placed it back on the coffee table.

"Do you have to do that while I'm here?" I asked.

He stopped and looked at me as though I had destroyed a yearlong plan.

"You wanna light some of those candles over there?"

"Do *you* wanna put that away until I leave?"

He laughed and, without even glancing at me, said, "We don't know exactly how long that will be."

I ignored him, got up, and lighted six candles before turning the lights out.

"You have any incense?" I asked.

"Over in that basket," he said, pointing to the corner where many of his plants were stationed.

"You know the crowd was feelin' you tonight. They loved y'all. See, people get tired of that commercial shit. They wanna learn, wanna wake up. Nikai, somebody was in the audience watching you all night."

I smiled and retreated back to my place in the middle of the living room. Thought about how the crowd made me feel. The way that we were accepted. And how I wished Rob had been there to see it—see people demand to hear more from me and *not* want to see me go.

"Who?" I asked.

"A record executive. He's local, but he has some serious connections. He wants to sign you."

"Me?" I asked, sitting up straight.

"Just you. I told the girls already, and they're happy for you."

"Are you sure? Because I don't think they like me."

"Trust me, they like you. They just want *you* to like you."

Kalif finally filled the cigar with its inappropriate contents and then lighted it. Took a long drag, then leaned back on the couch and stared at the ceiling.

"Success won't take long. You just have to pray." Then he looked at me and asked, "You pray, Nikai?"

"Sometimes."

"Why just sometimes?"

"I usually pray when I don't know what to do about a problem or when I'm visiting my father."

Kalif fell silent again and stared at whatever it was on his ceiling that kept calling his attention.

"What kind of problems do you have?"

I sat up and looked at him. Wondered if talking to him was what he had planned all along. Letting my guard down was a sure way for Kalif to get uncomfortably close, in more ways than one.

"Nothing, nothing that really matters."

"To who?"

"To you."

"You think that I would volunteer to listen to something that I really didn't want to hear? If it's bothering you, it must be important. Is it the brotha you live with?"

"I don't live with anybody!"

Kalif finally looked at me and put his cigar out.

Then he calmly asked, "Do you talk to him the way that you talk to me?"

"Sorry, but we live *together*. I have just as many bills in my name as he has in his."

I got up from the floor and sat down next to Kalif on the couch. Grabbed a throw pillow and held it close to my chest.

"Nothing that you tell me now will be more embarrassing than him not showing up tonight."

"Do you have to be so insensitive, or is it the *drugs*?"

"No, actually, it's the truth. And you don't wanna hear it. You think that you are the only person in the world with relationship problems?"

He'd never mentioned having a relationship or problems. And where was this mystery woman while I was relaxing in a candlelit room with her man?

Kalif took the rubber band off of his dreads and shook his head as though it were his first taste of freedom.

"You know how to braid hair?" he asked.

"Yeah, but I've never braided locks before."

"You think you can do mine?"

"I can try."

He pushed the coffee table back and sat on the floor between my legs. Made me want to ask for a pair of shorts or even tell him that I had changed my mind. I hadn't had a man that close to my womanhood in months, and it almost seemed unfair to let Kalif beat Rob to the punch.

He rested his elbows on my thighs and asked, "So what happened to your father?"

"Lung cancer."

"How long ago?"

"Too long."

"You ever dream about him?"

"No. Why?"

"Because I dream about my mom sometimes. I see her so clearly. It's almost as if she's still here."

"What happened to her?"

"Suicide."

I felt my legs stiffen and, apparently, so did he.

"You all right?" he asked.

"Yeah. How did she take her life? I mean, if you don't mind talking about it."

"She took a bunch of sleeping pills one night and left me in this world alone."

As I took more of his hair between my fingers, a million questions ran through my head: How often had he visited her? Had he taken her presence for granted, the way I had with Daddy? Where was his father? And did he think that maybe his mother had gone to hell?

"Kalif?"

"Whassup?"

"Have you ever heard that when you kill yourself, your soul doesn't go to heaven?"

"Where else would it go?"

"I don't know. I heard that it would go to hell."

"I believe that we are already living in hell, right here on earth. There's no place to go but up."

"That sounds like something *you* would say."

"It's the truth. But let's talk about you and your husband."

I gave him a good squeeze with my legs and said, "I told you, I'm not married."

"Oh, that's right. So he wouldn't mind if I did this."

Kalif pushed my dress back and kissed the inside of my thigh. Sent chills up and down my spine and scared me. Not because it felt so good but because it felt so right. I let out a soft moan and had to remind myself that this was possibly someone else's man. I placed the palm of my hand on his forehead and moved his face back.

"Did you say that you were in a relationship?"

"No. Did you ask?"

I sighed and attempted to close my legs, when he grabbed my foot. Massaged my toes in those laced-up sandals as he talked.

"Listen, I'm seeing someone."

I snatched my foot away and asked, "So why isn't she ever here?"

Kalif grabbed his cigar out of the ashtray and glanced at me out of the corner of his eye, "She's here now."

I blushed and looked around the room.

"Where? I don't see her."

"Ah, you got jokes tonight." He laughed. "C'mon, I wanna show you something."

Kalif stood in front of me with his arms extended. I looked into his now-mellow face and then down at his rough hands, which were inviting my touch.

"Okay, but bring some lotion."

I rose to my feet and lost my balance in Maurie's heels, which I was still wearing. Twisted my ankle and damned the shoes.

"You can take those off when we get where we're going," he informed me.

"And where are we going?"

"Physically or spiritually?"

I started to say "Both" but then paused for a second. Was intrigued by the idea of doing the latter.

"Spiritually."

"Spiritually, anywhere you want to be. Physically, on the roof."

He turned and disappeared into the bathroom. Fumbled around in the linen closet for a minute and then returned with a bottle of cocoa butter lotion. We headed toward what could be considered an ancient elevator and slowly rode to the top floor. Kalif on one side, controlling the lever, me on the other, hoping he wouldn't try to touch me the way he had downstairs, hoping that I wouldn't let him.

The elevator stopped on the top floor. Made me lose my balance again for a minute. Kalif pushed the wooden cage up and stepped out into a long corridor. Turned left a couple of times and then right. Walked through another open loft, which appeared to be under construction, and then out onto the roof.

The night sky was beautiful—the shade of navy blue, with a hint of purple. The stars looked like confetti that had been tossed into the air during a celebration of life and maybe even creation, too.

It was warm outside, with a very slight breeze. Just enough to cause Kalif's now-braided dreadlocks to swing back and forth. He had two dark green lawn chairs stationed a couple of feet from the edge of the building. A crate rested between the two, balancing plant life. In fact, there was plant life for as far as I could see. Apparently, everyone in this neighborhood frequented their rooftops, and for some reason, his participation in this ritual made Kalif seem more approachable, normal, or just closer to the regular world. My world.

I sat down in the chair on the right and crossed my legs.

"You want me to undo your laces?" he asked.

I blushed and extended my ankle. Noticed that his lotioned skin looked so much better under the night sky. His nails were immaculately clean. Beside the scent of myrrh blowing off of him, I caught a whiff of fabric softener from his clothing. It all made me second-guess what I perceived brothas like Kalif to be. His hair was supposed to be unsanitary and infested. His body was supposed to reek of week-old funk. And his clothing was undoubtedly supposed to be nothing short of filthy. But I found my prejudgments to be totally incorrect. To be honest, he looked a lot better than most of the guys in the club that night. But it could have been the fact that I was turned on by him al-

ready, combined with disappointment in Rob, worry over
Mama, and the rum and cola that I'd drunk before going on-
stage.

I turned to Kalif and asked, "How long have you been growing your dreadlocks?"

"You mean my locks?"

He stared straight ahead, the way that Uncle Lucky did when
he was zoning.

"They're labeled as 'dreads' or 'dreadful' by those who *fear*
them, those who cannot *achieve* them. Some brothas and sistas
like that shit, but it's a stigma as negative as the word *nigger.* We
didn't give *ourselves* either name. There's nothing *dreadful*
about my hair."

"Oh."

I sank in my seat and tried to find that star he was focusing
on. But I couldn't help but wonder what he was thinking about
me, my relationship, and my stupid comments, as well.

Kalif turned to me and asked, "You ever thought about letting your hair lock up?"

"Yeah. I've thought about it."

"And?"

"And I don't know if I'm in a position to do that right now."

"Do what? What you want to do?"

I gave a nervous laugh. Shifted in my seat and hoped that
maybe he would grin and then agree to let it go. But his expression didn't change.

"So you're saying that you aren't in a position to do what
you *want* to do?"

As he sat forward in his seat, the look on his face quickly
changed, but to one that conveyed a disturbance. Like my ignorance was throwing off the peace that he had come up to the
rooftop to find.

"I'm saying that in my world, it's not acceptable."

Kalif was silent as he leaned into the back of his chair.

"You comfortable in your world?" he asked.

"None of us can ever be totally comfortable, no matter
where we are."

"You really believe that?"

I didn't answer. Basically, because I did believe that, but I knew that Kalif would come up with some philosophical way of saying that I had my head stuck up my ass.

"I can see you believing that, because a lot of people do. It's part of what separates us all."

"What do you mean?"

"Your reality is not my reality and vice versa."

I folded my arms across my chest and sighed heavily.

"And what *is* my reality?"

"Living life as though you have absolutely no idea what's coming next. Waiting for the right time instead of making the time right. Pleasing everyone but yourself. Probably because you don't know what it would take to please you."

"Well, I *do* know that kisses on my thighs don't!"

He laughed and looked over at me.

"That depends on who's doing the kissing."

"No one but Rob *should be*."

"So why was I?"

"Because you obviously have a hard time respecting other people."

"Maybe it's that you don't respect yourself."

My mouth fell open as I rolled my eyes in embarrassment. Ashamed that I had lost my ability to reason, all because of a pair of full, wet lips between my legs. Outdone by the nerve he had telling me this, telling me the truth.

"Close your mouth. You're not the only one out here doing it, but the difference between you and them is that you care. You just don't know where to draw the line with people. For example, the situation with the brotha never showing up tonight."

"What about it?"

"What do you plan to do about it?"

"Why?"

"Because I wanna know."

"But why? Does it have anything to do with you?"

"No. But that's only because I don't allow things like that to happen to me."

I looked back off into the night sky. Searched for some kind of transitional phrase, some way of getting off of the topic of my pitiful relationship.

"Come up with any new tracks lately?"

Kalif laughed.

"No. Have you?"

I turned my mouth up in annoyance.

"Why do you always have to talk in circles?"

"Is that what you think I do?"

"It's almost as if you try to trick people into answering their own questions."

"What makes you think that I talk to everyone else the same way that I talk to you?"

"Then why with me?"

"Because I believe in you. I see something in you that you don't, something that most people don't."

I blushed and looked out across the skyline.

"And what's that?"

"Potential to be free."

I waited for him to elaborate.

Then I asked, "Free from what?"

"Whatever it is that's keeping you from being in the position to do what you want to do."

"I thought freedom came along with living in this country." I laughed.

"It does, but your mind isn't free. Free to make choices."

"I chose to be here tonight."

"It's not that you didn't think you had anything to lose. Can you honestly sit here and tell me that the thought of him wondering where you are hasn't crossed your mind?"

"Actually, it hasn't."

"Then maybe I'm wrong about you; maybe I was wrong about everything. I have no problem admitting error."

We both fell silent on that rooftop. Changed the subject to the stars and the moon. Got deep. Or at least he did. I was too busy doing just what he'd accused me of, thinking about Robert. Wondering if he was worrying about me being out at two o'clock in the morning with a bunch of people I hardly knew. Wondering if maybe my absence had sparked at least an ounce of jealousy in his heart. Just enough to shape up before the right time came for me to ship out.

But that wasn't the only truth unfolded that night; I wasn't free. I was actually being held captive. By my world. You remember, the one with all of the confusion in it. It seemed strange how someone like Kalif, with a lot fewer worldly concerns, could find peace and serenity so easily. While those of us trudging to the office every day, keeping up with what the most popular magazines say we should wear, finding debt around every corner to maintain what society says is standard, never take notice of the simple things that keep people like Kalif going. The sun, the stars, the moon, and the gifts of the earth. Knowledge of self, the energy in the universe, and the blessings from the Creator. Karma, the beauty within every one of us, and, most importantly, the courage to let that beauty show.

That night, Kalif was extending me an invitation. Into his world and out of mine. An invitation that required me to leave all of my negativity and preoccupations behind. An invitation I wasn't quite sure that I was ready to accept. It was the same invitation that Sheila had extended. The only difference was the packaging.

When I got in late that night, Rob was already in bed, either sleeping or doing a great impression of someone in a coma. I chalked it up as him not wanting to offer an explanation for not showing up for the performance. But he really didn't need to. Sheila once told me, "People do what they want to do and everything else simply falls by the wayside." Robert's behavior hurt me a lot, but I was tired. Tired of fighting and crying. Tired of trying to make sense of it all. Tired of falling by the wayside. Honestly, I was getting tired of Robert.

The next night, while Rob was asleep, I sat at the round table in our bedroom, which I had reserved for papers and folders, and wrote a letter to send to Saint Croix. I wanted to fill Sheila in on what was happening to me. How Taylor had snapped, how sexy Kalif was beginning to look, how I was about to get a record deal, and how I was holding on until the right time came for me to leave Robert.

So much had changed since the last time I had spoken to her, and as inappropriate as it seemed, I found myself comparing her to Kim. I wanted Sheila to meet the people I was beginning to spend so much time with. I wanted her opinion of the man who had moistened the seat of my pants the night before. But to be honest, I just wanted Sheila back.

After pouring my heart out, I signed my name and read the letter over one last time. As I was folding it, the phone rang and almost woke Robert. I rushed over to pick it up before he did.

"Hello?"

"Yeah, Nikki. Did you want to talk to me?" Mama asked.

"You feelin' okay?"

"Yeah, why do you ask that?"

I sighed heavily and sat down on my side of the bed. Held the phone between my shoulder and chin and climbed under the sheets next to Robert.

"Mama, Taylor mentioned the other day that you went to the doctor."

There was silence on her end.

I said, "Mama?"

"Yeah, I'm here."

"Is there anything that you want to tell me?"

"Nikki, it's nothing, really. I have a small malignant lump in my breast. The doctor told me that once it is treated, there will be nothing to worry about."

Robert turned over on his stomach, moved closer to me, and placed his arm across my waist. I winced.

"So why hadn't you told me about this? You took Taylor to the doctor with you and didn't even bother to call and let me know that something was wrong."

"Taylor just happened to be here that morning. I needed to go, and I wanted someone to go with me. That's all."

"I just don't like the idea of you keeping secrets from me. Listen, I know I've let you down before, but that was the past. Don't you trust me enough to share your health concerns with me?"

"I wasn't keeping a secret, Nikki. Look, it's late and I need to go to bed."

I said, "Taylor knows that you told me about her being pregnant."

"And how did she figure that out?" she asked brusquely.

"It accidentally slipped out when we were arguing. That's when she told me about the lump."

"How could you do this, Nikki? I didn't tell you that for you to throw it in your sister's face! You act as though your life is full of bliss, like you're unable to make mistakes. And then you have the nerve to wonder why she keeps things from you!"

I sat up straight in the bed, pulled the phone from my ear, and looked at it for a moment.

"Mama, I told you it was an accident."

"You accidentally lose your keys. You accidentally lock yourself out of the house, Nikki. But you don't accidentally tell someone you found out that she's pregnant!"

"I'm sorry. What do you want me to do?"

"I want you to let me go. It's late."

"Okay," I mumbled.

I gave Mama her wish and let her go. Only I had no idea how long she meant. In the days that followed, I called her, but I only got the answering machine. I didn't bother to leave a message, because it was obvious that she had no more to say to me than Taylor did.

It was beginning to seem like I didn't fit in over there anymore. Like I was an outsider making trouble for a family I wasn't even a part of. So I slowly began to drift away from them. Made no more attempts to contact either of them and soon learned that my presence wasn't missed at all. No one had a problem with me disappearing. No one even cared if *I* had fallen ill, had a lump on my *head*, or had gotten pregnant myself. Maybe because they didn't really care about each other.

An entire two weeks went by and then one day, out of the blue, Mama called me over to the house for a big dinner she was cooking because James was coming into town. I guess she wanted to show him the sort of meals he could look forward to from his fiancée. Poor guy still didn't know that Taylor could easily turn morning oatmeal into a lethal weapon.

I looked in my closet, threw on a black short-sleeved shirt and a tan skirt, along with a pair of black-and-tan heels. Oiled my hair and pulled a frightening amount of new growth back into a bun. Grabbed my black purse with Travis's money in it so I, the queen of procrastination, could stop by the grocery store after leaving my mama's house. Dinner was to be served at four o'clock, so I figured I could be out of there well before the customer service counter closed at eight.

When I pulled up out front, I realized that it wasn't a private family affair, but another attempt to showboat on Esther's part. She had friends over whom I hadn't seen since I had gotten my period. And I'm talkin' *at least* fifteen years. I spotted Lula Mae's car next to Mama's, sighed, and counted backward from ten. I had no intention of turnin' this dinner out, but if either of them mentioned that little briefcase-carrying munchkin man, it was gonna be on.

I walked in the door and noticed that Lucky was holding his ground. His recliner was still stationed in front of the television, even with five hens cackling all around him. I headed upstairs to the guest room and put my purse on the top shelf in the closet. It would've been too much work to try to keep an eye on it with all of those people walking in and out of the living room. As I pulled the door closed and headed downstairs, I could hear the guest of honor arriving.

My mother announced, "Ladies, this is Taylor's handsome husband-to-be, James."

The room filled with the most annoying feminine greetings I had ever heard. I made it downstairs in time to see them all getting the back of their hands kissed. Then watched them fan their faces as though there were a snowball's chance in hell that he could've meant that.

Taylor stood back in a white short-sleeved shirt, a pair of pecan-colored drawstring linen pants, and matching pecan brown heels, watching the normal swooning over a man who truly looked too good to be true. James wore a pair of black linen slacks and a tan shirt that looked like it was made for him and him only. Looked like he had just stepped off one of the pages of *GQ.* And smelled like the men's fragrance section of a department store. He had the kind of flawless smile that demanded attention from most, and obviously, attention was what he usually got.

Taylor asked in front of everyone, "Nikai, did you speak to James?"

See, that's how stuff usually got started. One of those smart-asses had to make a comment to impress the majority. I assumed she and Mama had played rock, paper, scissors for it while I was upstairs and Taylor must've won.

"I'm sorry. James, c'mere. Normally, you would've been over here giving me a nice *loonnnnggg* hug by now. How've you been?" I hugged him and gave his tush a good squeeze.

Taylor's gasp was likely to be heard all the way in Mexico. She rushed over and pulled James by the hand as I went and sat in a chair next to Lucky.

"You eatin' with them?" I asked.

"Not unless they all plan to get together and push this chair, with me in it, over to the table."

I laughed and said, "I wish I didn't have to."

"I wouldn't have come if I was you. I see how Esther treats you, and it ain't right. But just wait and see. Taylor will be the one to break her heart someday."

"You think so? Seems like she's done everything right all of these years."

"Yeah, it *seems* that way. But everything ain't always what it seems. Mark my word, she'll be the one to shock us all."

"Guess I'd better get on in there and make myself a plate. I figure the sooner I eat, the sooner I can leave."

Lucky patted me on the arm as I got up and said, "Slim, just remember God takes care of all babies and fools. And you ain't a baby no more."

I walked into the kitchen and joined the hen session. James had left the room while all of the ladies made an airtight circle around Taylor, asking her all of the questions that had anything to do with a wedding. She took her time answering and appeared to be loving it. Every question Taylor didn't jump on, Mama had sewn up. You would've thought that it was gonna be a double wedding, the way they were acting.

Then one of the ladies asked me, "So, Nikai, when are you gonna settle down and tie the knot with a nice young gentleman?"

Lula Mae said, "Some women don't know one when they see one."

"Well, if your son was actually *tall enough for me to see,* I probably would be able to tell whether or not he's a nice young gentleman."

She gave a loud huff and looked at my mother, who had jumped up from the table and was busying herself with the food.

"Esther, I think you should speak to your other daughter."

Mama said, "Nikki, I think you should apologize."

"For what? She threw the first punch."

I was starting to sound like a child. And I imagined that I was looking like one, too. At the very moment that I *wasn't* in the wrong, my mama didn't even defend me. Taylor was so busy telling the lady next to her about the wedding gown she had ordered that she didn't even notice what was going on. Not that she would've defended me anyway.

"Look, this dinner isn't supposed to be for me! Why are you all asking *me* questions? I've got a question for Taylor! Where is James?"

"Right here," he said, descending the stairs.

He was straightening his shirt and wiping sweat from his forehead. I found both to be rather strange, because his shirt wasn't a button-down, so it wasn't like the thing was gonna move, and since Mama and menopause had hooked up, she usually kept the central air up, as though she were entertaining Eskimos on a daily basis.

Taylor gave all of us an uneasy look and asked, "Sweetheart, you okay?"

"Yeah," he said, struggling to fake a laugh. "Just a little hungry. When are we gonna eat? I heard this cooking is the *best.*"

Mama blushed and set a plate of smothered chicken, green beans, mashed potatoes, and warm dinner rolls in front of James. His eyes lighted up as he dug in.

One of the ladies asked, "Not gonna wait for us, huh?"

"Oh, sure" he said, dropping his fork and wiping the corner of his mouth with a napkin. "Sorry about that."

Then Lula Mae said, "So, James, Taylor tells us that you will be moving back here when you return from the honeymoon in Cancún."

He looked at Taylor and pulled a half smile. "I see Taylor has been doing a lot of *talking*."

"Well, sweetheart," she explained, "they were asking, so I told them that we were thinking about it."

"No, you didn't, Taylor. You specifically said that y'all would be moving back here."

"Mama! Please. It's my wedding, my husband, my honeymoon, and my life. When we've decided, we'll let y'all know. Excuse me."

Taylor jumped up from the table and headed upstairs to the bathroom. I could hear her slam the door as the hens all went back to cackling. I sat there and waited for somebody to volunteer to comfort her, but they were more concerned with what Mama was serving for dessert. As for James, well, apparently he had become just as upset as Taylor, because as he sat right there in front of the food, his nose began to bleed. Consistently. Ironically, those hags were stumbling over one another to help *him*. So I assumed that the only right thing to do would be to go up and check on my big sis.

I knocked on the bathroom door and asked, "Taylor, you okay?"

"Go away, Nikki."

"I will once I know that you're okay."

"I'm fine, but I'm not coming outta here."

"So what do you expect everyone to do about the dinner?"

"I don't care. They can all go home with a doggy bag."

Shit, she didn't have to say it twice. All I needed was the go-ahead to leave and I was outta there. I walked into the guest room and opened the closet to get my purse. Put it over my shoulder and returned to the bathroom door.

"Taylor, are you sure you don't care if everyone leaves?"

"Nikki, I'm not coming out of this bathroom *until* everyone is gone."

"It's your call. I'm gone."

I took off down the stairs and made the announcement that Taylor would prefer that everyone go on home. I even lied for her and said she wasn't feeling well, that she was upstairs lying down, and that she only wanted to see James. That part was thrown in just to make Mama feel bad. A little payback for not defending me when it came to smart-ass Lula Mae.

I gave Lucky a kiss on the cheek, waved good-bye to everyone else, and made tracks. I was an entire hour early to the grocery store to get a money order for Travis. When I pulled into a space on the lot, I grabbed my purse to count the bills one more time so that the transaction would go as smoothly and quickly as the dinner.

I unzipped the inside pocket and found nothing. Nada. And I'm talkin' *nada goddamn* bill anywhere. I became frantic as I ripped that handbag to shreds. Even bent one of my nails back to the nail bed. Now I was more pissed 'cause I was in pain. Where could the money've gone? It had been there when I put the purse up. And everybody was downstairs except, except . . . James. Nah, it couldn't be. He had too much going for him. He made more in a week than Robert and I made together in a month. But who else could've touched it?

I ran to the pay phone in front of the grocery store and dialed Mama's house.

"Parker residence," Mama answered.

"Mama, go upstairs to the guest room and look on the floor in the closet. I think I dropped some money up there."

"Hold on."

She put the phone down and didn't return for at least two minutes. When she did, I could tell that she was talking to Taylor.

"Nikki? I didn't see any money up there. You sure that's where it fell?"

"Either there or in James's hands!"

"What? *What are you saying?*"

"Mama, I think James stole the money out of my purse!"

She put her mouth close to the phone and whispered, "Do

you know how stupid you sound? Why would he take money from you when he makes more than you ever have?"

"I don't know, but he did. And I'm gonna prove it!"

I slammed the phone down in her ear because I honestly couldn't figure out why somebody like James would take from me. I couldn't even say for sure that he'd done it, because I didn't pull any fingerprints, but something inside told me that that joker was up to no good—as far as Taylor was concerned *and* as far as my money was concerned. But in the meantime, I had to figure out how I was gonna duck and dodge Travis. And more importantly, how I was gonna come up with another five hundred dollars that *I* definitely didn't have.

That next morning when I arrived at work, I was tempted to unplug my phone. Didn't want to take any chances on getting a three-way call from the jail. How would I look trying to explain to a man with absolutely no freedom that I had lost his five hundred dollars, which I was supposed to have mailed off a month ago? I was lucky he hadn't sent whoever was watching me up to my job. I was willing to bet a dime to a dollar that Travis already knew about what I was going through and how I'd gotten so caught up that time hadn't permitted me to worry about him and his finances. But what was even uglier was that he probably didn't give a damn.

I called over to Mama's house to get James on the line, but he had caught a flight back to New York that morning. The sneaky bastard had probably used my money to fund the trip. The moment I asked Taylor, she started yelling in a pitch that was too high for me to understand, so I just hung up on her. I didn't have money to send Travis, so an eardrum replacement would really be living above my means.

I spent that day and many that followed gazing out of the window. And I don't mean a lost in thought, daydreaming sort of gaze. I was watching to make sure nobody was watching me. Looking for unusual employees. Even became skeptical of the usual UPS man. I was losing my mind waiting . . . and waiting . . . and waiting. Until one day I got that call that I hoped would never come.

"Nikai Parker speaking."

"Where's my money?"

"Huh?"

"Nikai, where is my money?" Travis asked.

"Travis, is this you?"

"Who else's cash are you toying with? I hope you and the fireman didn't spend my money."

"No. He doesn't know anything about that money. I kept that between you and me. Well, sort of."

"What do you mean, 'sort of'? Do you or don't you have it?"

"I don't have it right now, but I'm gonna get it. It was stolen from me, but I'll take it out of my next three checks."

"What makes you think I have that long? I've got needs, too."

"I know, Travis, but please just be patient with me."

"You've got until next month, Nikai. If you don't have my money, you'll find out who's been watching you. Next month, Nikai. Next month."

Part Three

Who's Lovin' Who?

Robert

It was early October and Kim was begging again. This time, it wasn't for twenty or thirty dollars; it was for room and board. She told me that Moms had thrown her out over money. Moms said that she wanted Kim to start helping on the bills as a way of learning responsibility. It was supposed to be a motivational tactic to make her independent, but all it managed to do was send a grown woman running into the arms of her big brother.

I was letting her use the extra bedroom until she got on her feet *or* on her knees to beg Moms to take her back, whichever happened first. She'd been staying with us for almost a month, and for Kim and Nik, it was like a nonstop slumber party. I'd slip her a twenty every now and then to keep Nik busy while I dealt with the lunatic who was possibly carrying my child. I never told Kim where I was going, because if I had, I might as well have told Nik.

But the day before, Kim had stepped to me before I left for the engine house and said that she needed to talk to me. Her hands were still in her pockets, so I assumed it wasn't about money. I told her to meet me back at the apartment around noon the next day, in hopes that maybe she wanted to say good-bye and thank me for letting her stay.

That afternoon, I was in the kitchen making a ham sandwich when she got there. I heard her drop her bags in the bedroom and immediately go to the bathroom. I was halfway done with my lunch when she joined me. She stood on the threshold with one hand high on the wall and the other on her hip.

"Big bro, now, you know I'm gonna get straight to the point."

I didn't look up at her, just continued with my lunch.

"Yesterday, after I got back from the cleaner's, there was a car parked outside."

"What kind of car?" I asked.

"Just listen. I don't remember what kind it was because that's not the point. But there was a woman in it who looked like she might have been five, maybe six months pregnant."

I dropped the sandwich and choked on a piece of bread that was left floating in my throat. I knew she was gonna say that Karen had been by there, knocking on the door, because Kim had dropped Nik off at work and had her car all day.

"You all right?" she asked.

"Yeah, I'm fine. Now, what happened?"

"Well, she said that she was looking for the leasing office because she wanted to rent a two-bedroom. But anyway, to make a long story short, she said that her two roommates just moved out on her last week and that she couldn't afford a three-bedroom apartment. Especially with her baby coming."

"I thought you said that you were making a long story *short*."

"I am, I am. Give me a chance. So I introduced myself and told her that my brother stayed in this complex and that I was tired of leeching off of you. Rob, you should have seen her face light up when I pointed up to this apartment. You would have sworn she knew you from a past lifetime or something. But anyway, we exchanged numbers and everything and I told her to call me so we could make arrangements for me to go over and look at the place. She's a real pretty sista. Looks like your type, but you're taken; *plus,* I know you don't do the *baby's daddy thing.*"

"Did she look mentally stable?" I asked.

"Don't most mentally disturbed people look stable? What kind of question is that? You ought to be happy that I'm trying to get out of your hair. And you can tell your evil, wicked mama that I'm moving in two weeks!"

"What do you mean, *two weeks?* You don't even know that

woman! And how do you even know that you'll like the apartment that she's staying in?"

"Listen, how many raggedy three-bedroom apartments have you seen out in West County? I'm trying to do the right thing! I'm not a kid anymore! It's like you and Mama don't even want me to be responsible!"

"We want you to be out on your own and responsible, too. But how responsible is it meeting some crazy woman in a parking lot and then moving in with her two weeks later? You need to think about that."

"Why do you keep calling her *crazy?*"

"Because, she's got to be just as crazy as you are to offer to let someone she met in a parking lot move into her apartment!"

"Fuck you, Rob! I didn't ask for your permission, I just wanted your opinion. I'll be out of your hair in two weeks. Until then, I'll do my best to stay out of your way."

Kim turned and stormed out of *my* kitchen like she had put in on the bills that month or something. It's funny how you have to see for yourself what others have already warned you about. Moms ran all of this down to me before Kim even had a key made, but I was so used to getting her butt out of binds, instinct kicked in. Had me doing the right thing for Kim before I could even figure out what the right thing really was.

The last thing I needed at that point was Karen gaining the favor of my family and friends. But I had to give it to her—that stunt she was pulling was definitely low. Far more clever than I had imagined her to be. But that was beside the point. I had to keep Kim out of that apartment, no matter what.

Nikai

Girl, yo' hair is bad as Jesse James totin' *two* pistols!"

Dorothy stood outside my office door, yelling like she was at a barnyard boogie. I shook my head and got back into my work. I wasn't in the mood for her comments or her negative energy.

"What in the hell did you do to your head?"

"I beg your pardon."

I finally looked up at her as she walked into my office *without* an invitation. She ran her hand over the back of her black skirt and took a seat without me even nodding in the direction of a chair. She tucked a number-two pencil behind her right ear and set the pile of folders that she was carrying down on my desk.

"I said, 'What in the hell did you do to your head'?"

"What are you talking about?"

I wanted to make her get ignorant with me so that I would have a reason to read her for once. I knew exactly what she was talking about. I had taken some extensions out of my hair the day before and paid my beautician one last visit to get the rest of the relaxed hair cut off. Washed it, doubled-strand-twisted it for a wavy effect, and let it go that morning. Then I put a cute brown headband on and teased it to give it a full look.

"Good morning, Dorothy."

"All of that pretty long hair you had . . ."

"How are you feeling today, Dorothy?"

"Has your mother seen this?"

"No, she hasn't. I thought I would let you do the honors of seeing it first."

"What were you thinking?" she asked, emphasizing each word with waves of her hand.

"The same thing you were when you got that French roll done to your hair."

Dorothy sat in the chair across from me and continued to shake her head. I looked down at the paperwork that I was working on before she came in and began twirling the ends of my hair around my index finger. I could hear her breathing becoming heavier and knew she was getting more upset. She was sounding extremely close to disgusted.

It seems my life was the only one left for her to offer her input about. It was almost as if she felt that when her daughter died, she'd been left all alone in this world, the same way Kalif felt after his mother died. Looking at it from that standpoint, I could understand why life sometimes seemed like an uphill battle. Always waiting for things to level off, for a moment to exhale and grasp a sense of accomplishment. But for some, there was no one to share victories with, no one to acknowledge their efforts, and no one to make them feel needed.

At first, I was certain that Dorothy wasn't in control of the rest of her life and that was why she tried so hard to control her dead daughter's, through me. But now I see that Dorothy truly *had* no other part of her life. The guy she'd been dating three months prior went back to an old girlfriend, and her cat, Ivory, ran away. Every time she got close to someone, she engulfed that person with concern, when there was hardly ever any needed. That person's life *was* her life. She knew nothing but to take care of other people, and, as sad as it seems, without other people with other problems, she felt that she was no one and might as well be dead, too.

"Oh my God! Oh my God! *Nikai!*"

Linda walked into my office and stood next to Dorothy, her mouth open, speechless. Tears filled her eyes and made me a bit concerned about exactly what it was that had surprised her. I glanced out of the window behind me to make sure there wasn't a meteorite coming toward my head and Dorothy just wasn't saying anything in hopes that it would blow my hairstyle to pieces.

"I can't believe you did it! C'mere, give me a hug."

She came around the side of my desk with her arms extended. I stood to give her a hug, and she insisted that I do a twirl so she could see my hair from every angle.

"Isn't she beautiful?" Linda asked Dorothy.

Dorothy's eyes narrowed as she scooted to the edge of the chair and waved her finger at both of us.

"What in the hell is *beautiful* about that? She looks like a fool. How are you gonna listen to Little Miss Lily White? I'm telling you, it looks *ridiculous!*"

"But Dorothy, this is Nikai's natural beauty. She's being herself."

Dorothy rose from her seat and came within inches of Linda's face.

"Don't you ever in your life call me Dorothy again. Am I not your elder?"

"Dorothy, she was just trying to make a point," I interjected.

Linda came two steps closer to me and looked at me as though I had said the magic word to get us both knocked out. Dorothy turned her neck as if a screw had come loose and the *Exorcist* spin were moments away.

"You're supposed to be so into your people, but you will stand here and let her speak to me this way!"

"If anybody said something out of line, it was you!" I yelled.

The blood in my right arm stopped circulating, so I tugged at it to try to get Linda to loosen her grip. The phone rang and sliced through some of the tension in the room. I attempted to answer it but soon realized that with every step I was gonna be pulling 125 more pounds with me.

I tapped Linda on the hand and said, "I need to get my phone."

She let go but remained within inches of me.

"Nikai Parker.

"Whassup witcha?" Kim asked.

"I'm kinda in the middle of something right now. Can you call me back?"

"Wait. First, I wanna tell you something."

"I'm in a hurry right now," I said, stretching across my desk.

"It's about an apartment that I'm gonna be moving into," she sang.

"That's great. Can you leave a message on my voice mail?"

"You *and* Robert can both go to hell!"

"All right, thank you, Ms. Hayes. I'll speak with you later."

By the time I had hung the phone up, Dorothy was gone. Disappeared without saying another word, at least not to me.

"You okay?" I asked Linda.

"Yeah, I'm fine. I just don't know what's gotten into Dorothy. She's usually so nice."

"Don't worry about her," I said, fanning my hand. "Dorothy has got a lot of issues that she isn't addressing."

"I hope she isn't mad at me."

"Well, I wouldn't worry about that. There's always gonna be somebody in this world who doesn't like you for some reason. And then there will be the ones who don't like you for no reason. Now, I don't know about you, but I've got better things to think about."

"I guess you're right. But I still say your hair is beautiful, even if Dorothy disagrees. It actually looks better this way. It's you. You're a black woman. I can't see why you wouldn't want to look this way."

"Thank you. It took a lot to get to this point, and you just saw why."

"I know. Well, I've got to get back to work. See ya later, and remember, I love the hair."

Linda left my office looking as though she wished she hadn't said anything at all. Maybe Dorothy thought Linda was being sarcastic, or maybe Dorothy hated the way she looked so much that she was mad at me for looking just like her—for being the person she thought she had convinced the world she wasn't anymore. I mean, it's got to be extremely difficult for white people to know when to compliment a black person who isn't emulating them. It seems that we are so busy paying homage and borrowing from other races and cultures that when someone compliments us on our natural, coily hair, we get defensive, assuming that they are making fun. How could something that we've spent the last thirty years fixing not be broken in the first place? How could our churchgoing, God-fearing mothers be wrong about us being so undesirable and repulsive until we corrected *God's* error, whether it be through painful, burning scalp irritation or the possible tainting of our bloodstreams? The irony of it all is that we become upset with others, when the problem really lies within. If we *felt* beautiful and, as a result, *liked ourselves as ourselves,* we would respond with a thank-you and not blow up at someone like Linda for trying to be nice.

Dorothy actually left me feeling embarrassed. Mostly because one of my elders didn't approve, but also because she didn't know. She didn't know that she could be beautiful no matter what she was wearing or how she looked. It didn't take harsh chemicals, a four-hundred-dollar pantsuit, or the approval of someone whom she *didn't even resemble* to make her attractive. All it would take would be for her to *feel* beautiful, but she couldn't even master that. She had years and years of brainwashing to undo, and as much as I liked her, I just didn't have that kind of time on my hands. It was just that simple. Her reality was definitely *not* mine.

Nikai

Nikki, we need you over here, now. There's been an accident."

This was the message left on my answering machine while I was in the shower the next morning. Mama sounded pretty calm, but whenever someone says that there's been an accident and your presence is needed, something bad has usually occurred. I went down a mental checklist, looking for possibilities, beginning with the most far-fetched: Uncle Lucky left the house alone. Nah, impossible. Mama was diagnosed with cancer. That probably wouldn't classify as an accident to her, and if it did, she wouldn't be the one making the phone call. Maybe Taylor had miscarried. That would be a surprise to us all and probably an omen, since the wedding had been postponed until after the baby was born.

I lowered my head as I stepped into my jeans and said a silent prayer for whoever and whatever it was that had my family on edge. After throwing on a navy blue sweater, black boots, and a pitiful voice in order to call in sick, I grabbed my keys, purse, and leather coat on my way out of the door.

On the way over, I felt a sadness come over me. And the closer I got to the town house, the more I feared knowing what this was all about. When I pulled up out front, I could see Uncle Lucky sitting in a kitchen chair in front of the window. This was extremely unusual, because he was practically *always* glued to his recliner, and in his eyes, he was now making himself a target for the make-believe loan sharks. He looked out at me and then went back to that place where he found peace. I put the car in park and leaned back on the headrest. Exhaled, closed my eyes, and shook my head because I could feel that something definitely wasn't right.

I walked up the front steps and into the house. The door was unlocked. They were either expecting someone or the last person to arrive had had news so big that locking the front door became insignificant.

"Mama?" I called.

There was no answer. I ducked my head into the living room and spoke to Uncle Lucky.

"Where is everybody?"

He didn't turn around at all. Just pointed up the steps and placed his ashy gray hand back in his lap.

"You okay?" I asked.

He breathed deeply and continued to focus. When he heard me suck my teeth, he pointed back upstairs again. I took his nonverbal advice and began to climb the stairs as Mama came walking down. She jumped for a second, grabbed her heart, and then closed her O-shaped mouth. Mama took me by the shoulders and gently turned me around. We descended the stairs and walked into the kitchen.

"I got your message. What's going on?"

"That's what I want to know. What did you do to your hair?"

"Oh God, here we go again. I cut it, Mama."

I took the ends of my hair in my hand and twirled it around my finger to show her that this was *no accident*. She shook her head and mumbled something to the Lord about her children being retarded.

"Mama, why did you call me over here?"

"Your sister needs us all right now. There won't be a wedding."

I covered my mouth and asked, "That no-good, thievin' dog dumped her?"

"No, Nikki. He died."

There was more silence. Then Lucky coughed in the living room and called Mama to get him some water.

"All right, I'll be there in a second," she answered.

She went about getting him something to drink, walking lightly, as though that was going to make anyone feel better.

"How did he die?"

"He was shot during a robbery."

"Where?"

"In New York."

"No. I mean shot where?"

"What different does that make? *The man isn't alive!*"

"It makes a lot of difference, Mama. Now, *where?*"

"*In the face!*"

She stormed away from me as if she felt I didn't have a sensitive bone in my body. But that actually determined a lot. For example, when Taylor got the news, I'm certain she tried to imagine the actual shooting—James's expression, whether he felt pain or not, and whether she would be able to look at him one last time. And in this case, it wasn't looking too promising.

The house was so quiet, you would have thought we were standing in the middle of a funeral home. Lucky always had the television on or at least a game on the radio, but even he seemed moved. It made me wonder if they had shared the news with him. If he had joined us in this world long enough to mourn by the window or if he was simply begging to be on the other side of it.

"It's a beautiful day, isn't it?" I asked him.

I stood behind him and held on to the back of his chair. He nodded his head in agreement, folded his hands, and sighed aloud.

"Somebody is here," he whispered.

"What?"

"Somebody is in here."

"Uncle Lucky, what are you talking about?"

He fell silent again.

"You expecting company? One of your friends coming by today? You must have been the one who left the door unlocked."

Uncle Lucky nodded his head. Tension built up in his face as tears began to roll down his wrinkled cheeks. Clear, heavy tears. They flowed so quickly that I didn't know if he was afraid or happy. Both would have made it difficult for me, because I had no idea of how to comfort a man who had seen and was seeing more than my eyes ever would.

I wrapped my arms around him and tried to rock him, but his body was cold and stiff. He didn't move. Neither did his eyes. He stared out farther than the complex, way beyond the place that Kalif focused on, past each and every one of our wildest dreams, and began to whimper.

"I'm ready to go," he said.

"Ready to go where, Uncle Lucky? Where do you wanna go?"

I stooped down in front of him and took his ice-cold hands in mine. I rubbed his fingers as his loose skin moved back and forth with each stroke.

"You want me to take you outside? I will, if you want me to," I assured him.

He didn't say anything, but I could feel the life coming back into him; I felt warmth. He slumped over in the chair and finally looked at me.

"Did they tell you what happened?" I asked.

"They didn't have to."

I should have known that neither Mama nor Taylor would have given him enough credit to understand something like death. He had probably seen more people come and go than they would ever imagine, but they treated him like a child. Insisted that he be seen but not heard. That had to hurt him, had to make him want to go. Something inside of me knew that he was aware of James's death, and wherever James was was where Lucky was asking to go. But I didn't want that. I didn't want that so badly that I was determined to make him not want it, either.

I walked up the stairs, down the hall, and knocked on the door to the guest bedroom. Mama opened it and put her index finger up to her lips. Taylor was lying on her side, facing the window. I walked around to the side of the bed and sat down next to her. Her hair was matted and her skin looked flushed. She had dark circles around her eyes and dried tears made her face appear to be ashy.

"She's not talking much," Mama said.

I placed my hand on her back to let her know that I was there. She didn't move. Felt as cold as Lucky did, except she was empty, even with the baby inside of her. Her stomach had gotten slightly bigger since the last time I had seen her, but she seemed detached from her child, detached from us all.

"How's the baby?" I asked Mama.

"The doctor says that the baby is fine. They're just worried about her."

I asked Mama to get me a brush out of the bathroom and leave us alone for a while. She closed the door behind her and told me not to be too long, because Taylor hadn't been asleep all day. I took the brush and ran it softly through my sister's tangled hair.

"Remember when we were little and you used to brush my hair like this before I went to sleep? I used to love to let you practice on me once you had cut all of your baby doll's hair off. Never knowing that you had no idea what you were doing. I trusted you with just about anything, even my life. Yep, nobody could tell me anything about my big sister. Taylor, you were so smart, so beautiful. You made everybody proud. I just wanted to be close to you. Have people know that *I* meant something to *you*. And you know what? I still do."

A tear fell from her eyes, across her nose, and down the opposite cheek. I wiped it away and then did the same with the ones that were issuing from me. I bent over and hugged her as tightly as I could without disturbing her or the baby.

"I love you so much, girl. And now I need *you* to trust *me* when I tell you that you will be okay. You hear me? This baby needs you now. You've got to be strong, the way you've always been. I know you're hurting, but James wants a strong, healthy child from you. Don't let him down. He's here with you now. Even Lucky said so."

I put my hand on her stomach, closed my eyes, and rubbed it. I wanted him or her to feel that Mommy wasn't alone. That we were gonna make sure that she was okay. I sat down on the floor facing the window and crossed my legs. Grabbed the arm that she was lying on and rested my head on it.

I felt bad for mentioning that money and making that our last conversation. I wanted Taylor to know that she was not my enemy, but my sister. The only person in the world with the same blood flowing through their veins. That should've been enough to make us tighter, but something that appeared to be stronger than both of us was preventing that.

I must have been sitting there on the floor for about thirty minutes when Mama came back and reminded me that Taylor needed to get some sleep. I stood up, kissed her on the cheek, and left with Mama.

"Did you get her to talk?" she asked.

"No."

She must have seen the dried tears on my face.

"You okay?"

"Yeah, I'll be all right. When is the funeral?"

"It's supposed to be on Tuesday, in Atlanta. I don't know if she'll be able to handle it, though. I was thinking that maybe you and I could go in her place."

"Oh, Mama. You know I don't like funerals."

"And your daddy didn't, either, but you see that he eventually had to show up for one."

"That's sick, Mama. You know his birthday is in two weeks. I was wondering if maybe you guys wanted to go see him with me this time."

Mama looked off and busied herself with coupons and things of that sort.

"Mama, you think that he doesn't know that y'all don't visit him?"

"Listen, Nikki. I told you that I'm just not ready. Besides, somebody has got to be here with Lucky at all times."

"What if I get Robert to come over and sit with him? They can watch the game together and everything. Lucky might like having a man around."

"And whose gonna look in on Taylor?"

"Well, I'm assuming that by then, she'll be up and about."

"Don't assume things like that! This was her fiancé, much more than someone to shack up with like that child molester you fell head over heels for and that *man* you're livin' with now!"

I couldn't believe my mama, who didn't even have the decency to look at me while she insulted me and my relationship. Not to mention her stick-and-move tactic of bringing up Travis.

"Are you saying that I would feel less pain because Robert and I aren't married?"

"Listen, I've got a lot to do. While you're here, you can make yourself useful and help me clip these coupons."

"I'd like to, but my love slave/bed buddy is waiting on me at home. We have to talk about having some illegitimate kids to tag both of our last names with, and confuse them."

She cut her eyes at me and went back to clipping coupons or killing time, whichever she preferred to call it. I grabbed my things and said good-bye to Lucky on my way out. Out of the very place he was trying to escape. It made me feel guilty for not taking him with me, not being able to. But he knew better than anyone what he wanted, where he wanted to be. And it hurt me to think that it was much further than any living person could ever taken him, no matter how many tears he shed.

Robert

Kim was spending the night out, the apartment was quiet, and Nik, with her exotic new hairdo, had just stepped out of the shower, smelling like peaches and cream. Her skin was shining like a layer of silk had been placed across her chest and shoulders. She put one foot up on an open dresser drawer and lotioned her legs as I pretended that the sight of her thighs glistening from my reading light didn't bother me. She wrapped the white towel that she was wearing around her breasts a little tighter and lifted it in the back to oil down the mothership. Slid into a pink satin gown and had forgotten her panties. By the time she was done freshening up and getting all feminine on me, I had the sheets looking like a goddamn tepee.

Nik climbed into the bed, humming a tune that I wasn't familiar with. Laid her head down on the pillow and turned onto her side. Kicked the newspaper that I had at the foot of the bed down on top of the cedar chest. I looked at her, sucked my teeth, and continued reading the sports page. Once I was finished, I pulled the blankets up and caught a glimpse of my old roaming grounds, which were covered in silk. But before I could invite her to a game of hide the sausage, she was snoring loudly enough to wake the dead. Rolled over on her stomach and began mumbling in her sleep.

I cleared my throat in an attempt to wake her, but she only got louder. She tossed and turned for another minute, then started with an annoying laugh—a bashful, teasing, flirtatious laugh. I listened. Waited to see who it was that interested her like this, even in her sleep.

"I can't be here for that. . . . Yeah, he can be. . . . I love him. . . . What—Kalif, stop!"

I sat up straight and pulled the blankets off of Nik.

"Wake up!"

"What?" she asked.

Nik looked up at me and then rubbed her eyes with her knuckles as though she was unsure of her surroundings.

"Wake your ass up! You're at home and I ain't Kalif! What, you got some feelings for him or something?"

"What are you talking about?"

"I'm talking about you calling his name in your sleep! What's up with that?"

"I didn't call his name in my sleep, and don't wake me up again for some silly shit like this!"

She turned over on her side and pulled the blankets over her head. I snatched them back. She tugged from her end. I pulled from mine. Except now I was on my feet, yanking with all of my strength and trying to send her lying ass flying across the room. But she let go. Sent me stumbling backward into the closet. Hit my head on the corner of the door and the buckle of one of her stupid handbags. I snatched them all down and threw them at her. Accidentally hit her in the face. *And what the hell did I do that for?* Nik stepped up on the bed and then down the other side. Looked like Ms. Sophia in *The Color Purple* coming for Harpo.

Just as I thought she was gonna punch me in the chest or something, she left the bedroom. Swung the door wide open and grabbed a blanket out of the hall closet. Stomped back into the bedroom for her pillows and stretched out on the couch in the front room. I listened to her toss and turn again for about twenty minutes. She searched for a comfortable position to get a good night's sleep, the very same way I had to all of the times that I'd messed up and come home late. But that's what she deserved for dreaming about another man while sleeping next to me. She didn't want to do what it would take to make me happy, so I'd be damned if she'd make someone else happy in her dreams.

After watching the end of a flick, I dozed off into a light sleep. Began to dream about a little hottie of my own. One who didn't hold out on me when she saw my piece was hard enough for a midget to do pull-ups on. Still aware of my surroundings, I heard a distant noise in the bedroom. Assumed she had come to her senses and gotten back in the bed. Then I felt a nudge in my shoulder and then a hand in my underwear. A warm hand massaging my sack and then suddenly placing a death grip on it. I opened my eyes, to find Nik standing over me with sweat dripping down her arm and onto my piece.

"Now, *you* wake *yo'* ass up! Get up, now!"

"Baby, what's goin' on?"

I put my hands in the air, like she was attempting to take something more than my dignity and pride.

"Don't you ever wake me up like that again! You hear me?!" she yelled.

Her hand was shaking and her body was sweating profusely. That sexy gown began to stick to her nipples, but it failed to turn me on this time around. She was blinking quickly, like she didn't know what she was doing or how she had gotten to that point.

"Baby, calm down. Let my sack go before—"

The grip got tighter.

"Nik, goddamn it—"

Tighter.

I was seeing colors by then, so I shut up and let her speak.

"I have enough problems in my life right now, Robert, without you adding to them! My mama might have cancer, my sister is hurting, her fuckin' man died owin' me five hundred dollars, I'm bein' watched, and I don't need no extra stress from you!"

The gown must have begun sticking to her butt, because she used the free hand to scratch it and gave the mothership room to breathe. I watched her movements as though my life depended on it.

"I have tried to be nice to you, but you are really making this hard for me," she continued, her wrist locked in place. "Can we start being decent toward each other, Rob?"

"Yeah, yeah, baby, whatever you want," I uttered as a tear streamed down the side of my face.

"Repeat after me."

"*What?*" I yelled.

She secured her hand at the base, grabbed a few pubic hairs while she was at it, and said, "*Repeat after me. I will do my best to create a peaceful environment for Nikai.*"

"I will do my best to create a peaceful environment for Nikai. Now please let me go."

"You know, you gave me a bruise on my forehead from those purses?" she said as the bright spots disappeared from my sight.

"I'm sorry, Nik. But you keep toying with a man's piece. You could've caused some serious damage."

"Whatever, Rob. I just needed to get your undivided attention. I wasn't gonna turn my wrist any further."

I sucked my teeth, when I actually wanted to call her bluff, but I remembered that there wasn't enough distance between us. Didn't need an instant replay to convince me that her elevator had stopped going all the way to the top.

I was beginning to wonder who was crazier, Karen or Nik. That wasn't the first time she had snapped on me, but there was something strange about the argument that night. She managed to touch on everything *but* the accusation. Even some off-the-wall stuff about being followed. Nik couldn't have been laughing and having a good time with Kalif in her sleep and not doing so when she was awake. Something inside was telling me that there was far more than music being mixed at that damn studio.

Nik took another shower, climbed back into bed, and nuzzled up to her body pillow as if nothing had happened. Even had the nerve to rub the mothership on my thigh before dozing off. She asked me to wake her up before I left for the engine house. My mouth said, "Sure." But after what she'd pulled this last time I tried to wake her, my mind said, Fuck it. Let her sleep.

Nikai

Hi, uh . . . my name is Karen and I'm calling for a Kim Hayes. I would appreciate it if you would give a call so that we can set up a time for you to come by and look at the apartment. I believe you still have my number. If not, it should have shown up on the caller ID box. Thanks."

This must be the apartment that Kim was talking about, I thought. The sista sounded as though she had it all together to me. Other than the way she took it upon herself to assume that we had a caller ID box. Robert kept me on the phone at work half of the morning, calling her crazy and sick. Bad-mouthed the woman like he knew her. When I tried to calm his suspicions by offering to go with Kim to see the apartment on my lunch break, he left the engine house, met me in the parking lot, and refused to get off of the hood of my car until I went back inside. Made me wonder if *he* was the one who was crazy. I decided to let it go but to look into it later. There was obviously more to this woman than either one of them was telling me, because every time that I asked him to elaborate, he'd change the subject to Kalif.

Robert accused me of talking in my sleep the previous night. Said I was calling Kalif's name and everything. I played dumb but didn't really find that too hard to believe. He'd been on my mind constantly. I didn't spend as much time with him any-more, because of personal issues in my life, but for some reason, I felt strong around him. It was like he'd become my touch of sanity in an otherwise-insane world. My world.

Violently grabbing the testicles of a sleeping man twice my size, comforting an elderly man who suspects spirits of the dead are present, trying to convince my mother that the revelation of my ex being a child molester was *not* a turn-on, trying desperately to save up money that I really couldn't afford to give, and consoling a sibling who felt as though she had lost her reason to live—all this had begun to take a toll on me. This wasn't normal behavior and I was beginning to feel as though I were living a double life. Wearing a mask from nine to five and then letting my hair down—or should I say tearing it out—when I wasn't working.

After Rob left, I called Kalif and accepted an invitation to meet him down at the loft the next morning. Scheduled a time to meet with the record executive to discuss signing me. Got up the nerve to tell him that I missed his company and then shared the drama from the night before with him. I expected him to be flattered by the idea of showing up in my dreams, but he sounded agitated, damn near pissed. He repeatedly asked me if I was okay, and he wanted me to run through the story in detail when we got together.

I let him go and decided it was time to make up with Kim. After all, she would say that we were friends first and sisters-in-law second. I dialed the Southwestern Bell Human Resources Department and then pressed her extension. She picked up on the third ring.

"Human Resources, this is Kimberly. How may I help you?"

"You can knock the chip off of your shoulder," I joked.

"What do you want, you lousy wench?"

"Oh, sweetie, you still mad at me?" I teased.

"You *and* your man can still go to hell."

"Okay, but I'll be waiting for you at the door," I joked. "Where did you sleep last night?"

"Far away from you two losers."

"Seriously, girl. I almost had to hurt your brother last night."

"If I'm lucky, y'all will do each other in."

"Shut up. Now, are you ready to be serious?"

"Whatever. I went over to that girl Karen's apartment and ended up staying."

"How does the place look?" I asked.

"It's nice. Big bedroom, and she's got some nice furniture,

too. A lot of glass, flowers, and leather. You know, the sista has got some class about herself."

"Are you saying our place is a hole-in-the-wall?"

"You said it, not me." She laughed.

I was relieved to finally hear that sound. Kim usually makes it hard on people when she's mad at them. Won't get in contact for days at a time, and when she does, she's calling them everything *but* a child of God.

"I wanted to see the apartment with you, but when I told Rob, he lost his mind. Drove up to my job and everything. He either doesn't like that woman or *really* likes you. And since he doesn't know her, it's got to be you. You think your mother is behind this?"

"Probably. But that fool was acting strange when I first brought up the idea with him. I think that smoke is affecting his brain. But anyway, I want you to meet her. She's real cool. Not silly and catty like most women. We stayed up late last night talking about her baby *and* her baby's daddy. She'll tell all of her business if you listen long enough. She's like one of those lonely sistas who's looking for female friends to bond with."

"So when are you going over there again?"

"Actually, she invited me back over there tonight. I told her about you and she said she was really interested in meeting you personally. Said something about reading peoples lives through their eyes. She claims to be psychic."

"Really? Maybe she can tell me if there's a marriage in the future for me and talk to me about some other issues that I'm dealing with."

"We'll see. I'll get dropped off at the apartment around seven and we can go from there."

"Okay."

As soon as I put the phone down in its cradle, I spotted Dorothy walking down the hall, carrying a box. She slowed down, rolled her eyes, and shook her head at me. I could see the other leasing consultants whispering across the room and behind her as she walked back and forth. I went to the door and called Linda into my office. She was talking to an older white guy who did janitorial work for our property. She put up her index finger and told him something to the effect that she would be back with him in a minute.

Linda strolled into my office wearing tan corduroy pants and a navy blue cotton long-sleeved shirt. She closed the door behind her and stood in front of my desk, when normally she would have sat down.

"Do you know what's going on with Dorothy?" I asked.

"I heard that she was fired."

"For what?"

"It's a long story."

"And I think you've got time to tell it!" I barked.

"Well, I happened to tell Casey, across the hall, about what happened the other day with Dorothy and your new hairstyle. And well, you know how a snowball effect can get. One person starts out telling the story, and by the time it's done, it's blown way out of proportion."

"So what was said?"

"Casey told Jamie what *actually* happened and then Lindsay told Julie some wild story about Dorothy slapping me once I left your office."

Linda lowered her head as she finished telling me what had happened. Maybe she felt ashamed for not saying anything, or maybe she felt weak for not being able to ensure that I didn't find out.

"Well, did you clear it all up? I mean, you didn't just let them believe that, did you?"

"I tried. I even offered to bring you in, but they said that your word meant nothing, since nobody was around to see it. I don't know why, but everyone found it easier to pity me than to believe that Dorothy didn't do it."

"Has Dorothy said anything to you about this?"

"No. I'm kinda afraid to say anything. She's been breathing fire for the past two hours, and I'm trying not to get burned."

"Okay, thanks."

I let her get back to whatever it was that she'd been doing before I called her, then dialed Dorothy's office. There was no answer. Then I spotted her walking past my window again with her phone packed on top of a box. She was really close to being finished—with packing and with all of us, as well.

I grabbed my coat off the hook on the wall and did a rapid dash for the elevator. Caught the doors as they were closing and tried desperately to pull them apart. I lodged my foot between them and looked to Dorothy for assistance. She placed the box that she was carrying down and pushed the button to close the door. Held it down until I let go of the doors, and the idea of her ever speaking to me again.

"Karen, this is my best girlfriend, Nikai. Nik, this is Karen, my new roommate."

Kim wasn't lying about her having a baby. Her stomach sat out like her water was about to break any minute. She was pretty, though. She had a smooth, even complexion and the kind of long hair that most brothas love. It made me think about the fact that Robert hadn't really said too much when I cut mine and started wearing a natural like N'Bushe Wright. I guess every man isn't caught up on hair after all.

The part about her apartment being nice was true, too. She had a thick white carpet with a pastel-and-gold color scheme. She invited us into her bedroom, which, of course, was the largest one, with a queen-size bed and a canopy. There were lots of flowered pillows at the head and satin belts tied around the foot of the bedposts.

"You all can take your shoes off, climb up there, and make yourselves comfortable. Want anything to drink? I've got white zinfandel, soda, orange juice, and water."

Kim said, "I'll take zinfandel."

"Me, too."

Karen left the room and Kim gave me an "I told you so" look.

I said, "Check this out. She's been tying some brotha up and serving him up proper."

Kim grabbed one of the belts off the bedposts and nearly fell onto the floor laughing.

"I know that's right, sistagirl."

Karen walked back in on the conversation and noticed Kim holding the belt. She gave me an extremely nervous look, then tried unsuccessfully to snatch it away. Gave us our glasses and then climbed up on the bed.

"Girl, you are crazy. Gimme that."

"You've been giving somebody something to think about," Kim said, pressing the point.

"Yeah, I try to. You know how it is."

"No, I don't. Maybe once I've moved my things in, you can run down the rules for me."

I looked around the huge bedroom at her vanity stand and the pastel floral paintings that decorated the walls. Handcuffs on the dresser and the very *same* kind of motion lotion that Robert had tired to use on me one.

They went on talking for a while, but I kept noticing Karen paying more and more attention to me, even when she was talking to Kim.

"So, Kim tells me that you can see the future."

She cracked a half smile and took a sip of her wine.

"Yeah, everybody's but my own."

"How did you find out that you had this gift?"

"I began to see things happening before they actually did. For example, I knew that I would meet you before I ran into Kim that day. And when she pointed up to the apartment that she was staying in, I could see tension on the other side of the door. Are you and her brother having some sort of problems?"

I glanced at Kim and she nodded for me to go ahead.

"A few."

Karen put her index and middle fingers up to her temples and then leaned her head back to the ceiling. Her eyes began to blink so fast that I thought maybe she was having a seizure.

"There is a lot of tension in your relationship, a lot of secrets, and not much intercourse between you two."

My mouth fell open because I couldn't believe how close she had come to talking about Rob and me. I looked at Kim, who was just as surprised as I was, and nudged her in the shoulder. Put up an okay sign with my fingers and tried to get some more insight.

"You're right. We haven't had sex in almost a year."

Kim yelled, "Damn!"

"Shut up!" I said, nudging her again. "You're messing up her train of thought!"

"I see him sweating inside a lot of clothing. He's hot. I see fear in his eyes."

"That must be because he's a fireman!" I yelled.

"But his worry is not about the fire. It's about something else. He's being indecisive in his life right now."

"About what? Can you see it? Is it about marrying me?"

"No. I don't see marriage anywhere on his mind. . . . Uh-oh."

Karen got quiet, opened her eyes, and took her hands away from her head.

"What? What did you see?" I asked.

"I don't think you want to know. I try not to give any bad news, only good."

"*Please* tell me what it is."

"Yeah, tell her!" Kim added. "I wanna know, too."

Karen tilted her head back. To get back into that trance, I guess. Her eyes began to blink quickly, like they had before, only now she was shaking.

"I see him watching his surroundings. Making sure that you aren't around."

"*Mmmhmm.* Go ahead."

"I see another woman. A beautiful woman. He's spending a lot of time with her."

Karen snapped out of it. Took another deep breath and shook off the visions. I looked at Kim, who was now shrugging her shoulders and taking big gulps of wine.

I asked, "Can you tell me her name?"

"I don't see all of that. Just faces and emotions."

"Well, do me now!" Kim insisted.

Karen went on predicting the future for Kim as I soaked in this revelation. That dirty bastard woke me up over a damn dream, when he's actually living out his fantasies. Doing all of the things that I stopped Kalif from doing because I felt guilty. I felt I owed Rob an opportunity to knock the webs off of my sweet haven below.

We stayed at Karen's apartment all night. Talked about the coincidence of her wanting to name her baby Robert and finished another bottle of zinfandel. By the time the night was over, we all had bonded, and found that girlfriend group that we all needed. And with one of us being able to predict the future, I could see that relationship blossoming quickly.

The next morning, we woke up to sausage, eggs, and pancakes. Karen said that she felt domestic, so we let her be just that.

"How did you ladies sleep last night?" she asked, standing in front of the stove, wearing a pink apron that read KISS THE COOK, and holding a spatula.

"Okay, considering what I learned," I answered.

"I'm really sorry. I told you that I didn't like giving bad news."

"That's okay. *You* have nothing to do with *Robert* cheating."

"So, what do you think you're gonna do?" she asked.

"I don't know. What do you think? I mean, what do you see me doing, later?"

Karen turned back to the skillet of pancakes and began flipping them over and over again. Punched holes in each with the corner of the spatula and then placed it down on the counter. She rubbed her stomach, sighed, and turned back to me.

"You ever thought about dating someone else?"

Immediately, Kalif came to mind. But so did the fact that Kim was sitting right there at the kitchen table with me. She was half-asleep, not half-deaf.

"No. I couldn't do that."

"You afraid of getting back out into the dating pool?"

Kim looked over at me with her eyes half-opened.

"No. I love him."

Karen hit the hot skillet with the back of her hand and then began to curse at no one in particular.

"You okay?" I asked.

"Yeah, I'm fine. But maybe you need to think about making yourself happy."

I listened to what she had to say because, after all, she could see what was going to happen anyway. But also because that wasn't the first time I had heard this. Kalif had told me the same thing the night that we watched the stars together. The night that *we* bonded.

"I haven't been doing this long, so don't get me wrong. I don't know everything. I'm still kind of rusty."

The strangest feeling struck me when she said that. Not a feeling of being convinced, but that maybe I was psychic, too. For some reason, I felt that I had heard her voice saying the word *rusty* before.

Kim slowly came to life and said, "Well, I don't appreciate y'all sitting here talking about my brother like I don't exist."

"I'm sorry. Let's change the subject. So when are you gonna move your stuff in?" Karen asked.

"I'll have to ask Robert to help me move my bed and things, but I was looking at this weekend, maybe."

"Sounds good. Well, Nikai, you know there's another room. So whenever you get tired of Robert, you can move in, too."

I nodded and began to eat the breakfast that she had placed before me. Laughed with my newfound friend until I was full of her food, funny stories, and foresight.

Once Kim had eaten, she decided to stay a little while longer. She reminded me that she would be by the apartment that afternoon to get some things. Asked if I would mind talking to Rob about moving her bed for her. And then warned me not to take all of Karen's advice. Said that Karen couldn't be too psychic or she would foresee the ass kicking that Kim was gonna give me if I even *thought* about dating someone else while I was with her brother.

I headed home about 1:00 P.M. Thinking the whole way. Thought about my man, my life, my decisions, my world. And my reality, which was becoming more and more self-destructive.

I pulled up to the apartment as the sound of Karen's voice saying that Robert was "making sure that you aren't around" rang louder and louder. Remembered her telling me that she could see him with a "beautiful woman." One that he was "spending a lot of time" with.

I put my car in reverse and drove to the drugstore. Bought a box of condoms and then went down to the loft. Prepared to make some of *my* dreams come true.

Robert

W here are you?" I asked Kim.

"Why?"

I sighed and leaned back in the black swivel chair at the engine house. I was in the kitchen, alone. Keates and Hodges were lifting weights upstairs and Don had taken the day off to look for engagement rings.

I was half-dressed and breathing heavily. Water was dripping from my hands and the phone. Kim had paged me while I was washing up from a run and put in 73-911, our emergency code.

"Moms called and asked about you. I haven't seen you in days and didn't know what to tell her."

"I told you to tell her that I was moving into an apartment in two weeks."

"And *I* told *you* that you couldn't!"

"How in the hell do you think you can tell me what I can and can't do? If you need to be worrying about anybody, it's *Nik!*"

"What are you talking about?" I asked.

"My roommate is psychic and—"

"More like psychotic."

"Anyway. I said she's psychic, and last night she told Nik that she could see you with another woman."

The phone slipped from my ear and my heart skipped about six beats. I picked it up somewhere between Nik moving in over there and Karen naming the baby after me.

"*What* did you just say?"

"She told Nik that she could have the extra room in her

apartment. And even though she likes the name Robert enough to name her baby that, she didn't see anyone by that name in Nik's near future. She also suggested that she start dating someone else. And to be honest, Nik looked like she might consider it. So instead of worrying about where *I'm* resting *my* head, you need to worry about where *Nik* is resting *hers*."

"Have you talked to her today?"

"Not since she left here this afternoon. She said she was going home, but I didn't get an answer when I called."

"Yeah, me, neither."

Kim laughed and asked, "You think she's somewhere getting served up?"

"You better hope not, because this is all *your* fault."

"How is it *my* fault that you can't manage two relationships? And by the way, why haven't I met this lovely lady you're spending so much time with?"

"*There* is *no one else*. And if your friend is so *goddamned psychic*, why isn't she getting paid for it?"

"I don't know, but if she wasn't the real thing, how could she manage to see you in a lot of hot clothing, with fear in your eyes? Isn't it strange how she figured out that you're a fireman?"

"Not as strange as you think."

My pager vibrated on my belt. It showed that someone had left a verbal message instead of a numeric one. I hoped that it was Nik, but then again, I didn't. I hadn't had enough time to come up with answers to all of the questions that Karen had put in her head the night before.

"Listen, are you gonna be there for a while? I need to make a phone call."

"Yeah, I'll be here. Hey, if you talk to Nik, tell her to call me at Karen's."

I agreed, but the sound of my sister and my woman making themselves at home with the side show, who could possibly be carrying my child, sent chills down my back. I soon learned that the message wasn't from Nik at all, but from Karen. Requesting my company again. And, as usual, ASAP. I called her back on her cell phone.

"What, are you with the fuckin' psychic network now?"

"You know you've been on my mind, don't you?" she sang.

"How can I not be, when you're predicting my next move?" She laughed hard.

"You are so funny, Rusty. I forgot to mention that I met *Nik*. Isn't that what you call her? She's a lovely girl. Not as pretty as I expected, but I guess I can't foresee everything. And the natural."

"What about it?"

"It's so . . . not you."

"*Nik* is me."

"Yeah, *whatevah*."

"Where is Kim now?"

"Oh, she's out in the living room. She can't hear me. I'm in the bathroom."

"What are you doing, stocking up on EPT tests that you don't ever plan to use?" I asked sarcastically.

"What the fuck is that supposed to mean?"

"What do you think it means? You're the only woman I've seen get pregnant and go to the doctor before using a pregnancy test, one located twelve feet away from her bed."

"What do you know about women being pregnant, anyway? I thought you said that Nikai wasn't fertile."

"And I thought you said that all of this was just between *me and you*."

"It is."

"So why are you trying to get my sister to move in with you?"

"*She* asked *me* if she could move in here. So I figured that I could help a sista out and have a little fun with you."

"You call this fun?"

"Well, I didn't guarantee that it would be a barrel of laughs for you, but the look on Nik's face last night when I told her that you weren't considering marrying her was worth it."

I fell silent, because I had learned that the lack of an audience was the only thing that would calm her down. When there was no one around to acknowledge Karen's antics, she was decent and sometimes even desirable.

"So, how do you expect me to see you with my sister living there?" I asked.

"You have a place, don't you?"

I sighed and held the phone again.

"Okay, okay. I'm just kidding. Meet me in the food court at the Galleria in an hour."

I truly didn't like the idea of meeting with Karen out in public, but it was better than waiting to find out the next day what she had done to Nik. Clearing up the lies she had told and praying that she hadn't come *too* close to the truth. The larger her stomach became, the more serious Karen got about us ultimately being together. And that meant that I had to work even harder to cover my tracks and try not to get burned. Even when I wasn't on duty.

Nikai

Oooohhh. *Yeah, right there. Don't stop. Oh God. Just like that.*
Kalif had been rubbing my feet for almost an hour and a half.
Stimulating other parts of my body through my soles. Sending
seductive messages with a tickle between my toes and an occasional kiss around the ankles.

I surprised him when I showed up at the loft that afternoon.
Apologized for not calling first but explained that I *needed* to see
him. He said that he had been working on tracks all day and
thinking about us. As if there actually was an *us* to think about.

"Okay, that's enough," I said.

"You sure?"

"Yeah, I don't want your hands to get tired."

"Why? You have something else for them to do?" he asked,
giving me a devilish grin.

I blushed and looked away. Specifically over at my purse, where
I had left the condoms. Kalif pulled a previously rolled blunt from
behind his ear, lighted it, and sat down on one of the other futons. He took slow, short drags and then held his breath like an
underwater scuba diver. Exhaled and handed the blunt to me.

"What am I supposed to do with this?" I asked.

He looked at me sideways and, without uttering a single
word, let me know just how dumb that question was.

"Are you gonna hit that or let it burn up?"

"I don't know how."

"The question is, Do you want to? I'm not trying to pressure
you into anything."

I examined the cigar that had been taken apart and then reconstructed. Put it to my lips and inhaled. For much longer than I should have. My throat began to burn as I coughed and gagged on oxygen that never seemed to reach my lungs. Kalif jumped up and ran over to me. Patted me on the back and then held me. Sucked up all of the clean air that I was gasping for.

"You okay?" he asked. "Put this down."

He took the cigar from me and set it in a homemade ashtray created from foil. Pulled me up from the floor and lifted my arms above my head.

"You feel any better?"

"Yeah. I don't see how you smoke those things!"

"It's something that you have to get used to. There are some things that you just aren't ready for."

"I guess so. Can I put my arms down now?"

"Can you breathe?"

"Yes. I'm fine now."

Kalif let me go and sat back down on the futon across from mine. Picked up a pen and paper and started writing.

I asked, "What's that?"

"I'm writing a poem."

"What's it about?"

"Entrepreneurship."

"You're supposed to write poetry about love and things of that sort."

"Maybe, if that's all you're concerned about. But what's important to me is our people living with an African frame of mind. You ever heard of the saying, You can take the person out of the ghetto but you can't take the ghetto out of the person?"

"Yeah."

"Well, that's how I feel about the motherland. It's right here in my heart, no matter where I am."

Kalif leaned over, rested his elbows on his knees, and began rubbing his hands together.

"Nikai, what I'm concerned about is our children having safe community centers to go to after school, instead of hangin' on the corners like I did when I was young. There should be computer classes, plenty of food, clothing and shelter, fair employment opportunities, collective responsibility for the youth. And we should be providing this for ourselves, *not* waiting for someone else to have pity on us. A proud people wouldn't do that. That's how you know it's all mental. Our minds are locked up. Locked into dependency. We don't want change because with that comes responsibility for our own actions and that means that we can't cry foul when things go wrong. When funds aren't recycled back into our community, when the youth's preconceived notion of beauty is the opposite of its mothers. When we begin to love ourselves from the inside out, it makes it harder to kill one another. If I love me, I can't harm you, because you *are* me. These senseless deaths have got to stop. The dependency has got to stop. We are so used to having someone in charge of us that we are afraid of freedom. Afraid of the unknown.

"A friend of mine was talking about the unknown. She says it's like a prison and knowledge is the key. Once you know, you are free to grow."

Kalif smiled at me and leaned back on the futon like a pleased professor.

"Why are you running from me?" I asked.

"Running from you?"

"Yeah, you afraid to get close to me?"

He laughed and then glanced down at the cigar on the wooden coffee table.

"You must be feelin' that, huh?"

"I don't need that to want to be close to you."

I was trying desperately to get him to touch me. I felt as though Kalif's embrace was a blow to Rob, and I wanted to hurt him— *now.*

"Hey, you need to chill, 'cause you're talkin' out of your head."

"No, I'm not! Come here," I called, beckoning for him.

"Seriously, Nik you need to stop that. That's not even you."

"Then what is me?"

"At what point are you gonna stop looking for me to define you? When was the last time you asked yourself that question?" Kalif asked, raising himself up from the futon, a bit of anger in his voice.

I dropped my head and covered my face with my hands.

"What does that brotha do to you?" he asked, slowly pulling my chin up.

I could see misunderstanding in his eyes. He couldn't understand how I'd allowed myself to get nowhere this fast. How I could not know who I was, what I wanted, and where I was going, *all of the time.* I had cut the perm from my hair, and kept the company of those who believed that the search for oneself in the world is the pursuit of illusion. And still, I was willing to sacrifice something as sacred as my womb to a man who didn't love me for a man who probably never would.

"It's not so much what he does to me as it is what I do to myself."

"So what's the problem? I mean, you know what you need to do."

"No, I don't. If I did, don't you think I would have done it by now?"

He sighed and leaned back. Took one of his locks in his hand and began twisting it at the root.

"How will you ever know how strong you are if you don't spend any time by yourself? You don't give yourself a chance to grow, because you're afraid to. I think you're afraid of what you might become."

"And what's that?"

He sighed harder a second time.

"Enough with the questions, okay? If I tell you everything, there will be nothing to figure out on your own."

I nodded and he shook his head at me. Laughed and patted the large pillow next to him on the floor.

"Come here."

"You sure you want me that close?" I asked.

"Positive."

He wrapped his arm around my shoulder and put my head in his lap. Ran his fingers through my coiled hair, the same way I had done with him before. Kalif took frankincense oil and massaged my scalp until I had calmed down enough to *feel* what he was saying. It made me realize that Robert had never expressed affection or concern toward me like this. And that Kalif's platonic touch was more powerful than a sexual one. We shared a spiritual moment. One that even sex-craved Robert would envy. Because even without coming to each other in our most naked form, we were still connecting.

Kalif said, "Tell me about your dream."

"I don't really remember it. All I know is that Robert woke me up and told me that I was calling your name."

"What was his reaction to that?"

"He was mad and we got into an argument."

"Did he touch you?"

I didn't answer. I knew that if I was going to be honest with him, I would have to tell him about my attempt to squeeze any future offspring out of Rob. I didn't necessarily want him to know that part, that part of me. Kalif continued to run his fingers through my hair, until he realized that I was avoiding his question.

"Tell me what you want," he said.

"Um, I want to sing. I want to be successful. I want to be in love."

"Stop right there. You said that you want to be in love. Is someone else's love for you more important than your love for yourself?"

"It shouldn't be."

"Well, is it?"

"I guess sometimes it is."

"See, a lot of sistas have that problem. They validate themselves through their relationships with other people. So if your relationship doesn't work and you find it almost impossible to keep a particular individual happy, you feel as though you've failed. And in your eyes, that failure illustrates to the world that you are not worthy, not suitable to be loved. Otherwise, you would be in a relationship."

I lay there quietly, enjoying the moment. Kalif didn't say much more. Actually, there wasn't much more for him to say. He had shed light on the obvious. I was afraid of being alone in this world. Hanging on to Robert in hopes that he would eventually fall back in love with me. I couldn't really say if waiting for the right time to leave was a good idea anymore. We had begun to lay hands on each other, and not in an intimate fashion. Things were getting serious. I had begun to stash some money away for an apartment. Fifty dollars every check. And before I knew it, I was only able to take fifty from every check for Travis, too. And at that rate, it would be two months before I had all of his cash.

All of my relationships were plummeting at a scary pace, but none of that had anything to do with my internal dilemma. I had issues that *I* wasn't addressing. And until I did, I would be looking for Kalif, Karen, Sheila, and anyone else who was willing to answer them, to supply alternatives, and to free me from the shackles that society, my family, and life experiences had convinced me were rightfully mine.

Robert

Karen said, "Ah, so glad that you could join me. You wanna get something to eat, maybe catch a movie?"

She sat at one of the round tables in the food court, sipping on a clear soda. Her perfect nose was now plump and her face had a glow. She had done away with tight jeans and replaced them with pants that had elastic waistbands. And large blouses now covered her D cups, which had recently graduated to a double D.

Still in my blue uniform, I took a seat across the table from her and rested my arm across the back of a chair.

"I'm not hungry. Have y'all eaten?" I asked, pointing to her stomach.

She grinned and rubbed her belly in a circular motion.

"Yeah, we had a little something before we came."

"That's cool. So what did you need to see me about?" I asked.

She looked down at the table and began ripping a napkin into shreds. I noticed a white gauze on the back of her right hand had been secured with tape.

"What happened to you there?" I asked, pointing at her bandage.

Karen gave me a fake grin and put her hands in her lap.

"I had a little accident while I was cooking. It's okay, though. I want to talk to you about what you plan to do as far as Nikai is concerned."

"What do you mean?"

"I mean, I feel bad being her friend *and* her man's lover."

I tapped my heel on the floor repeatedly in order to calm myself, because this woman never ceased to amaze me. Sometimes, it seemed that she had convinced herself that the way she was acting was sane behavior.

"You know, you are one of the *sickest* people I've ever met in my life."

She locked her fingers under her double chin, smiled, and asked, "Really? I've outdone *everyone* you know?"

"What is your problem?"

"You know, if I didn't know any better, I'd think that your feelings for me were decreasing."

"Damn. Earth to Karen. They have!"

"Well, that's fine, too. But Kim is taking me over to your mother's house tonight to help her pack the rest of her stuff. If you plan to keep this thing under wraps, I suggest you be there."

"For what?"

"For free!"

"Don't play with me, Karen."

"Do you see a smile painted on my face? I'm serious. I told you that I wanted to meet your mother, but you just keep writing me off like some kind of joke. I also told you that you were eventually gonna give me a ring, but something tells me that you haven't accepted that, either."

She nonchalantly waved her swollen fingers around as she toyed with my future. I wanted to reach across the table and give her a *ring*. Right around the eye. Karen continued sipping on her clear soda and then rattled off some bullshit about the baby missing me.

"By the way, how's your son doing?" I asked iniquitously.

Her eyes narrowed and her nostrils flared as though my delving into any misfortune of hers was the straw that broke the camel's back.

"He's fine. Why?"

"Because, that's a part of your life. I was just concerned about how you and the father were working things out."

"We aren't! He wants him and that's it."

Her demeanor switched from arrogance to innocence. Karen calmed down considerably. But what bothered me was that she humbled herself to this man and then gave me the blues every chance she could get. It all made my next idea even more intriguing.

"Well, you do realize that the baby will need to know its brother."

"I guess you're right."

"So, listen. I can talk to his father for you and maybe see if we can work something out so that you can spend more time with your son. But I need a favor from you."

"And what's that?"

"I need your word that you won't go over to Moms's house with Kim."

"My favor doesn't even compare to what you're asking me to do."

"Don't you miss your son? How can you sit here knowing that a part of you is walking around in the world and you can't even contact him? Give me a chance."

"No, I don't think Derek'll go for that," she said in a helpless tone.

"That's probably because you've taken the wrong approach in the past. Give me his number and I'll talk to him. This is important to me. Family should be close, especially when they share the same mother."

She tore off a piece of the napkin that she was ripping earlier and wrote the brotha's name and phone number down, reluctantly handed it to me, and then thanked me for my sincere efforts to make the wrong, right.

"It's okay," I assured her. "By the time I'm done talking to Derek, you'll have joint custody. Now, do I have your word?"

"I guess," she said, sounding disappointed.

I looked at Karen and saw something in her eyes that I had never seen before: fear. She wore a terrified expression for the remainder of the conversation. But she never told me why. Not that it would have taken a rocket scientist to figure out that Derek had instilled a fear in her even greater than the one I had of losing Nik.

I could tell that there was something she wanted to say. And that it hurt her to know that she needed to keep it inside so that she could remain in control. Too many secrets unfolded might cause her to lose some of her leverage over me. And in her eyes, it wasn't worth it. Not even if it meant a momentary taste of sanity.

Nikai

About a week later, on the day that I was scheduled to meet with the record executive, Sheila called. Byron's mother had passed away the night before and Sheila was preparing to move back to the other side of the island with Rastaman.

"Are you all right?" I asked her.

"Yeah, she went in her sleep. Byron's been taking it pretty hard, though."

"Really?"

"She was all he had. He's got no more family anywhere, at least that he knows of."

"Oh, tell him that I am so sorry about his loss. But guess what?"

"What, sweetie?"

"I'm going to meet with that record guy I was telling you about. You know, the one who saw me singing in the club that night."

"Really? You nervous? Don't be nervous. You'll do good. I just know it. Take your time, do your breathing, and blow his mind."

"I will. This is my big break. Hopefully, things will be looking up when I leave there. Lord knows, I need it."

"Is everything else okay?"

"Oh, I didn't fill you in, did I? You leave too much time between phone calls, Sheila."

"Quit complaining and tell me what's been happening!"

"Well, Travis called me, asking me to put some money on his books."

"Why *you*? It's been over two years since he's seen you!"

"Same question I asked, but he gave me some line about me being the only person that he could trust. So I went and got five hundred dollars from his mother, with the intention of sending it right off."

"Don't tell me you spent it!"

"No, no! Let me finish. I was really busy and couldn't do it right away. So my mother throws this dinner for Taylor's fiancé, and I planned to get a money order immediately after I left there. But the dirty *muthafucka* went upstairs, stole it out of my purse, and then had the nerve to die on me before I could cuss him out and get it back!"

Sheila was laughing so hard that I was certain she hadn't heard every word of the story. She even dropped the phone a couple of times, only to come back laughing some more.

"So now, I owe Travis five hundred dollars that I *don't* have because I'm trying to save up to move into my own apartment."

"Can't make it work with Rob, huh?"

"Nope. I've tried, too."

"I don't think you've tried as hard as you say. I think you've still got something for that producer you wrote about in your letter. Whassup with him?"

"Kalif? I like Kalif, but there's so much other stuff going on right now. . . ."

"Kai, what did I tell you about being afraid to show how you feel? If he makes you happy don't be afraid to say that he does. Hell, even show it!"

"You said the same thing about Rob."

"And?"

"And look what happened with us."

"That's a part of life. And guess what?"

"What?" I asked.

"It'll probably happen again and again and again and again. That's just the way it goes. You just keep livin'. And if you're still plannin' to leave Rob, don't let him know that until you have all of your money *saved up* and an apartment *picked out.* Remember what I told you."

"Yeah, watch my mouth. And don't cut my nose off to spite my face."

"Bye, sweetie."

"Bye."

I got out of bed, jumped in the shower, and hopped out at the speed of light. I was running late for my meeting with the bigwig in the music industry. I rambled through my closet and grabbed a wine-colored pantsuit and matching heels. Snatched the shower cap off of my head and shook my twists into place. Rubbed some jojoba oil on my scalp, sprayed perfume on, and headed out the door.

I pulled up in front of a building downtown, near the St. Louis Centre and the Mercantile Towers. Practiced my breathing on my way up to the tall glass doors, just in case he wanted me to sing a cappella. I was more nervous than I'd ever been in my life. My hands were shaking and I was starting to sweat like James had right after he stole my money and came trotting down the steps like he was just about to receive an award for Best-Dressed Pickpocket.

I was supposed to have been looking for a man by the name of Leon Lovejoy. I hoped I didn't *look* as silly saying his name as I sounded. It had a certain ring to it, though. Like a woman in heels and a cheesy dress would be bringing him cocktails every hour on the hour and calling him "Daddy" as she took his order.

I hopped on the elevator and took it to the fourth floor. Got off and roamed the hall until I came to Suite 423. I stopped, adjusted my jacket, checked my breath, and then rang the bell. I waited, but no one answered. I rang it a second time and a tall brotha with that Alonzo Mourning sex appeal opened the door. He was wearing a white tank top and black basketball shorts and was talking on a cell phone as he waved me in. I mouthed a silent *hello* and did a dainty wiggle with my fingers. Stepped inside to admire the studio and office space that he had turned into a playhouse. There was a pool table in the center of the floor, pinball machines along the wall, and a basketball hoop at the end. Leon was apparently a six-foot-seven kid living like a king. The entertainment center was like something out of the movies. I had never seen a television cover that much wall space in my life. He had speakers coming out of the ceiling, for God's sake, and a dance floor in case you felt moved to get up off of his long leather couch and shake yo' booty.

He finished with his call and walked over to me as I gawked at the place like somebody who hadn't ever been anywhere nice.

"Leon Lovejoy," he said, extending his hand.

"Nikai Parker. Nice to meet you. This is a very interesting place you have here."

"Thanks, I guess. You want anything to drink?"

"No, I'm fine. Thanks."

"You can come in here and sit down," he said, leading the way to the area where I assumed he entertained. "I wanna check something out and then we'll be ready to talk business."

He sat down and grabbed a remote off the arm of the couch and turned the television on. I sat back, crossed my legs, and waited for the SILENCE IS GOLDEN sign to flash across this theater-size set.

Then Leon asked, "So whassup with Kalif? He tell you that I saw you the first two shows and loved your voice?"

"Yeah, he did. Thank you. I just try to sing from my soul."

"It shows. You have a certain look about you, too."

He pressed the play button and a video started up. It was the usual scene of brothas pulling up to a rented house in rented 4x4s, sipping drinks, and dancing with rented models.

"You into hip-hop?" he asked.

"Mostly people like Common, Mos Def, Talib Kweli."

"This group here is definitely *hot*. I just signed them and got this video under way. There's a lot of local talent right here in St. Louis. People are really sleepin' on the Midwest's potential."

"Where are you from?" I asked.

"Jersey. The East Coast is a lot faster than out here. For me, coming to St. Louis is like going to the South. I can kinda slow down and relax a bit."

He grabbed the remote to turn the volume up. Had the thing blastin' in my ears like I might've mentioned that I was hard of hearin'. Leon started doing a dance right there on the couch. Was even throwin' his hands in the air and wavin' 'em like he just didn't care, if you know what I mean.

Then he looked over at me and asked, "You like that, don't ya'? That shit's hot, ain't it?"

I wanted to tell him, Hell no! But before I could even fix my mouth to fake a smile, something popped up on that screen that caused me to lose the air in my lungs. Not the half-naked sista with her dress over the head of one of the emcees and not the brotha who was tossing dollar bills into a fireplace that he couldn't afford even if that song had gone platinum, but *Travis's* face. He was sitting next to Tyrone and three skanks, who were falling all over him. Leon noticed me gasping for breath and turned to me again.

"You can be on the big screen like this, too, you know."

"Um, can I ask you a question?"

"Whassup?"

"Who is this group you just signed?"

"You see my man right there, there, and there? That's them. And that's their manager," he said, pointing to Travis. "He just got back in town and hopped right on this project with them."

He could've knocked me over with a feather or just by turning his system up another notch. I suddenly felt weak, like I hadn't eaten in twenty-four hours or something. Leon went on talking about how *hot* his new group was, while all I could think about was *money* and the fact that I didn't have the amount I owed Travis. He was fresh out of jail, hungry, and trying to make it as a manager for Tyrone. And by the looks of things, they were doing a lot more spending than they were saving. Which ultimately meant that he would be looking for me, or should I say his five hundred dollars?

Leon turned to me and asked, "So, where do you see yourself musically in the next five years, let's say?"

"Um, right now really isn't a good time for me. I'm feeling kind of sick to my stomach. You mind if we do this another time?"

"No problem. Just have Kalif give me a call when you're feeling better."

"Thanks," I said, walking to the front door. "I really appreciate your understanding."

"It may just be anxiety from seein' those bruhs in the video. Kinda makes you ready to make your mark, huh?"

"I must admit that video *definitely* has something to do with it."

James's funeral was finally scheduled for the following day, because of a lengthy FBI investigation and Taylor still wasn't in any shape to view a closed casket, not to mention an open one. Mama told me that the funeral home had managed to partially reconstruct his face by using clay and that they suggested a veil be placed over the top half of the casket. She said that his mother had been hospitalized for a nervous breakdown and, seeing how Taylor was carrying the only child he'd ever produced, we were responsible for showing up on her behalf. This was all before she asked me to press and curl my hair so that I wouldn't embarrass our family. Now, what do you think my response was?

Naturally, I was accused of being self-absorbed, inconsiderate, and, for the first time, jealous of my older sister. It really surprised me to hear that coming from Mama's mouth. I guess because after a while, you get used to the feelings of the heart staying there and never passing the lips. But obviously, she was fed up with me and my uncompromising ways. I mean, how dare I refuse to call in sick and take a chance on losing my job, not alter the texture of my hair for a bunch of strangers, and then resist putting my car on the road for 1,120 miles both ways for a dead man whom I hardly knew anything about other than the fact that he had kleptomaniac tendencies and was five hundred dollars richer when he left St. Louis? The nerve I must have.

That morning, I went by the house to try to explain to Taylor why I was unable to make the trip. She and Uncle Lucky were sitting side by side, wearing sweat suits and staring out of the front window. I wondered for a second if maybe he had convinced her to join him on his journey to escape the state that they were in. To be his copilot in reuniting with James.

"Hey, everybody," I greeted them, standing behind the two wooden chairs.

There was no response. Then Lucky looked at me and smiled. I returned the gesture and massaged his shoulders for a brief moment. I turned to Taylor and pulled her uncombed head close to my waist. Her arms fell limp by her side. Without making any eye contact, I tried to let her know that I really *wanted* to understand how she felt. But that was all. I didn't need personal experiences like this to make me appreciate my current woes. I caressed the side of her face and felt her arm come up behind me and wrap around my waist.

I looked at Taylor and asked, "You wanna talk?"

She nodded and slowly pulled herself up from the chair. Made her way up the stairs and into the guest bedroom. Her walk was stiff and almost looked painful. Not physically painful, but the kind of pain that occurs when the heart hurts. When you don't know if tomorrow will be better and you don't really care.

I took a seat on the full-size bed and asked, "Did Mama tell you that I wouldn't be able to make the funeral?"

"Yeah, she told me."

Taylor sat down in a light blue recliner next to the closet. Pulled the lever on the side and extended her legs. She folded her hands on her stomach and sighed heavily.

"It's just that I don't have the time to take off from work. I've used up all of my vacation days."

I was lying and, believe me, I felt bad for doing it. But events like funerals and burials weren't enough incentive to travel that kind of distance. Besides, I hadn't lost sight of the fact that I couldn't have *paid* Taylor to drive *three* miles to represent me at Robert's funeral. Even if his *entire* head had been blown off.

"I didn't really want y'all to go anyway. There's just too much still going on."

"What do you mean?" I asked.

"James's mother didn't really know the person I knew."

"And I'm assuming that we didn't, either."

"No, y'all didn't. He was kind and sweet. Gentle yet power- ful. He made people listen when he spoke. Had the criminals in that courtroom shaking in their boots."

She laughed and rested her mouth on her fist as she stared outdoors.

"I wonder how he felt. You know, like if he was lonely or if he thought of me and the baby. Sometimes, I even wonder if he cried. Or if he even saw it coming."

I saw no use in bringing up the money issue at such a touchy time, so I decided to drop it. Resolved myself to the fact that I was either gonna hustle it up or admit the truth. But in the meantime, I had to be there for Taylor.

"He ever come to you in your dreams?" I asked.

Taylor suddenly came to life and answered, "Actually, he did. Just the other night. We were at his apartment in New York and he came home right on time, the way that he always did when I visited him. We sat down for dinner and watched a movie. I asked him how he was and he told me that he was okay. The awkward thing about it was that I wasn't afraid of him, even though I knew that he had passed away."

"You think that it was really him coming to you, or do you think that you *wanted* to dream about him?"

"I don't know. I guess maybe a little of both. But what I *do* know is that his mother is upset with me."

"But why? Doesn't she know that you shouldn't be traveling in your condition?"

"I don't think she really cares," Taylor said, rubbing her stomach. "It's not *me* she wants present; it's the baby."

"That's crazy."

"No, that's Clara."

Taylor fell silent and let her head fall backward. She closed her eyes and allowed a few tears to seep through her lashes. Shook her head and ran her fingers through her matted hair. I let her have her minute, because she deserved an opportunity to cry as freely as she wanted to. But it was when I witnessed her brows come to a point and the rest of her face ball up in disbelief that I held her hand.

"It's okay. Let it out."

She began to whimper like a scorned child. Fluid ran from every opening on her face. She cried until she sweated. Then she wiped away the old tears to make room for the new, which weren't too far behind.

"Nikai, I told him to leave that stuff alone."

"What stuff?" I asked.

"The drugs, the guns . . ."

She went on to explain how James was *not* the wonderful guy we all thought he was. I was shocked as hell. Not that I originally thought the brotha was perfect, but he was *way* too fine to be caught up in drugs and guns. I mean, James was the kind of brotha who you never broke wind in front of. On the outside, he appeared to be flawless. Like there could be no imperfections in his life. The sad part is that he was just that. Flawless on the outside and a mess on the inside.

"He dealt with a guy he met in court one day. He promised that it wouldn't amount to much trouble. Swore that he would never jeopardize my life. I trusted him, with everything, and now he's left me here like this. How am I supposed to raise a baby on my own? That was the whole purpose of getting engaged—to have a family. Now I'm no better off than some unwed mother whose boyfriend ran off."

"Taylor, I don't really think this is the same thing. I mean, James would never have left you once you'd gotten pregnant."

"I wish that were true. He didn't really want a baby just yet. He said twenty-eight was too young for children. And he didn't want to be like all of these other brothers out here with *baby mamas.* So that's when the idea of getting engaged came up. But soon after that, the drug situation got worse, and I gave him an ultimatum. It was either me or the drugs. He chose the drugs. That's why I told everybody that the wedding was postponed. It was actually canceled."

At that point, it all began to come together. The nosebleed, the uncontrollable sweating, and the sudden urges to steal from an in-law-to-be. James had an addiction that Taylor knew all about. That's why she'd been so adamant about us staying out of her business, because she thought that part would somehow seep through the cracks.

"So do you think that he was really killed during a robbery?" I asked.

"Who knows. I had not talked to James all of that week. That night, I called him and didn't get an answer. I didn't leave a message, but I guess it didn't matter, because he never would have gotten it anyway."

Taylor started with the waterworks again.

"Why didn't you tell us any of this?"

"Because no one would envy a marriage to a drug addict. It was embarrassing. I've waited for my big day all my life. The moment when I could take center stage and show the world the way it's *supposed* to be done."

As I listened to Taylor, I realized that my older sister was actually as confused as I was. She was taking a dose of fantasy every morning. Except hers was twice the size of mine. She was not only living a lie but making an effort to paint a false picture for the world to see. At least I just refused to talk about mine; therefore, I didn't have to lie. There were no stories to clean up and no confessions to make later.

"So what did Mama say about all of this?"

"She doesn't know. I couldn't tell her that James didn't want to marry me. I can't tell anyone that."

"So why'd you tell me?"

"Because Lucky didn't understand," she said, bursting into laughter.

"You told Uncle Lucky before you told me?"

"I knew it wouldn't go any further with him. You might've felt the need to share it with Robert or his *low-class* sister."

"I wouldn't tell them something personal like that," I said, scooting down to the other end of the bed. "I've got a secret for you, too. Robert isn't ready to marry me, either."

Taylor chuckled to herself and shook her head.

"This is pitiful. You think it's us or our choice in men?"

"Maybe both," I answered, shrugging my shoulders.

"I need a man like Lucky, one who'll speak when spoken to and do as I ask him."

"No, I think I need a man like Daddy. Someone strong and loving."

"Shut up, Nikai, 'cause Daddy could have killed cats for a living and you would still want somebody who looks like him and acts like him."

"Hey, he was a tough act to follow."

"Yeah, I know what you mean. I miss him so much sometimes."

"You know, his birthday is next week. I'm gonna go see him. You wanna go with me?"

"No. He's right here in my heart. I don't need to go to the cemetery to see him."

"I know, but it's just the whole principle of it. At some point, you have got to go and visit him. He's upset with you and Mama right now."

Taylor looked at me as though I were speaking German.

"Have you been sniffing those markers at work again?"

"No, I know what I'm talking about. Once James is gone long enough, you'll see what I mean."

I must have hit that weak spot, because she started up with the tears again. Leaked like a punctured waterbag. Slow and steady. This time, I got down on my knees in front of her and tried to shift her thoughts in another direction. I placed my hand on her stomach and the other on the arm of the chair.

"How does it feel?" I asked.

"It feels like change. You ever reach a point in your life when you feel things will never be the same?"

I wanted to say yes but decided that telling a lie would bring me no closer to understanding *or* my sister. I never allowed myself to get to that point. I wanted to play it safe. Made sure that I didn't necessarily *have* to change.

"Are you afraid?"

"Of what?"

"This sort of change."

"Not really. Some things you have to welcome. Besides, I thought that this would improve our relationship."

"You feel like you've wasted your time?"

"At first I did, but then I realized that this is just as much my baby, as it is James's, if not more. I wish that he were here with me, but I guess you can't have everything in life."

You can't have everything in life. That phrase left me wondering one thing. If you can't have everything, then how much can you have? I mean, I've seen people who look like they have it all *and then some*. Enough good luck to spread around two or three times. And then there are those of us who look like we cut out of line to go to the bathroom and missed out on our share totally. I'm talking *relentless cycles of misfortune.*

Some would say that Taylor had it all—an excellent job, a fine man, an engagement, a beautiful baby on the way, good health, and a youthful look. But to her, it was a mediocre relationship, skeletons in her closet, and a boatload of insecurities. In Taylor's eyes, James's death was just another one of God's sick jokes, but to me it seemed like deliverance. Deliverance from her little make-believe world. It was almost as though she was eating what she thought were prunes, in the dark. When God turned the light on to reveal that she was really eating water bugs, she got pissed. Not only because she couldn't deny what was going on but also because others were allowed to view her misfortunes.

Mama used to tell us, "If you think you've got it bad, lay your problems down on the table with a bunch of other peoples', and I can guarantee you that before they're done, you'll be snatching your own back up." I never thought that I could apply that when comparing my life to Taylor's. Now I could see why she was always so edgy. She really believed that her world was supposed to be picture-perfect. Even to the point where she had convinced others of the same. Everyone *but* God.

Robert

I'd been sifting through the loose change and lint that I pulled from my pockets before I turned in the night before. My end of the dresser was in complete disarray. Deodorant, cologne, pieces of torn paper, lotion, nail clippers, and other stuff contributed to the clutter.

I was looking for Derek's number and a few more quarters to dry my laundry. Since Nik had started hanging out with Karen, she'd been slacking on housekeeping, staying out late, and acting real *touched in the head*. Believing that bull about Karen being psychic.

The other night, she started talking in her sleep again. Uttered something about her uncle Lucky seeing ghosts, and Taylor selling drugs. Her mama being crazy, paying five hundred dollars to the St. Louis county jail, and the elevator doors closing on her at work. You know I listened closely for a word that even rhymed with Kalif. *Belief, relief,* or *handkerchief* would have earned her another rude awakening.

I never heard his name anymore, until one day I was on my way down to the laundry room and the phone rang. I ran back up the stairs in time to catch the answering machine picking up.

"How's everybody doing? This is Kalif calling for Nikai. Sista, don't forget I need you back down at the loft this evening. Got some more tracks for you to listen to. Call me when you get in. Peace."

Don't get me wrong, I understood his need, as a producer, to review the tracks with Nik. But wasn't she supposed to be part of a *trio*? She was skipping out of there on a solo mission too frequently just to be listening to music. And way into the late hours of the night at that. They'd given only seven performances in four months. The demo tape was *still* in the process of being made. And the brotha had never officially introduced himself *or* thanked me for allowing so much of Nik's time to be taken up.

It was almost disrespectful the way that he called, casually greeted me, and then asked to speak to *my* woman. A couple of times, I lied and told him that she wasn't home or couldn't come to the phone. I didn't want him to think that he possessed some kind of power to move Nik, when I couldn't even maneuver a conversation, if I caught her on a bad day.

Nik came through the front door, dropped her bags, and headed to the bathroom. I passed her in the hall and ran down to the laundry room. By the time I had made it back upstairs, she was kicking her boots off and pulling a sweater from over her head. She completely disrobed and jumped in the shower without uttering a single word to me.

"Nik, where are you going?" I asked, ducking my head into the steamy bathroom.

"Down to the loft."

"For how long?"

"I don't know. Why?"

"I'll wait until you come out."

I sat down on the bed and started folding towels. She rushed out of the shower, still dripping water, and proceeded to get dressed. Made sure that her black panties and bra matched, as though she was expecting to be modeling them later. She put an unnecessary amount of raspberry body splash on and then stood in front of the open closet with both hands on her hips.

"I was thinking that maybe we could do something tonight."

"Uh, tonight wouldn't be good for me," she said while getting dressed. "I don't exactly know when I'll be back."

"Well, why don't I rent some movies and pop a little popcorn? And when you get home, we can kick back for a while."

She continued lacing her boots and checking out her own butt in the full-length mirror.

"I don't want to make a promise that I can't keep. We've got a lot of music to go through."

"So when will I get a chance to be with you?"

She stopped moving around for a second and exhaled heavily.

"As soon as I've had a chance to be with myself."

"Maybe if Kalif wasn't getting more than his share, you could evenly dispense your time!"

"Whatever, Robert."

She fanned her hand at me and grabbed one of her purses off of the closet door. Picked up the one that she was currently carrying and dumped its contents onto the bed.

"Nik?"

"Yeah."

"Do you still love me?"

"Why would you ask me that?"

"No reason."

She turned and looked at me like I had asked to borrow a lung. I just walked away, because there was no reason to speak on that topic any further. She had answered my question by *not* answering it. Nik picked up the few things she needed and left the rest. Mumbled a pitiful "I love you" and walked out of the front door.

I sat down in the bedroom and inhaled the scent that she had left behind of her freshly bathed body. Probably assuming that it was all I deserved to get of her. I gathered up the rest of the junk from her purse and placed it on the dresser. Stretched out on the bed and beat the mattress a couple of times. Felt a small package about the size of an Alka-Seltzer. I moved the ruffled sheets back and found a condom, a brand that I didn't particularly care for. As a matter of fact, condoms were something that I never bothered to buy because Karen was usually prepared and Nik had let me know that I had nothing coming in that department. So, if it wasn't mine, it had to be hers. Or *Kalif's*.

I hopped up, grabbed a pair of damp jeans and a sweatshirt from the laundry room. Called Don at home for the address to the loft, but I didn't get an answer. A lack of response had become a common thing around here. No one seemed to be available anymore. I paced the floor, gritting my teeth, until my head hurt. Tried to look through the mess Nik had left on the bed, for some kind of lead, but came up empty-handed.

I walked into the kitchen and put a pot of water on to boil. Made some hot coffee and poured it into a thermos. Grabbed as many of Nik's things out of the closet as my arms could hold and then threw them in the trunk of my car. I went back up to the apartment, got the condom, the thermos of coffee, and a hundred dollars from my stash. Then I drove to Karen's place.

Nikai

Maurie, Janae, and Ahmad had arrived at the loft long before I did. They had dinner on, and some beats that Kalif had arranged for our project were blasting through the speakers. The smell of baked whiting and vegetables lingered throughout the entire fourth floor. It all had me feeling peaceful. Like I didn't have a care in the world.

Kalif lighted candles and turned out the lights in the living room, where he and I sat. The rest of the loft was bright, but not enough to disturb our vibe. He had managed to find a comfortable spot between my legs while I braided his locks again. He explained the energy he felt from the heat on his back and its connection between us. Then told me that since the womb was where he'd come from, it was only natural for him to want to return, and that its closeness brought him serenity.

"Tell me your deepest secret."

Kalif rested his elbows on my thighs and asked, "Why?"

"Because I want to know."

"If the secret is that deep, shouldn't I be keeping it to myself?"

"Is it that you don't trust me?" I asked.

"No. But I just don't see the purpose of revealing things that are irrelevant."

"Do you think that you can suppress a part of your life so long that it almost seems like it never happened to you?"

"Yeah. That's how it is with that deepest secret. When I think about it, it seems distant. But it was so long ago that it doesn't matter."

"What is it? I'll tell you what mine is."

"Let me see if yours can compare. Tell me."

I glanced up at the others, who were still in the kitchen, cooking up a storm, and took a deep swallow.

"I don't think I'll ever be able to have children."

"Why do you say that?"

"Because I've tried before. Several times."

"And how do you feel about that?"

"It makes me sad when I see other people with children who are the spitting image of them. The way that people describe the feeling, the amount of love that they have for their children—it all makes me sad. I messed up the chance that I was given by having an abortion. It probably wouldn't be so bad if everyone around me wasn't coming up pregnant and reminding me of my disability."

"Is that how you think of it? As a disability?"

"Well, yeah. I mean, sometimes. Birth is supposed to be natural."

"Have you seen a specialist yet?"

"No. I don't want those people looking at me like some kind of hopeful welfare recipient who wants to have a baby without a husband in order to keep a roof over my head."

"There you go again, caring about what other people think. What about how *you* feel? Isn't the mental anguish that you experience more important than the opinion of some physician you don't even know personally?"

"I guess it should be. But a little support would help."

"Support from who?"

"Robert."

"Why do you think he doesn't support you?"

"Probably because a child is one of the things that he can do without."

"And you?"

"And me what?"

"Is it something that you can do without?"

"Right now, yeah. I mean, I want a baby sooner or later, but

I guess knowing that I can have one when I get ready is what stays on my mind. What about you?"

"What about me?"

"Is it something that you want?"

"Someday."

"When is *someday*?"

"When I've found my queen. But I wouldn't say that marriage is necessary."

"Why not?"

"Because true love can exist only in the heart. I can sign my name on a sheet of paper all day and never give a damn about the person whose signature is next to it."

"I guess you're right. Kalif?"

"Whassup?"

"Do you find it hard to make it in this world, living by your own set of laws?"

"If I was caught up in the ways of this world, it probably would be. But I choose the universal laws as opposed to man-made ones. Hey, you never told me how things went with Love-joy."

"I'm not really sure about signing with him."

"Why not?"

"I just get a bad feeling about the whole thing. I can't explain it."

"Nikai, kindred spirits are usually drawn toward one another. If you aren't feelin' it, then maybe you should check him out one last time to know for sure."

"You mind setting up another appointment?"

"Didn't I tell you that I had something planned for you?"

"Yeah, you did."

"Then if there's anything I can do to help you, you know I will."

"Thanks. So tell me your secret."

Kalif got quiet and put his arms down in his lap.

"I felt responsible for my son's death."

I gasped slightly and wondered if I were swimming in water that was too deep for me.

"Why?"

"It's a long story."

"I've got time."

"Well, when my son's mother and I hooked up, we were both pretty young. Probably about twenty-one. She was into hanging out a lot, drinking, smoking, whatever. I didn't trip, 'cause I wasn't into taking care of adults. After a while, I came into the knowledge, but she wasn't feelin' it. Talked about me bad, asking me what the big point was. Said I was only one person trying to change the world. Had me questioning myself for a minute."

"Questioning yourself how?"

"Wondering if I really was wasting my time, wondering if maybe I was just trying to stand for something in order to give my life purpose in other people's eyes."

"And?"

"And I realized that that thought was impossible, because in other people's eyes, I was already wasting my life, so the satisfaction that I felt was because I knew that I was doing what was right. And that a lot of those people, like my lady at the time, attacked me because they felt I was challenging them to be who they already were; I was the reflection that they didn't want to see.

"I stopped drinking and smoking. Took my health a lot more seriously. Didn't concentrate on spending money unnecessarily and saved instead. Started praying, reading, doing community service whenever I could. But Tasha couldn't get with that. It was too much work, I guess. One day, she came to me cryin' and sayin' that she was pregnant. Didn't know what to do. Acted like she wanted to kill my seed or somethin'. I told her she needed to have the baby, that it was divine will from the most high. She got mad and said she couldn't afford it, didn't even know if she wanted the relationship anymore, let alone the child."

"So what did you do?" I asked.

"Prayed. She came to me a month later and said that she would have the baby if I quit buggin' out with the knowledge. I couldn't do that, so into the fourth month, she started with the drinking again. Supposedly tryin' to wait me out, but the shit didn't work. I just prayed even harder, while she made her drinks doubles. We went back and forth until the eighth month, but by then she was bedridden and the baby was almost fully developed. We knew there were complications the moment he got here. When Mawali died, Tasha went back to her same old ways, but I sank into a depression. I felt a level of responsibility to Mawali. I'd stood back and let someone harm my child. That alone made me a bad father. Every day, I thought about how I could've stopped her, how I could've done more than prayed."

"But that's what faith is all about, knowing that divine will is gonna take over anyway. It's believing that the Creator wants the best for you and sometimes blessings are disguised," I said.

"I know, but that was my *son*, my seed. It was hard to handle, especially with her dancin' her ass back to the club the following week. I started smoking herb again soon after that, but as far as the other stuff goes, history. I left Tasha and everything else in the wind."

Kalif sat between my legs and took an extremely painful walk down memory lane. Unleashed a sadness that I wasn't sure I should have pulled from the depths of his soul. As he talked about holding his lifeless firstborn in his arms, he shed tears. I watched him fight the urge to cover his pain, convince himself that he hadn't done anything wrong. In his mind, he was just as, if not more, guilty as Tasha. He felt that infamous silence had let him down.

Kalif became quiet for a while. Didn't say a single word, just stared at the middle of the coffee table.

"You okay?" I asked.

"I'm better than I was. It's just wild how you can see yourself in a situation but at the same time not be able to imagine how you managed to handle it."

"Yeah, I know. That's how I feel sometimes when I think about my relationship with Robert."

Kalif calmed down and placed his elbows back on my thighs.

Then he asked, "Can you describe your relationship in three words?"

"*Leave me alone.*"

Kalif burst into laughter and leaned forward. Turned and looked at me.

"You are a trip. What's goin' on with you two?"

"I think we've grown apart. It's like we've been boycotting each other for the past year. He won't compromise, and neither will I. So now we're just waiting to see who will get fed up and move out of the apartment first."

"And why won't you?"

"Basically, because I don't have anyplace to go. I refuse to move in with my mother, and right now I can't afford to live alone."

"What if I told you that you could live here?"

"That might interfere with our professional relationship."

"Not if we balance it with an intimate one."

I blushed and tightened my grip on his locks. He had no idea how much I would have loved to do just that. But jumping out of one relationship only to jump into another didn't seem to make much sense, either.

"I guess not, huh?"

"I didn't say yes and I didn't say no."

Not out loud anyway. My spirit was telling me to lean in the direction of positive energy, while my heart was telling me to hear what Rob had to say at least. Maybe he'd turned over a new leaf. And then again, it could be a desperate attempt to salvage a relationship of convenience. It was beginning to look like he was just as afraid of change as I was. Learning to trust and consider another human being is not an easy task. You either succeed or you don't. And those who don't usually end up like Robert and me. Unsuccessfully filling the same space. As for those who do, well, that remained to be seen.

Robert

"W ho is it?"

"It's me."

"Who is me?"

"Karen, open the door."

It was freezing cold outside and the fact that the clothes I was wearing were still wet didn't make the situation any better. I'd knocked off the thermos of hot coffee on the way over and fired up at least four cigarettes. My legs were shaking, my hands were stiff, and my head hurt from gritting my teeth between each drag.

Karen came to the door wearing a flannel gown and bunny slippers. She scratched around her navel and grinned when she realized that it was me.

"Hey, baby."

I hesitantly stepped inside of her apartment. Didn't want to take a chance on Kim being home while I responded to Karen's informal greeting.

"Who's here with you?" I asked.

"Nobody. Kim had a date and Nik won't be over until to-morrow."

She grinned and looked at me out of the corner of her eye. I sucked my teeth and took a seat on the couch. A response, what-ever it may have been, would've probably landed me in jail that night.

Then Karen asked, "Have you talked to Derek yet?"

"No. Been too busy to worry with that right now."

She closed her eyes, laughed, and put her hands up to her temples.

"Yeah, I can see a lot of worry in your life."

"*Knock that shit off!* I'm not here for your games, okay?"

"So why *are* you here?"

"I was looking for Kim."

"Relax, I don't expect her back anytime soon. You want something to drink?"

I put my feet up on the coffee table and rested my eyelids for a second. When I opened them, Karen was next to me, on her knees and holding a glass of wine.

"Thanks," I said as I took it from her and finished it off with one long gulp.

"What's going on with you?" she asked.

"Nothing. Can I get another one of those?"

She went into the kitchen and returned with a larger glass, this one filled to the top.

"Drink up."

Karen stood over me, smiling as I knocked off my second glass of wine. Then offered to get me another. And another. And another. By the time I had finished my fifth glass, she didn't have to give a psychic performance, because I was telling her everything that was on my mind.

"And a fuckin' condom was laying on the bed when she left!"

"*What?* Oh, that is *so* wrong. What do you think she had it for?"

"There's no question what she had it for, *to fuck Kalif!*"

I rested my elbows on my knees and cupped my forehead in both hands. Karen scooted closer to me on the couch and rubbed my back. Tried to comfort me as much as she could.

"Rob, I just can't believe she did this to you. Some sistas just don't know."

"Don't know what?"

"They just don't know a good man when they see one. I mean, there are so few of y'all out there, getting one is a blessing. You do know that you are a blessing to her, don't you?"

I lifted my head and asked, "Am I?"

"Yeah. Fit to be a king. And only a *fool* would treat you like any less."

Karen and the zinfandel were beginning to put things into perspective for me. I mean, it wasn't as though she hadn't gotten to know Nik. She could see what was what. Maybe she saw something that I didn't. Maybe Nik had told her some things that were never supposed to be known by any other person.

I turned to Karen and asked, "Has she ever mentioned him to you? I mean, she's lied to me before about some guy in jail. I *know* she's said something about Kalif."

She twisted her lips to the side and looked away. Had a look on her face that showed clearly that she was holding something back.

"Robert, I love you. And I don't want to see you get hurt. I couldn't bring myself to tell you anything that she's said about you *or* Kalif."

My head was spinning. I was desperate. I needed to know what I needed to know.

"Karen, I love you, too," I said, reaching out and rubbing her stomach. "And I trust that we have a close relationship. I wouldn't keep anything from you and the baby."

Karen's eyes lit up like 75-watt bulbs. Moved even closer and blushed like a virgin schoolgirl.

"Please, tell me what's going on."

Her expression quickly shifted.

"If you love *me* so much, why do you care?"

"Because I want to make her pay for playing with my emotions. She just can't treat me like this over some *Bob Marley wanna-be!*"

"Oh, is that how he looks? When she described him, she only told me that he was a fine brotha and that he knew how to treat her. Now, I don't know if she was insinuating that you *don't*, but that's kind of how it sounded."

"Did she really?"

"Yeah. But what other people think of you doesn't matter, Rob. You have to be true to yourself. Besides, the people who *really* love you see you for who you are. As long as *we* don't fuck you over or *fuck somebody else*, you'll be okay."

I sat on the couch, quietly listening to what she had to say. Repeatedly rubbed the palms of my hands together until the warmth between became irritating.

Then Karen asked, "Baby, you okay?"

I didn't respond. I was too busy picturing Nik giving my lovin' away. It had been marinating for almost a year. The juices were still in place; walls were good and snug. Could probably catch a grip on a piece, tight enough to have a man speaking in tongues.

"Baby, you want another glass of wine?"

"Nah. I'm okay."

"It's just not fair how she treats you. You deserve so much better."

Karen leaned back on the couch and actually appeared to be more upset about that situation than I was. And she hadn't even had anything to drink. She sighed aloud a couple of times and folded her arms across her breasts. Slowly rocked back and forth and then burst into tears.

"What's wrong?" I asked.

"I don't like to see the people I love hurting."

She wiped her face, got up, and walked into the bathroom. I didn't know whether to follow her or if she was asking for a little time alone. I mean, she was tripping like Nik was messing her over. After about a minute and a half, I heard her call my name. Then she asked me to come into the bedroom and talk her to sleep. I stood up and attempted to catch my balance. Held on to the walls until I reached her bed.

"Be careful, sweetie. Why don't you take those wet clothes off?"

Karen was being supportive, attentive, and everything that I needed, when I needed it. And that was so much more than I could say for Nik. Karen was trying to give me the family that Nik probably never could. She didn't want anybody else *but* me. Not to mention that she was determined to be there whether I was with someone else or not. Now, I hadn't been in love very many times and didn't exactly know it when I saw it, but as far as I was concerned, Karen was coming pretty close to being my woman.

"Come and lie down next to me," she suggested, patting the spot on the bed reserved just for me.

I climbed up on the bed as she wrapped her leg around me and held me close. Rocked me as though I was our baby and hummed a tune. She was *way* off-key, but at least I could say that I was the only person she was singing for. That wasn't necessarily true with Nik.

"So what did you plan to do?" she asked.

"I was gonna come and see if Kim knew where the loft was. That's where Nik does her music and *everything else*."

"But specifically, what are you gonna do?"

"I don't know."

I lay there and stared at the ceiling, cupping the back of my head with my hands. Resolved myself to the fact that if Nik was gonna get her freak on, she was doing it by then. I calmed down a bit and slowly drifted off to sleep. Karen went on humming that off-key tune she liked so much. It seemed easier to doze off than to stay awake and be tormented by a pitiful imitation of the woman I thought I loved.

My eyes couldn't have been closed any longer than ten minutes, when I was awakened by a hand in my boxers. My piece was being stroked slowly. The warm palm was laced with some kind of lubricant. Had me doing pelvic thrusts in my sleep. I didn't want to open my eyes. Afraid that I would throw off the flow of things. I moaned and moved. Moved and moaned. Called God's name a few times and then Nik's. The massage stopped as I heard the sound of phlegm being coughed up from the middle of somebody's chest cavity. Then came a glob of mucuslike fluid landing right between my mouth and my chin. My eyes popped open in time to catch Karen backing away from me and almost tripping over her shoes.

"*What the fuck is wrong with you?*" I yelled.

"You called me *Nik!*"

"I don't give a damn what I called you. You don't spit in my face!"

"Well, you need to try to remember my name! I won't be disrespected in my own *damn* house!"

"If you spit in my face again, I'll do more than disrespect your ass!" I warned.

"Rob, you don't scare me!" she said, standing on the other side of the bed, her hands planted firmly on her hips. "I'm not Nik, and don't you forget it! Shit, now I don't blame her for going to be with a *real* man. Your sorry ass—"

I think I might have levitated across the bed at the speed of light. All I know is that I ended up on top of Karen, and not in a very flattering position. My hands were around her throat and her face had turned red, almost the same color that I was seeing. The alcohol had my adrenaline pumping, and the anger that I had built up about Nik was being released on Karen and, unfortunately, my unborn child, as well.

She kicked, screamed, and clawed at my arms until she had no more strength in her body. Flashbacks of her threatening to break up my relationship came to mind. All of the times that she'd called the apartment and circled the apartment caused me to press her neck deeper and deeper into the carpet.

I had been pushed so far that there didn't appear to be any point of return. Everything that I knew to be real was falling apart and all I had to look forward to was a baby I wasn't necessary sure I'd created.

The spit that Karen had hawked up on my face dripped from my lips down toward hers. She turned her face away as the long line of thick mucus settled along her neckline. My salty sweat fell into her eyes and blended in with the tears. It all made me want to let her up, until she narrowed her eyes, adjusted her hips, and kneed me in the groin. I quickly went from seeing red to seeing stars. I landed on top of her. All of my weight made it hard for her to breathe and just plain hard for the baby.

"Get the hell off of me!" she screamed.

I rolled onto my back as she went on damning me to hell. Then she stood over me, raised her foot to stomp the life out of my piece, when there was a knock at her bedroom door.

"Karen, open up. What are you doin' in there?"

It was Kim, back from her date, and with the best timing she'd ever had.

"I'll be out in a second," Karen called.

"No. My date is out here and I want to show you something."

"No! You can't come in here. I don't have any clothes on."

"Girl, I'm not tryin' to look at you," Kim insisted as she opened the door and slipped inside.

Her mouth fell open so wide that I could have shoved a tire

in it. Kim batted her eyes constantly and then rubbed them as though the sight that she was seeing would change.

"What . . . what . . . what . . ." she stuttered, pointing at both of us.

Karen was sitting on the bed with her face resting in her hands. Appeared to be leaving all explanations up to me. Kim covered her mouth and gasped for breath a few times. Took a seat in the chair next to the door and continued pointing back and forth.

I searched for the right words to say as I slipped my piece back into my boxers and rose to my feet.

Then Kim said, "Wait a minute. I don't understand this."

"What is there to understand?" Karen asked.

Kim looked at me and asked, "Do you know that she's pregnant?"

"How could I not know?"

"It's his baby, Kim."

My eyes shot in Karen's direction as she nonchalantly put my sanity on the front line. Acted as though she was simply giving Kim the weather forecast.

"Wait, wait, wait. You mean to tell me that y'all have known each other all along? You knew who he was when I moved in here and you pretended like we just happened to be in that parking lot at the same time?"

Karen sat down on the bed and shrugged her shoulders. I guess she saw this as a personal problem for Nik, Kim, and me. She had come into our lives and toyed with us until she was done. Now that the game was over, she was ready for everyone to disappear, including me.

"Hold up. You faked like your ass was psychic to fuck with Nik because you really wanted Rob for yourself? *Bitch, are you crazy?*"

And there she went. Kim was all over Karen like a tacky silk outfit on a pimp. I grabbed Kim by her feet and pulled her back across the bed. It almost felt as though I was plowing a field, the way she insisted on swinging at Karen.

After she pulled herself together, Kim looked over at me with flared nostrils and balled-up fists.

Then she asked, "Where is Nik?"

"Out with Kalif!" I answered.

"*What?* What would make you say that?"

I pulled the wrapped condom from my pocket and held it up in the air.

"So what's that supposed to mean?"

"It means that this came out of her purse."

"And how do you know she didn't buy it for *you?*"

"Because we don't do anything that would require a condom."

Karen straightened her ripped gown on her shoulders and snickered aloud. Then Kim cut her eyes in a fashion that demanded silence from both of us.

"Now, what makes you think that she's even interested in Kalif?"

"I don't know, maybe it was the way she called his name in her sleep," I answered sarcastically. "Or it could be the way that she rushes to be with him *almost every evening.*"

"Well, maybe if you spent more time at home—"

"And less time in *my* panties!" Karen added.

"Shut up!" I yelled.

"Why don't the *both* of y'all get out of my house!"

"Shit, I've been thrown out of better places than this! C'mon, Rob, let's go home."

" 'Let's'? What do you mean, 'let's go home?' "

"I mean that *you* need *me* to keep *that* a secret," she explained, pointing at Karen's stomach. "And frustration from being homeless might cause me to pour my heart out to Nik."

Then Karen smiled at me, winked, and said, "Don't worry, because if she doesn't tell it, I *promise* I will."

"You don't want to do that," Kim warned. "Unless, of course, you plan on wearing that little raggedy gown to the emergency room, and *I* can promise *you* that labor pains won't be the symptoms."

"Who put those handprints around her neck?" Kim asked, walking around to the passenger side of my car.

She had sent her date home and gathered up the rest of her things to move back with me.

"I did. She started talkin' crazy and I just couldn't take it anymore."

"So you *choked* her?"

"Like I was being paid to."

"That's wild, but the sad part is that there's a child involved in all of this."

"Yeah, tell me about it."

Kim tossed her purse onto the seat and walked to the back of the car. Yelled for me to pop the trunk and then took longer than anybody I had ever seen just to throw a few bags in it. I took a glance in the rearview mirror but only got a clear shot of the trunk, no Kim. Then out of nowhere, she appeared at my window, holding one of Nik's dresses in one hand and a pair of shoes in the other.

"What the hell is *this* about?"

"Ah, I was planning on taking her things down to the loft."

"And you had to come by *here* to do that?"

"No, I came by here to get you so you could show me where the loft is."

"And what if I didn't know?"

"Then . . . then—"

"Then what, Rob? You were gonna take your ass right back to that apartment and wait for Nik no matter how long it took her to get home? Don't you love her? Don't you even want your relationship to work anymore? People like me are out here in this world searching and praying every day for that special someone to come into our life. You have that someone already, and all you can think to do is to sweat inside that *dizzy broad* who has way too much free time on her hands. I mean, this is ridiculous."

Kim shook her head and walked to the back of the car. Shut the trunk and got inside like she had just lost her best friend. Then looked over at me as though I had caused her to. I guess, in a way, she felt I had. She knew that in some small fashion, my actions would affect her and Nik's relationship and it bothered the hell out of her to know that my *piece* was what had put us all in that position.

Everybody was hurting, except for Karen. She had what she wanted, and that was power. She had little power or control over the rest of her life, so she found her womanhood in making me move—to the left, right, or whatever direction she felt at the time. And when the cold, cruel world came down on her, like it always manages to do on all of us, she called me. But what she had forgotten was the call that I still had to make to Derek.

Nikai

We had all just sat down to eat, when Kalif's pager went off. He took it from his pocket and excused himself to make what he referred to as "an urgent phone call." Dragged the 150-foot phone cord into his bedroom and closed the door. This all seemed sort of strange, until I realized that there was actually so much more of him that I hadn't connected with. A past that even *he* tried desperately to forget. A past, I realized, that I just might never know about in its entirety.

After about four minutes and three bites into my fish, he came marching out into the living room. Grabbed me by the arm and took me back into the bedroom with him. Kalif stood over me as he paced the floor, twisting one of his locks at the root.

"I need a favor."

"What is it?" I asked, hanging on his every word.

"Don got burned in one of those fires and he needs me over at his place as soon as possible. Can you give me a ride?"

"Sure. Is he okay?"

"I don't know. He called himself, so I'm assuming that he's not burned too badly. But I just want to be there for him."

"No problem. You ready now?"

Kalif took a few long breaths and clinched his fists a couple of times. I could see the sensitive side of him surfacing, a characteristic that he rarely showed in the presence of others. But I guess now was different. Or maybe I was different. Whatever it was, it sent my heart racing just as fast as his was. Had me wishing for something that just might happen, something I had heard him wishing for out loud, a me and him.

Robert

I should have known that when I made it home, Nik wasn't going to be there. The apartment was just the way I had left it. Pieces of her underwear and clothes were strung across the floor from the living room to the bedroom. It all helped me see what I'd been thinking at the time, or just the fact that I *hadn't* been thinking at all.

I walked into the kitchen, where Kim was getting a glass of juice from the refrigerator. Hopped up on the island and playfully kicked her.

"Don't touch me."

"You still mad?" I asked in a playful, whiny tone.

"Dogs get mad. But you ought to know all about that anyway."

"Oh, that was a low blow. You feel better now?" I laughed.

"No, Robert. I'm still disappointed in you."

"Well, would a hundred dollars make you feel any better?"

Kim drank juice from her glass and rolled her eyes at me. Held her hand out and did the snake roll with her neck that a lot of sistas are famous for.

"I see that now I have your undivided attention," I said, peeling each twenty back.

Her eyes grew large as she slammed the half-full glass down on the counter. I was about to lick my thumb and count it off to her, when my pager went off. Whoever it was had left a verbal message, giving me enough time to make Kim sweat.

"Hold up a second. I gotta return this page first."

I grabbed the white cordless off of its base in the kitchen and got the surprise of my life.

"Hey, Rob, it's me. I was calling to let you know that I got caught up and couldn't beat the flames this time. Wanted to know if you could come by for a while. If you can, come now. Peace."

"Listen, I need to make a run right now. Can you stay here and straighten this stuff up before Nik gets home? I don't want her to know about any of this. And try to cook a little dinner if you can. I want to surprise her."

"And why should I do something to help you?" Kim asked.

"Because if you don't, you won't have this extra money in your pocket," I said, waving the bills around.

I ran out to the car and gathered up the rest of Nik's clothes. Went back in the apartment, gave Kim a kiss on the cheek, and thanked her for doing this for me. Then I jumped in my ride, opened a brand-new pack of Newports on the way over to Don's, and prepared myself for the worst.

Nikai

I asked Kalif, "You gonna be okay?"

"Yeah, I just need to see him first."

Kalif had smoked half of a blunt and had leaned the car seat back so far, I couldn't tell whether he was snoring or sighing. He had one hand resting over his face and the other on his chest, close to his heart—right where I wanted to be.

We pulled down from the house because there were so many cars parked on Don's street. And all of them appeared to be within walking distance of his house. Kalif jumped out before I'd even shifted into park, did a light jog up to the porch, rang the doorbell, and then beckoned me to put some pep in my step.

I turned my back from the front door and prepared myself for first-, second- or third-degree burns on a man who had practically become a brother to me. But when the door opened, there were people everywhere. And I don't mean consoling one another. They were holding champagne glasses and laughing like someone had popped *Friday* in the VCR.

Don was standing next to the chair that Theresa was sitting in. I wondered for a second if that hurt, and then I questioned whether he was hurting at all. Kalif had already blended in with the crowd. Hugging what appeared to be family members who hadn't seen him in a long time. Watching him work the room, it became clear to me that he was the black sheep of the family. But because everyone else was acknowledging his presence, those who looked as though they wouldn't spit on him if *he* were on fire spoke, as well.

Don silenced everyone and said, "We'll be able to make the announcement in just a second. We're waiting for someone very special, my best man, Rob."

I felt faint. And if it hadn't been for Kalif, who happened to be on his way over to me, I'm sure I would have hit the floor.

"Did you hear that?" he asked.

"Yeah, but what is this all about? I thought you said that Don was burned in a fire."

"That's what he told me. But that was only so that his friends and the little family we have in St. Louis would come immediately. This was a surprise to *everybody.*"

I wanted to say, Who gives a damn? Jealous-ass Robert was on his way over and would find me at his best friend's engagement party with another man, and I was in no mood to go for twelve rounds. Everybody carried on having a good time. Everyone except for me, that is. I was nervous as a hooker in church. I sat quietly over in the corner, sweating my hairdo out. The perspiration from my upper lip trickled down past my chin.

"You all right, baby?" an elderly woman sitting next to me asked.

"Yes, ma'am. I'm fine."

I wiped my face and tried desperately to stop my right knee from bouncing. Every time that annoying doorbell rang, my heart skipped a beat. And with the number of people packing that house, I should have been dead three rings ago.

Kalif pulled a chair up next to me and asked, "Where do you want me?"

I was thinking the west side of Chicago, but my mouth told him to make himself at home. I mean, after all, we were at *his* cousin's house. It wasn't the other way around.

"Are you sure? Because I can move across the room and pretend I'm not here with you."

"Does Don know that we're here together?" I asked.

"Yeah. He said something about mentioning it to you later. That doesn't bother you, does it?"

Before I could answer, the doorbell rang for the gazillionth

time. I did a ninety-degree spin with my head just as Rob walked
in. The crowd gave a loud cheer, like *he* was the man of the hour.
They rushed up to him so quickly that he could see nothing but
arms and faces. I just sat tight, fanned my blouse, and hoped to
the high heavens that he didn't see me.

Robert

I'm tellin' you, there's nothing like receiving endless amounts of love from people who aren't even your family. I stepped into Don's place expecting to smell burned flesh lingering in the air, mixed with the aroma of the nerve-settling tea that Theresa drank so often. But what I got was generations of approval.

I worked my way through the crowd and asked Don, "Whassup?"

"Hold up. You'll see in just a second. Hey, everybody, listen up. Theresa and I have an announcement to make."

Don draped his arm over my shoulder and walked me back over to where Theresa was sitting. On the way, I passed familiar and unfamiliar faces. But one—or should I say two?—stood out. Nik's and Kalif's. They were seated next to each other, but Nik had her back to him. Made me wonder if they'd had the nerve enough to show up there together.

"Theresa and I have been dating for almost three years now and we've come to the realization that there can't possibly be anyone else out there in this harsh and lonely world who can fulfill our needs. So we've decided to get married."

The room filled with cheers, toasts, and laughter. Don and Theresa looked at each other as I stared at Nik and Kalif. Neither one would look in my direction. I was brought back to reality by Don pulling me over to meet some old man whose conversation would do me no good at that moment. I was on a mission.

I leaned into Don and whispered, "Listen, I'll be right back."

He nodded and went on holding meaningless conversations with people who were too blind to recognize the blatant disrespect that was occurring right before their eyes. As I got closer, Nik shifted in her seat and adjusted the jeans she'd been wearing when she rushed out and forgot her *contraceptive* on the bed. The very one that I was still toting around in my pocket. I was ten feet away when Kalif got up and darted in the opposite direction. And to top it all off, Nik got up and followed him. Looked like they were heading for the kitchen, but, as if it were planned, they doubled back and headed upstairs. I followed.

Nikai

Kalif and I walked upstairs and split up like the Jackson 5. He went into a bedroom at the end of the hall and I ducked into the bathroom. The tension that had built up downstairs was too much for us. Although I know Rob's presence made me far more uncomfortable than it did Kalif.

I could hear footsteps in the hallway, coming toward the end where I was located, and then a knocking on a door. Only it wasn't the one that I was behind. It became louder and eventually turned into a banging.

Then I heard Kalif ask, "Damn, brotha! Whassup with all of the noise?"

"Is she in there?" the other voice asked.

"Is *who* in here?"

"Tell Nik to get her ass out here, now!"

"I can't do that."

Kalif's tone was peaceful yet firm. It was the kind of sarcastic behavior that usually sent Rob through the roof.

"What the fuck do you mean, you can't do that?"

"I don't talk to sistas like that. Now if you want to see her, I would suggest you *ask* her to come out. You might get better results."

I paced back and forth on the pink carpet in this highly decorated bathroom. Tore off a piece of a plant on the back of the toilet and put my ear back up to the door.

"Look, I'm missing my best friend's engagement party. Now, would you move so that I can get my woman and rejoin him?"

There was a silence for a moment. Had me wondering what Kalif's response had been, or if he'd even had one at all. Then Robert began yelling again. Asked where I was and whether or not I was fuckin' Kalif. I took a deep swallow, balled up the plant leaf in my hand, and opened the door. Stood there with clenched fists and clicked my heels. Silently wishing I were at home.

"Here I am, Robert."

Robert looked at Kalif, who had emerged from the bedroom. Looked at every inch of him, from the locks on his head to the large Timberland boots on his feet. Turned his nose up in disapproval and, without glancing in my direction, reached out for my hand. But I didn't take it. I didn't want all that came along with the bond that Robert and I had—the rude awakenings, the uncertainty of outside relationships, and the general negative energy that he put out. I was with him only for one reason—to buy myself a little time. Time enough to save money so that I could go. Freely.

Kalif watched me as Robert did the same. Both were applying pressure, only in a different sense. Robert wanted me to make a decision that coincided with his, while Kalif simply wanted me to make a decision, whether it be one of weakness and dependency or strength and self-awareness. He just wanted me to stand up for something and to do it right then.

I started playing a game of "He loves me, he loves me not" with the plant leaf in my hand.

They continued to stare.

I continued to tear. Piece by piece, until I was down to one.

"What are you gonna do, Nik? Are you coming home or not?"

Kalif gripped the panel on the doorway and leaned heavily on one leg.

"Nikai, make yourself happy," he said.

"No, she's gonna do what she knows is right!"

"And how do you know going home with *you* is the right thing for me to do?"

Robert looked at me as if I were a child getting smart with her father. His lips parted as he began to yell again.

"*Get whatever the fuck you brought so we can go, now!*"

Kalif stood up straight and took a deep breath. Flexed a chest that was considerably smaller than Robert's and put his hands in his pockets. His subtle movements made me remember the fact that there was more to him than met the eye.

"Nikai, if you want to leave, you should leave."

"Oh, what, are you giving her permission now?" Robert asked.

"No one gives me permission to do anything. And that goes for you, too, Rob," I said.

Kalif said, "If you need to go, I can get a ride home."

Robert sucked his teeth and said, "So, I see y'all really *are* doin' more than just music. Well, you forgot this!"

Robert pulled a condom from his pocket and threw it at my face. It hit me in the same damn spot on my forehead as the purse buckle that he'd sent flying across the bedroom the night I called Kalif's name in my sleep.

"Don't look surprised. You left that shit this evening when you were rushing out to be with this sucka!"

If there were ever a time to do a disappearing act, that was it. I could feel Kalif staring at me, but I was too ashamed to look in his direction. And the condom at my feet was only adding more embarrassment to the fact that he had rejected almost all of the previous passes that I made at him.

Robert stood in front of us with a crazy look in his eye. Kalif, as if nothing had been said, was still anchoring his pockets with his hands. So I figured the only way that I would be able to save face in this situation was to play crazy right along with Rob. So crazy that I even scared myself.

I dropped the last piece of leaf—"he loves me not"—stepped deep into his comfort zone, and said, "All right, so I *fucked* him."

If you've ever seen the open palm of a large hand racing toward your throat, you know what I felt at that very moment. And if it hadn't been for Kalif, that hand might have made it to its destination. He grabbed Robert's wrist in midair and quickly caused all of the anger to shift in his direction.

Now, I already told you that Rob puts out fires for a living, and the heaviest thing Kalif carries while working is a clipboard of sheet music. If all of that healthy eating, meditation, and African holistic behavior were to pay off, now was definitely the time.

Robert's first blow landed on Kalif's cheek. The second on his chin. As for the third, it never made it. Kalif charged at Robert and pushed him into the hall closet. It sounded as though he shook the entire wall. They fell to the floor and rolled around for a while. One on top of the other, until Kalif made up his mind that he wasn't gonna take any more blows. He straddled Robert's chest and pounded into his face. I watched Robert's eyes attempting to focus on me, but before he could form an expression, he was being hit again. Kalif's fist went up and down, relentlessly crushing the bones in the face of a man I still loved.

I covered my ears, closed my eyes, and yelled, "Kalif, stop! Get off of him!"

It seemed as though the plaintive tone of a woman was the only thing that got through to him. The beast in Kalif disappeared as he cut his eyes at me, a disturbed look on his face.

"What is it you want? This man wants to hurt you!"

"I know, but hurting him won't stop him from hurting me. Please, get up."

He looked down at Robert, who had stopped moving. He lay there with his eyes closed and his head shaking from side to side.

As Kalif backed away, Don hit the top of the stairs and immediately looked at me, then at his practically motionless best man, and then at his sweaty, bloody-knuckled cousin.

"What in the hell is going on up here? Nikai?"

"I . . . I . . . I really don't know."

"Kalif?" Don asked.

"Look, I gotta go," he said, calmly wiping the sweat from his face and darting down the stairs.

I gave Don an apologetic look and followed behind Kalif, who had sped up to a rapid jog. Their family and friends were still mixing and mingling. Obviously *pretending* to be undisturbed by the noise that we had created. I opened the front door and ran down the sidewalk. Caught up with Kalif at the corner, under a streetlight, and pulled him by the back of his black leather Avirex bomber jacket.

"Where are you going?" I asked.

He stared straight ahead and said, "I can't finish your project, Nikai."

"What do you mean? Why not?"

"Because that shit back there wasn't necessary! You know how fucked up your relationship is! Why would you want to invite someone else into some bullshit like that?"

"I'm sorry. But you knew a long time ago that I was involved with someone. You knew what you were getting yourself into. I mean, did you honestly expect Robert to be happy about it?"

"No, but I didn't expect that you would choose confusion over sanity. I'll send the remainder of your fees for studio time to Don. You can pick it up from there. Good luck, sista."

Kalif stepped off of the curb and slowly blended in with the darkness. I turned back to the house and remembered that my coat was inside. I felt the cold, emotionless chill that Kalif had left inside of me and decided not to return to that madness right away.

I needed to relax, unwind, and think my next move through. Doors of communication were quickly closing before me, leaving me speechless. And what hurt more was that even if I did have something to say, I had no one who was willing to listen. No one but Kim, who was usually just as confused as I was. Sheila still hadn't moved back to the other side of the island. Mama was preoccupied with Taylor, Taylor was preoccupied with James, or the lack of him, and Lucky was simply preoccupied.

The dispiriting part of it all was that the decisions that I was afraid to make were still waiting for me. They were keeping me from home, happiness, and sanity. Or was I? Was Kalif's friendship worth my losing everything that I'd built with Robert? Was I making the right choice to stay until I could afford to go? Was Robert afraid of losing me, or just the convenience of my presence? Had I actually grown in his heart, or just on him? And ultimately, could I honestly go without both of them?

Robert

I said, "I'm all right!"

"You sure you don't wanna go and get checked out?" Don insisted.

I glared up at him. He was leaning against a counter in the kitchen and I was sitting at the table, holding a towel with ice wrapped in it, against my mouth. Don had cleared the house out after Nik and Kalif left. Everybody had questions, but none of us was giving answers.

I pulled a pack of Newports from my pocket and asked, "Theresa mind if I smoke?"

"You know she does. I can't even light incense."

"That's your fault. You ought to be able to do whatever it is you want in your own house."

Don shook his head.

"Stop talking and put that ice back on your mouth."

"I'm serious. Nik would never try and tell me what to do. You better break Theresa from that now, before it's too late."

"Too late for what?"

"Too late for you to establish yourself as man of the house."

"So in other words, too late for me to do what you've done?"

I leaned back in my chair and placed the ice on my lip. Heard Nik screaming at Kalif in my head a couple of times and then envisioned her smacking the hell out of him in the cold.

"Don."

"Whassup?"

"In your opinion, does Nik act like she wants to be with Kalif?"

"I think Nik wants to be *happy*."

"Aside from the past couple of months, don't you think I do a pretty decent job at that?"

"Honestly?" he asked, hopping up on the counter.

"Honestly."

Don locked his fingers, leaned forward, and said, "I think you've done a pretty decent job of hiding an unborn child from her. You've done a remarkable job of pushing her into the arms of another man and a rather impressive job of lying to yourself."

There was no need to respond, because Don had just said a mouthful. When Nik and I used to argue about women, money, or my time, she would tell me that the truth is always more painful than a lie. And I had danced around that hurt for too long.

"So what do you think I should do?"

"It all depends on what your motivation is. Do you want that relationship? Because if you don't, you should let her go, so that she *can* be happy. That's what a real *man of the house* would do."

"Of course I want the relationship. I know that no one would stick by me the way that she has all of this time. But what about children? She can't give me that."

"Is that her fault? And besides, I thought you said that you weren't ready for kids right now."

"Well, I'm not ready for a nursing home, either, but when I am, I want to know that I'll have the funds to secure myself a spot."

"In actuality, Nik not being able to have kids has nothing to do with you having one on the way. It sounds like more excuses. You're justifying your behavior by what someone else can or can't do. Like it or not, you have made yourself a father without making Nik a mother."

"But is that my fault?"

"Listen, it's nobody's fault that she hasn't become a mother by now. But it is your fault that you've become a father. How do you even know for sure that she can't have children?"

"Because we've tried more times than I can count," I said.

"And I bet you've been with Karen more times than you can count, but that hasn't stopped you from showing up at *her* door."

"Look, I don't need a lecture. Just a little advice."

Theresa walked into the kitchen, carrying a stack of paper plates and looking as though she hadn't missed a single word of our conversation. She silently glanced at Don, tossed the trash into the wastebasket, and turned to me.

"You want *my* advice?" she asked.

"Sure."

"If you love Nikai the way you say you do, then you should tell her about the baby. Being honest is all you can do at this point. Truthfully, you have no other options. Depending on where her heart is right now, she will either decide to stay with you or to move on. But whatever decision that is, you have to respect it and take care of your child. The one that you made without her. Imagine how you'd feel if you spotted her on the streets five years from now pushing a stroller. Robert, things aren't always what they seem. Open that third eye."

Theresa spoke her peace and left the kitchen quietly. Don looked at me with raised brows and shrugged his shoulders, then jumped down off the counter and stood in the middle of the floor, grinding his fist into the palm of his hand.

Then he said, "Well, that was simple."

"Where'd you find her?" I asked, laughing.

He looked into the direction in which she had walked and answered, "Somewhere close to heaven."

Don walked into the living room and began playing a stupid game of tag with Theresa while they helped each other clean the place up. I stayed where I was and held that towel close to my face until the pain went away. But like all pain, the disappearance was only temporary. It was bound to resurface at the most inopportune moment.

By the time the ice had completely melted, I decided that I was gonna tell Nik the entire story and deal with the consequences like a man. If she decided to leave, I'd know she'd never been mine to begin with, and if she stayed, I'd thank the heavens for blessing more men than just Don.

Nikai

I drove home, hoping that Robert was staying at Don's place that night. And that maybe Kalif would give me a chance to explain myself. I had planned to call when I got in, but it appeared that Kim had cooked and cleaned her way back into the apartment.

She said, "Whassup? You talk to Rob?"

"Yeah."

"So he told you why he rushed out of here like that?"

I hung my coat in the hall closet and said, "Oh, you must mean when Don invited everybody over for an announcement."

"What kind of announcement?"

"He and Theresa are getting married."

I sat down on the couch in the living room, leaned my head back, and closed my eyes. I had been crying and smoking the entire way home and was exhausted. Kim was asking question after question. And I mean frivolous ones, like what Rob's reaction to the announcement had been, if we had talked over there, and whether or not I had heard from Karen.

"We spoke briefly, and I haven't talked to Karen since the other morning. Has my mother or sister called?"

"Yeah. Your mother called and said that she wouldn't be able to make it. She also said that Taylor didn't have the energy."

"Yeah, right," I said skeptically.

I hadn't necessarily expected them to pull through, but a pleasant surprise was well overdue.

"Is there someplace you need me to go with you?" Kim asked.

"No, I don't really think you'll want to join me in a cemetery. Besides, it's my father's birthday, and I wanted the family to go to see him together."

As Kim got up to check on the baked chicken, the phone rang.

"Hello?"

Karen said, "Nik, it's about time you made it home. I wanted to talk to you about something."

"What is it?" I asked.

Karen chuckled a bit and then said, "I don't quite know how to ask you this."

"Well, whatever it is, could you do it quickly, because I'm really tired."

"Okay, okay. I was sitting here meditating, when a vision came to me. I saw Robert holding a baby in his arms. Are you pregnant?"

"*What?*"

"I can't really explain it, but I think y'all need to take out some time tonight and discuss children," she added.

"We aren't considering a family right now, Karen. Robert doesn't want any babies at this point."

"Trust me on this one. Why don't you come over here for a little while?"

I said, "I would, but Kim is cooking for everyone."

"Oh, she's there?" Karen asked, sounding unusually nervous. "Well, don't tell her I called. I was supposed to be calling her back later."

"You wanna speak with her now?"

"No, no, no. I'll talk to her later."

Karen hung the phone up in my ear before I could thank her for sharing her thoughts with me. As absurd as they were. I got up and joined Kim in the kitchen. She was pushing a pan covered with foil back into the oven and stirring some mashed potatoes in a pot.

"Your girl Karen just called," I said, taking a seat at the table.

Kim stopped stirring the food and turned to look at me.

"And what did she say?" she asked, anger in her voice.

"She said something about Robert and a baby. I told her that Robert wasn't ready for children."

Kim's mouth was in the shape of an O. Tears came to her eyes as she dropped the spoonful of mashed potatoes and reached out to hug me.

"Girl, what is wrong with you?" I asked, pulling back.

"Women do this all the time. She can see how much prettier you are, and she's jealous."

"Who? What are you talking about?"

Kim pulled away and held me by the shoulders.

"What did you say Karen told you?"

"I don't remember word for word, but it had something to do with Robert and a baby. She said she had this vision while she was meditating. She wanted me to go over there, but I told her that you had already cooked for everybody."

"And what did she say when you mentioned me?"

"She started acting real strange and jumped off the phone. She said that she was gonna call you back, or something like that."

Kim turned the oven down, wiped her hands on a dishrag, and took my hand in hers. Pulled me toward the living room and sat me down on the couch. Her upper lip was sweating and her knees began bouncing beyond her control.

"There's something that Robert needs to tell you, but I don't know how long he plans to take with this. We all know that things have been kinda shaky between you two for a while, and I'm sure you wonder sometimes how long y'all will make it, but—"

We both heard keys in the front door and then the lock turning over. I wondered what Rob's reaction would be at seeing me without Kalif for protection. Kim looked even more disturbed, then continued talking as Robert walked through the door. He glanced at both of us and then focused in on his sister.

"Rob, I have to," she said.

"No, you don't!"

Robert snatched his key out of the door and slammed it behind him.

"What are y'all talking about?" I asked, taking my hand from Kim.

"Are you gonna do it or should I?" she asked.

They stared at each other like two rivals as I patiently waited, wanting to know what the big secret was that must have skipped over me. The secret that had created so much tension between sister and brother. A secret so costly that people were afraid to reveal it, out of fear that I might never be the same.

I asked, "Will *somebody* tell me *something?*"

"Yeah, Rob has been—"

All of a sudden, Robert broke his silence, fell to his knees, and took my left hand in his right. I thought for a second that he was gonna tell me that he was planning to move out of the apartment or that maybe he had gone after Kalif, but the words that passed through his lips were the very ones that I had longed to hear since the beginning of time.

"Nik, will you marry me?"

Robert

I don't know where it came from, but I dropped down on one knee, parted lips that were swollen to the size of bratwursts, and asked Nik to spend the rest of her celibate life with me. It was either that or allow Kim to recount the moment that she'd found me in my boxers, on Karen's bedroom floor, with a hard-on and phlegm running down my chin.

Nik didn't give a response right away. She glanced back and forth at Kim and me for about five minutes and then silently got up and ate dinner. I decided to follow her lead, but Kim never could take a hint.

She whispered, "What was all of that, Rob?"

"What do you think it was? Whassup with you making my confessions for me?"

"Well, someone has to do it. How long do you think you can let things go on like this?"

"For as long as you mind your business," I said, getting up to join Nik in the kitchen. "I'll tell her, Kim. Just promise that you'll let me do this."

She folded her arms like the stubborn ten-year-old that had followed me around and kept notes to report back to Moms when we were growing up. I knew that I was asking a lot for her to keep her mouth shut, so I wrote her another check for one hundred dollars and went back to covering my tracks.

"I hope you know that Karen called a little while ago, telling Nik that you have a baby on the way."

"Are you bullshittin'?" I asked.

"No. Nik didn't understand what she meant, but if she puts two and two together, she'll probably remember that she already told Karen that y'all haven't been together, sexually, in almost a year. You don't realize it, but your jig is up."

Later that night, long after Nik and I had gone to bed, she woke me up, unintentionally. She was crying, softly and to herself. I rolled over and rubbed her back until the subtle whimpering ceased. Until she felt that I was aware of her pain. I didn't know what the hell was going on with her now, but for the moment, she was mine. She had fallen into my arms. Weak and in need of something. Something that Kalif just wasn't around to give.

I turned her over and lifted the light blue satin gown that she was wearing and began massaging her thighs. She didn't stop me, which was a good sign. A few months ago, she would have clamped down hard enough to sever my wrist. Her tense muscles suddenly loosened as I decided to test the waters and go a little higher. She moaned and moved to the right a little. I watched her and moved north.

Just as I was reaching for her panties, she grabbed my hand. Shocked me into a limplike state. Her eyes were open and she had lifted her head up from the pillow.

"Do you have anything?" she asked.

"Uh, I did have an erection, until a second ago."

"No. I mean a condom."

"For what?" I asked.

"For this to go any further."

"I thought we were getting married. What sense does it make to use a condom when we're gonna be together without one eventually?" I said, entertaining the thought that maybe I'd pushed her into Kalif's arms. "This is you and me that I'm talkin' about, Nik."

"Who, in this room, gave an answer to a wedding proposal? It sure wasn't me. And besides, if I do decide to marry you, there's no guarantee that you won't need to wear one then."

All of the visions that I held about being inside of Nik again had dwindled away. Moments like those were to be cherished. I could practically feel her moisture. The way that her soft walls would hug and massage my piece until the friction was no longer bearable. Then suddenly, I realized that the overwhelming sensitivity that she brought about with every pelvic thrust would remain just that, a vision.

For me, that is.

Nikai

Go ahead and call me stupid, because I was actually about to give him some. See, Robert's problem was that big mouth of his. He would say whatever he thought, no matter how twisted it was, leaving me to unravel it into a logical sentence.

He started rubbing my legs and I didn't say anything, basically because it felt good. I wanted the massage, but that was all. Until I felt him rising against my thigh. This was a first for the both of us, because I would never let him get that far, and after a while, he stopped trying. We usually crawled into bed and pretended no one else was there.

That night started out the same way, until I accidentally woke him with my crying. And that's when the rubbing started. What the *dirty dog* didn't realize was how backward his actions were. He didn't even have the decency to ask me what was bothering me. Not that I would have shared it with him. Something told me that confessing my desire to see Kalif again would have kicked off another knock-down-drag-out fight, which even Don King would have been willing to invest in.

So I figured that if he was willing to propose in such a desperate fashion, then the least I could do would be to break him off a little somethin'. But then the condom issue came up. Now, what made that fool think that I'd forgotten all about his previous infidelity? Not to mention the yeast infection we shared, which actually hindered me from walking in an upright position.

Don't get me wrong. I know that any woman in her right mind would have told him to take his proposal and stick it where

the sun don't shine. Especially if he stepped up to the plate without the ring. But I was determined to seize the moment. I had
every intention of basking in the glory of finally having Robert
in that submissive position. Believe me, when I was done,
Robert would be the one shedding tears in the midnight hour.

"Happy birthday, Daddy. I brought you some more flowers."

I bent down and cleared the orange-and-rust-colored leaves
from his tombstone. Set the fresh flowers into his pot and tossed
the old ones in my bag. The cemetery was pretty much quiet,
except for a burial across the way. There was a huge turnout for
whoever had died. Someone had either had a lot of friends or a
lot of enemies who wanted to verify that he was gone.

I pulled a blanket from my sack and placed it on the ground
next to Daddy. Made sure that I was blocking the burial. I didn't
want Daddy feeling bad because I was usually the only person
that ever came to see him.

I sat down on the blanket, folded my legs, sighed, and said,
"Well, I've got so much to tell you, I don't even know where to
start. You probably know all about everything, but I just need to
talk. Never imagined you'd be a therapist in your afterlife, huh?"

I looked out across West Florissant Avenue, through massive
falling snowflakes, at the outdated pumpkins still resting on
porches; they should've been thrown away weeks before. The
wind was blowing, but it was unusually cold for that time of
year. I lifted the hood on my black sweatshirt and shoved my
hands into the pockets of my dark brown bomber jacket.

"I'm assuming you've met James by now. Yeah, he ought to
be the snob with the drug habit. But then again, maybe you
haven't met him. He may not be up there. Taylor told me all
about the dirty cases that he was taking and the double life he
lived. Mama still doesn't know. I think Taylor sees James's failures as her own. You know, as far as her poor choice in men goes.

"Speaking of choices in men, Robert proposed to me last
night. What do you think about that? I never thought I'd see
the day when he'd get down and pop the question. Am I
happy? To a certain degree. I guess I expected more. Like a surprise get-together for it or maybe even a ring. That's right, he

still doesn't have a ring for me. But to be honest, I'm in no hurry. The sooner he gives the ring, the sooner I'll have to give an answer. And I've actually got a little interest in someone else. Nope, he's nothing like Robert. His name is Kalif. He was the producer for a singing group that I was in. But after he and Robert met, Kalif decided to drop me from the trio. We were called N-Sight. Yeah, the very thing that I'm in need of right now. Know what else I need? You guessed it. Money. I think I might need to take the money I've been saving for an apartment and put it with the share that I've been saving to pay Travis off. I just want him out of my life, Daddy. I'm tired of worrying. About money, Robert, Kalif, Sheila, Mama, Taylor, Lucky, and even about what other people think. I just want to be free to be me."

The burial across the cemetery was breaking up and everyone retreated back to the limos or other vehicles they rode in. They slowly dragged along, heads hung low, as though there was nothing to be had once the dirt was tossed into the hole. Like that person was gone forever and was never to be heard from again. It all made me think about Mama and Taylor. Their view of Daddy's death was so different from mine. If everyone felt the way that they did, no wonder people are afraid to die.

"Mama and Taylor couldn't make it today, but they put in on the flowers. You know, Taylor's in no condition to go out, and Mama has to keep a close eye on Lucky. I think he's becoming suicidal. He's been talking about James almost as much as Taylor has. Only in an envious sense.

"Well, I'm gonna get going before I catch pneumonia out here," I said, standing and shaking the grass from the bottom of my blue blanket.

I tucked it securely under my arm, readjusted the flowers in the pot, and asked, "If you see me making any mistakes, bad calls, or just messing up in general, would you give me a sign? I haven't forgotten what you told me before you left. And I still believe that if there's anything you can do to stop me from being hurt, you'll do it. I love you, Daddy. And everybody else does, too. They're just afraid of what that love might do to them. Like make them as strong as you and I."

Robert

Don asked, "You did *what?*"

"I popped the question, Mr. Follow My Lead."

Don and I were in the TV room at the engine house, having a private discussion about the night before.

"But what about Karen?"

"What about her?"

"If you were gonna ask any question, it should've been how Nik will feel about that baby," he suggested.

"I was gonna do that, but when I walked in the front door, Kim was preparing to drop the bomb *for* me. I had to do whatever it took to change the subject."

"Rob, changing the subject is commenting on the St. Louis Rams this season! Changing the subject is talking about the early winter we're getting! Changing the subject is *not* asking somebody to spend the rest of their life with you!"

"And exactly how would you have gotten out of it?" I asked.

"First of all, I wouldn't have gotten myself in it."

"Yeah, yeah. All right, I already understand that, since Theresa is running your show."

"I don't really see it as letting someone else run my show. Think about it. Where would we be as men if we didn't have women to keep us on point? I love what my woman does for me. You would, too, if you'd let your guard down and allow Nik to work her feminine magic."

Don was talking out of his head. Luckily, the fire alarm came on and cut him off before I was forced to get up and walk away.

A call came over the audible, informing us that there was a fire in a four-family flat and that people were trapped inside. We jumped into our turnout gear, which was lying on the floor next to the pumper, and buckled up for the ride. The entire time I was strapping the tank on my back, Don rambled on, more concerned with my personal problems than securing his gear.

"Tell her, Rob," he yelled over the alarm. "Man, if you don't tell her, you don't really love her."

I nodded my head and signaled that I got what he was saying but that was as far as it went. If Nik decided to leave me, Don's relationship would still be intact. I would be the only one left suffering.

Hodges pulled up in front of a burning building. Families were standing on the sidewalk, wrapped in blankets. A teenage mother was crying and pointing in the direction of the fire. Led me to believe that maybe there was another child in there. I saw Keates speaking with her briefly and then a female police officer attempting to calm her down.

Keates stepped up to me and said, "There's another girl trapped inside, on the second floor. You and Don take it while I check the first floor."

Don and I looked at each other and, without uttering a single word, understood what the plan was. Keates was gonna be on anther one of his rescue trips. The woman he was speaking to had pointed to the first floor, not the second. There was no reason for us to be up there. But there was no time for a debate, either.

I took the ax and swung at the front door until the wood shattered. I could hear Don behind me, breathing and bitchin' all at the same time.

"This is bullshit, man! Keates knows there's nobody up here!"

"I know. Let's just go through once and get the hell out."

We walked quickly through the living room area and down the hall into the kitchen. Don and I stuck close to each other as we listened for a cry for help, a call in the dark, or something to let us know that we weren't wasting our time and possibly our lives over some silly hero shit that Keates had in mind.

I felt my way into the bathroom, just to make sure that no

one had tried to break a window for fresh air and maybe passed out, and then I heard a thump in the other room. It was loud enough to make me forget about checking the rest of the house.

I yelled, "Hey, Don!"

I didn't get an answer. He was supposed to be right behind me, but I figured that he had wandered into one of the bedrooms. All of a sudden, the loud shrill of his pass device going into alarm mode rang throughout the apartment. I cringed, because I knew the only reason I would be hearing it was if it was unable to detect motion from him for at least thirty seconds.

"Yo, Don!"

I used the sound of the alarm to try to locate him through the thick smoke. I rounded the corner of the hallway and spotted Don sprawled out on his stomach, lying on the living room floor, with a curio cabinet on top of him. His helmet had been knocked forward, off his head. There were large sheets of glass surrounding him and a small one piercing the back of his neck. His eyes were open wide, revealing the shock that he must have suffered. Blood slowly rolled out of the side of his mouth and formed a small puddle at the base of his air mask.

I grabbed my radio and yelled, "Firefighter down! Stop all fire-suppression operations! I've located him on the second floor, in the northwest corner of the living room! Send EMS now!"

I rushed over, too afraid to move him, too afraid I'd sever his spinal cord.

He whispered, "My chin strap wasn't tightened. I didn't even see this thing coming."

His breaths were few and far between as it became more and more apparent that he wasn't gonna be walking out of that fire with me.

"Don't sweat it, man. You're gonna be all right."

I was sweating now, even more than before. Started experiencing a shortness of breath myself. The room began to spin as I heard Don call my name.

"Whassup?"

"Tell her, man. Tell Nik about the baby."

And then everything went black.

Nikai

I started to pray again—for wisdom, peace of mind, reconciliation, and, of course, some *dinero*. Had made up in my mind to call Mr. Leon Lovejoy on my own for another meeting. Chemistry or none, my money was funny and I needed a contract from him as soon as possible. I figured that maybe once I had given Travis his package back, he would be kind enough to remove the candid cameras from wherever they were. To be honest, so much was going on that the thought of being watched wasn't upsetting me the way he probably had hoped. But that was only because I had never actually seen a face, a pair of binoculars, or unfamiliar cars following me. Between the United States and the Virgin Islands, folks were droppin' like flies, and with the cemetery chances that I was taking by messin' with money belonging to somebody fresh out of an orange suit, I wasn't gonna be too far behind them. But even with all of the fear I had reserved for that part of my life, the fear of never seeing Kalif again still lingered.

After leaving the cemetery, I parked outside of the loft, with the heat on full blast, listening to Will Downing's "I Try." It seemed that all I could do would be to *try* to get Kalif to understand how difficult my choices were and that once they were finalized, they couldn't be undone.

The clock on my dashboard read 1:15. I had been sitting there staring up at the fourth floor since 12:30, waiting to see if I'd be lucky enough to catch him coming out, going in, or even watching me watch him. All I needed was an opportunity to explain to Kalif that I wasn't choosing Robert over him. That the way he made me feel was different from what I had at home, different from what I'd ever had. I just needed time to get myself in order.

The door to the main entrance opened halfway and then closed again. I sat forward in my seat and held my breath long enough to see that it was only a sista running out to the car in front of me for something. She stretched across the passenger seat, grabbed an object, and closed the door. Folded her arms across her breasts, paused to look at me, and then darted back in the building.

I slumped back down and resumed my position. Waiting for fate to lean in my favor, I rewound the tape and sighed to myself. It was beginning to look as if Kalif was running from me. Trying to make me pay for dragging him into such a hostile situation, when actually we were both looking for the same things, a touch of sanity and a record deal, if possible.

Surprisingly, the way that this all affected our professional relationship was becoming irrelevant to me. I didn't care if I ever got access to Kalif's studio again. I could always find another producer. What I wanted was his friendship and his touch. I wanted him to look across a candlelit room and say he believed in me. I wanted him to find a spot between my legs and let me feel his energy as I rubbed his head. I wanted to study the sky with him until it was hard to tell where it ended and our spirits began. I wanted Kalif back in my life again.

The next song on the tape started as I leaned forward and stared up at his window. To my surprise, Kalif was standing there, looking down at me. I beckoned for him to meet me at the door, but he didn't move. Pulled the navy blue material he used for curtains closed and walked away.

I started my car and drove around the corner to the pay phone to call but found that it was out of order. I stood out in the cold, banging the receiver against the phone booth for about thirty seconds. I was tired, frustrated, and running out of ideas. Daddy used to tell me, "Where there's doubt, Nikki, there's always hope." I leaned my head against the booth as frozen tears began to fall.

"Help me, Daddy, please!" I cried.

I walked back to the car and got in. Started it up and cranked up the heat. Drove back around to the loft and pulled into the same spot. The sista who had run out before was now sitting in her car. I reached into my purse to find a piece of paper or something to write a note on to ask Kalif to call me later. All I could seem to find was a catsup-stained sheet that I had wrapped up in a dollar the first day that I visited the loft. The older man who took my change that day had mentioned that it was valuable, but he probably never imagined how desperate I would be for a simple piece of paper. I grabbed a pen and opened the paper, which read: *Sometimes we're afraid to lose what we never really had.* I sighed, wiped away another tear, and looked up in time to catch Kalif walking out of the building to get in the car with the sista, who was now staring at me out of her rearview mirror. As I pulled away in shame, she leaned over and kissed him, validating my suspicions. By the time I made it back to the apartment, I had balled up the note and tossed it out into the cold, along with all hope of ever seeing Kalif again.

"Where have you been?" Kim yelled, meeting me at the front door.

"Out! Why?"

"Robert is in the hospital. He passed out in one of those fires!"

"Yeah, right," I said, fanning my hand at her. "And who's getting married now?"

"You won't be, if you don't come with me now!"

Kim grabbed me by the arm, snatched my keys, and pulled me to the car.

I asked, "When did this happen?"

"This morning. I got the call a few hours ago. I'll drive, because we have to pick my mama up. She's too nervous to take her car."

My bones were shaking, not from the cold, but from my nerves being on edge. And when combined with a broken heart, the outcome usually isn't very good. I fastened my seat belt and said a silent prayer for my possible fiancé. That's right. I said my possible fiancé. I mean, what other options did I have at that point? Kalif had made it painfully obvious that he was moving on, Robert had had a change of heart, and I *still* needed someone to hold me in the late hours of the night.

Kim and I stopped by and got her mother, whom I'd never particularly cared for. She spoke to me when she sat in *my* car, but as soon as I got in the backseat to let her have the front, she began to complain to Kim about *me*.

She asked, "What took so long? That boy could've been layin' up in that hospital dying, for all we know!"

"Mama, I told you I had to wait for Nik to get back. You know I don't have a car."

"And I also know that it doesn't take four hours to say happy birthday to a *dead man!*"

I let that one ride because of the situation. I was sure that she was as on edge as I was. Starting an argument with Robert's mother before I even knew his condition didn't seem like such a good idea at the time. Kim glanced back at me with an apologetic look on her face. I just shook my head and stared out of the window.

"So, Nikai, when do you plan to have children?" Mrs. Hayes asked.

"Mama! Why would you ask her a question like that?"

"Because I would like an answer to a question like that."

I squirmed in my own damn seat and said, "Sometime after I'm married."

"So have you figured out what's keeping you from being a bride?"

"I didn't imagine that there was something that I was personally doing wrong."

Kim said, "It may just be Rob."

"I don't think so. When a man finds the right woman, he will definitely be ready for children and a wife."

I said, "I thought it was the other way around. The wife and then the children."

Mrs. Hayes cleared her throat and shifted in her seat. I turned my nose up behind her back and entertained the thought of pushing the back of the seat into the dashboard.

Women like that always want a daughter-in-law and grand-children but aren't willing to prepare a man for that family. They raise their daughters and love their sons. So much so that by the time the son is old enough to consider marriage, he doesn't have a clue what it takes to keep a woman happy enough to *want* to have a child with him. They raise men who are used to being waited on, and can't do for themselves simply because they never imagined that some woman, any woman, wouldn't be there to do it for them. They won't open a door, pull out a chair, or remind themselves not to walk in front of a sista when they're together. What pissed me off was that Mrs. Hayes wouldn't have wanted a man like that in her life, but she'd raised her son to be nothing more. Instead of seeing other sistas as the enemy, we women should work together. Prepare our sons to respect young women. Stop telling them that all sistas are gonna take their money or cheat on them, use them so we don't have to work, want someone to take care of illegitimate children, and just need a good steady piece to call our own. If every woman kept that in mind as they instructed their little boys on how to wash a dish, vacuum a carpet, and, for God's sake, treat a woman, the divorce rate wouldn't be so high.

Kim cut in a parking space and did a half-assed job of park-ing my car in the hospital lot. She and her mama were shaking as they walked quickly up to the revolving door. I took my time and lagged behind. Not that I wasn't concerned; I just didn't want to be around Mrs. Hayes any more than she wanted to be around me. We all hopped on the elevator and got assistance with locating his room.

When we found him, Robert was sitting up on the side of the hospital bed, in a gown, watching a commercial on television. He gave sort of a half grin when we walked in and stood around him. First he looked at his mother, then at Kim, and finally at me.

Mrs. Hayes said, "Don't worry, sweetie. Mama's here to take you home and make sure you're okay."

"Hey, punk, I expected tubes to be hanging all around your head," Kim teased.

Robert gave a soft laugh and winked at me. I smiled back, mostly because I needed that wink badly.

"So how are you feelin'?" Mrs. Hayes asked.

"Better than others. Don's dead."

Robert dropped his head and cupped his face in his hands. Whimpered out loud until his mama sat down next to him and joined in on the waterworks. Kim and I looked at each other and then stepped out into the hall.

She asked, "You believe that?"

"I just saw him last night. How can he be gone that fast?"

"I guess that's just part of the job."

"But it's just not worth it," I said.

"What it is is unfortunate. But we've all got a role to play in this world."

"And what role was Don playing? The fool?"

"Think about it, Nik. If somebody doesn't put the fires out, no one would be able to survive them."

"And what about the firemen who get injured? What about their families, their fiancées?"

"I'm sure Theresa isn't taking this very well, but time heals everything."

"I guess I see it differently, because I could have been Theresa today. Rob could've been the one in that fire."

"I know, I know. By the way, your friend Sheila called and said that she had something important to tell you. She wouldn't say what it was, but she wants you to call her."

"Good. That must mean that she's back on the other side of the island."

"What island?"

"It's a long story."

We walked aimlessly around the hospital until Mrs. Hayes was willing to let another human being within ten feet of her son. She asked Robert if he was okay at least twelve times before we even got a moment alone together. And when we did, she left, clawing at the walls.

I said, "Hey. You hurting?"

"Nah, not much. How are you?"

"Okay, now that I know you're still in one piece."

"How has Moms been treating you?" Rob asked.

"Like she wants to push *me* into an open flame. You know what she had the nerve to ask me on the way over here?"

"What's that?"

"When I planned to have a baby."

"She's been asking me the same thing for years now. Get used to it. That's just Moms."

"I don't know if I can."

"So what do you think you should do?" Rob asked.

Before I could answer, he pulled a chair from across the room and propped his feet up on it.

"You okay?"

"I will be when you answer my question."

"What? I don't know what you mean by 'what you should do.' "

"Maybe you should have that baby she keeps bugging us about."

I lost the smile on my face and looked down at the keys in my lap, nervously fumbled with them until Robert pulled my chin back up.

Then I said, "You know we've tried."

"I know, but let's try again."

"And if we fail?" I asked.

"And if we fail, then we'll try again and again and again."

"I don't know, Robert. Trying is what soured our relationship the first time."

"No, me not being patient with you is what soured it. Listen, that could have been me today, instead of Don. He's downstairs in the morgue, waiting to be put six feet under, and he doesn't have any children to carry on his name. Hell, not even a widow."

"How is Theresa, anyway?"

"I don't know. I haven't seen her. She called and said that she may stop by, but I told her to take her time. She's got enough to worry about."

"It just doesn't seem fair. Don was such a good person."

"I know."

Robert put his arm around me and comforted me with a *sincere* hug for the first time since I had gotten a home HIV test. He kissed my forehead as I laid my head on his shoulder. We stared out of the window for a while and then he broke down again. The void in his life was becoming apparent. Don was gone and no one could fill his space. But at least a baby could fill Robert's life with a little joy.

"Baby," I called.

He looked at me and wiped his face with the back of his hand.

"The answer is yes."

"Yes what?"

"Yes. We can try for a baby again. But only under one condition."

"What's that?" he asked, smiling broadly.

"We have to get married first. Nothing big. But it has to be done the right way. Is it a deal?"

"How soon can we get started?"

"How about now?" I asked, running my hand up the inside of his thigh.

"Uhnn, Nik. You're nasty."

"Yo' mama."

Robert

I was walking out of the bathroom and being careful to keep the back of my hospital gown closed, when Keates appeared in my doorway. He searched my face for some kind of indication of how I was feeling toward him. I nodded my head and sat down on the side of my bed.

"Mind if I come in for a minute?" he asked.

"Nah."

Something told me to seize the opportunity to put him in the hot seat.

He pulled up one of the chairs, sat down, and asked, "So how ya feelin'?"

"Inside or out?"

"Well, both, I guess."

"On the outside, I'm doin' great. The inside, I'm not so sure about. Been downstairs to ask Don the same question?"

Keates quickly stood to his feet, turned his palms to me, and said, "Look, I just came by to say . . . to say . . . well, to say that I know I was wrong for making that call. I just . . . it's just that fighting fires has become a part of me. I just seem alive when I—"

"Sit down, man," I told him, uncertain of why I didn't desire to kill him myself. "It's cool."

"Hayes, I can't say I'm sorry enough. Since Alice walked out on me, I just haven't been the same."

"Keates, don't sit there and blame some woman who probably doesn't even know that the fire occurred. *You* caused Don to die! *Nobody else!* Just *you* and yo' ego trippin'!"

I could see tears forming in his eyes as I looked away. I didn't want to see this man cry. It wasn't like his tears would bring my best friend back, so he could save them.

"You're right. You're totally right. That's why I turned in my resignation today. I realized that I was at the point where I couldn't separate my private life from my profession, so I quit."

"What do you plan to do now?" I asked.

"I don't know. Been thinkin' of movin' to Utah with my daughter and her family. If not there, I'll probably just try to re-build my life here."

"Well, good luck. Rebuilding a life isn't an easy thing to do. I should know. That's gonna be my first order of business when I get out of here."

"So I guess I should be wishing you luck, as well?" he asked, extending his hand.

I glanced at it for a second and thought about the fact that I would never touch Don's hand again to dap him up. Got the sudden desire to smack Keates's away but couldn't. For some reason, it just wasn't in me. It felt good, but it felt strange. I'd been able to bring myself to smack the shit out of Nik months ago, choke the air out of Karen yesterday, but I couldn't turn away a man who was responsible for my best friend's death. It was obvious that my rebuilding was occurring right there, even before I had left the hospital. If there was any way that I could ask the big guy in the sky to help Nikai to forgive me, I knew I *had* to forgive Keates. After all, he never meant to hurt anyone. And truthfully, neither did I.

I grabbed his hand and gave it a firm shake and then pulled him in for a quick hug.

"You take it easy, Keates."

"You, too, Hayes."

And just like Don, he was gone. Never for me to lay eyes on again.

That night while I was lying in bed, the phone rang. I tried to raise myself up and answer it, but I realized that Karen was sitting on my back. Her big stomach was resting against my neck. I looked over and noticed that Nik was undisturbed by the phone, and Karen's presence, as well. When I finally answered the ring, Don was on the other end, begging me to tell Nik about the baby. The moment I promised that I would tell her, the load on my back got lighter. I turned around and Karen was gone. I placed the phone back in its cradle and realized that I was sleeping on a bed of broken glass. My flesh was being ripped apart while Nik slept silently next to me. I tried to wake her, but she seemed oblivious to everything that was occurring. I called her name louder and louder every time.

"Nik, Nik, wake up! Nik! I've got something to tell you! Nik!"

I woke up to a dark room. I had soaked the sheets on the hospital bed with sweat. I placed my feet on the floor and poured myself a glass of water from the pitcher. Stood up and walked over to the window. Caught a glimpse of a shining star in the sky as I drew the curtains.

"Don, man, if you're listening, I promise I'm gonna tell her. I'm just waiting for the right moment. I promise. It'll happen sooner than you think."

Nikai

After trying to get in touch with Sheila numerous times and figuring up how much more I needed to be at a smooth five hundred dollars, I got in bed. I hardly slept a wink that night. I kept thinking about Don and Theresa, Robert and me, and the little one that we were planning to work on. Surprisingly enough, when I woke up the next morning, I was ready for the new day to begin and ready for my fiancé to come home. He was scheduled to be released from the hospital that afternoon and I wanted to be there to give him any support that he needed.

I arrived at work about fifteen minutes early in order to alert my supervisor that I would only be working half of the day. When I made it to my office, there was a note on my desk, informing me that Dorothy had called. She wanted me to meet her for brunch to discuss her termination of employment with the company. And, I imagined, a little blame assessing, too.

My horoscope that morning read that I shouldn't use my eyes to see the truth: "What looks like heaven just might be hell. Moments of clarity will be frequent. And a Cancer will play a top role." I couldn't think of any Cancers I'd met in the past five years, but I kept this warning in mind. The day was only beginning.

I grabbed a cup of coffee in the lounge and spotted Linda across the room, talking to the sista who had taken Dorothy's place a little over a month ago. She looked like she was in her late twenties, petite, with a short, permed hairdo. Reminded me of Anita Baker back when "You Bring Me Joy" was the jam. They both glanced in my direction and waved before carrying on with their conversation. I smiled back and retreated to my office to kill a little time before meeting with Dorothy.

As soon as I sat down, my phone rang.

"Nikai Parker speaking."

"Nikai?"

It was Mama, sounding as though she had been crying for a while, maybe even all night. I assumed that she felt guilty for crucifying me over past circumstances that were beyond my control.

"Mama, what's wrong?"

"I'm ready. I'm ready to see your father."

I sighed and leaned back in my chair. She had finally realized what this meant to me and how important it was for her to be strong. How important this was for her own personal growth.

"When do you wanna go, Mama?"

"I don't know. I was thinking about maybe going next weekend. Would that be okay?"

"Anytime you want to go is fine with me. How about Taylor? You think she would like to come?"

"Well, she promised to look in on Lucky for me. If you would rather she go this time and then I go another, that'll be okay."

"No, no, no. You're going next weekend and that's that. I'll be over in the morning to check on y'all. How's the baby doing?"

"Taylor hasn't been complaining lately. You know her ankles had swollen up to the width of a streetlight, but now she's all better. I made her cut that salt out and move her butt out of that bed."

"You know, she isn't the only one who needs to get out of the house. Lucky needs to take a walk more than anybody. Even if it's around the parking lot, it would help him."

"I don't know, Nik. You can't save everybody. Some people are content the way that they are."

"Mama, do you really think Lucky is content living in that make-believe world? Raising the window next to him is not the kind of fresh air he needs. He needs a walk in the park, a ride on the MetroLink, a stroll through the mall. Something to let that man know he's still alive."

Mama fell silent. I wondered if maybe I was throwing too much at her at once, but this had been eating me up inside.

Every time I saw him stare off into the distance and then snap back, I became sad. It seemed that I was gonna be the only person who was willing to take him farther—farther than the parking lot, farther than the television screen, and farther than that musty recliner that he'd been anchoring for twelve years.

"Nikki."

"Yeah."

"I'll be ready next Friday around noon. Maybe we can stop for some flowers or something."

"Sure, Mama. That'll be nice."

I let her go and turned around to the window behind me. Looked out across the street and spotted a large dark brown brotha carrying I LOVE YOU balloons, with a child by his side. He hopped up on the curb, helped the kid dodge small mounds of snow, where grass used to be, and came into the building.

The young sista who had taken Dorothy's place shot down the hall, past my door, and into the arms of this attractive brotha. Made me think about the days when Robert used to do things like that. The other leasing consultants walked out into the hall and stood around, observing this man and his son getting down on one knee.

They asked, "Will you marry us?"

The sista stood teary-eyed, with her hands covering her mouth. By then, I was standing on the threshold of my office and could hear every woman in the building yelling, "Tell them yeah!"

"Yes, I'll marry y'all!"

Both guys rose to their feet, one hugging her around the neck and the other around the waist. There was laughter, applause, and a roar in the building that brought tears to my eyes. Linda rushed to her side, carrying a cake. Set it down on a nearby desk and then hugged the brotha.

The sista turned to Linda and asked, "You were in on this?"

"Yeah, it took everything in me to keep from telling you that Derek and Alex were coming."

They hugged each other, revealing a closeness that I hadn't known about until today. It left me wondering how much of my personal information Linda had issued out or decided to keep to herself. The four of them grabbed the cake and headed back to-

ward the lounge, where juice had been set out by another one
of the assistants. When they got down to my door, Linda
stopped to introduce them.

She said, "Nikai, this is Derek and his son, Alex. Lauryn is
marrying them, as you heard."

I bent down to the cute little boy, who looked to be about
four years old, and said, "Congratulations." He blushed and
grabbed his father's leg. Made it apparent that Lauryn was *not*
his mother, but about to become his stepmother. Yet surprisingly enough, he didn't look a lot like Derek, either. I also offered congratulations to the fine brotha standing there next to
them and then hugged Lauryn.

"I don't want to stop the celebrating. Carry on, and I'll be
down to the lounge for a piece of cake. You gonna save me a
piece?" I asked Alex.

He frowned and let me know he'd had enough of my friend-
liness.

"Congratulations again," I told them.

Linda said, "Nikai, I've got something that I want to show
you. I'll be back with it."

"Okay, I'll be here."

I stepped back into my office in time to catch the phone ringing.

"Nikai Parker speaking."

Dorothy said, "Good morning, Nikai."

"Can you hold on a second?"

"Sure."

I closed my door and walked around to the other side of my
desk to sit down.

"Yeah, I'm back."

"Did you get my message?" she asked.

"I sure did. You aren't calling to cancel on me, are you?"

"No. I'm calling to confirm."

"Okay, so where do you want to meet?" I asked.

"I can come by the office and pick you up, if you don't mind."

"That's fine. What time are we looking at?"

"Let's say ten-thirty."

"All right. I'll see you then."

I hung up with Dorothy and headed toward the lounge, not for cake, but to keep my word. Mostly, everyone was just sitting around, fascinated by how cute Alex was, including me. He had taken his heavy tan coat off and now began playing with the little miniature men that he had stuffed in his pockets.

I noticed Derek taking a glance at his pager, sighing, and then placing it back on his waist. He kissed Lauryn, whispered something in her ear, and then asked to use a phone.

"You can use the one in my office," I offered.

He followed me down the hall, into my office, and over to my desk.

"Dial nine to get an outside line," I told him.

I busied myself at a file cabinet as he talked on the phone.

"Yeah, whassup?"

Derek suddenly seemed irritated and unpleasant. Whoever it was he was speaking to had the opposite effect on him that Lauryn did.

He snapped, "Karen, do you know how far I am from your place right now?"

Derek looked at me and asked, "This is what, twenty to twenty-five minutes from Shadow Oaks apartments in West County, isn't it?"

"Just about."

I remembered that those were the apartments that Kim's old roommate lived in, and I made a mental note to ask her exactly why she had decided to move out.

"Alex is busy right now! You can't jump in and out of his life when you get ready to! Besides, you have a baby to prepare for. Learn from your mistakes and wait on that one!"

Derek slammed the phone down as though he was doing it strictly out of habit.

I asked, "You okay?"

"Yeah, she's just tryin' to take me through some more changes. Bad timing is her specialty."

"That was Alex's mother?"

"Yeah. I guess you could say that. But Lauryn has been more of a mother for him than Karen."

The coincidence of him stating that she was pregnant, named

Karen, and lived in Shadow Oaks triggered like a night-light coming on in my head.

"Did you say that she has a baby on the way?"

"Yeah. She probably tricked some sucka into givin' her another child to abandon."

He ran his hand across his face and continued. "But I've learned my lesson. I'm just lucky enough to find a good woman who doesn't mind being there for me and my son."

"Yeah, lucky is what you are. By the way, what's your sign?"

"Cancer. Why?"

"Oh, no reason."

I let Derek get back to his celebration as I prepared to meet with Dorothy for brunch. Then it occurred to me that he was the Cancer in my horoscope that morning. Once I was certain that he was gone, I picked up the phone and called Kim at work.

"Kim Hayes speaking. How may I help you?"

I asked, "Does Karen have another baby?"

"What?"

"I just met this brotha named Derek, who has a baby by a woman named Karen. But check this out—she's pregnant now *and* lives in Shadow Oaks apartments."

"What? She never mentioned having another child to me. You think it's the same Karen?"

"What are the odds of it not being?"

"Sounds like slim to none."

"Why don't you call and see?" I suggested.

"Girl, I don't deal with her anymore."

"Why not? You never did say what brought you back to our supposed 'hole-in-the-wall.'"

"Nik, I don't have time to talk about that right now."

"What? Don't act like your job is more important than gossip. If you can make a nail appointment while on the clock, surely you can discuss something as juicy as this."

"Look, my supervisor is coming. I've got to go."

Kim disconnected us and left me sitting at my desk, holding the receiver in my hand. And wondering what the hell had gotten into her.

*　　*　　*

Dorothy was parked outside of my window at 10:30 on the dot. I grabbed my purse and coat off the back of my door and darted out into the cold. She had the heat in her car on high, and Phyllis Hyman in the background singing "Old Friend." I checked Dorothy's expression to see where she was coming from and possibly where our conversation was headed.

She smiled and said, "Well, long time no see. How've you been?"

"I've been pretty good. How about yourself?"

She sighed and pulled off of the lot. Didn't give an immediate answer but began nodding her head.

"Been keepin' busy. I've got a lot more time on my hands than I used to."

Dorothy reached over and grabbed my hand. Shook it back and forth for a second and continued talking.

"I missed you, Nikai. I was sure I would've heard from you by now."

I looked at her out of the corner of my eye and wondered if she even remembered the elevator incident. I mean, that was *my* foot she watched get jammed in those doors.

"Well, I've had a lot of personal issues to deal with. But I kept you in mind."

"That's good, real good."

She fell silent again and watched the road with an unusual amount of attention.

Then she looked up at my hair and said, "I see you're hangin' on to that hairdo, huh?"

Oh God, here we go again. I was sick of feeling my way through the conversation, trying to figure out where she was coming from and exactly what the hell she wanted from me.

"I see you're hangin' on to that one, too," I answered.

Her fake smile fell somewhere down by the floor mats. And so did mine.

"Have they found anyone to fill my position yet?"

"Actually, they did. About a month ago."

"Is she nice?"

"I don't know her personally, but from what I've seen, she seems to be okay. Why?"

"No reason. I was just wondering. I'm assuming that Linda is still there."

"Then you're assuming right."

Dorothy shook her head as though to say that the whole company was a pitiful bunch of fools. She turned a sharp corner and made me grab the handle on the door.

"So how's that young fella of yours?" she asked.

"Oh, Rob? He's fine. I'm picking him up from the hospital today. He was in a fire and passed out."

"Oh my goodness. Do you need me to come by and help you with him?"

"No. I told you, he's fine."

Her disposition shifted as quickly as the gears that she was stripping, all because she had a chip on her shoulder. She pulled up in Applebee's parking lot and then turned to me.

"Nikai, I might as well be honest with you. I haven't been okay. I'm alone most of the time, and the rest I spend sleeping. I tried to dispute the whole ordeal, but it was my word against theirs. I wanted to know if you would help me get my job back."

"*What?* Dorothy, I told you they already filled your position. And besides, I don't have enough pull to get you hired again. You were there when I came."

She calmed herself and gripped the top of the steering wheel with both hands.

"I'm sorry. I shouldn't have tried to put you in a situation like that. I guess I was only thinking of myself."

I took Dorothy's hand in mine and said, "It's okay. We're all selfish from time to time. I know you didn't mean any harm by that."

"So what now? I mean, what do I do with myself? I have no job, no man, no hobbies, no life."

"I have to disagree with you on that last one. You have a life; you just haven't decided to start living it. There's a lot you could do. Ever thought about getting in a book club, church choir, social club, or even jumping back into the dating scene?"

Dorothy laughed and said, "I never thought I would live to see the day that you were advising me on life. I guess maybe this old soul can still learn a lot, huh?"

"True, and you can start by not feeling sorry for yourself. You catch my drift?"

"Yeah, I caught it, right between the eyes."

"Dorothy, I want to apologize about what happened that day in my office. I hope you don't think that I was challenging you in front of Linda."

"You know, I sometimes wish that you were my daughter. You're so bright and beautiful. I guess I thought that we had built a relationship that Linda was trying to tear down. She was always talking to you about her problems and everything. It made me feel like you had forgotten about me."

"I could never forget about the person who made my transition into that job so smooth. Linda didn't take me under her wing; you did. And as far as my talking to her goes, I was using some of your wisdom. You were like a second mother to me."

"Were?"

"I mean, you *are*," I said, correcting myself. "I couldn't force her to straighten out the misunderstanding. I only left it up to her."

"Well, you see what she thought of you leaving it up to her. She didn't bother to mention the truth to anyone."

"I know, but she knows in her heart what happened. And she also knows the effect that it will have on our relationship. I'm sure this means nothing to you, but in time, she'll break. She's human, just like anyone else who has spoken falsely against someone."

Dorothy looked down and then over at me.

"I guess you mean me, huh?"

"Do I?" I asked.

"I guess I need to apologize for lying about her, as well. I'm sure you found out that it wasn't Marion who had the problem with Linda spending so much time in your office; it was me."

"You didn't have to do that to get my attention. All you had to do was ask for a little of my time."

"Well, can you spend a little of your time inside of this restaurant with me? Because I'm starving."

"Only if I can have a hug first."

I held Dorothy to let her know that she wasn't alone, that I hadn't forgotten about her, and that it didn't take all of that to get my attention. I think she held me because it was something that she hadn't done to anyone in a long time, because she wanted to seize the moment with me, and because we had wasted enough time in that parking lot. We really were starved.

Dorothy dropped me off in front of the office about 12:30. I assured her that I would keep in touch, closed the door, and ran into the building to get my briefcase. It was right about the time that I needed to pick Rob up from the hospital and make things all better with him. It seemed that this was becoming my duty. I was turning into a rock for everyone to lean on. The very person who was deemed irresponsible, shunned because of unfortunate circumstances, the vulnerable woman everyone once doubted was now being called upon to soothe others. And the ironic part was that the one person who had always seen this in me wasn't around to witness me blossom. Kalif had basically given up on me.

By the time I made it to my office door, Linda was coming down the hall, waving a light green sheet of paper.

"What's that?" I asked.

"It's what I've wanted to tell you about. Lauryn brought this flyer in yesterday. It's for an audition for a band. They need singers and they give local performances. I just knew that this was something you would want to look into."

"Let me see it."

I took the flyer from Linda, and, sure enough, it was for an audition in just two days. I had scheduled an appointment to see Leon Lovejoy the day after the audition, but I figured if I threw enough mud against the wall, something would have to stick. I had to consider my singing career. Everything couldn't be put on hold according to whether or not certain people wanted to take part in it. I wasn't asking for love from Kalif anymore. What I wanted was music, the part of me that would always be there. I had to go to this audition. I owed it to myself not to be a disappointment to *me*. It didn't matter anymore if I let Mama down. I might not ever be as successful as Taylor. There still remained the possibility that I wouldn't be blessed with children like Karen was, but I *did* have purpose. I had a role to play in this world. And now was my turn to perform.

I asked Linda, "Can I have this?"

"Sure. That's why I brought it to you. You never know, this group might be better than the one you're singing in now."

"Oh, I'm not singing with that group anymore. Things just didn't work out."

"Anything you want to talk about? You know, I'm still your friend, Nikai. I wish you didn't keep your distance so much."

"Is that what you feel like I do?"

I was starting to sound like Kalif. He was inside of me, becoming a part of me at the very moment that I wanted to forget all about him.

Linda explained. "Well, I would have come to your office by now, but I was sure that you were still angry with me about Dorothy getting fired."

"How do you feel about that?"

"About what?" she asked, looking as though I had lost her somewhere in the conversation.

"About Dorothy getting fired, and you being able to prevent it."

Linda sighed as her shoulders fell. She tucked her hands behind her back in a humbling position.

"I don't know. I'm really sorry about that, but as time goes on, I think things will be okay."

"With whom?"

"With everybody. That's why I was hoping to patch things up with you. Nikai, you were an important part of my life, and you don't even realize it."

Linda broke down crying in my office while my door was still open. I hoped this wasn't an attempt to set me up to look like I had smacked the mess out of her, but when a couple of consultants began to crowd around my door, I angrily insisted that she close it.

"Look, I like you a lot, Linda, but you make poor choices, and I can't take chances with someone like that. You were able to control that situation and you just chose not to. Now, how do you think Dorothy feels? She doesn't have a job because you *just didn't feel like talking* at one particular time. To have your whole life resting in someone else's hands is devastating! While you skip around this office pretending that time will make everybody forget, Dorothy is sitting at home wondering which way is up! She didn't have a net to catch her the way that you do. Life is not all roses and candy! How do you expect me to trust you as a friend when I've seen how you toy with other people's lives, without a conscience?"

Linda wiped the tears away and looked up at me with insult all over her face. Then her brows did that "I'm pissed" dance as she raised her voice, as though sanity were no longer a part of her being.

"So just what are you saying?"

"I'm saying that if I have to watch you with my eyes in the front *and* back of my head, then it's too much work to be around you!"

"And all of this stemmed from Dorothy not knowing how to be politically correct and keeping her personal opinions to herself? All she had to do was mind her own business and stop trying to cut into our friendship."

"You don't get it, do you?"

"Get what?" she asked.

"This has nothing to do with Dorothy at all. This is about *your* insecurities. You were the one doing all of the clinging. Up here in my office, sharing your personal business as a way of saying you trust me, that you were my friend. Don't you see that friendship has nothing to do with how much you give, how many secrets you share, or how many others you can beat out for an individual's time. Friendship is free. It's about concern for another human being. It's about wanting the best for them, not being able to *buy* the best for them. You gave a lot of your time, but, Linda, you never really gave me your friendship."

Linda sighed and looked up at me.

"You know, Nikai, we really are from two different worlds, and it has nothing to do with color. My parents have always used money as a way of getting a rise out of me. It was there to substitute for time, attention, and sometimes even love. I've never had someone break things down for me like this. Nobody ever showed me what it was like to show love without a wrapped gift or sharing something near and dear, like secrets."

I tossed my arm over her shoulder and moved her blond hair from in front of her face.

"Well, girl, life is all about elevation. If you're not going up, or at least trying to, you're not living. Think of this little talk as a step up. You're just that much wiser, girl*friend*."

"Well, I guess I better get back to this party in the lounge. You coming?"

"No, I've got something else planned."

"Okay."

Linda turned to walk out of my office, when a thought occurred to her.

"You think you could give me Dorothy's number so I can call her? There's something I want to say."

"Like what, exactly?"

"Starting with I'm sorry and ending with the fact that I'm gonna try to clear this mess up."

"Sure."

I gave her the number and watched her hop out of my office like new. I was happy to know that I could help her, but even happier to know that she understood. She understood that the sweet parts of life are what keep you going. The times when one can laugh for the moment, even though everything looks bleak.

She was right: We were from two different worlds, and it had nothing to do with color. But in a sense, I grew up in the same way that Linda had, doing without. I didn't have approval or reassurance, just like she didn't have genuine concern for her or attention. But there's one good thing that I can say about growing up without: It builds character. And it builds something else inside of you: It builds your spirit.

Robert said, "I missed you today."

"Oh, baby, I missed you, too. How are you feelin'?"

"I'll be great when I can get out of this hospital and go home."

I grabbed a bag of his clothes, which I brought from home, and asked, "You think you can get dressed by yourself, or do you need some help?"

He laughed and said, "Depends on whether you plan to leave *your* clothes on or not."

I playfully tapped him on the arm as he took his bag and walked into the bathroom to wash up. I sat down on the side of the hospital bed and began gathering the clothes that Rob had worn to the hospital, when his pager vibrated across the food stand. I picked it up. It was the *same* number that had showed up on our caller ID box at home when Kim was staying at Karen's apartment.

Now, I know I'm not the brightest person in the world, but this woman's name and number were popping up all over St. Louis. And I'm talking in just *one* day. I pressed the review button to see if I saw it again. And there it was. Karen's phone number was on Robert's pager *twelve* times since the night before.

I walked over to the bathroom and banged on the door.

Rob yelled, "It's open!"

"No. I think you need to come out here for a second."

He walked out with his pants and sneakers on but no shirt. I held the pager up in my hand and waved it from side to side.

"Did you know that Karen's number is on your pager *twelve* times since yesterday?"

"Let me see that," he said, taking it from me.

Now, I don't know about you, but I was waitin' to hear something along the lines of "Who the hell is Karen?" Rob continued wiping his face with the washcloth as he pressed the review button. I guess to count and see if I had gotten the number of calls right. Like that would have mattered.

Then he said, "That must be Kim calling me again. You know how persistent she is when she wants something."

Before I could respond, he carelessly tossed the pager on the bed, turned around, went back into the bathroom, and locked the door that time. The thing that didn't make sense was that Kim had told me she didn't deal with Karen anymore. And since she and her mother had been with me at the hospital the day before, there was no way she could have paged Robert from that number. I was getting the feeling that everybody, possibly even Don, knew something that I didn't. Which meant everybody who was still breathing was gonna have some questions to answer.

Robert

To say that I wanted to shove my foot up Karen's ass would be an understatement. There I was, stuck in a hospital bathroom, mourning the loss of my best friend and trying to figure out how I was gonna explain to Nik why that dizzy broad had been paging me for two days straight.

I'd called Karen back the night before and told her what had happened in the fire. Let her know that I was okay and warned her to allow *me* to contact *her*, not the other way around. I also informed her that Nik and I were planning to get married and were about to work on a baby of our own. That was right about when she snapped.

"I thought you told me she couldn't have any kids!" she yelled.

"We've decided to try and try again."

"And what about the one you have on the way?"

"What about it? If it's mine, I'll take care of it."

"If it's yours?"

"You heard me. I'm tired of playing these games with you. Call me when you're ready to talk paternity tests!"

At that moment, I hung up on her. Around three minutes later, my pager was being blown up. She might've paged me seven times that night. But you know it didn't just stop there. Karen had to give me an early-morning wake-up page, and then blew the damn thing up every hour on the hour. After the last one, I was so relieved that she had given it a rest, I dozed off.

Before I knew it, it was 1:30 and Nik had come to take me home.

Nik asked, "Rob, what are you doing in there?"

"I'm on my way out."

"Hurry up, baby. I've already had time to go to the desk and check you out, and all you have to do is put your shirt on."

Nik had the gift of keeping her voice very low in order to convince me that she wasn't pissed. I knew her. She'd call me "baby," and then once I opened the door, I'd have a mad-woman in my face again. She'd done it in a hospital before, and I couldn't think of anything that would keep her from doing it again.

I unlocked the door and peeped out first. Nik was sitting in one of the chairs, watching the television. She quickly darted her eyes in my direction and tilted her head as if to say, Come on. Stood up and put her handbag on her shoulder. Turned the television off and silently placed both hands on her hips.

Then she said, "Your pager just went off again."

My heart stopped as I looked across the room at it slowly crawling across the bundled sheets.

"Did you check to see who it was?"

"That's *your* pager. I know the call isn't for *me*."

I picked it up off of the bed and looked at Karen's number flashing on the screen. Put it back on my waist and said, "Remind me to call my mother when we get home."

"No problem. You talk to Theresa today?"

"No, have you?"

"I was at work all day. You were the one lying up here with free time to reach out and touch someone."

I sucked my teeth and said, "All right, Nik."

"Don't 'All right Nik' me!"

One of the nurses appeared in the doorway with a wheelchair to give me a ride to the hospital entrance. She stopped and looked, as though the tension in the room had maybe floated out into the hall.

She asked, "Everybody okay in here?"

"Yeah, we're fine. My wife is just excited about me coming home."

Nik faked a smile and walked outside to pull the car around.

"Looks like you're in the hot seat," the nurse commented.

"Like you wouldn't believe."

During the entire ride home, Nik played Lauryn Hill's "Ex-factor."

"You let go and I'll let go too," Lauryn sang.

And when the song was over, Nik rewound it to make sure that I understood the message. I imagined that this was her subtle way of telling me she felt we should go our separate ways. But until I saw no other avenues to travel back into her life, I was gonna do whatever it took to keep this woman involved with me. Even if it meant severing all ties with Karen and the baby.

Nik pulled up in front of the apartment and left the engine running.

"You're not coming up?" I asked.

She stared straight ahead and answered, "I've got a run to make. I'll be back. Don't forget to call your mother."

I stepped out, closed the door, and missed getting my foot run over by about four millimeters. I threw my bag over my shoulder, walked up the steps to the apartment, and found a long envelope taped to the front door. I opened it and unfolded a photograph of an ultrasound. The note on the back read, "It's a boy! Love, Karen." I balled it up and went inside to find a cigarette. The phone was ringing as I lighted a square and took my first drag.

"Hello?"

Kim said, "Nik has been asking questions."

"What kind of questions?"

"She called me at work today and wanted to know why I moved out of Karen's apartment. But that's not the clincher. She said she met a guy today who said his son's mother is named Karen, that she's currently pregnant, and that she lives in the *same* apartment complex that your Karen does."

"Did she say what his name was?"

"I think it was something like Darren, Darryl, or something with a *D*."

"Did it sound like Derek?"

"Yeah! That's what it was."

"So what did you say to her?"

"I told her that I had to go. I've gone along on this ride with you for long enough. Rob, this is where I get off."

I took a deep long breath, let Kim go, and tried to remember what I had done with that number Karen had given me in the food court that day. Nik obviously had cleaned the house for my arrival back home and literally rearranged all of my junk. I found myself ripping through the house the same way she had when she'd misplaced that special brown paper bag, carelessly leaving items that weren't even mine overturned. I looked in a miniature wicker basket that she had placed on the dresser and found the piece of napkin among some loose change, nail clippers, and a tube of Chap Stick.

I grabbed the receiver from its cradle and dialed the number. After one ring, a woman picked up and instructed me to leave a numeric or verbal message after the tone. I chose the latter.

"Yeah, uh, Derek, my name is Rob Hayes. And, uh, you don't know me personally, but we've got something in common—Karen. I understand that you have a son by her and, um, from what she tells me, I do, too. Well, at least on the way. Ahem. If you can, give me a call at five five five-three nine four two. Leave a message and I'll get back to you right away. Peace."

Nikai

Lies. Lies. Lies. If that man told me one more lie, I was going to *scream*. I'll give it to Rob, he was pretty smooth with the pager thing. And I might've believed that *shit* about the last page being from his mother, had I not been the one to put Karen's number in there *myself*.

I dropped him off at home so that I could take a ride and cool off. It just didn't seem like a good idea to be cooped up in that apartment with all those sharp knives while Robert continued to test me the way that he was. I didn't have a particular destination in mind. But when my wheels stopped turning and I had finally shifted into park, I found myself outside of my mother's town house, looking for my big sister to listen to me.

I rang the doorbell a couple of times but didn't get an answer, so I decided to use my key. Mama's car was gone, but Taylor's Infiniti was parked a few spaces down. I walked in and met Uncle Lucky as he was coming out of the bathroom.

"Hey, where is everybody?"

"Your mama went to the cleaners and Taylor should be upstairs. How you?"

"Pretty good," I said. "I'm surprised to see you up and about."

"Well, I don't need nobody to help me use the toilet. After all of these years, I think I've caught the hang of it. Tell 'Ugly' to come on downstairs. She can't keep you to herself all of the time."

I laughed and headed upstairs to see what Taylor, or Ugly, was doing. I knocked on the guest bedroom's door and waited for permission to enter.

"Who is it?" Taylor asked.

"It's me. Open up."

"Come on in."

I opened the door and allowed the strong odor of fingernail polish remover to smack me in the face. Taylor was sitting at the head of the bed, with a pillow propped up behind her back, giving herself a manicure. She was still in her nightgown from the night before and had a red satin scarf wrapped around her head.

"Hey, where have you been?" she asked.

"Around. How's the baby?"

"Oh, I'm doing okay, too." She laughed.

"I'm sorry. How are you *and* the baby doing?"

"That's more like it. We're both fine. Mama told me about Robert being in the hospital."

"Yeah, he's okay. His friend didn't make it, though."

"Really?" she asked, filing her nails down. "That's a dangerous profession. It almost makes you wonder if it's worth it. Was he married?"

"Engaged."

"That's a shame," she said, patting the other side of the full-size bed. "Sit down."

I walked around and moved the rest of her clothing, which she had sprawled out, over onto the recliner that was stationed near the window. Taylor went back to concentrating on her nails and then looked over at me, paying particular attention to my hair.

"Hey, Nikki. I wasn't gonna say anything before, but I've got to know where you got the idea to do your hair like that."

I ran my hand over my short but neat Afro and said, "One day, I just decided to be me."

"What does that mean?"

"It means I got tired of running. Running from who I am, and running *toward* the person everyone else thought I should be."

"Is that what you think you were doing?"

"That's what I *know* I was doing. What is meant to be will be. I mean, I knew when I did it that I would get the sort of reactions that I did get from the very people who mirrored the look they so hated."

"And what were those reactions?"

"Don't pretend like you didn't look at me like I'd lost my mind the first time you laid eyes on it, little Miss So So Soft and Beautiful."

Taylor laughed so hard that she messed up the polish on her index finger.

"Look what you made me do! And for your information, I didn't look at you like you had lost your mind."

Taylor got quiet and grabbed a cotton swab off of the night-stand next to her.

Then she continued. "I looked at you like I was proud."

"Proud?" I asked.

"Yeah, proud. I mean, we both know that I've always had the beauty and the talent," she said, dodging the playful swing that I was taking at her. "But you've always had the courage. While you were envying my shallow attributes, I envied the ones that were gonna carry on with you for the rest of your life. Think about it. Out of all of us, you are the only one who has the nerve to hang out in a cemetery, chop off all of your pretty hair, and chase your dreams relentlessly. Lucky is too chicken to cross a threshold, I was about to marry for status, and Mama won't even go visit a man she spent twenty-five years of her life with."

"Girl, if you only knew. I don't have it together the way you guys think I do."

"But that's the thing—you don't give up trying. I was sitting downstairs, next to Lucky, a month ago, not knowing if I even wanted to go on living. You remember the day when we found out that James had been killed?"

"Yeah."

"You don't know it, but when you brushed my hair that morning, you brought me back to life. The tears you saw on the outside were nothing compared to the ones that I was crying on the inside. I wanted to call you back, ask you not to go, not to leave me just yet. I miss that, Nikki. I miss us being close. When it was just me and you against the world."

I reached over and held my big sister until I could no longer refrain from crying myself. Held on for all of the years that we allowed what the world considered standard mark the differ-ences between us. I held on for all of the lost moments when we should have been there for each other, when neither one of us was able to see the wedge that had been driven between us.

Taylor pulled away and said, "All right now, you're crushing my baby."

I laughed aloud and placed my hand on her belly. She looked at me, grabbed my hand, and directed it to where she thought the head was. I smiled at her and decided to reveal that deepest secret that no one had known except for Kalif, Sheila, and Robert.

"Taylor, this is what I envy."

"What, these swollen ankles?" she asked, pulling the covers back.

I laughed and explained, "No. The ability to conceive."

"What? What are you talking about?"

"Robert and I tried about a year ago, but nothing ever happened."

"How long did y'all try?"

"I don't remember. I think it may have been ten months or so."

"Did you go see a doctor about it?"

"No. When people ask that, it just makes the condition sound even worse."

"'The condition.'? You act like you're terminally ill, girl!"

"Sometimes, that's how I feel."

"Listen, calm your nerves. Sometimes it can take women five years to get pregnant. There are only so many days out of a cycle when we are fertile anyway. While men, on the other hand, produce semen all year round. Sometimes, it has nothing to do with health. It's just that the timing has to be right. Just let me know if you want me to go with you to see a specialist."

"I guess I wanted the baby for the wrong reasons."

"And what were those?"

"To make Robert love me more. To keep him at home."

"Well, that's probably why you didn't get pregnant. God knows, *no* baby will make Robert love you more. And if you felt he didn't love you the way he should, you shouldn't have wanted a baby with him anyway. Having a baby would only make it harder to leave if you needed to."

"What do you mean, emotionally?"

"Hell no! I mean *more clothes to pack!* Take it from me. I love this baby inside of me, but I'm scared as hell. I wasn't prepared to have to raise a child on my own. But maybe that's why I'm pregnant."

"What does that mean?"

"It means that maybe God had a plan to make me as strong as you are. And this is what I have to go through."

"And what happens to those of us who are already strong?"

"Well, you only become stronger. I'm sure you're going to have times when you're uncertain."

"Hell, I've got those now. I think Robert is cheating on me, but I just can't prove it."

"If that's the case, you won't have to. The truth will come out sooner or later. He won't be able to hide it forever."

"And what should I do until then?"

"Live, Nikki. Don't be like me, Lucky, and Mama. Don't let circumstances and situations determine your actions. You're better than that. Besides, my baby doesn't want a weak aunt."

I hugged Taylor one last time and got up to leave.

"Where are you going?" she asked.

"To try to get Lucky to live again."

"Good luck," Taylor said, shaking a bottle of clear nail polish.

I pulled the door closed behind me and then opened it again.

"Hey, Ugly, Lucky said its okay to come down and sit with him sometimes."

Taylor laughed and threw a pillow at the door, but she missed. I went back downstairs, to find that he had fallen asleep in front of the television again. I grabbed the blue-and-white-checkered afghan off the back of his recliner and covered him with it. Kissed his forehead and left the haven in which my loved ones dwelled. It was the place that I now called home.

On my way back to the apartment, I thought about Robert being there and the games that I was sure he was preparing to play. I passed the church that usually had different words of inspiration posted outside on the lawn. I pulled up to the red light and looked over in time to catch an elder completing the sign. It read: "The truth needs no support; if it limps, it's a lie." I nodded my head as the light turned green and gave an amen to that.

Robert

Yeah, this is Derek. I'm returning a page from a Robert Hayes. Man, give me a call at home as soon as you can. You don't know what you just got yourself into. I should be home by the time you get this message. The number to reach me at is five five five-eight nine eight eight. Peace."

This was the message left on my pager about fifteen minutes after I paged Derek. Nik still hadn't made it home yet, which meant that I had time to talk and not whisper. I straightened the dresser back up and sat down on the side of the bed to call this brotha back.

"Hello? Is this Derek?" I asked.

"It depends on who's calling."

"Oh, my fault. This is Rob, Rob Hayes. I left a message for you on your pager about Karen."

"Oh, yeah. Whassup? I wanted to ask you how you got my number, but I'm assuming that she gave it to you."

"Only I didn't tell her what I was calling to talk to you about."

"Can you hold on for one minute; my fiancée is coming in."

Through the muffled receiver, I could hear a woman and a child in the background and then what sounded like Derek moving to another room.

"Yeah, whassup? So what can I help you with?" he asked.

"Well, first, I want to let you know that I was the brotha in the bedroom that day that you came over about the money."

"Mmmhmm."

I was pausing for Derek to acknowledge the incident with a

little more concern, but he remained quiet. Continued waiting to see what my point was or if I actually had one at all.

"I wanted to let you know that there was no offense taken," I added.

"None intended. The purpose for me saying what was said was so you wouldn't end up in the situation that you're in right now."

"Brotha, believe me, I know. But Karen has been taking me through some serious changes. She's tried to destroy my relationship with my woman *and* my family."

"It all sounds like a familiar story."

I asked, "Oh, you know another brotha she's done this to?"

"Hell, I *am* the brotha she's done it to! At one point, I was just like you, but with no one to warn me. She had my girlfriend's phone number, work number, and license plate number, too. Karen has destroyed more relationships for me than I can count. A little over three years ago, she gave up and started harassing someone else. I'm assuming that was you."

"Unfortunately. But I do have an advantage over you, brotha. I'm not certain that this baby is mine."

Derek laughed so hard that he dropped the phone. I could hear him pounding his fist on something hard and then trying to grab the receiver with hands that were too weak from the comedy that I was providing.

"I'll do you one better. I *know* Alex isn't mine."

"So why do you have custody of him?"

"Because as far as my love for him is concerned, he is. Karen pulled the same stunt on me five years ago that she's probably trying to pull on you. We were in a relationship, and one day she pops up pregnant. Wouldn't allow me to go with her for ultrasounds and dared me to speak to her doctor about her condition. This was all to keep me from knowing how far along she was. She had me out buying a high chair, a crib, a stroller, a changing table, sleepers, and a playpen. Shit, I even started paying for her health insurance.

"A year or so went by and I started noticing that Alex looked nothing like me. So one day, I decided to get a blood test done. The results showed that he didn't belong to me."

I asked, "Did you tell her that you knew he wasn't yours?"

"For what? By then, I loved that baby more than life itself. I needed him. Alex became the glue that held me together. And I wasn't gonna let Karen destroy that. But what I didn't know was that she had no intentions of doing that anyway. She simply wanted her freedom. I took Alex and got my own place downtown. Then when I had taught him to walk, talk, and use the toilet, she decided to pop back up again. The sad part was that she wanted us both back. Taking custody of just Alex would cut into her time, which was something that she couldn't allow to happen, so she tried to win me over. After a year or so of rejection, she gave up. Told me one day that she was willing to settle for *occasional visits* from the child *she* brought into this world. Can you believe that? That shit fucked me up! Talk about a lack of maternal instincts. But as it turns out, Alex never really became comfortable with her and didn't want to visit at all. And naturally, I stopped making him. Now if I ask her for a little financial assistance, she gets flip at the lip or hangs up. Which is fine with me, because my fiancée is helping me more than I would have imagined."

"Damn."

"Sistas nowadays are a trip."

I asked, "So what did you do as far as stopping her from ruining your relationships?"

"Let me guess. She's calling your place when she knows that your woman is there, parking outside of your home and waiting for you to come out, and announcing to the world that you're the baby's father. Am I close?"

"Close enough. You left out the part about pretending to have psychic abilities, threatening to tell my woman that she's sleeping with me, and coercing my sister into becoming her roommate in order to keep me on my toes."

"Damn, she's advanced in the past few years. Well, Loose lips sink ships was always her motto. But look, my family and I are about to sit down for dinner. If I were you, I would lose contact with her until that child is born. Get a paternity test and then go from there. I don't know what your situation is, but you could be losing a good sista by messin' around with Karen. Take it from me. Don't let her any closer to home base than she already is."

I said, "Listen, man, thanks for the info."

"No problem. And I hope there aren't any hard feelings about what was said the day you were visiting her."

"Hey, it's cool. Take it easy."

"Peace."

As I was hanging up the phone, Kim came in from work. She dropped her bags at the door and did her usual dash to the bathroom. I stepped out of my bedroom and into the kitchen to make a ham and cheese sandwich, and she joined me. Kim sat down at the table and folded her hands together, a condescending look on her face.

She said, "I don't like having to lie to Nik."

"And you think I do?"

"Well you're making a conscious effort to!"

"Look, I'm gonna have this thing all cleared up before Don is even buried. Trust me, things will be back to normal in no time."

Kim turned her mouth up in skepticism.

"And if they aren't?"

"Then I will have been wrong for the first time in my life."

Four days had gone by since the fire and I still hadn't heard from Theresa. I was on leave of absence for the rest of the week and decided to turn down the suggested counseling, even though the city was going to be paying for it. This left me with a lot of time on my hands and just as many issues on my mind. That evening, I decided to run by the house to check and see if Theresa was all right, make sure she wasn't spending too much time alone and ask if she needed anything. I knew in my heart that if things had been the other way around, Don would have done it for Nik.

Theresa came to the door wearing a loose-fitting pink sweat suit. Her hair had been pulled back into one of those buns that Nik used to wear before she cut all of her hair off, and her eyes looked heavy.

She said, "Hi, Rob. Come on in."

She was home alone, with all of the lights out. There were about three candles lighted in the corner and Stevie Wonder's "Never Dreamed You'd Leave in Summer" was playing in the background. She rushed over and turned on a couple of lamps before wiping away the obvious tears. I noticed an eight-by-ten photo on the couch of Don in his uniform, when we first got hired. He was smiling, which was something he'd never had a problem doing, unlike me. His full face, bushy eyebrows, and the distinct cleft in his chin brought back memories.

I asked, "How is everything going for you?"

"As to be expected. I'm sorry that I didn't get a chance to make it to the hospital. I've just had a lot to do. His family has been by every day, trying to see what things of his they want. At first, I tried to monitor what was taken, but now I show them what was his and go lie down in the bedroom. I just close my door and let them pick and fight over that petty stuff. None of it matters to me. Not a single object will bring him back."

Theresa broke down crying, which was to be expected. But there was one thing that seemed rather peculiar to me. She never said Don's name. Kept referring to him as "him." It was as though she felt the less informal she was, the more distance she could put between him being in her life and the way that her life was now. Like maybe one day it would go from "him" to the dim memory of a man she used to love.

I asked, "When is the funeral?"

"Friday, in Chicago. I don't know how I'm gonna get there, though. His aunt insisted on taking his car and giving it to her son. She told me that he bequeathed it to her son and that she was sorry that I wasn't informed of this before he passed."

"So how have you been getting around?"

"With nowhere to go, it hasn't been too much trouble."

I sighed and rested my elbows on my knees. Cupped my face in my hands and listened to Stevie over and over and over again. What bothered me was the fact that the family of such a good man would be this cold and inconsiderate of the woman he loved. It was beginning to make sense that he'd decided to live in St. Louis and not go back to his hometown.

"Theresa, what are your finances like?"

"We had a little savings, but not as much as we needed. You know, we were thinking about opening a wedding account, but he never got around to it."

There she goes again with that "he" and "him" shit again.

"Listen, I've got to run, because there are a lot of things that I've got to get done before Friday, but I want you to get the details on where the funeral is gonna be held and be ready at about five that morning. I'll be by to get you, and I just may have a small package for you."

"Rob, I'm a grown woman. And besides, you and he had the same occupation. There's no way that you can afford to take care of me for him."

"Theresa, I hear what you're saying, but Don would have done it for me if things were different."

"But that's it—they're *not* different! *You're* here and *he's* not! Nikai won't be alone tonight like I will. She won't have to pack clothes in boxes that you'll never be able to fill!"

Her tone became hostile as she balefully spoke about everyone and anyone who hadn't at least tried to understand her pain. She grabbed framed certificates that Don had earned and violently tossed them against the wall. I watched the glass shatter and fall like rain during a midday storm. The same storm that had been brewing inside of me since I watched Don lie amid broken glass, literally begging me to relieve my conscience of the burden I had been carrying. I slid down the wall Theresa was taking her frustration and resentment out on and cried. I cried for every time that I'd wandered off. Off into that bathroom when I should have been watching Don's back, off into the arms of Karen when I should have been home looking out for Nik, and off into my own world when reality had become too much for me to handle.

I stayed there and held Theresa late into the night. So long that she had started calling Don by his name again. I think it was that I wanted to prove her wrong about having to fall asleep alone that night. But then, it wasn't that I actually wanted to prove *her* wrong; I just wanted to prove *somebody* wrong. I wanted somebody to know that I could be a good man. That I didn't always seek personal gain before getting involved. That I had a real heart and not one made of steel. That even though I always appeared to be in control, I wasn't. That I had fears, concerns, and a need to be understood. I wanted somebody, anybody, to know that after all I had been through, I still needed someone to catch my drift.

Nikai

Robert was late getting home again. I was sitting up in bed, wearing a red teddy with the thong up my butt, waiting for him to walk through the door. And every time I heard Kim get up to go to the bathroom, my heart raced a mile a minute. I'd gone through just about every emotion imaginable, starting with worry, then anger, anxiety, joy over the fact that no news usually meant good news, and then back around to worrying again.

I had planned to break Robert off a little somethin', not because he deserved it, but in an attempt to conceive. The kinky outfit was just a perk. I watched the *Laverne and Shirley* marathon on Nick at Nite until my crack was rubbed raw. Every time I tried pulling the thong to the side, it went back into hiding, as if it were being drawn by a magnet. Made me more impatient. I was anticipating the moment when I could snatch it off and shock Rob into a stuttering state.

I had gotten down on my knees and prayed at least five times that God would bless me with a spot in that band that I'd auditioned for that morning. (And believe me, it ain't a pretty sight for a sista to be wearing a sizzlin' red thong teddy, with carpet burns on her kneecaps, if ya know what I mean.) The other members seemed like fun people to be around. Real eclectic, yet down-to-earth. We did a couple of sessions and I showed them some songs that I had been working on but never got to share with N-Sight. If you ask me, we connected well, even before we all went out to lunch. Made me wonder how many other people they took out to eat, and if this was an attempt to cushion the blow of rejection. They told me that I should be hearing something by the next week, since everyone still had to vote, but the day went by slowly and, thanks to Robert, so did the night.

I looked over at the nightstand at a message that Kim had written down for me. Sheila had called for the third time, saying that it was important that I get back to her. When I tried to call her back that night, the operator said that the line had been disconnected. I tried it over and over again in hopes that the operator was wrong, but she wasn't. There was no telling when I would be able to speak with Sheila again.

Once my clock read 2:46 A.M. I undressed and tossed my useless outfit across the room, onto a chair. Got the sudden urge to get down on my knees and open my cedar chest at the foot of the bed. The one in which I had hidden my beaded gowns that Sheila and I loved so much. I grabbed a long green one and shook it out. Pulled it over my head and then stood in front of the mirror, modeling it for myself. The memories that surfaced brought tears to my eyes. I turned around and picked up a bag of sage out of the metal box that I had found Travis's personal items in. Put some in an ashtray, cracked a window, and struck a match. The smell filled the air as I lighted a candle on the dresser.

That night, I lay in bed and meditated heavily. Envisioned myself doing all of the things that needed to be done. Making the right decisions, growing, and finally being free. Gave the Creator full control of my life and turned my problems over: the void in my life from Sheila's absence, the lack of money to repay Travis, whether signing with Leon Lovejoy was the right move, whether to stick it out with Robert or to walk away, whether to encourage Lucky to live, and whether to wrap my arms around my mama and be the first to say "I love you." In that instant, the candle began to shine brighter. Bright enough for me to be able to see the difference even with my eyes closed. Something was definitely different; I was different. Although I still had no idea what was gonna come my way, I knew that I could handle it all.

I got undressed and dozed off into a light sleep, and then the phone woke me. I grabbed the caller ID box and prayed that it wasn't someone calling from a hospital, telling me that Rob had been in an accident. The word *Anonymous* flashed, along with the time, which was now 3:20 A.M.

"Hello?" I answered.

There was silence. Not even breathing.

"Hello?"

"Were you asleep?"

The voice was distant but familiar.

"No. Who is this?" I asked.

"Kalif."

I curled my naked body up under the satin sheets and began to whisper. There was no telling how many trips Kim was gonna make to the bathroom that night, and I didn't want to give her any reason to put her ear to my bedroom door.

Kalif said, "I couldn't sleep. I miss you."

"I didn't think you had time to miss me, with all of the company you've been keeping."

"You *did* notice that she kissed *me*. It wasn't the other way around. And besides, if I had known that you had become a private investigator, I probably would have told her to keep the public displays of affection to a minimum."

"I guess it's better that I see certain things. What gave you the courage to call here like this? You know, Rob could have answered."

"You've never taken chances for the things you want?"

"And what exactly is it that you want?"

"Your company. Can you come out for a while?"

"I don't know. It's pretty late."

"Do you *want* to come out for a while?" he asked.

I didn't answer.

"Still afraid to do what you want to do, huh?" he continued.

I looked over at the empty space next to me. Placed my hand on the cooler half of the bed, where Robert should have been, and pulled the covers back.

"I'm on my way. Look out for me."

*   *   *

I pulled up to the loft and found Kalif leaning against the building in the same B-boy stance as the first day I met him. It was
cold as hell outside.

I closed my car door and said, "You didn't have to wait outside."

"I wanted to make sure you came."

"You think standing in the cold would make a difference?"

"If I can ask you to come out in this weather, then I ought
to be able to stand here and make sure that you're all right."

I shrugged my shoulders and hurried inside of the building.
We hopped on the elevator but kept our distance from each
other. It almost seemed like we were starting all over again. Like
we hadn't known each other.

"What did your man have to say about you leaving?"

"He wasn't home."

Kalif didn't respond. He simply nodded his head and pulled
the lever on the wall. Without showing any emotion, he lined
his floor up with the bottom of the elevator.

"What did your woman have to say about you having company? Or is that why you waited so late to call?"

"I didn't wait until late. I was just getting home."

"Oh, from her place?"

Kalif turned to me as we walked into his dimly lit loft.

"Is there something you want to ask me?"

I said, "Actually, there is."

"Then do so."

"All right. Why did you call me over here?"

"I thought we covered that."

"You said you wanted my company. There's got to be more."

"Sounds like you want more."

I blushed and said, "Would that be so wrong?"

"What would be wrong is for you to pretend that you don't.
You want anything to eat or drink?"

"At this time of the morning?"

"I've got the munchies. I've been lifted all day long."

"Lifted?" I asked.

"Yeah. Lifted, blasted, high. Nikai, you know what I mean.
Stop acting so flawless and untouched."

"Maybe I am flawless and untouched."

Kalif shook his head and walked into the kitchen. Tossed himself a salad in one of those plastic four-for-a-dollar bowls, grabbed a white envelope off of the counter, and sat down next to me in the living room. He wasted no time eating and putting away half of a liter of water. Picked up the package and handed it to me.

"What's this?" I asked.

"The remainder of your fees. I didn't get a chance to get them to Don in time. So here you go."

I opened it up and found fifteen twenty-dollar bills. I couldn't believe that I had forgotten all about the money for the studio time. But something wasn't right. It was way too much.

"Kalif, some of this is yours."

"No, it's not. What I got was priceless."

"What was that?"

"Your time."

I blushed and silently thanked the Creator for being right on time.

Then he asked, "Have you been singing lately?"

"It's been kinda hard to since I've become an outcast. I have an appointment to meet with Leon Lovejoy in the morning, and I'm waiting to hear from a band that I auditioned for. It looks promising, though. I've still got to go on."

"Sorry about that. You can understand how I felt at that moment, can't you? I guess I let my emotions get in the way. All I could see was that brotha tryin' to do harm to you. The kind of psychological harm that shows every time you lack the confidence that was once inside of you. Back when you knew who you were, what you wanted. Back when you went after what you wanted."

"Why do you talk to me like that?"

"Like what?"

"Like you really know me. Like you maybe even look up to me or something."

"Maybe it's because I do. Does that bother you?"

"Which one? You knowing me or you looking up to me?"

"Both."

"I think it mostly confuses me. I mean, I haven't done anything that would make you look up to me. Things have been coming together for me only lately. You said yourself that there was a time when I knew who I was and what I wanted. You just implied that I'm totally lost now."

"Is that the way it sounded?" he asked, placing the bowl on the coffee table. "That was my way of letting you know that it *is* inside of you. It's what brought you here tonight."

"That, and you, too."

Kalif blushed, ran his hand over his head, and began twisting one of his locks at the root.

"You want me to do that for you?" I asked.

"Only if the need to be close to me is that strong."

"Will you stop with the complicated answers! Yes, I want to touch you. Yes, I want to be near you. That's why I'm here now. I missed the hell out of you."

"That's interesting."

He walked over and sat down between my thighs. Rested his elbows the way that he used to and massaged my ankles. Kalif began toying with the anklet that he had given me. The one I'd made sure not to remove, no matter what happened between us.

"I see you kept this."

"Some things are forever. Remember?"

"Too bad everything isn't," he answered, relaxing from the scalp massage.

"Like what?"

"Like life. Seems like the Creator's timing was all wrong with Don. He hadn't done hardly anything."

I closed my eyes and pictured the look on Theresa's face when they made their wedding announcement. I thought about all of the funny stories that Rob used to have about him and how he treated me like a sister when he hadn't even known me for more than two and a half years. How his death had inadvertently given me life. He reminded me of what I had and what I *could* be without. To cherish this time and live as though tomorrow would never come.

"Yes, he did. He left a lasting impression on us all. He left a lot of memories, food for thought, and inspiration. I believe that was his purpose."

"Seems like there should be more."

"There is. What you do with it all."

Kalif asked, "You going to the funeral?"

"I hadn't gotten any information on it. When and where is it?"

"In Chicago, on Friday."

"I'll think about it, but I don't know what kind of effect me being there with you and Rob at the same time might have on the occasion."

"I don't have a problem with it. I'm comfortable with the way that I feel about you."

"Oh yeah? And how is that?"

"I care about you a lot, but I also respect the fact that you're in a relationship."

"So much that you would ask me to come out and see you at three-thirty in the morning?"

"It's so much easier to put things off on me, isn't it? Nikai, you got up out of your *empty bed* because *you* wanted to be here."

"Whassup with the emphasis on my bed being empty?"

"My way of reminding you what you had to have considered before coming. When you think about it, it doesn't make sense to go back."

"What are you saying?" I asked.

"What does it sound like?"

"Sounds like you're asking me to stay here."

"Well, now that we know your hearing is working, what's your answer?"

"I don't know."

"Not true."

"Yes, it is."

"Don't lie to yourself."

"I'm not!"

"Then stay."

"I can't."

"Why not?"

I continued rubbing his head as I perused my mental file cabinet of excuses.

"Because I promised Robert that I would try to make our thing work."

"And I'm assuming that coming to see me was in an effort to keep that promise."

"No."

"Then why are you here, Nikai? Why now? Why me?"

My hands stopped and it seemed as though everything else did, as well. Including my fear of rejection. It was time for me to acknowledge that sense of courage that no one in my family had, that the people who surrounded me envied me for. It was time for me to make a decision. Not as far as being with Robert or Kalif, but about being *without* them. I needed to be with myself for a while. That didn't necessarily mean that I couldn't *date* someone, but I couldn't *dedicate* myself to someone. There was a difference just as plain as the difference between these two men. The same difference that was drawing me closer and closer to one—self-awareness.

"Because I think I'm in love with you," I confessed.

Kalif stood up from the floor and sat on the futon next to me. Placed his tattooed arms around me and brought his soft lips up to mine. He gave me sweet, gentle pecks until my tongue invited his to a five-minute tango. I allowed my hands to roam freely, to touch all of the places that had left me speechless when Kalif casually strolled throughout the loft without a shirt.

The moisture in my seat increased as I encouraged him to continue unbuttoning my pants. I wanted to go too far, to seal this uncontrollable desire to bond with this special man. The man who supported more than just my career. Kalif supported my need to live. My need to know that with tomorrow would come disappointments as well as euphoria. And that my fear of both was okay. That in the midst of harmony yet imbalance, *I* was okay.

That night, Kalif and I made more than love. We made a spiritual pact to grow without reservations, to trust without violations, and to elevate without stipulations. And I didn't have to rub the crack of my ass raw to do it.

Robert

At about six o'clock in the morning, the sun woke me from a deep sleep. I thought that I was having another one of those strange dreams, when I looked around and realized that I was in Don's living room. Theresa had given me a blanket, gone to bed, and that was all. The mess she'd made the night before was there to greet me when I stood up.

I crept down the hall and lightly tapped on her bedroom door. She didn't answer. I cracked it a bit and stuck my head inside.

I called, "Theresa!"

She didn't budge.

"Theresa!"

This time, she rolled over, sat up, and looked at me with eyes that had not yet focused.

"I'm gonna go on home now. Come on, so you can lock the front door."

She threw the sheets back and revealed that she hadn't even bothered to get undressed last night. Without saying a word, she ran her fingers through her ruffled hair and scratched at her hips. She slowly dragged her feet as she followed me back into the living room.

I opened the front door and said, "Don't forget about tomorrow morning. I'll be here at five."

She nodded her head and rubbed her puffy eyelids. I reached out and gave her a sympathetic hug. She hugged me back with the little strength that she could muster up. It was apparent that

Theresa was still tired—not just physically but emotionally, as well.

Theresa silently held on to the edge of the door as I turned to leave. After all that she took the time to share with me the night before, she couldn't find anything to say now that she was about to be alone again. I walked out to my car, opened the door, and glanced back in time to catch her beckoning for me to step back up on the porch.

"Robert, thank you for listening to me."

"Anytime," I assured her.

"Now it's your turn to talk."

"I should be okay—"

"No," she said, grabbing me by the arm. "Not to me. To Nikai. I could tell last night that you still haven't shared your secret with her. Tell her, Rob. Tell Nik about the baby."

By then, her eyes had widened, but not half as much as mine. She stood mourning and reciting the last words to come out of Don's mouth. She always said Nikai, not Nik, and she never would've given her opinion unless it was absolutely insisted upon. Something told me that *Theresa* really didn't have anything else to say that morning. *Don* did, through her.

Kim met me at the front door with a serious *attitude*. I hadn't even gotten my key out of the door before she was in my face, yelling.

"You know what? I'm sick of you two people wasting each other's time! You don't want that relationship, and neither does she! Both of y'all have more nerve than a brass-ass monkey to walk out of here and not return until the next day. . . ."

"Nik isn't here?" I asked.

"Not as of right now! But you wouldn't know that, because you were too busy playin' house with Karen!"

"*What*? I was at Don's place with Theresa all night."

"Oh, and that's the weak-ass line you plan to run by Nik when she gets home?"

I locked the door and walked into the bedroom, with Kim still on my heels. I noticed a red nightie lying in a chair, sage ashes, smoke in the air, and one of those voodoo dresses tossed on Nik's side of the bed, which appeared to have been turned down the night before.

"You know, we aren't as close as we used to be, and this is all your fault!" Kim continued, "There was a time when she would have told me where she was going in the middle of the night! Now look at the way things are! Use your dick to destroy your own relationships, Rob, not mine, too!"

"Look, if Nik didn't tell you where she was going, it's probably because she didn't feel like she could trust you. And I don't have nothin' to do with that!"

"So what now? I mean, what do y'all plan to do?"

"Why?"

Kim's anger quickly turned to frustration. Tears formed in her eyes as she stood on the threshold of my bedroom and broke down.

"Because if y'all break up, our friendship will, too."

I took my baby sister by the shoulders and attempted to calm her.

"You can't live through Nik and me. We can't be your completion. Our problems can't become yours just because you're too afraid to get in a relationship of your own. I know it's safer to stand on the sidelines and narrate than it is to have loved and lost on your own, but you've got to get back out into this world and take chances. I won't always be there for you to hide behind. And I definitely won't always be there to smooth over your mistakes.

"I'm not gonna stand here and tell you that once I've told Nik all about Karen that she'll cry for a day or so and things will be back to normal, because something inside tells me that too much damage has been done for that to happen."

Kim said, "This is crazy. I did everything you asked me to do. I tried persuasion, I played dumb, and I even lied for you. That's probably why she doesn't trust me anymore."

She pulled the checks that I had given her, along with the three hundred dollars, from her pocket and threw them in my face. Then she started with the yelling again. Kim was so busy poking me in the chest and blocking my vision with her swinging arms, I didn't notice that Nik had made it home and was standing behind her in the hall.

Nik asked, "Lied about what?"

It took every nerve in my body and every ounce of love for her in my heart to form my lips and say the words.

"The baby inside of Karen is mine."

I kept my eyes fixed on her and prepared myself for whatever spit, hits, or kicks that were going to come my way. Which was more than I could say for Kim. She complained so much about a friendship gone bad yet she couldn't even look Nik in the eye during *my* confession.

Nik asked Kim, "And you've known about this?"

"Girl, I just found out a little while ago, and as soon as I did, I moved out."

"Well, y'all's mother must be ecstatic."

I said, "She doesn't know. Nobody knew except the three of us, and, of course, Don."

Nik remained strangely calm as she fondled the purse on her shoulder.

"See, Kim, that's a faithful friend. As close as I thought Don and I were, he still grinned in my face and held a secret like this for what, four or five months? All because he didn't want to see his best friend hurting. Now that's dedication if I've ever seen it."

Kim and I looked at each other and silently shared the same thought: Nik has lost her mind. She even dragged what looked like a smile across her face. Had a peaceful glow about herself. It kinda reminded me of Angela Bassett in *What's Love Got to Do with It* after she beat Ike upside the head in the limo and meditated her way into a new life.

Nik scooted past the two of us and began snatching clothes from the closet and laying them out on the bed. Grabbed her luggage, jewelry boxes, shoes, and beauty supplies from the bathroom. Started pulling framed prints down from the walls and even neatly folded up the satin sheets on the bed.

I asked, "You don't want to talk about this?"

"Everybody's been so tight-lipped up until now. It really

wouldn't make sense to talk. Besides, I'm sure you'll be too busy with Lamaze class and all."

I deserved that one. Which is why I didn't try to explain that I hadn't planned to speak to Karen again until after the baby was born and I had taken a blood test. None of that would have lightened the load that I had just placed on Nik.

Kim dared to ask, "Where are you going?"

On that note, I snatched my keys up and tried to leave the apartment. If looks could kill, Nik would have left us both for dead.

"No! The question is where is *he* going! Robert, come back here."

I turned around to face her, my head hung low.

"Nik, I just want to say that I didn't mean for—"

"You didn't mean for what to happen? For me to find out? Or for Karen to get pregnant?"

"Both."

Kim finally stepped up and added, "Really, Nik, he tried—"

"What do you mean, 'he tried'? How can you stand there and defend him when you *know* he's wrong?"

Kim lowered her eyes and said, "Nik, he's my brother."

Nik sucked her teeth and then looked back and forth at the two of us.

"Well, I guess it was my fault that I trusted either one of you. I guess everybody plays the fool sometimes, huh?"

She gave a smirk and went back to packing her things. I walked up behind her and tried to hold her by the waist.

"Don't touch me!" she yelled, pulling away.

She turned around, wielding a wire hanger and waving it like she was looking to puncture someone.

"You know, it's a damn shame that *Karen* has been the most honest one of all in this shit! She was the only one with enough balls to step up to the plate and acknowledge what she did. Your sorry ass," she yelled, pointing at me, "always managed to tell me when you wanted to *fuck!* Why in the hell was *this* so hard?"

As she carried on waving that hanger, the corner of it got caught in the tennis bracelet on her wrist. She looked down at it, before pulling hard and snapping it in half.

"And you can keep the pathetic-ass *guilt gifts!* That's not an expression of love. An expression of love would have cost you a lot less. But you couldn't see that all I wanted was your time, affection, and to know that you belonged to me. Was that too much to give? Was it, Robert?"

Before I could answer, she had started up again.

"I spent night after night lying here hoping that one day you would fall back in love with me."

"But baby, I do—"

"No, you don't, because you don't even love yourself. You're just *in* love with yourself, and there's a difference."

Nik fell silent again and took a deep breath.

Then she said, "Well, it looks like you got that baby you wanted after all."

"You know I don't want a baby with her. I want a baby from the woman I'm with."

"Well, I've learned something that I think I'm gonna share with you. Sometimes, Rob, we're afraid to lose what was never really ours to begin with."

Nikai

Where was I going? That wench had the *nerve* to ask me where I was going. I threw a self-explanatory scowl in her direction, told her brother off, and finished gathering my stuff. Packed things in the same order that I had done before, only this time, Robert was aware of my departure and there was no need to speak my mind any further. He understood exactly how I felt at that moment. He understood so well that he left in a hurry.

As soon as I heard the door shut behind him, I calmed down considerably. Even surprised myself how much better I felt about doing exactly what *I* wanted, what I felt would make *me* happy, and that was to leave Rob, that apartment, and everything behind me. Didn't know *where* I was going after the confrontation that morning, but the Creator had brought me too far to drop me off then. I walked around the apartment whistling and wondering how long it was gonna take his sister to follow his lead. Kim hadn't moved from that spot. She stood with her mouth half-opened, looking as though there was something else she wanted to say.

I turned to her and asked, "Would you do me a favor?"

Her expression softened. I could see in her eyes that I could have asked her to go play in traffic and she would've been out of the door before I could tell her which highway I meant.

"Can you take this box and put all of those pots and pans in it? I would really appreciate it."

Kim looked confused. Her feet were still planted as though

moving them would've allowed our last few moments together to escape.

"Nik, don't go," she begged softly.

I stopped packing and sat down at the foot of the bed. Sighed and placed the empty hangers in my hand on the floor. I reached out for her as she quickly joined me on the empty mattress.

"I can't stay here, Kim. It has nothing to do with you. I understand your loyalty to Robert, because I would have done the same thing for Taylor. But think about what you're asking me to do. You want me to be unhappy so that you're comfortable. Now, you know that's not fair. It wouldn't be fair to me or to our friendship."

"So we still have a friendship?"

"Listen, so much has happened in just a few months that it's really hard to say. I haven't even had a chance to digest what just went down here, but I do know that a line has been crossed. And everything we had won't be salvaged, but what we can do is keep in touch. Without Rob swaying your loyalty to me, maybe we can try it again someday."

"Who will I talk to?" she asked.

I placed my hand on her shoulder and said, "I don't really know, Kim."

She opened her mouth again but appeared to be at a loss for words.

"Nik, I want you to know that I wasn't in on this with Rob and Karen. Like I said, as soon as I found out, I moved. That's why I told you that I didn't know about her having another child. I didn't allow them to drag me into the situation enough to know information like that."

I began rubbing her back and told her, "I believe you. But none of that even matters to me anymore."

"So where are you going to live?"

I looked Kim in the eye, hugged her one last time before I finalized the death of our friendship, and said, "I wish I trusted you enough to say."

She stood up from the bed and silently made her exit. I think it was the fact that she had humbled herself that upset her the most. She had taken her pride and tossed it out of the window in an effort to get me to do what she wanted. And once I refused, she decided that nothing was worth humiliation. I guess that sort of thing ran in their family.

The thought of where Robert had gone crossed my mind, but only in passing. It was like his love, there for a while and then, like the tears of a lovesick fool, it dried up.

I sat down with some newspaper to wrap my Afrocentric figurines, and the phone rang. I waited to see if Kim was gonna pick up, considering she knew that I was busy, but she didn't. I stretched across the bed and grabbed the receiver on the last ring.

"Hello?"

Mama said, "Nikki, I've got a surprise for you."

"What is it?"

"I'm not telling right now. You'll see when you come over tomorrow. I can't wait to see the look on your face."

Mama had the surprise sounding like James had returned from the dead with my money or something. I explained my situation to her and asked that she pass the news along to Taylor. She offered to let me keep my stuff at her place and did that motherly worrying thing, until I had to remind her that I was in the middle of packing up my stuff and wanted to be gone before Robert made it back from Babies "R" Us or wherever the hell he'd darted off to.

To be honest, I wasn't really upset with Karen. Even after all of the games she'd played. The main reason was because *she* didn't owe me anything. Robert was supposed to be loyal to me, not some woman I hadn't even really known. I was giving *him* all that I had to offer. All that I felt I could afford to sacrifice, and sometimes even more. Karen would do *only* what Robert *allowed* her to, and that included becoming pregnant with his firstborn.

I didn't want to be like all of the other ex-girlfriends in the world, putting on a grand finale in order to save face. It was apparent that Karen had won hands down. The game was over. One that had really been too dangerous to play in the beginning. But after all that Rob had taken me through, it was still in me to be pleasant and bow out gracefully. To be the lady who had captured Robert's heart in the beginning and boggled his mind in the end.

I picked the broken tennis bracelet up and placed it on top of the red teddy, which I had no use for. Where I was going, there was no need for either. After piling my stuff into the trunk and backseat of my car, I walked back up to the apartment. Took a tube of lipstick from my purse and scribbled a message on the dresser mirror, where I knew his shallow ass would find it: "About that wedding proposal—I think I'll pass."

Then I headed back to Kalif's place for the night.

Robert

I rode around the city for hours in an attempt to get used to being alone. Up Interstate 70 to 170 and then over to 270. Got off on West Florissant and traveled all the way back toward downtown. Normally under circumstances like these, the track or Don's place would have been my next move, but he was long gone. And the following day would be my last chance to say good-bye. There wasn't going to be anyone special in my life anymore. No one to understand what made me tick. And no one who really cared.

I had decided to leave the apartment because there was actually nothing left to say. To beg Nik to stay would have been an insult to her intelligence. And I still loved her too much for that.

I imagined that she'd been with Kalif the night before because he had brought a part of her to life, even when she wasn't singing. That, and the fact that the smell of sex on her clothes was thick enough to be sliced with a knife.

I pulled up in a 7-Eleven lot and went inside to load up on beer and Newports. Something told me that I was gonna need to be *out* of my right mind for a while. At least until I was used to sleeping in the middle of my bed again. As the cashier totaled up my snacks, drinks, and smokes, I felt my pager vibrating on my belt. Afraid of who it might be, I ignored it. That is, until it went off again and again and again. My suspicious finally settled, because no one could blow up a pager like Karen.

I stepped over to the pay phone outside of the 7-Eleven and called her back.

I asked, "Whassup?"

"I thought I asked you not to greet me with 'Whassup?' " she scolded.

I breathed heavily and said, "I'm at a pay phone Karen."

"How far are you from my place?"

I knew what her next question was going to be. I also knew that I was gonna accept that invitation because I didn't feel like being alone anymore.

"I'm about seven minutes away."

"You think you can stop by for a while?"

"I'll be there."

I hung up the phone, turned the collar up on my black leather three-quarter-length coat, and took my groceries back to the car. Flashbacks of the conversation I'd had with Derek kept popping up in my head. How he'd warned me that Karen meant me no good. How he'd pointed out the obvious patterns. How he'd run down the results of his contact with her.

As a man, I'm subject to flaws, and with temptation being in abundance, I was bound to get caught up. What concerned me most now was that Nik didn't hate me for what I had done. The way that I had irresponsibly toyed with her feelings was unacceptable, yet hopefully forgivable someday.

I pulled up in front of Karen's place and lighted up a smoke. Grabbed two brews and put one in each pocket. This time, I was gonna be drinking something I knew that I could handle. I remembered what had happened the last time I allowed her to supervise my intake—things started to fall apart.

She opened the door. She was wearing a large—and I do mean large—white terry-cloth robe. Her hair was in rollers and the stench of alcohol on her breath was strong enough to make a small boy dizzy. I considered scolding her, but we had traveled down that road before, and besides, I was too tired to argue with a grown woman about her choices.

She said, "Have a seat. I'm gonna put some clothes on."

Karen disappeared into another room. I could hear her rumbling through drawers and wondered what the special occasion was. She'd never bothered to wear anything more than a T-shirt or maybe a gown before. She returned to the living room in a pair of black leggings and a red fleece pullover. Sat down across from me on the love seat and turned on the television.

Then she asked, "You okay?"

I couldn't tell her that her sick and twisted plan to destroy everything that I knew to be normal had worked. I couldn't let her know that she had won.

"I'm still upset about Don, but I should be all right."

"Thank God it wasn't you."

"Maybe it should've been."

"What?" she asked.

"I said, 'Maybe it should have been.' I can't imagine things being any worse than they are right now."

Karen looked down at her swollen hands, which were resting in her lap. The expression on her face was one of disappointment.

"You hate the idea of me being pregnant, don't you?"

"*Hate* is a strong word."

"I know. That's why I chose to use it. Derek called last night. He told me that he had spoken with you, and that the topic of joint custody never came up. Said you didn't want me to have this baby."

I sighed and leaned back on the couch. Rested my head in my hand and looked across the room at her stomach. Her body had stretched so far out of shape that I began to question if I had even roamed those grounds.

"There was a lot that I needed to know. A lot that I knew you weren't gonna tell me."

"And how do you feel about it, now that you know what happened between Derek and me?"

"Let's just say that I've got my eyes open. For a while, I wanted to believe you. I had convinced myself that with you was where I might've needed to be."

"And how do you feel now?"

"Like I'm dreaming. Like I've lost all control of my life."

"Is it me or Don's death?"

"A little of both, combined with the fact that Nik has left me."

Karen's eyes grew wide with surprise. She covered her mouth

with her hand and turned the volume down on the television. I waited for her to fall out laughing. Maybe even high-five her fetus, but instead, she didn't crack a grin. In a way, it appeared that she was just as tired of winning as I was of losing.

"She knows about the baby?"

"Yeah. I told her this morning."

"How did she take it?"

"Better than I imagined. She was pretty calm. Just started packing her clothes. Kim stayed and talked to her, but I left. Felt like it was the least that I could do. She deserved all the time she needed to get herself together and swallow the news."

"Robert."

"Huh?"

"How would you feel if I told you that I was sorry?"

"Like your timing is bad. But I can accept an apology."

I nodded my head and parted my lips so that it would at least *look* like I was smiling. I was at the point where all I could do was accept her apology. The human side of Karen surfaced and made her more attractive. Not in the physical sense, but in a sense that assured me that she did have a heart. A sense that allowed me to sit in that room and not lunge across the table at her for all that she had done to me. All that she had helped me do to myself.

"You know, I really loved Derek. I wanted us to be a family so badly. He used to tell me that I had no maternal instincts. Sometimes, I think he's right. I miss Alex, but now that I know he's going to be taken care of, I can prepare for this little one. Derek never really wanted much, now that I think about it. Just wanted me to be at home most of the time. And I couldn't do that. If I stayed home, I was facing myself and the fact that I was living a lie. And taking them through the lie, as well. Derek doesn't know it, but Alex isn't really his."

I held my poker face and quietly allowed Karen to continue spilling her guts. Her eyes begged me for a reaction of some sort.

"And I guess I should tell you that this one isn't yours," Karen said, touching her belly.

"Why did you decide to tell me now?"

"Because, for one, it was becoming too much work. For two, paternity tests don't lie. And for three, I'm tired of my babies growing up not knowing who they are and who they came from."

"Do you know who the father is?" I asked.

"Yes. He isn't around, though. He lives in Indianapolis. Moved after I became pregnant."

"Does he know about the baby?"

"Yeah, but having a wife and family of his own sort of put a damper on things, if you know what I mean."

I started to ask why she would let herself get involved with someone with a family, but then I answered my own question. Because men like me saw women like Karen as a gold mine. She was every married and taken man's fantasy. There were no expectations or strings attached, because she understood the situation going into it. There were endless hours of enjoyment, because consciences were being removed with the panties and boxers.

I asked, "So what do you plan to do now?"

"I don't know. But I'm off to a pretty good start, don't you think?"

"I guess you could say that. Karen, I'm sorry that this is happening to you for the second time."

"I made my bed, so now I have to lie in it." She chuckled. "Maybe this time I'll acquire those maternal instincts that Derek says I'm lacking."

"Maybe."

I was relieved to learn that I wasn't going to become a sucka. I wasn't gonna be taking care of a child who wasn't mine. But what I didn't want was Karen to crucify herself for the lies she had me believing. She could have told me anything at that point and it wouldn't have moved me. I had lost everything that mattered. And if the things that didn't matter disappeared as well, it would have hardly been noticeable.

I no longer had a woman at home to go to, a friend to confide in, or a child to expect. I guess the truth gave me a feeling of relief, but it took away a lot, too. The truth took Nik from me and the truth took expectations away, as well. I didn't know what to look forward to after the funeral. The days that followed were gonna be open game. I had become a soul wandering about aimlessly. A man with no direction, in need of a good woman to take me where I needed to be. To show me what it would take to make her and only her happy. To understand that the weaknesses that I possessed before were no longer mine. That I was elevating from a grown boy to a man.

As I began to pull away from Karen's place and mentally prepared myself to celebrate the life of my best friend, I took a five-by-seven photo of Nik from my wallet and set it on the dashboard. Decided to leave it there as I drove around aimlessly. I thought about the good times that we'd shared, the trip I'd planned to take her on back when cheating wasn't even taken into consideration. When Nik and I knew where we stood. When Nik and I both made sure that things were good.

I see now that happiness is one of those things that don't come around and meet you halfway. One has to make a conscious effort to achieve it. And once it's obtained, there's the daily task of maintaining it. Treating it as precious as it is.

I'd made my mistakes and gathered up a load of regrets along the way. I'd broken Nik's heart, disappointed Kim, and let Don down, too. But it wasn't all bad. I'd given Karen an opportunity to be honest with herself. Which was something that she hadn't done in a long time. To be honest, neither had I.

My mother says that when the right woman comes along, she'll know what to do to keep me happy. The dispiriting part is that it's taken me this much time and this many errors to know how to be a good man for that woman, whenever heaven decides to drop her my way.

Nikai

The next morning, I hopped on an elevator, and rang the doorbell to Leon Lovejoy's suite at exactly 9:45. He opened the door, a bottle of beer in one hand and five cards in the other. There was rap music blasting behind him, along with several male voices.

I said, "Hi, did I come at a bad time?"

"No. Come in. Actually, you're early. I needed to talk to you anyway."

I followed him inside, only to find my worst nightmare coming true. Travis, Tyrone, and his posse were all sitting around a card table. Fifty-dollar bills were falling off onto the floor and women were picking them up on cue. Travis and I made eye contact for the first time in well over two years. At first, he looked surprised at the changes I had made in my appearance, and then he simply laughed, got up from the table, shook the half-naked hoochie off, and gave me a genuine hug.

"Damn, Nikai," he said, holding me by the shoulders and standing back. "I don't know what to say."

"Probably give you your money, huh?"

"Don't you know that if I really needed that money, I would have contacted you by now? Keep it. I'm doin' good. That's your half for the living room furniture that we bought together."

"Sounds funny to hear you say that word—*together*."

"Yeah, it does, doesn't it?"

He continued smiling as I looked him over. He hadn't

changed one bit. Was still the spitting image of Shemar Moore, only now in a more ghetto sense. I contemplated asking about the person he had watching me, but I decided to leave well enough alone, considering the fact that I'd never been approached. It was water under the bridge. And he probably didn't want to talk about it any more than I did.

"I heard you're singin' professionally now."

"Trying to make some things happen."

"Me, too. You see Tyrone?"

"Yo, whassup, Nikai? Long time no see," Tyrone greeted me.

I nodded my head. Couldn't think of anything else to do. Whatever came out of my mouth would've leaned in the direction of our last encounter. One I really wanted to forget. One I had done such a good job of forgetting.

Then Leon said, "Nikai, you wanna step into my office?"

We went inside a small room near the pool table, where he had a large oak desk, two brown-cushioned rolling chairs, a file cabinet, a plastic tree in the corner, and a small lamp. Leon sat behind the desk and waited for me to get comfortable. I set my purse down on the floor by my feet and folded my hands in my lap.

"What I wanted to talk to you about was the contract I was willing to offer you. It seems your illness gave way to another artist, whose look is a little more in demand right now.

"It's nothing personal," he said, holding his hand up and then looking back down at a sheet of paper that I was sure had nothing to do with what he was saying. "So, what I'm gonna do is keep you in mind just in case things don't work out with her, because I dig your whole vibe. You know, the nappy hair, the loose clothing, and the whole nine. It's cool; it's just not what the world wants right now. You get what I'm saying?"

"I sure do. Point well taken."

I thanked him for his time, said good-bye to Travis for good, and then left it all behind. Because that was what I needed to do. Just like Sheila trusted that the power in the sky was gonna lead her in the right direction, I had to do the same. And I knew that it was all for a reason.

"The nappy hair and loose clothing . . . it's just not what the world wants right now." Leon was speaking the sad, ugly truth. But as I left, I asked myself, What exactly does the world want? And second, How does it differ from what I want? All I could come up with was that the world wants fantasy. The same addiction I'd once had and successfully kicked. The world wants what it's used to, because it knows what the risks are already. It was as simple as that; their reality was definitely not mine.

That afternoon, I pulled up in front of my mama's town house and parked. The bright sun had begun to unsettle the oil-stained piles of snow along the sides of the road. The grass was beginning to peek through slush blocks in the yard and the temperature had risen to a comfortable fifty-three degrees.

A feeling of warmth came over me as I stood at the door in my navy blue pantsuit and blue all-weather coat, my double-strand twists resting neatly on the back of my neck. I felt good, inside and out. I had laid down a huge burden. Didn't feel the need to have a man in hopes that he would make me complete. I'd made myself complete as soon as I'd started to realize who I was, what I deserved, and exactly what I was capable of. I now had money to move into a place of my own, my mama was willing to let me store my things at her house until I had moved, and Kalif and I were back on speaking terms.

I put the key in the lock, turned, and tried to push the door open, but it didn't budge. I applied a little pressure and then heard giggling. I stood up straight and removed my key. I tried knocking, but the waiting seemed to go on forever. Finally, I could hear feet running toward the front door, and then my mother stood there grinning and holding her hand out for me to come inside.

"Good morning, Nikki. I guess you're ready for your surprise. Step right around this corner and have a seat on the couch. I'll bring it right out."

I slowly walked into the living room. Checked to my left and to my right but saw nothing. No big bow, wrapping paper, or tissue. Mama stood on the threshold and waited until I was sitting down, then turned, ran out of the room, and began yelling through the house.

"Nikki, you ready?"

"Yeah."

"All right, here's your surprise!"

I assumed the surprise was something large, because it was taking whoever was carrying it a long time to bring it to me. The footsteps were slow and light. Not quite a drag. I heard a throat clear, a man's throat. Mama stepped around the corner and moved to her right to reveal the surprise of my life.

Uncle Lucky stood there smiling proudly, his hands in the pockets of a black suit. The burgundy-gray-and-black tie that he was wearing drew attention to his clean-shaven face and recent haircut. Mama helped him do a half spin as she described his outfit from head to toe.

He laughed and looked happy to be transformed and, I guess I should say, included in an activity that called for him to do more than change the channel. We carried on whistling and applauding him so loudly that Taylor came downstairs to see what was so interesting.

"Hey, look at you! Where are y'all supposed to be going?" she asked.

Mama answered, "We're all going to see Nicholas."

I said, "You're welcome to come, if you want."

Taylor shook her head, rubbed her belly through her flannel gown, and returned to her bedroom.

Mama said, "Give her time, Nikki. Everybody needs their own time."

I turned to Lucky, to see that he was at the front door, grabbing his winter coat off of the coatrack.

"You ready?" I asked.

He nodded his head and slowly held his arm out to escort me to the car.

"Thank you, sir. Gentlemen like yourself are so hard to find these days."

I turned to Mama and Lucky and said, "All right, we're all gonna go up together and then give one another a moment to talk to him alone."

They both nodded in agreement as we opened the doors of

my car and walked up the hill to Daddy's plot. We stood holding hands and giving our personal greetings. Lucky seemed the
most nervous, as he continuously shifted his weight from side to
side. He dropped my hand and grabbed a handkerchief from his
pocket. Covered his face and walked away. I lightly tapped
Mama's back and joined Lucky under a leafless tree.

"Remember when he used to say that you would outlive everybody in spirit?" I asked.

"Yeah. I wonder if he meant the body, too. I've been waiting
for this old thing to conk out on me for about ten years now."

"Be careful what you wish for or you just might get it," I told
him.

"Trust me, Slim. I know what to wish for. I've been at it a
long time."

"What made you decide to come out today?"

"I don't know. It must have been the fear. Fear will weigh
you down and tire you out. I was tired of being down-and-out.
So I figured that God was waiting me out. I was seeing how
long it would take him to bring me on home, and he was waiting to see how long it would take me to get out of that house.
And you know something, Slim? He always wins."

I leaned over and hugged him tightly. Rested my head on his
shoulder and waited for Mama to give me a turn to talk to
Daddy. She took three steps forward to the tombstone and
began to move her lips. I hoped that she was telling him all of
the things that had been on her mind since he left her. I hoped
that she would find the peace and the courage to come back on
her own. And I hoped that he heard her.

After gripping the tombstone with both arms, Mama decided
to give me an opportunity to share some time with my father.

"Hey, Daddy. You see who I brought out with me this time?
Surprised ya, huh? Well, as you probably know, I've left Robert.
I'm alone now, but that's not a bad thing. It's sort of like being
in transition. I'm interested in a wonderful brotha named Kalif.
He treats me good and he's very spiritual. You would have loved
him. Lucky's back there waiting to talk to you. He was really
nervous, but he decided to come and see you. Let me see. What
else is there to tell you before Lucky jumps up to bat? Oh, Tay-

lor and the baby are fine. Just waiting to see if he or she is as pretty as I am. Hey, Daddy, if you happen to meet a nice guy up there by the name of Don, tell him that I said thanks for everything and that I know where his heart was."

Mama yelled from across the cemetery for me to give Lucky an opportunity to speak. I put up an okay sign with my fingers and fell back into my good-byes.

"Well, your baby girl is starting over again. As you can tell, my outlook is a little different. I'm happier and more content with my job, career situation, and health. That's right. Kalif is helping from the inside out. We're getting our diets on point starting tomorrow. It's called 'holistic health.' I'm also gonna start running again, when I'm not singing. Since it wasn't meant for me to sign that contract, I've decided that if I don't get a call from the band I auditioned for, I'm gonna work on a solo project. You believe that? I know you do. It's what you told me to wish for. You know what, Daddy? I can honestly say that I'm happy right now. Well, I've taken up enough time. I think we're gonna take Lucky to the mall to hang out and then maybe out to dinner. He deserves it. I love you, Daddy. And Taylor sends her love, too."

Mama yelled, "Nikai! Nikai, come on!"

I readjusted the flowers that Mama had placed in front of the tombstone and joined them under the tree.

"Go ahead," I told Lucky. "He's waiting for you."

He took off walking up the hill and stood in front of Daddy's grave. At first, he didn't say much, just stared at the tombstone and then removed the fedora from his head. Looked around the cemetery as though he was checking to see if anyone else was there and then started holding a conversation.

I asked Mama, "What do you think he's saying?"

"I don't know. Probably asking Nick what heaven is like."

"If he could answer, what do you think he'd say?" I asked.

"Something corny, like 'the opposite of hell.' You know your father, always full of jokes."

"Mama, you glad you came out here today?"

"Yeah, I guess I am. It's not as hard as I imagined it would be. You know, they say the people who really loved you while you were living are the very ones who visit you when you're dead. I didn't want Nick to believe that I didn't love him. He still means the world to me."

"I think he knows that, Mama. Have you been to the doctor lately?"

"Just the other day."

"And what did he say?"

"He told me that the cancer was still in remission. That's part of the reason I decided to come out today. I wanted to make peace with your father just in case."

"Just in case of what?" I asked.

"Just in case I go to see him sooner than I imagined."

"Don't talk like that. You won't be going anywhere for a long, long time. I love you too much to let that happen."

She smiled at me and said, "Nikai, baby, I love you, too."

Mama hugged me under the tree and sent a warm feeling through me despite the cool breeze. I laid my head on her shoulder and exhaled. Kissed her on the forehead and silently promised never to let her go. Even when she *is* called to join Daddy among the angels.

Robert

I picked Theresa up at 5:30 that Friday morning and we immediately hopped on the road to Chicago. She still looked bad, even after dressing up in a black dress and black coat. She didn't bother with makeup or nail polish or any of those extras that I was so used to seeing her with. I reached over and handed her an envelope with four hundred dollars in it. She looked down at it, grabbed my hand, and decided to hold it instead.

"I need this more than I need the money."

So I left it there for her. Drove two and a half hours with her hanging on to me for dear life. We were an hour outside of Chicago when Theresa drifted off to sleep right as we pulled in front of a Clark gas station.

I turned to her and asked, "You need anything?"

She didn't answer. I asked her again.

"Theresa, you need anything?"

Still no movement. I put my hand on her shoulder and shook her lightly. Waited to see if her eyes would open, but they didn't. She wasn't even breathing. I jumped out of the car and ran around to her side. When I opened the door, her limp body fell out in my direction. I held her up and tried to yell for help.

"Hey, somebody, I need help! There's a sick woman over here!"

A heavyset truck driver with a full beard and long blond hair ran over to see what the problem was.

"Anything I can do?" he asked.

"Where's the nearest hospital?"

"About five miles down this road. Get her into my truck and I'll drive you guys down there!"

I literally dragged Theresa's limp body from the car, tossed her over my shoulder, and hauled her over to the truck. Started doing CPR in an effort to revive her, but she wasn't coming to. I pulled her arms together and a bottle of sleeping pills fell down by the floor mats. The trucker and I both looked down at them and then up at each other with the same expression. Theresa was in big trouble. He put the pedal to the floor, and just as we were pulling up to the hospital, she came to.

I stared sweating as I pulled her from the truck and actually found myself praying. As much as I complained about Nik doing it, it seemed so natural at that time. I mean, when it really came down to it, I realized that there was no one else who could help me. No one *but* God. It was becoming apparent that the bottom line was that I needed him, and at that moment I prayed relentlessly. Sat in the waiting room, oblivious to everyone else around. Prayed until I was blue in the face. I wanted forgiveness, *and* mercy. But not necessarily for me. I wanted him to take mercy on Theresa. For him to leave her here on earth.

Surprisingly, the truck driver, Bob, didn't leave. He stayed there with me for hours. Long past the scheduled funeral time and on into the late morning, early afternoon. Bob walked the halls for a little while and then brought me a cup of coffee.

He asked, "So you heard anything yet?"

"No," I answered, running my hands over my bald head. "The doctor said that they would be pumping her stomach. I don't know what's going on."

"I'm sure she'll be fine. You're all dressed up. Where were ya goin'?"

"To my best friend's funeral—her fiancé."

"Damn, sorry to hear that. It must've been tough to look over and find her that way."

"You've got no idea."

"Well, look. I was thinking that if you needed me to, I could hook your car on the back of my truck and bring it to you."

"Thanks, man. You don't know how much that would help."

"No problem. You just keep your head up."

Just as Bob was leaving, the doctor came walking into the waiting room. I couldn't tell much from his face, so I just stood up and braced myself for whatever was to be.

"She's doing fine. You want to come in and see her?"

"Of course."

I followed the doctor back to a room, where Theresa was all hooked up the way that I'd been not so long before. She was lying in bed with her eyes closed. I pulled up a chair and sat down next to her. Called her name and waited for a response of some sort.

Again, I called, "Theresa?"

She looked over at me and tried to pull a smile across her face.

"How are you feelin'?"

She nodded her head.

"You know, we missed the funeral. But we can still have our own little memorial right here."

She closed her eyes tightly and tears began to stream down her face. I felt bad for her. I didn't want to see her cry. I stood, leaned over, and hugged her. She shook and whimpered in my arms like a helpless baby.

I told her, "It's okay. Don's been watching over you."

She nodded her head again and then finally spoke.

"Robert, you're an angel."

I took her hand in mine and thought about what she had said. The real angel was Bob, who had come out of nowhere and helped two total strangers.

"You know how we got here?" I asked.

"How?"

"God sent a real angel. He's gone to bring my car out here."

"I want to meet him. Hey, Robert?"

"Whassup?"

"I'm sorry for doing that to you. You know, taking the pills while you were around."

"It was supposed to happen that way, Theresa. That's why you did."

"Did you ever talk to Nikai about that situation?"

"Yeah, and she left me."

"And what about the baby?"

"It's not even mine. Can you believe that?"

"You serious?"

"Yep. Now I've got no baby and no woman, either."

"Maybe it was for the best."

"I've learned that nothing is coincidence. Some people just have harder lessons to learn."

Theresa held my hand tighter in agreement as a sexy young nurse walked in to ask her how she was feeling.

"I'm doing good. Thanks."

She turned to me and asked, "And how about you?"

"Fine. Thanks. Can she get some water?"

"No problem."

She walked out of the room, swaying hips that reminded me of Nik's. The way she would sit on my lap and they'd spread like warm butter over morning toast. Theresa gave my hand another good squeeze and then laughed.

"She wants you."

"You think so?"

"Yeah. And she's cute, too. I think you should go for it. What've you got to lose? You're a free man."

I looked out into the hall, where I'd first come to realize the power of prayer, and then down at Don's lady lying helplessly in bed. Thought about the past three years, how I'd grown and how I hadn't, and shook my head.

"You got the free part right. But I'm still working on being a man."

Nikai

We pulled back up to the town house after going to eat and walking through the mall. We were all exhausted from showing Lucky everything he had missed out on. He was so fascinated by "this new invention called the escalator" that we took turns riding it for at least two hours. I had Mama go on it most of the time with him. Had to make her pay for giving up on Lucky and not forcing him to come out before now.

He was sound asleep in the backseat when I threw the gearshift into park and turned the engine off. I offered to wake him and help get him in the house, but for some reason, Mama insisted that I go in first. I took the key out of the engine and walked up to the front door. Turned the knob and realized that it was unlocked. I eased in out of fear that someone had walked in on Taylor while she was sleeping. Afraid for both of us, I ducked my head around the door and screamed as loudly as I could. My heart stopped beating and all I could think to do was cry. The tears flowed heavily as Sheila grabbed me and held me in her arms.

"Sweetie, don't cry," she kept saying. "Kai, stop crying."

Rastaman appeared by her side with a broad smile and joined in on the hug as Taylor stood at the bottom of the steps laughing and rubbing her belly.

"That's why you didn't want to go to the cemetery!"

"Yep. Who else was gonna let them in?"

By then, Mama had awakened Lucky and was up to the front

door. He was still too tired to do anything more than wave a hello and go on up to bed.

I asked Sheila, "When did you all get here?"

"Byron's been here for about a week, finding us an apartment."

"A what?"

"An apartment. We've moved back here, girl. That's why I kept trying to contact you. I wanted to let you know, but you were so busy with your little friend Kalif."

"Sheila, Rastaman—I mean Byron—I really want y'all to meet him and the rest of my friends. They've become as special to me as y'all are. Kindred spirits truly are drawn to one another."

Sheila hugged me again and said, "I know, sweetie, that's why we're back home."

Nikai

Kalif and Byron had just finished putting some of my things up in the loft, stuff that Mama had no room for. They found spaces for my boxes of knickknacks and extras that I'd brought with me. Maurie, Janae, and Ahmad were there as well for a welcoming dinner/jam session. We plugged in my record player and put on some old cuts from way back. (I'm talkin' '73.)

I introduced everyone and watched the chemistry happen before my eyes. No one wondered why Rastaman had locks, because we all did in one way or another: We had locked ourselves into self-love. No one questioned the significance of the mud-cloth dress Sheila was wearing, because it was understood where her heart was—stretched from here to the motherland, and ours were in the same place. Maurie's and Janae's cowrie shells were admired and not criticized. They all traded bottles of frankincense and myrrh, healthy recipes, and wisdom. Burned sage, lighted candles, and vibed. We may not have been what the world wants, because I doubt the world really knows what to wish for.

The girls begged me to rejoin the group, instead of the band that I told them about, but I wanted to wait. I needed to see if I could do it. I needed to break away from what was familiar and venture out. I figured it would all be good for me if I remembered where home was—where I was loved.

As Kalif and I, wearing sweats and sneakers, shared a futon in the candlelit living room, he turned and asked me to twist his locks again.

I said, "It'll cost you."

"How much?"

"How much are you willing to give?"

"To have you close to me, whatever it takes."

I blushed and asked, "And how do I know you're not just saying that?"

"Because you know what I've gone through to get you here with me now."

"I guess you have a point."

He took a seat between my legs and rested his elbows on my thighs as I arrived at another question to answer myself. What happens when two people try to find peace of mind and common ground in a world where influence is strong, fear is crippling, and secrets can be costly? They grow. Up and away from what is comfortable and closer to what they've always feared. Even when that fear is of being alone and cast out.

As I sat and looked back at the way that Robert and I had grown apart, I was grateful. Grateful for experiencing the disappointments of love, the strength of renewal, and the joy of certainty. I looked into the face of adversity and removed all doubt that I could be who I wanted to be, that I could be the person I was born to be.

Today, my horoscope read that career moves would fall in my favor. "Don't expect a smooth journey. But the outcome looks promising for new love." As I looked down at Kalif, I saw a future. Not necessarily full of promises, but of hope. And with that being all that I could do, hope seemed the most logical at that moment.

I stopped twisting his hair, got up, and thumbed through my box of oldies. Grabbed one of Donnie Hathaway's old albums and threw it on. As the old sweet vinyl sound poured through the speakers, my favorite song floated from one end of the loft to the other. We all joined one another in the darkness, that now *unfamiliar* darkness, and sang in harmony: "Take it from me, someday we'll all be free."